BLIND ANGELS

EARTH'S EXILES

BLIND ANGELS

TERRY MADDEN

Cursed Dragon Ship
PUBLISHING

For A.J. Maulhardt, my favorite son

CONTENTS

Retrieved from *Vera Rubin* database 2345-05-16

Image capture from video dated 2119-10-05

Description: Subject Lt. John Lauretta in a recorded message to unspecified future recipient holds up a sheet of paper with encrypted writing. Translation provided by Dr. Camber Maypole.

John,

When I hit the ground, Ru Shi Zhu was waiting for me. She claims she knew nothing about those embryos. She owns the fucking company. How could she not know?

But she bought me dinner and picked my brain about them.

Find out why those embryos are on board and who is responsible. Don't let anyone know what you're after or they'll send your ass back here with me. I wouldn't be too sad about that. But wait 'til you're out of system before you ask any questions.

Live your life, John. But sometimes, think of us. I will.
Cam

Beside the signature is a cartoon drawing of a flower and a smiling bee, determined not to be part of the encryption.

1

SKIN

2345-02-03 *Earth Standard, Colony Village, Varanasi*

SKIN WAS the organ people missed the most. Analogs, though functional, could not preserve memories like the real thing, scars and all. The feel of a breeze playing over the fine hairs of the arms, the sweet shock of diving into a mountain lake, the touch of a lover's lips. Camber Maypole missed her skin as much as anyone, but she wasn't expecting much from this venture capital meeting. The demand for biologicals just wasn't there anymore, not even for real skin.

The security door to the colony greenhouse buzzed open, and Maypole stepped inside. It was an odd place to hold such a meeting. Then again, Rishi Corp was known for their showy product reveals. The place was crawling with Varanasian orchids in colors Maypole had never seen—fuchsia, plum, variegated. Maybe she could talk them into letting her take some cuttings.

A mech attendant met her in the atrium and scanned her ID. "The meeting is on the top floor, Dr. Maypole." It motioned to a glass elevator car partially hidden behind a small grove of what looked like apricots.

Maypole reached out to pick one, but the attendant launched a warning to her system. *No touching the crop.*

Yeah. No touching.

Skin analogs had improved in two centuries, certainly, but most people had forgotten what skin was really like: flaky, itchy, full of zits and scars. The interface between real skin and machine hardware had to be more complicated than draping a hide over a bundle of gears and wiring. Touch analogs on their holo-prints had become sophisticated. Pressure sensors in the chassis of a new generation print could translate touch with reasonable accuracy, even a subtle change in wind direction. Rishi's "New Skin" might be a hard sell.

With no money to invest, Maypole might not get to stay long enough to see how this skin worked, which was all she really wanted anyway. Well, that and the price tag.

The view from the glass elevator opened onto rows of uniform aquaponics racks alive with plants of all kinds. Mindless mechs were scurrying over the greenhouse in double-time, pruning, pollinating, whatever else they did to maintain the multi-level hothouse. A tiny pollinator bot found the glass of the elevator and bounced off it a few times before going back to work. Maypole guessed the ag specialists wouldn't trust native pollinators with their engineered crops. A mistake, in her opinion.

The elevator opened onto an antiseptic hallway that terminated at a conference room door.

Inside, a handful of investors were scattered around an oval table centered inside a glass bubble. The whole thing was suspended above the main greenhouse. Below them, native vines and migraters intermingled with engineered species. The plants climbed the garden walls in competition for the green-gold radiation of their star, Upsilon Andromedae A. The sunlight through the droplets of condensation on the greenhouse panes cast a glittering spell worthy of Virtual.

Rishi Corp had probably been using this garden as a pretty place to entertain rich assholes for a century.

Maypole took a seat at the table with three other mechs. Their carbide skeletons were clothed in stylish holographic projections that covered the mass of sensors, wiring, and actuators. This projection was the aesthetic part of their holo-prints—a canvas for personal style. Tattoos must be in fashion again. She scanned the variety she saw on the others. A blue-skinned creature had a glowing golden message around his neck that read, *Prepare Ye.* Tacky.

She sent the guy a backchannel text. *I bet this skin won't come in your color.*

He replied with a *fuck you* emoji.

She gave him a smile.

His eyes flashed to her only tattoo, the NASA meatball on her wrist.

Eight drones hovered nearby. Most no bigger than dragonflies, they landed on the slick table, one after the other, the red light of their IR sensors transmitting the scene to the minds that controlled them from Virtual. One of the drones was not the standard issue mech, but a spendy holo-print of a little red bird that ruffled its feathers periodically and tipped its head as it eyed each of the visitors in turn.

That brought the number of prospective investors to twelve. If she'd been running this show, Maypole would have convened in a smaller room to make the low turnout less obvious.

They busied themselves IDing each other, scrolling through their backchannels.

Except for Maypole, these people consisted exclusively of Vested, the ultra-rich who had signed on to Rishi Corp's immortal retirement scheme back on Earth—the promise of life everlasting in a pristine paradise.

Looking from one to the other, Maypole offered her most confident smile. She'd successfully infected this little coffee klatch with her commonness. Let them try to throw her out.

"Just think of me as Kolya Lemkos's drone," she finally said. "He's quite interested in the potential of synth-organics. He sent me to scope it out for him." It was partly true. She'd had to promise not to make a scene. Considering this privileged assembly, it might be hard to keep that promise.

"How is Dr. Lemkos?" asked the little red bird drone. The accent and voice were familiar. Maypole ID'd the drone as Martine Sommer, shoe company magnate turned server host. Martine thought of herself as a social justice warrior and had even built a free virtual realm as a refuge for penniless minds. Lemkos claimed she was the first one to discover the long-term effects of bit rot, but Maypole had decided to opt out of Martine Sommer's treatment. The process involved total immersion in her rebirth realm, Samsara. Maypole had found her own treatment for bit rot—stay out of Virtual.

"Lemkos is just fine," she told Martine. It might actually be true. It was hard to say with him. She added, "He had a case today that was impossible to reschedule. You know how it is."

"I was hoping to catch up," Martine said. The wings of her red bird flapped excitedly.

"Well you know where to find him." Maybe she shouldn't have said that, but it wasn't like Lemkos to turn away a well-connected admirer. He might be rich, but he'd never be Vested.

The door opened.

A sleek carbide chassis appeared, without any holo-print, just a naked skeleton. All the gearing and actuators were fully visible, like the original mech bodies they'd had two hundred years earlier. Interesting marketing strategy. The servos of the naked chassis whirred and hummed without the usual dampeners imposed by a holo-print, and the visual receptors stared straight ahead. Maypole knew the mind inside was scanning each of them in turn. Without his holo-print, Maypole couldn't tell whether this guy was disappointed at the turnout or not.

Her onboard system slapped an ID over his gleaming skeleton that read, *Noah Dutro, lead research and design for Rishi Corp.*

Maypole called up his biomass image and stats: senior neuroscientist and co-developer of the neural net salvage system. Shit, big dog on deck.

"My friends, welcome to Rishi Corporation and an opportunity I think you'll appreciate." He spread his arms in a gracious gesture.

Maypole's onboard system projected a variety of images of Dutro as it narrated his bio on a backchannel. A rapid carousel of images showed a fortyish man in mid twenty-first-century fashion: tight-fitting white viscose tee and shroom-leather jacket. He was good looking in an outdoorsy way with his blond man-bun, jeans, and a silver nose ring. In fact, silver and turquoise circled every finger, and a pair of tattooed snakes ran up both jugulars, flicking red tongues. He'd probably started the retro-tattoo fashion himself.

The clacking of Dutro's mechanical feet on the polished floor brought the guests to attention as a steel box was wheeled in behind him.

"No need for a lengthy preamble." He reached into the steel box and removed a tray, saying, "Let's talk science. An opportunity to own skin far superior to the real thing. Brings new meaning to the term 'skin trade.'"

No one laughed at his joke.

The drones rose from the table, flitted, and repositioned them-selves around the room like mosquitos.

"I hope you've had time to glance at the prospectus."

Maypole didn't get one, of course.

Dutro spoke without the usual projection of moving lips on a holographic face. It was unsettling. "In conjunction with Body Perfect, who makes this state-of-the-art chassis"—he indicated his blindingly slick skeleton—"Rishi Corp will produce an incomparable sensory interface. Because it will be real. Organic. It does not depend on holograms to project an image, but real skin."

With the arrival of the colonists not more than six weeks away, such skin would be a benefit. For Maypole, examining a patient with her chassis hands would give the humans the uncomfortable sensation of being prodded with a bundle of articulated steel twigs, whereas hands made of skin . . . This advantage gave Dutro's research relevance, at least.

Dutro gingerly deposited the culture tray on the table. Maypole and the others leaned over it to stare while the drones hovered closer. The tissue had the appearance of true epidermis. Under higher magnification, Maypole could see it was complete with a gelatinous layer of dermis.

"What you see is skin grown from genetically tailored cells from native creatures here on Varanasi. The cells carry 89.87 percent human DNA reverse-engineered from native precursors. Tough work, mind you, as the molecular building blocks in this world are backward."

That was an understatement. The luck of the draw in this world was that it chose to fashion its life out of molecules that were related to those that made up life on Earth, but the geometry was predominantly mirror image. So even engineered DNA sequences from the native molecules required tedious biochemistry.

Engineered dogs were still a fantasy, sadly.

Dutro went on, "This has presented technical problems in engineering Earth life from genomic data as was originally planned. Until now."

Blue guy interjected, "What about the work out in Shivi Desh? That would be better than skin."

Dutro initiated his holo-print image. It faded in to cover the skeletal chassis with a more conventional image of his biological self. The servo sounds ceased. Dutro stared down the blue guy for so long he was probably sending a threat on a back channel. After a moment, he put on a smile and clasped his hands. "We will discuss that work when it's complete, Mr. Fillory. Today we are here to present a hybrid tissue. It provides the illusion of human skin, complete with hair follicles, dermis, and subcutaneous fat."

Shivi Desh? What could possibly be happening in that remote canyon that would interest blue guy? Maypole used to climb the cliffs in that gorge and hunt for plant specimens, but there was nothing there except a few mines, hellions, and forests.

A drone chimed in, "To think of all the pain we endured trying to rid ourselves of subcutaneous fat."

That one got laughs.

Standing just outside the open door, the holo-print of a woman appeared. She wore a scarlet cheongsam, her hair bound with Varanasian orchids, around which a halo of projected butterflies fluttered. If she was trying not to draw attention, she had failed. She blocked every attempt Maypole made at IDing her. Yet Maypole felt a tug of recognition, or at least, of the image she was projecting. East Asian certainly, or a hereditarily large percentage. Maybe the image was that of a twenty-first-century movie star? No, Maypole *knew* her. But from where and when? This world or Earth?

She met Maypole's gaze openly, then gave her a hint of a smile, an imperfect right eyebrow lifting. Whoever she was, she recognized Maypole as well.

The others were all gazing down at the cultured skin.

"I have the illusion of human skin right now," said blue guy, holding out his muscled arm. "Why do I need biomass to do what a holo can do easier and cheaper? If it's not *real* human skin . . . I don't know how you'll spin a good marketing campaign."

"It *is* real, Fillory. Just not fully human," Martine Sommer said with a sweet chirp. "But, Dr. Dutro, where's the circulatory system required to feed this skin? It must eat and excrete like all other living things."

"I'm glad you asked." He said it as if the question was a plant, which maybe it was.

As Dutro talked, Maypole had the distinct feeling she was being observed by the beautiful woman. A message popped into her peripheral from a Tanbo Khando. It had to be the woman. *Dr. Maypole, allow me to escort you out. This meeting is privileged.*

Maypole gave the woman a wink.

"These cells photosynthesize." Dutro was saying. "They feed and excrete via passive gas transfer. They grow, die, reproduce, and heal when injured—"

"The *real* obstacle to making a go of this," Maypole said, leaning in with the others, "is the fact that 94 percent of the people on Varanasi have never even ventured out of VR. They're all gophers. If they ever had a desire to see this planet, it faded a long time ago. Most of them have forgotten a planet exists outside of Nirvana Virtual. Most of them have forgotten they ever *had* a biological body."

"When the colonists arrive, that will change," Dutro argued. "We'll want to interact with them as one human to another."

I shall have to call security, Khando messaged. *Please, follow me.*

"What if they don't make it?" It was a drone with a male voice.

"They're almost in system," said another. "How could they *not* make it?"

"Even more reason to build more human-like holo-prints," Dutro said.

"What about the option of tissue samples?" Maypole blurted. If she kept talking, this Khando couldn't throw her out. "I mean tissue from the colonists themselves. Harvest would be a snap. Maybe even more than skin—"

"I'm sure you could answer that yourself, Dr. Maypole." Dutro gave her a look rather like the one he'd given blue guy when he'd mentioned Shivi Desh.

Security mechs appeared at the door. But Dutro held up a hand and dismissed them, then shot a scathing look at Tanbo Khando. Who was in control here?

Dutro continued, "Human skin requires a circulatory system, which you, as a doctor should know. It needs a *body* to feed it. This skin does not. We can, therefore, interact with humans as equals. No 'uncanny valley' issues. No rubbery silicone. It could be argued this skin's more sensitive than human skin. Real touch." He reached out the distal phalanx of his index finger to touch the holo-image of Maypole's cheek.

Predictably, she felt the cold of his mechanical hand and sensors, the nest of wiring running from his fingers to his hand and arm. His finger certainly did not feel like skin.

"Tanbo, love, please."

In response, the beautiful woman came forward. Making her way from one investor to another, she touched them each in turn, at least, those who wore holo-prints. The interface was organic. Tanbo was actually *wearing* the new skin. When she touched Maypole's hand, her sensorium registered a tactile description of real skin. The warm, soft, pliable sensation contrasted with the daggers Tanbo's eyes directed at Maypole.

"Thank you for coming," Dutro said, the cue that the show was over. He pressed his palms together and offered an abbreviated bow. "You'll find all investment info in your inboxes. Oh, Dr. Maypole, we'd like to include you in that list, though I understand you represent Dr. Lemkos."

"I make my own decisions. But yes, I look forward to more information." But Maypole was thinking about the woman wearing the skin, Tanbo. The name rang no bells.

Maypole headed for the elevator with the others, but the little red bird hovered close to her shoulder.

"It has been a while, Ms. Sommer," Maypole said, remembering the slick sales talk Martine had delivered so long ago when her "experience" was first available. "How is your Samsara realm going? I understand it's become crazy popular."

The elevator dinged, the door opened, and they all piled in.

"It has done quite well," Martine replied. "I'm sure Lemkos has shared his experiences with you?"

"Some." He had bored her to death with it.

Martine's server, Samsara, was free of the Black Stack. She was Rishi Corp's biggest, no, only competitor. Her presence at the venture capital meeting certainly gave Rishi execs reason to wonder why. Maypole was mildly curious as well.

Maypole added, "What do you think of the skin? I mean, it has some definite applications with the colonists arriving."

"Quite useful," was all Martine said.

On the ground floor, Maypole exited onto the main street that ran through the middle of Colony Village. Martine's bird fluttered beside her.

"I wasn't here for the skin," Martine said, her voice a low whisper.

When they reached the first complex of vacant townhouses, Maypole stopped walking. The other investors had gone their separate ways, and she and Martine were alone now. "If not the skin, then what?"

"Can we speak privately?"

"Of course. My office isn't far."

Maypole led the way through the newly constructed residences awaiting the arrival of the smell and clatter of humanity. The Medical Center was nestled at the heart of the planned community, right beside the park and playground that might soon be loud with children.

"Please, come in," Maypole said to the bird and indicated her open office door. What could a Vested want from her?

She closed the door, offering all the privacy they could possibly get from a place like this. The lab was just as she'd left it . . . except for a lowland bluebelly that lay dead on her desk.

"Shit. It must have come in with one of the techs and couldn't get out." The rodents stashed their nuts and ended up inside buildings all the time.

With huge ears like membranous wings, the little creature lay there naked, its plumage having abandoned the poor thing upon death. Plumage lay scattered about like the remains of a plucked chicken. The feather-like symbionts were also dead and colorless, having failed to find a living host or sunlight.

"Shit, shit, shit."

"Not your fault," Martine said.

"Well, yeah, but . . ."

Maypole deposited the corpse in the trash bin and turned her attention back to Martine Sommer.

"What are those?" Martine asked, flitting over to the bank of humming fridges and freezers.

"Storage for meds." Was that why she'd come? To talk about meds? Maybe she thought the place was bugged.

Martine's bird alighted on the back of a chair, its wings ruffling and adjusting into a perched pose.

"Okay, Ms. Sommer. You can speak freely here."

"Dr. Maypole, I know that you were a member of the launch crew and were . . . relieved of your position."

Oh, this was going to get personal. Another attack on Maypole as NASA's charity case. She began calculating how to throw this woman out, professionally. "I have work to do here, Ms. Sommer—"

"Please, let me continue." Martine must have read her distress. Her bird hovered in the air and followed Maypole to the door.

"Go on, then." Maypole was only entertaining this Vested because Lemkos and Martine were friends . . . or something.

Martine said, "I have been doing some research on the ship's biobank. The contents are highly classified, so I have found very little. Lemkos mentioned that you were a medical officer aboard the ship and had some knowledge of the biobank."

Maypole would have to punch Lemkos in his virtual face next time she saw him. "Well, the biobank is just that, Ms. Sommer, a collection of plant seeds and animal and human embryos, all to be used in the genetic diversity program aboard the ship. What's so interesting about that?"

"You were relieved of duty," Martine said with certainty. "Removed from the crew after a conflict centered on the biobank."

She'd done some homework. "Look, Ms. Sommer—"

"Martine, please."

"Ms. Sommer, the reasons for my removal are classified. You'll have to speak to the Flight Director if you want more information. Now if you'll excuse me, I have work to do."

Feelings she had tried to forget flooded Maypole. Her future had been stolen, and she'd been dropped back to a dying Earth while the ship left the docking station. Her ship. The *Vera Rubin.*

Maypole opened the office door and held it. "Good afternoon, Ms. Sommer."

"Rishi Corp is working on more than skin," Martine said. "There are rumors."

"That's great, but I don't place much stock in rumors."

"Some of us are worried there is more going on than we know. Illegal research."

"Why bring this to me?"

"You have the, uh, the expertise to help us. You have information on some unauthorized embryos."

Jesus, how did this shoe designer know about the embryos? Maypole said, "Good day, Ms. Sommer."

Martine's red bird hovered just in front of Maypole's face. "You know, Dr. Maypole, not all the Vested are in this for themselves. Some of us still have a soul."

"Ms. Sommer, I doubt any of us have a soul. I'll tell Lemkos you said hi."

The drone flitted out, and Maypole closed the door. Lemkos had some talking to do.

2

WHEN THE DEAD SPEAK

2345-02-03, *Earth Standard. Aboard the* Vera Rubin, *205 AU from Varanasi*

SERAPH WAS in Farm A-3 when he got the message. He silenced his palmcomm and glanced at the sender's ID, a name he didn't recognize. He closed the message and turned his attention to the sickly zucchini leaves. They were smaller than they should be and yellowing. Stacked on top of tanks of tilapia, the racks of vines emitted the familiar smell of rot. Seraph weighed whether it would be better to recycle this crop or try to save it. Either way, he wouldn't be making those zucchini frittatas he'd promised Rain.

He checked the nutrient log on his palmcomm, confirming that his intern, Carl, had either missed A-3 or the lines were mucked up. Either way, it was Carl's ass. Feces. He liked Carl. Canning him was not what he wanted to do today.

He slipped the flask from the pocket of his jumpsuit and took a swig.

Two pollinator bots sat idle on the remains of a zucchini plant. No bigger than a peanut, the drones hummed, signaling that they could find nothing to pollinate.

"Funny thing." Seraph groaned. He collected the two polli-bots and dropped them in his pocket.

Water pumps hummed. Seraph opened the valve on the red tank and gave the crop a hit of chelated iron and micros. The slurry of minerals entered the water line at a junction of bundled plastic capillaries that fed the main aquaponics line. It would have been more effective to use the automated system despite its current problems. Even that piece of crap would be better than Carl. Time to move the kid to the fabber deck.

Seraph began inspecting and removing dead leaves, working quickly down the row. It would take at least a week to bring these plants around.

Runoff from the crop dribbled into the tanks where it would be enriched by fish excretions and then recirculated back to the main line to water the plants. The rusty smell of iron gradually mixed with that of algae and fish scales. The tilapia that eyed Seraph through the window seemed no worse for the lapse in chemistry.

He dragged his finger slowly across the glass. The fish followed it, pushing each other out of the way to get closer, as if his finger were a food pellet.

He'd be fish food soon enough.

Seraph's prison was a bit bigger than the tilapia's but not much different, right down to the recycling of his biomass. He had a few cubic kilometers of space to their few meters, but it didn't take much to feel the limits of his existence. He avoided trips to the Command Deck for just that reason. Beyond the skin of the ship lay nothing but infinite blackness and unreachable stars. The stuff of nightmares.

The prospect of leaving this wheel, of landing on a planet with a circumference twenty thousand times bigger than the only world he'd ever known . . . the weight of the approaching day pressed on him like spin gravity.

When tilapia left their tank, it never ended well for them.

His fingers found the hard edge of the flask in his pocket. It had to last him the day.

His palmcomm chirped again. He thumbed the dirty screen open. The same message was flagged.

Blocked message forwarded to Lt. Seraphim Stone from Lt. John Lauretta.

John who?

Seraph tapped to open it.

Vera's unsmiling face appeared. The ship's animated AI had full lips that enunciated the words with an impeccable standard American accent of two centuries ago. "Unauthorized communication. To unblock this message, contact your commanding officer."

"Why send it if it's blocked?" he asked the ship.

"It was in your message queue."

Seraph wiped the screen on his jumpsuit so he could check the time stamp. It was dated 2131-07-25. Somebody was yanking his wank. That was over two hundred years ago.

"Vera," he said, and the ageless face appeared. "Is the date on this message correct?"

"To unblock this message, contact your commanding officer."

"Sting me."

Seraph ran through a mental list of other ag specialists on other shifts. He'd known most of them longer than he'd known his wife. No John Lauretta. Must be someone from Torus-2. He spun the hatch seal to lock the farm, then shed his coveralls and stepped through the decontamination box. As he started down the corridor, Carl was coming from upspin, his head dangling over his palmcomm like he was watching a vid. Damn interns.

"Hey, you mucked up the chem on A-3, keso. If those fish die—"

Carl held up a hand to silence Seraph, and then tipped his palmcomm to show a close shot of the guy they called "The Harbinger," the popular preacher from Torus-2. He had a following of people who worshipped the First Flame, just a new name for the same old angry god.

"Don't tell me you follow this fish turd," Seraph said.

"Shh." Carl's forehead screwed up in concentration. "They're starving over there, LT."

From Carl's screen, the Harbinger spoke. "We understand the ship protocol is unyielding." The old man's chalky-dark face was bunched in concern. His voice was practiced at manipulative bull-shit, resonant and deep. His hair was twisted in strands of graying dreads and tied will little bells and baubles.

"We understand," the preacher said somberly, "that Captain Dela Cruz is abiding by NASA regulations. But we beg the residents of Torus-1 to consider donations of food. It could be left in the hub. No resident of Torus-2 will ever physically contact your population, no biomass of any kind will pass from T-2 to T-1. You must under-stand, we are hungry, and many will not last the next week, let alone until we reach Varanasi."

"That's not even possible," Seraph said. "What have they been doing with their farms?"

With that, the camera turned to the faces of children, clearly thinner than normal. Hand-picked and staged, no doubt, to stir pity from the residents of T-1. The camera then followed the Harbinger into the wreckage of their farm pods. Everyone knew that a third of their pods had been damaged by the debris strike two months earlier. Their shields had failed, but they should have had reserves to get them through while they made repairs. And they should have completed those repairs by now.

"This is on public wave?" Seraph asked Carl.

He nodded. "Everybody gonna see it."

The Harbinger talked while he walked beside the camera. "We appeal to the people of Torus-1 and to the human soul that is our captain, TJ Dela Cruz."

"Oh, feces," Seraph said. Calling out TJ—bad idea.

His palmcomm chirped again. He hoped it was TJ about this mess. But it was the blocked message again.

Seraph asked Carl, "You know some keso name John Lauretta?"

The kid shook his head.

Carl was less than two months out of occ training, a beard just a promise on his pale face. But he was taller than Seraph, his neck a stalk that seemed to have extra vertebrae. No late banking in this guy's blood. His starburst eyes confirmed it.

"Get back to work then. And if you miss your chem check on any pod again, you'll be the one going hungry. Got it?"

"You gonna talk to TJ?" the kid asked.

"None of your business. Go."

Seraph took a wheelie around the torus to his lift bay, passing the deafening pods of crickets and chickens, still loud through the sealed farm doors. He never understood how the workers in there didn't go deaf.

As he rode the lift down to the residential deck, he tried a few workarounds to get into the blocked message, with no luck. Once the doors opened to the commons, he was met by the projected face of the Harbinger. They were replaying his impassioned speech on the cinescreen. The preacher's face took up the entire holo. His real name, according to the tag at the bottom, was Alexandre Baakos. At least they didn't add "Prophet of the First Flame."

A good fifty people had stopped on their journey through shift change to watch the face suspended above the trade district.

Seraph made his way around them and turned downspin into the Dubai housing units. The road tonight was thicker than usual with wheelies and people on foot, many chanting, "Feed Retro!" Retro, or Torus-2, spun in the opposite direction to Torus-1, countering the torque produced on the ship by a rotating wheel. Retro contained a population of people, plants, and animals that were completely isolated from Command Torus, Torus-1.

NASA's love of redundancy was the reason, legend said.

The residential deck was twice as deep as other decks, allowing for two floors of living units with front patios that overlooked the main concourse. This was the only place trees had been planted, mostly hardwood, but some coniferous. It was supposed to make the first crew feel like they were living in a small town, something good for their morale. But for the people who lived here now, who had never known a town, it was their forest.

Seraph's unit was on the second floor. Each step felt like he was pulling a thousand kilos up the stairs. It wasn't just the increased spin gravity on this level. The only thing that brought him back to this trap was his daughter. He could see the sky through the branches of an oak that overhung his patio, festooned with paper images of some of the animals that awaited them on Varanasi. His daughter, Rain, had been adding to the collection every day, and now the menagerie was getting crowded.

Seraph had seen every one of Vera's sky collection at least fifty times, all recorded by the first bots on Varanasi. Today's was one of his least favorites—a gray rippling of low clouds peppered with flashes of lightning and thunder. In the downspin direction, a violet sunset had begun to show beneath the ghostly crescent of the gas giant, Majriti. In an hour, there would be a symphony of thunder and streak lightning followed by rain. Just the *sound* of rain, of course.

TJ's voice drifted from the front door. "Ominous."

Her unzipped captain's jacket hung open, revealing a dingy white T-shirt. It was like she was afraid to take that jacket off. The faded epaulets had been passed from one captain to another with exaggerated pomp. When she'd first made captain, Seraph thought she would sleep in the damn thing.

"Are you talking about the Harbinger? Or the sky?" Seraph asked.

She shrugged and offered him one of the two drinks she was holding.

"What's the occasion?"

Blank-faced, she held the drink out like bait.

He took it. Took a long drink.

He wanted to ask if he could help with this Harbinger situation, but he already knew the answer.

"Ominous is a good description of life," he answered for her. "We do our jobs and try not to think about the day that's coming. Then kesos like this Harbinger stir things up." That was a stupid thing to say. When had it become so hard to talk to her? "He's just looking for a handout and . . ."

"Yeah."

"Has he presented any real data to substantiate this claim?"

She pursed her lips and shook her head, then leaned on the balcony rail.

He swirled his drink. The ice clinked as he set it on the patio table.

The overwhelming urge to apologize for being who he was came over him. He wanted to be honest with her, tell her he knew where she was most nights. But that would do Rain no good. If he confronted TJ, it would end this game of playing house and she would leave them. Instead, he turned back to the oak tree and watched Rain's paper zoo twirl slowly in the air.

"What are you going to do?" he asked.

"I can't send them food. You know that."

He followed her inside. Rain's jacket and school tablet lay on the sofa.

TJ said, "If T-2 failed to complete repairs quick enough, it's not our job to save them." She was trying to convince herself of it, and she wanted Seraph to agree. She was just play-acting captain. The real captain was an AI. TJ was bound by protocol, by Vera. But Seraph wasn't sure TJ had accepted that on any level.

He took another drink of the amber hootch.

She added, "I've traded messages with the Torus-2 commander, and he says things are under control."

"Then this Harbinger is stirring the pot."

"Why?" she demanded. "Why would he?"

Seraph eased himself down beside her on the sofa. He took a

deep breath, smelling her hair and the vague ozone odor of the air purification system.

"Maybe the torus commander knows it's no use," he said. "Making the appeal to you, I mean."

She finally looked directly into his eyes, unblinking. "I'm sure they already tried querying Vera."

"What are you going to do?" he asked again.

Her stare was emotionless, her jaw set. She didn't answer.

"I think our reserves are well-stocked," Seraph added. "With the exception of the zucchinis, we're in full production. Can't we just leave some food in the hub, like the guy said?"

"You know that's a violation of protocol. Vera would never—"

"Vera's *not* human." He said it with more force than he'd intended. "She doesn't understand hunger."

"She understands the logic of protocol." TJ stood and started pacing, her hands on her hips. It was her job to jump to Vera's defense; TJ was the ship's human face. "I've sworn to uphold the ship's directives."

"Even if it means people will starve?"

"We don't even know that's true." She was right.

"Is it possible that evidence for this shortage has been censored by Vera? Maybe the T-2 commander has sent the evidence, but you never got it?"

She snorted a laugh. "Oh, the Vera-as-monster conspiracy again. Jesus, Ser."

Successive generations of people had been living in each torus. They were never to meet or mingle in the flesh, not until they reached the surface of Varanasi. That way, if one torus became contaminated, either crops or people, the second torus would be the backup. Seraph understood the logic. But the reality of that was a nightmare no one had considered. Until now.

"We're what? Four or five weeks out from reaching Varanasi?" he argued. "*Our* planet? When our feet hit the ground, we'll all be together, TJ. No Retros, no Command wheel. All of us. Together."

"Vera won't allow it," she said quietly. She was dead serious.

"Not a single one of *us* put these rules in place!" Seraph indicated the whole ship with a sweep of his arms. "We're slaves to a fucking computer built by people who never left Earth!"

A bedroom door slammed shut. He'd forgotten Rain was here.

"That's shortsighted, and you know it." TJ growled. "We could run into more problems. We have to eat when we get there. We have to brake, for God's sake. Yes, the first microwave beams have come online, but down the well? What about the moon-based braking beams? What if those joboxes that were supposed to have built all our infrastructure are rusted piles of trash by now? We fly right on by and head out into more fucking blackness!"

Sucking in a breath, TJ leaned back into the sofa. She downed her drink and slammed the empty glass onto the table. She was as scared as he was, just of something different, something she knew far more about than he did. The ship might skip off the atmosphere of Varanasi and tumble out of the star system. They'd lose the dream once dreamt by a bunch of space jocks. He wanted to hold her, tell her it was okay. But it wasn't okay. Nothing about this existence was okay.

"You're in contact with the ground—with, with the crew of minds that are responsible for building the braking system. Have they said anything about problems?"

She shook her head. "Whoever, or whatever, is responding could be nothing more than AI. Vera talking to another Vera."

"It'll be okay," he offered at last.

She gave him a surprised grin. "Who do you think you are? God?"

"There is no god. Only Vera." He forced a smile.

"Tell that to the Harbinger."

His palmcomm buzzed. The message again.

"TJ, this message has tried to come through five times today. It looks like it needs an override from you."

She took it from him and read the date. "What the hell?"

"I know."

She put in her access code and handed the palmcomm back to Seraph. He took it and headed out the front door. "I'll be back in a few."

"Secrets," she said after him, smiling.

No, she was the one with the secrets. Let her think this was a message from a lover. Whatever this message had to say, he wasn't sharing. Not until he knew what it was. Seraph headed for the stairs to the concourse below, stopped at the top step, then went back inside for the glass of hootch he'd left in the living room.

Outside, the commons were empty, the projected sky filled with the looming image of Majriti. The giant planet was a paisley shadow veiled by breaking clouds.

He took a seat on a bench under an almond tree, took a drink, and opened the message.

A video popped up. It was time-stamped 214 years in the past. A middle-aged man, graying, with a look of dread in his eyes, spoke to the camera. "My name is John Lauretta. I am the first agricultural officer on the launch crew of the *Vera Rubin*, and I have information that will be critical to those who reach Varanasi."

3

THE ENNUI OF PARADISE

2345-02-06, Earth Standard, Colony Village, Varanasi

A REMINDER SOUNDED from Maypole's onboard. She'd been tinkering with her stock of antibiotics in her Medical Center lab longer than she'd thought. It wasn't unusual for her to get lost in her work, but three days?

The work hadn't erased Martine Sommer from her mind. The woman knew why Maypole had been bumped from the ship, and there were only one or two people who could have told her about it. Maypole couldn't hide in her lab forever.

When she exited the Medical Center, it was already night. On Varanasi, this meant the natives would be hunkering down for a long sleep or waking up to hunt the sleeping.

Varanasi was an Earth-sized moon of Majriti, the largest of the planets orbiting their sun, Upsilon Andromeda A. As with most moons, Varanasi was tidally locked. It always showed one side to Majriti while the other side looked at the stars, making its day equal to the time it took to orbit its host planet. But unlike Earth, Majriti was a massive gas giant. So Varanasi's day cycle was thirteen Earth days long, half in darkness, half in light.

Maypole hailed a flyer and cruised over the dome of the great greenhouse. Night was rarely utterly dark on this part of the planet. The horizon was lit by the marbled hues of neighboring moons, and the limb of Majriti floated as a relentless crescent of storms in the direction of the sea, arcing from one horizon to the other, a swirling fractal masterpiece of turquoise and plum. The crescent waxed and waned but never darkened completely, even during an eclipse. The only location on Varanasi with no view of Majriti was the far side, a land of raging seas and archipelagos, and a wide, unhampered view of the Milky Way.

Maypole never tired of the views in this world and yet, that was all that was left to her. She'd become a spectator of life, not a participant.

She had postponed the inevitable long enough. She'd go home, dive into Virtual, and find Lemkos. If it was him who'd been feeding Sommer information about the launch crew, then he'd better have a damn good reason.

Martine's words repeated in Maypole's head, something about Rishi Corp working on more than skin. What could Rishi's tissue experiments possibly have to do with Maypole?

The flyer gained altitude and banked west for the coast.

She checked her timekeeper app. Three hours post-sunset—another five days, twenty-one hours of night to follow.

A message blinked in her visual field.

All NASA personnel report to Mission Control for immediate instruction.

This could only mean ground communications had received something other than the usual navigation ping from the *Vera Rubin*. She felt a rush of simulated adrenaline.

Maypole corrected her destination coordinates on the flyer and entered those for NASA HQ.

Mission Control commanded a rocky promontory overlooking the vast delta of the Ganges. A river far larger than its namesake on Earth, it drained most of the northern continent of Uttar Pradesh. The astronomer who first discovered the largest moon of Majriti was a native of Varanasi in India, so he named the moon for his hometown and the geographical features followed the naming convention of the Indian subcontinent. Maypole saw the irony in naming this world after the sacred city where devotees brought their dead to burn them on the banks of the sacred river in hopes they would achieve *moksha*, freedom from the curse of rebirth. Certainly, the twenty-first century astronomer could never have imagined that hundreds of thousands of human minds would one day have a digital "life" after death on his moon.

The Ganges Valley, this one, was couched in the lap of mountains whose peaks were higher than the Himalayas. Despite the scattered lights of manufacturing plants, mining operations, and mech storage, the landscape glowed in muted grays by the light of Majriti. A necklace of streetlights marked Colony Village below her as the flyer banked and came around to change course.

During the day, the valley stretched out in simmering pastels of leached minerals toward a swampy delta and the sea. But now, the river glistened like a paisley snake in the night.

Below her flyer, a spaceport stretched to the north in an array of illuminated landing pads where blinking drone craft launched and landed. They were shuttling mechs and materials to the armada of larger ships docked at a space station at geostationary orbit. It was busier than usual with the deployment of a legion of laser buoys which would be used to assist in braking the *Vera Rubin*.

The flyer left her on the roof of Mission Control, congested with arrivals. By the looks of their pricey holo-prints and chassis, many of her colleagues had been spending time in the Real. When a gopher leaves Virtual to walk topside, they don't bother with a pricey holo-print. They go with a rental, and most of them looked pretty much the same. The variety of styles Maypole picked out told her these weren't rentals.

A guy stepped off the flyer next to Maypole's. He jogged to catch up and walk beside her. "What will they be like?"

He smiled stupidly. His holo-print was that of a thirty-something guy who spent too much time in the gym. *His* idea of sexy. He was walking too close, so she stepped away.

He added, "I mean, they must have changed in two hundred years, right?"

This guy hadn't.

"Hard to say," she replied. "They'll likely be tall—lengthened bones from the low g. You know. Maybe some modifications to digestion too. And their diet may have changed depending on crop survival and choice."

"Riiiight," the guy said. By the look he gave her, that was too much information. Oh, he was just making conversation.

"It'll keep me busy for quite a while." Then she checked his ID. Brandon from accounting. She should have recognized his holo-print. He always wore that movie star from *Funk in the Punk*. He used to have parties at his house in Snowmass that included extreme skiing and a smorgasbord of drug experiences and weird mech sex. She'd accepted his invitation. Once.

They entered the crowded foyer.

Mission Control, a citadel with walls two meters thick, looked more like a bunker than a space facility, a response to the threat of refugee terrorism. No one could have predicted that terrorists would prefer Virtual. The havoc that hackers could wreak there was far superior to anything in the Real.

A holo of the NASA meatball filled the air above the AI receptionist. Once, that symbol had filled Maypole with pride. She'd worked her whole life to be worthy of wearing that thing. Now she was simply their charity case, rehired to fill a job that could easily be done by mechs. Was she supposed to be thankful? Fuck that.

The control room was packed. Everyone was shaking hands, slapping backs as if the mission were already over. The 2D images on either side of the scrolling logistics showed a braking-beam station. Telemetry scrolled off to the right in an unreadable blur. It was a perfect replica of the historical control room in Houston, the advanced tech hidden so it didn't take away from the effect. The big boss was an anachronist.

The flight director, Kaja Singh, was shaking hands with some political stiff.

A hand on Maypole's back turned into an embrace, and she found herself engulfed in the arms of Kolya Lemkos.

He wore his biomass holo-print, the way he had looked all those years ago: long, Ukrainian face with a heavy brow and sandy hair. A dimple in his long chin reminded her of what her dad used to say, "Dimple in chin, devil within." With Lemkos, that was clearly correct. It was what she liked best about him. His stubborn refusal to straighten his crooked nose reminded her that he shared Maypole's fondness for the unique imperfections of biology.

"Camber, Cupcaaaake," Lemkos crooned.

All attempts at putting an end to the nickname had failed. When they'd first arrived on Varanasi, Maypole and Lemkos had made the mistake of thinking there was more between them than friendship. They were new to immortality then. The affair had lasted no more than a decade, and if she had to explain why it ended, she would have to say that was on her. What she remembered of love was more than artificial sensory stimulation. It involved the real possibility of sacrifice. Love was the twin sister of pain, and she had come to believe both were unattainable in this immortal existence.

Their friendship had survived. At least, Maypole chose to believe it had.

Lemkos gave her shoulder a soft shove. "Oh, come on. You love that name."

"You're one long joke without a punchline, Lemkos. And the latest one requires an explanation. We need to talk about Martine Sommer."

"Oh, the buzzkill has arrived. So you went to the meeting after all. Should I slap down some credits on this new skin of Rishi's?" He crossed his arms and stood beside her as they both pretended to analyze the cache of cryptic messages between CapCom and someone or something aboard the *Vera Rubin*. Relativistic delay was still substantial, so it was more of a collection of lists than a back-and-forth.

"Well, *I* wouldn't spend good money on that skin," Maypole said. "Not unless you think the arrival of the colonists will draw the gophers out of Virtual. It's the only use I can see for it. For me, yeah, it would be brilliant. I could examine my patients with real skin, but . . . the novelty of having humans around will wear off quick, if you ask me. So," she said, steering back to her point, "you've been telling Sommer about my time aboard the *Vera Rubin*."

"Later," he said. "We have a pool going in Life Support." Lemkos nodded toward Maypole's fellow team members, Jim and Heather, waiting by their consoles.

"Did you even hear what I said?" Maypole asked Lemkos.

"Yeah, yeah. Did you hear what I said? Later."

Jim shrugged at her.

"What do you think?" Lemkos asked her in a low whisper. "Alive? Or Dead?"

"What do you mean?"

"The colonists." He pointed at the mass of data around them. "This could all be communication with the onboard system. I mean, Vera is perfectly capable of bringing a cargo of dead humans to Varanasi."

She said, "Don't you think Vera would have mentioned that the crew was dead by now?"

"Not necessarily," he said. "But she might have told the FD, and that's why she's called us here."

The Flight Director hadn't said it was an emergency.

"So are you in?" Lemkos asked.

"We have a Schrödinger's cat situation," Maypole said with a smile.

"That won't fly in the pool," Jim said.

"Well," Maypole reasoned, "in crew training, we read a paper about an experiment done back in the twentieth century in which rats were given a comfortable but limited environment with plenty of food and water and allowed to reproduce at will." Jim and Heather leaned in to hear more. "The populations invariably peaked and then declined, every rat dying out as they quit breeding altogether, succumbing to the ennui of paradise."

"Then dead," Lemkos concluded for her.

She had never allowed herself to consider the death of the crew, because it would make her existence even more meaningless than it already was. She held up a hand to prevent him from taking the credits she had queued.

"But the colonists are not rats," she argued. "And they were not left to breed unchecked—at least, I hope not."

"So alive," Lemkos concluded.

"I hope so," she said, releasing the credits. "Put me in for twenty on alive."

Maypole would soon be setting broken bones, prescribing antibiotics, and treating high blood pressure, no different than a village doctor on Earth. But the physical problems associated with adjusting to Varanasi would be substantial. The colonists' morphology had undoubtedly mutated in response to the conditions of space—low g, high radiation, spin gravity. There may be some challenges ahead, all of which she was prepared for. There was satisfaction to be found in this. Maybe.

The flight director, Kaja Singh, made her way through the crowd, wearing—as she always did for mission events—the holo-print of Gene Kranz, legendary flight director from the Apollo days centuries ago. Her projection was complete with red, white, and blue sequined vest, bow tie, and flat top.

Singh motioned again for silence and finally said, "We have

logged a communication with the captain of the *Vera Rubin* at 0313 Earth standard time." She even had a synthesized Gene Kranz voice to go with the look.

The room broke out in cheering.

"The captain," Maypole whispered to Lemkos. "Alive. Pay up."

"Torus-2 is suffering from the effects of a micrometeorite strike which took out a third of its farms, as well as its refrigeration. Their food is running low."

The room exploded in rumbles, and Singh called for attention once again.

"And," she called for silence, "the ship is off course by 0.756 au. A correction has been sent to the navigation program. If we bring it back into the proper trajectory, we'll see how much braking we can exert and how quickly. So orbital insertion time is . . . flexible."

Lemkos gave Maypole a sidelong wink. "I got this," he whispered. As a navigation engineer, he would be involved in any course corrections.

The Flight Director continued, "Regarding the food shortage, I have advised the captain that overriding Vera is not available to us here on the ground. We have no ability to assist in any other way."

Maypole expected some grumbling, some sadness at the loss of possibly half the colonists. Instead people were talking, laughing. These colonists were nothing more than a payload to these people.

"Why can't we override Vera from the ground?" Maypole whispered to Lemkos.

"We only have control over the nav system," Lemkos said. "NASA was always afraid of mutiny, and not just aboard the ship. They weren't sure what *we* would become in two centuries. So they made sure we couldn't access anything beyond navigation, and if I remember right, that was a fight I eventually won."

"Then we have no choice but to let them starve?"

"Not all. At most, half."

Singh was still talking. "The ship is broadcasting in severely reduced amplitude, suggesting power issues. She reports the firing of their laser cannon to deflect a rock too big for the mag-shield to handle."

"The cannon caused reverse photon thrust and deceleration," Lemkos offered.

"At the very least," said Singh. "The firing of the laser cannon to a location directly in front of the ship reduced their velocity, as Dr. Lemkos has suggested, as well as nudged them off course." She waited for the chatter to die down, then said, "We have work to do, people. Let's get to it."

Lemkos held up his hand for a high five, which Maypole grudgingly gave him.

"After this, you'll be coming over for a drink," Maypole ordered. "We have things to talk about."

"Yes, sir." He gave her a salute and followed the other engineers to the lab.

HAVING a home in the Real was an unnecessary expense. But Maypole cherished her house on the cliffs of the Gandikota coast. She had cobbled it together from castoff materials that were used to build Colony Village. All transparent siding, so there was nothing but sky and growing things and the view of the Great Green. Floating in the dim night sky, the sea stretched out in speckled white caps and phosphorescent currents to the Alexandrian Islands engulfed now in darkness and fog.

The flyer left her and Lemkos in front of the house, and then spun off toward the Ganges Valley to the east.

The glass doors slid open, inviting them inside.

Lemkos was acting overly defensive about Martine Sommer. "I can't say that our relationship was completely business. It didn't last more than a year, but for the most part, we got things accomplished."

"What kind of things?" Maypole asked. Before she shared what

Martine had told her, she wanted to know the foundation of this story.

Even in the dim light of the entry hall, she could see his evasive shrug.

In the living room, the orchids had moved to the western windows which meant it had been cold. The solar heater hadn't kicked in.

"Kiki?" Maypole called.

She found the mech servant out on the patio, calling for Puppy.

"He's just hunting," Maypole told her. "It's that time of year. He'll be back when he's eaten his fill."

"He worries me," Kiki said.

"No need for worry." Some AI emotion programs were getting out of hand.

Kiki's silicone skin had that obnoxious uniformity of all standard models. A moderately dark skin tone, as if they were trying for the look of a mixed-race, but it just came out sort of socially unacceptable anyway you sliced it.

"No need to find Puppy on my account," Lemkos said. "Leave him to his hunt."

For a gladiator, Lemkos was a pussy when it came to native pets.

"Kiki, make us two easy sours, please," then to Lemkos, Maypole said, "You still like that right?"

"Yours are the best." He walked out toward the cliff edge, hands in his pockets. "God, what a view. Even at night."

Majriti's pastel crescent draped across the glistening sea like the portal to another world.

"I ran across Henry Franklin in Fifth Fantasy," Lemkos said. "He's gone full gamer. He probably forgot there was a NASA or a job, or anything else. I wonder how many of the ground crew we've lost to bit rot?"

"People not backed up?" Maypole asked.

"Some would rather spend their money in the Realms. You know. Lose themselves."

"No, I don't know," she said. It had taken some fortitude but resisting the lure of endless fantasies in virtual reality was the only thing that Maypole felt kept her human—if she was that at all. It was at least partially responsible for the failure of her relationship with Lemkos. He had gopher qualities—too many for Maypole.

Kiki appeared with a tray bearing two drinks of lime-colored liquid on ice. The glasses were pretty. The smell registered as "citrus." Maypole had made multiple corrections to her software until the alcohol smelled closer to what she imagined it would be—a perfumy concoction of fermented stinger fruit. She'd decided it would taste like gin and passionfruit with a touch of almond. This one she'd done a fairly good job with. She'd have to make this available for download.

"Will the colonists actually be able to drink this?" Lemkos asked, taking a sip with his taste sensors. A chemical code in the drink would trigger a digital high.

"Maybe. But the residual sugar might give them the runs."

"Now there's one thing I don't miss." He took another long sip of his drink, then said, "Okay, here we are on the edge of the known world. Pretty safe, I'd say, unless Kiki is a spy. What did Martine have to say?"

Maypole recounted the strange meeting. Martine's red bird following her back to her office, and her fears of some experimentation on which she failed to elaborate.

"I figured I was being set up," Maypole said.

"Set up to do what?"

"Spread rumors," she said with a grin. "Like I am right now."

"So what if Rishi is working on some kind of tissue testing," Lemkos said. "I think it's given that they've been trying for years."

"Lemkos, she was asking about my time on the launch crew. About why I was canned. And . . . she knows something about the embryos."

"What embryos?"

"I know you and John were in communication after launch. He told you."

Lemkos sighed. "John told me that you had found something in the biobank that didn't look right. You questioned it, and *poof*, you're off the launch. Why would Martine be snooping around this?"

"Okay," Maypole said. She settled back in her patio chair and took another sip of her drink. Why not tell him? What could NASA do to her now? "The last shipment of meds from Earth contained human embryos of unknown provenance. We had orders to incorporate them into the biobank with the other embryos that would be integrated into the ship's population over time, through the genetic diversity program. But these . . . These had no family history, no phenotypic analysis, nothing. Not even a karyotype. And they expected me to load them up into the diversity protocol like all our other samples, which, by the way, had been extensively traced. These new embryos were an afterthought, *and* they came from Rishi labs."

"Wait, wait. Why do you need to use embryos from the biobank at all? I thought those were for building the population when the ship arrives here."

Maypole felt a lecture coming on, something she loved—boring Lemkos with necessary facts. "If you allow a population to interbreed over time, it leads to genetic problems: the magnification of both good and bad mutations, lack of genetic diversity, even sterility. So you have to inject new genomes in there, mix it up."

"So the ship's docs use frozen embryos from Earth to do this?"

"If a couple decides they want a child, they do a genomic scan and look for any common ancestors. If there are too many, Vera's algorithm will recommend a biobank withdrawal. Considering these 1400 people will be tasked with starting a new civilization on Varanasi, it's important to provide the semblance of a larger population so we hit no evolutionary bottlenecks."

"And I assume you brought up these suspect embryos to your captain," Lemkos concluded.

Maypole sighed and took another drink from Kiki's tray.

"And they canned you right there."

She nodded.

"Okay, so I don't get it," Lemkos said. "Martine knows about these embryos somehow. How? And why bother?"

"'Something more than skin.'"

"What?" Lemkos asked.

"That's what she told me. Rishi is working on something more than skin. It's a big fucking secret apparently, probably because it's illegal." She sipped her drink and watched clouds glide over the crescent of Majriti. Then she remembered. "Shivi Desh."

"What about it?"

"A guy mentioned something that was happening in Shivi Desh, some project of Rishi's. Peeved the Dutro guy. Maybe these two are related?"

"Sounds like a stretch, Cupcake."

Maypole said, "Maybe you should ask Martine yourself, Lemkos."

Lemkos sighed and looked off at the islands. Maybe they hadn't remained friends after all.

"I think I'm going climbing tomorrow," Maypole said and took a drink of her second easy sour. "You're welcome to come, Lemkos, but I know you've got lots to do with that navigation system and all."

"Where you climbing?" he asked.

"Shivi Desh."

"You can't go up that gorge in the dark," Lemkos protested.

"Why not? I'm a machine. I have lights. So do you."

Since when was Lemkos afraid of the dark?

PUPPY RETURNED from his plover hunt not long after Lemkos had left. The hound smelled like ocean brine and blood, so Maypole bathed him, trying not to loosen too much of his plumage in the process. The symbiotes weren't overly fond of water and at night, when they couldn't photosynthesize, many of them dropped off their host to look for better opportunities.

She liked to imagine Puppy as a dog. He was German shepherd sized. The first explorers had named them "seahounds," yet they had six limbs and could soar short distances with one set and swim underwater with another. They made noises that could maybe be construed as a bark, but mostly, they exhibited joy in companionship, even if their companions weren't exactly human.

She used to brush her dog's teeth back on Earth and had devised a chew toy that did the same thing for Puppy's dental thorns. Right now, his breath would stop a train.

Before he was dry, he ran back into the house and hopped up on her mostly unused bed, circled a few times and settled into his usual spot. The glow of Majriti streamed through the transparent walls of her bedroom and ignited Puppy's nocturnal eyes into a hyperreflective green. The lids soon drooped and closed. His breathing became rhythmic. His intestines rumbled with the lengthy journey of digestion. The air smelled of wet beast. She inhaled deeply.

She had a list of comms to answer, pinging her onboard. She went out to the patio again and started working through the messages, inventory from the medical center, notes from Jim and Heather. An idea struck her.

She accessed the updated NASA directory to find that it included the contact information for the current crew. The onboard medical officer would likely not share what became of the embryos, but she had to try. An incoming comm interrupted her message.

It came from the *Vera Rubin*. The only person that might have reason to contact her would be the current medical officer. She opened it.

A low-res video revealed the face of a living, breathing man in his thirties, heavy five-o-clock shadow, dark eyes, and skin that looked like he needed some sun. Maypole stared at a ghost.

"Dr. Maypole, you're going to think I'm fried, but I was told to contact you by a guy who's been dead for two hundred years. My name is Seraph Stone."

His accent was unique, probably developed on the ship over centuries. She could hardly understand him. He clipped words and ran them together. She slowed the speed.

"I received a message from Lt. John Lauretta," the man said. "Words cannot be plainly spoken here on the ship. We are watched. All the time. So I am sending his message, to ask if you might help me with finding an object."

"Object?" Maypole was already confused.

"Lauretta said you were the only one to ask." Stone swallowed hard, then repeated, "The *only* one. Watch his message."

She opened the file. There he was. If she'd had a heart, it would have stopped. To see John again. Gray-haired, wrinkled, his eyes were the same green seas she had loved so long ago. Pain shot through her imagined self. She still did. And his voice . . . She closed her eyes and listened.

"My name is John Lauretta. I am the first agricultural officer aboard the launch crew of the *Vera Rubin,* and I have information that will be critical to those who reach Varanasi. That information is stored in an object on the ship in a secure location. I trust that you, the current ranking agricultural officer, are authorized to contact the ground crew. Find Dr. Camber Maypole. She will know where to look."

In the video, John held up a sheet of paper with a single word written on it. But it was written in a cypher, one Camber had invented centuries ago. It took several minutes to recall the meaning of the scrambled hieroglyphs, little pictograms she had taken so much pleasure in creating when she was a teenager. With this code, she and John had shared their thoughts, all through training, all through prelaunch. They'd left notes in lockers, comments during briefings, and notes on pillows.

She finally formulated the word. "Legacy."

"Legacy? What does that mean? For fuck's sake, John, you couldn't give me any more than that?"

Whatever it was he was talking about was something he did not want Vera to know. Why? Because she would destroy it, whatever it was.

Maypole's mind raced. Not only had John been doing detective work on the ship, but he also knew that Maypole would be waiting on Varanasi. The only way John could have known that she would be salvaged and cast to Varanasi would be if Lemkos had told him.

The man who had identified himself as Seraph Stone reappeared, his ashen face bobbing in and out of view. He said, "Contact me, please."

Maypole closed her comms and looked past the orchids to the mist blanketing the sea. In her mind, she was back on the ship with John. What was it he had hidden? And what did "legacy" mean?

She found Puppy on her bed and curled up beside him. She reached out and stroked the seahound's head, smoothing the aqua-colored plumage, now darkening to forest green with the night. He shifted and settled under her touch.

She will know where to look. For what?

In her mind, she began walking the ship: the concourses, the offices, the farms, the commons. What and where? Most importantly, why? Was it coincidence this crewmember, Seraph Stone, had contacted her just days after Martine Sommer confronted her about the embryos?

Maypole missed tears even more than skin. Without them, the pain just built up inside with no way out. She reminded herself now was the only reality; everything else was data.

4

THE EYE OF THE SOUL

2345-02-10, *Earth Standard, aboard the* Vera Rubin

THERE HAD BEEN no response from Camber Maypole, not even an acknowledgement. Maybe she was gone, erased, or whatever they did to the mindware on that planet. Seraph had started looking for the "object" himself, tearing the office apart in the farm, the fertilizer storage, anywhere he could think of that this guy might have hidden something. Information was a broad term. It could be anything. A file, a photo, a drive.

Seraph risked only one search query for the name John Lauretta. Anything else might alert Vera. To what? What was happening here? Seraph had been contacted by a guy who held Seraph's job hundreds of years ago. Lauretta was sending him on a hunt for something deemed critical. But how? And by whose reckoning?

Vera's search produced a list of references from the ship's records —several schematics for mechs designed by one John Lauretta, a science article entitled "Radiation-generated Mutations in Soy," and a string of photos of a man who looked like he'd been born on Earth—stocky and compact, thick neck and small cranium. In a wiki dedicated to the launch crew, he found more. There was a short biography of the man who had sent Seraph the message.

Lt. John Lauretta, first agricultural officer, Torus-1. Born 14 December 2062 in Omaha, Nebraska. Died 9 October 2129 aboard the Vera Rubin.

In the first few days of his search for the object, the protests over feeding Retro had turned violent, stirred by moving sermons delivered by the Harbinger. A restaurant owner was dragged from his establishment while others pilfered his food stores. A great pile of soy, rice, and chickpeas sat in the T-1 commons, reserves donated by individuals and families. But TJ refused to allow it to be moved to the hub. She'd placed security forces around the food, as well as the lifts that led up to the ship's central linkage, the cylindrical hub about which the two tori revolved.

That night, Seraph served a loaf of powdered protein and mixed veggies. Rain picked at it, telling her gran about the VR excursions to Varanasi they were doing in school.

"We have to know the names of all the common plants and animals, especially the poison ones," Rain said.

"As long as you know the poison ones, you'll be fine, sweetie."

"Pearl," TJ scolded, "that's not how we do it here. The more we know the better."

Pearl shrugged, shot Seraph a look, and went back to her dinner, drowning it in barbeque sauce. As with all surrogates, Seraph looked nothing like his mother. Her short blond hair was turning white, and her waistline was rounding with age. Pearl's partner and Seraph's other mother, Clare, had died a few years ago, and Pearl had become a recluse, living on a steady diet of social media and courses on Bible study. Seraph had made a point of having her over for dinner as often as possible, just to get her out.

Pearl had come over for another reason too. Seraph had asked her to—no, begged, actually. He and TJ were less likely to fight with Pearl there. Since the food shortage, tempers were shorter than usual, and Seraph hoped TJ might listen to her. Pearl had been as much a mother to TJ as to Seraph.

TJ was quiet while Pearl chattered on about the Harbinger, the preacher from Torus-2 who was close to inciting a riot. She said he believed in a single mind or soul that encompassed the entire universe and linked all things by invisible threads, a belief that was at odds with Pearl's Christian philosophy.

"'Fireseed' he calls it, the part that links us all. Says the fireseed within us speaks to the First Flame, tells us where our fate lies. And we're all just some kind of projection. Simulation dreamt by the First Flame." Pearl dished out some salad. "His fireseed speaks to Baakos with the mouth of his god, whispers to him with orders, prophecies. Dreams and such."

TJ rolled her eyes and sighed as if she'd heard this a hundred times. She was tired and frayed. "Did it tell him, 'Don't fix your damaged farm pods?'" she snapped. "He should have been doing *that* instead of praying to his First Flame."

"His First Flame apparently told him to arm his people," Pearl said tentatively. "Some say they're ready to cut through our airlocks. Take the food we won't give them." At least Pearl had said it, not Seraph. Without looking up, TJ shoveled the loaf into her mouth as if she hadn't heard.

His mother cast a panicked glance his way.

"Look," TJ finally said, still chewing. "I understand what you two are doing, and Pearl, I love you. But you don't know what you're talking about."

"Do you want bloodshed?" Seraph asked her. "You know that's next. They're not going to quietly slip into starvation without a fight."

"So much for peace and love," TJ said, dropping her fork and leaning back in her chair, wiping her palms down her thighs.

"We could use a little more of that around here too," Seraph said.

TJ snorted a laugh.

Pearl stood and took Rain's hand. "Let's go take a walk, sweetie."

"But, Gran," Rain said, "they fight all the time."

"Well, let's find something better to do, eh?"

Rain looked over her shoulder at Seraph as the door closed. Her starburst eyes said this was all his fault. She was right.

For a long moment, the only conversation in the kitchen was between the ever-present air recycler and the clinking of ice against plasti-glass.

"I just want to feed those people, TJ." When she didn't respond, he pressed on, "I'll take the food myself. No open airlocks. I'll just leave it in the hub and go. I'll never contact them. I'll even wear a pressure suit. No possibility of contamination. We have enough food in reserve to feed everyone in Retro for a month or more."

"Will you help them get those farms back up and running too? Because without them, they'll die anyway."

"You think they're not capable?"

"You said it yourself, or Pearl did. They've been building a fucking army over there. They think we're going to have to fight the scary robots when we get to Varanasi. The rise of the joboxes." She made a frightened waggling of her hands. "The Harbinger says they're going to kill us. Now who's spreading panic, Ser?"

"If those guns exist at all, they're going to fight *us* first," Seraph corrected. "How do you think you'll defend *us*?"

TJ leaned across the table toward him. Her dark hair looked like a helmet, every curly strand tamed and plastered to her head. She'd tried to cover up the dark circles under her copper eyes with makeup that didn't match her rich skin tone. It made her look bilious, hungover. Maybe she was hungover.

"I'm saying Vera won't let it happen."

"What about you, TJ? What, or who, are you willing to sacrifice so you can stick with the rule book?"

"I've heard enough." She bolted to her feet and headed for the door, but Seraph blocked her path.

"There's no running away from this. From us. Listen to me." He took her shoulders and forced her to meet his eyes. "There has to be a way around Vera."

"All hail Seraph the savior! If you were smarter and stayed off the hootch, you'd know landing is not guaranteed. If by some act of God or the First Flame or the tooth fairy we do have to fight those joboxes? What then Ser? How will you save them then? Because I'm trying to save us now. I'm doing my job. So why don't you do yours."

She gave up with a long exhalation and ran both palms over her helmet of hair. She slumped onto the couch and held her head in her hands.

Seraph paced the room, rejecting every response that crawled to his lips, rejecting the belief that she was right. He finally asked, "What's the status of their farm pods?"

"Half are planted. The rest in various stages of repair."

"If it was Rain who was starving? What would you do then?"

She straightened up and set her jaw, muscles flexing. She met his eyes. "I'd do nothing different."

"I don't believe that for a second." Seraph held her gaze, willing her to see things as he did. "You would protect our daughter's life no matter what it took. And so will the parents in Retro."

She stared at nothing, her head shaking just perceptibly. "The problem with you, Ser, is you are blind to what's really going on here. With Retro. With us."

"I know exactly what's going on . . . with us," he said.

TJ levered herself from the couch, slipped on her pristine captain's jacket, and pushed past Seraph on her way to the door. He made no move to stop her.

"I've got work tonight." She turned back to him one last time. "Do me a favor and make sure you're not passed out when Rain gets back."

Then she was gone.

The hootch tasted particularly bitter that night.

SERAPH WAITED until Rain was asleep before he called the Harbinger. He wanted to hear it from the guy himself, not the edited social media circus that was going around.

The image of Alexandre Baakos bounced in and out of view on Seraph's palmcomm. The man talked while he walked, touring Seraph through the damaged farm pods.

"What is it you think you can do for us from over there, Lt. Stone?"

"Assess some workarounds for your farms," Seraph told him. "If the components are damaged, maybe we should try setting up temporary systems on the fabber deck."

"Already done. Unless you can make plants grow faster, you got nothing for us. Here," Baakos said, turning the palmcomm and pressing it up to an airlock window. On the other side, a swarm of mechs and waldos threaded wires and tubing down the length of new banks of aquaponics.

"This was all blown out," Baakos said, tapping the glass. "One quarter of our food. Gone. Then the freezers went down."

Seraph had seen no photos of the damage. He had to assume TJ had seen this.

The debris hit was far more extensive than she had let on. The offending rock had managed to breach the mag shield that protected them from interstellar dust. It had forced the shutdown of one of the three reactors, which in turn had led to power problems that had affected their temperature controls and grow lights. Mechs on the exterior of the ship had salvaged what they could of the remaining materials blown out by the collision. That stuff had to be re-fabbed into useable parts.

This was bigger than a few downed fish tanks. But why was TJ hiding it?

Seraph knew that overstepping his rank was unwise and making promises he couldn't keep was even worse. "Listen, Mr. Baakos, we are in negotiations right now about how best to handle this. You've already set up tanks on the fabber deck?"

"Check. And in my house too. We all got things growing in our units."

"When's the first harvest?"

"Crickets coming in real quick. We have eggs, milk from the goats. But it's not enough."

"Let me see what I can do. I'll get back to you tomorrow."

"And then what, eh?" Baakos said. His gleaming skin was the color of oak leaves just before they dropped. Baakos's eye filled the screen and blinked at Seraph. He had the eye mutation too, the red starburst around his pupil ringed by an algae-green iris. That was strange. The same mutation had arisen in Torus-2? With no genetic mixing? What were the odds of that?

"You gonna let us die?" Baakos said. "That's what the captain says. No food. No salvation for the Retros. But you, my friend, are named after the avenging angels of the old god, Jehovah. Seraphim? Right?"

Old god?

"My mom was into that kind of thing. Look," Seraph said, "nobody needs to die. We'll find a solution. But whipping up people about war with the joboxes? We got no reason to think—"

"Have you looked into the eye of your soul? Have you dreamed the same dreams as me?" Baakos's voice dropped into that sonorous preacher tone. "You know what's waiting for us on Varanasi, yes you do, I say. Bodiless minds longing for the flesh, longing for mortality."

"How do you know that?"

"I dreamt it, friend."

"And I dreamt the tilapia flew out of their tanks and attacked us, but I don't think it's going to happen," Seraph said.

Baakos squinted into his palmcomm, examining Seraph. Then he said, "You heard the voice of the dead, didn't you?"

"What?"

"Of course, you did," Baakos said, his face retreating from the screen. "You heard them whispering."

This guy couldn't know about the message from John Lauretta. Impossible.

Seraph said, "I don't know what you mean."

"'The devil's voice is sweet to hear,'" Baakos quoted somebody. "You're thinking I'm talking with the devil's voice. But you know better, Seraphim Stone, angel of the old god. You know I speak truth because our captor has not forbidden me."

Then the screen went blank.

Baakos thought the jobox—the minds on Varanasi—meant them harm. It didn't make sense. They had to be the same human minds that were cast out there at the speed of light almost three hundred years ago. NASA technicians and their AI programming helped them. Nothing to fear. But the question remained. Why had Vera, who censored everything, allowed Baakos to broadcast the truth of their hunger? He'd found a way around it. Maybe his fireseed had done it.

Seraph thought of the hundreds of thousands of refugee minds that had traversed the micro-wormhole to Varanasi. The lottery winners from a dying Earth. No, it wasn't just NASA waiting there. There was a microcosm of humanity itself. And look what they had done to Earth.

<hr>

IT HAD BEEN ALMOST five days since Seraph sent the message to Maypole. There was a delay, of course, but not more than twelve hours. He'd given up on a reply when it finally came. He locked himself in his bedroom and read.

No video, just text.

I'm sorry for the delay, Lt. Stone, it read. *Memories are odd things for us, prone to omissions and alterations. But about the object. I can only think of one place to look. The launch crew carried sentimental items to Varanasi, objects from Earth. These were stowed in the hub, aft. Our names are on the bags. Look there.*

The hub? Feces, no one was going to the hub right now.

You can do something for me, Maypole wrote. *I'm looking for information about the genetic diversity program. Records of embryo implantations through the centuries. Especially any reference to Rishi Corporation.*

"How does she expect me to get that?"

Seraph queried Vera about Rishi Corporation. It turned out this company had actually built Vera, *and* they were the lead contractor for all infrastructure on Varanasi. Back in the early part of the twenty-first century, Rishi launched the micro-wormhole that allowed information and nanobots instant transport from Earth to Varanasi. When they got there, those nanobots built something called the Black Stack.

Seraph had heard the term but had to look it up. Vera produced a data entry:

The Black Stack is an advanced quantum computer constructed in situ by the first nanobots that arrived on Varanasi soon after the micro-wormhole's distal mouth reached the planet. Information, streaming through the wormhole, enabled the replication and expansion of the nanorobots that built the earliest infrastructure. They, in turn, produced macro-bots and the first mining operations. It required fifty years for the Black Stack to reach its primary functionality and to receive the first mindware that was cast through the wormhole on low infrared waves.

"Huh." So the whole business was run on a single mainframe. Like the ship. The Black Stack was Vera's counterpart, except it had two centuries of upgrades that Vera lacked. The ship had stopped receiving transmissions from Earth at least a hundred years ago. No one had explained why, or maybe Seraph just never cared enough to ask.

"Vera," he queried, "is the micro-wormhole still functional?"

"Status is unknown," she replied.

Seraph went back to the Rishi entry and found a short video that looked like an advertisement. A guy was talking about immortality and how anyone with the means could live forever in a paradise unaffected by the devastation happening on Earth. "You have an option: Consciousness Salvage. Only available from Rishi Corporation. Think of it as Disneyland for your soul."

"What's Disneyland?" Seraph asked aloud.

Vera replied, "An amusement park in Anaheim, California, founded in 1956 by Walt Disney, known for his animated feature films and—"

"Vera, stop," Seraph commanded. He would find out more about this Disneyland later. First, this scavenger hunt. But he could only think of Rain. She would understand some day, he told himself. He had to trust that she would.

All he had to do was find a way into the hub. And if he was going to do something that stupid anyway, he better take food with him.

People had to eat.

5

SHIVI DESH

2345-02-12, Earth Standard, Varanasi

KOLYA LEMKOS COULDN'T THINK of anything he'd rather do than spend a day climbing a gorge with Camber. But he had convinced her to hold off until it actually was *day*. Besides, he had work to do, and she claimed she had medical files from the ship to analyze.

When his course corrections were locked in, the estimated time to the ship's orbital insertion around Varanasi was fourteen days, give or take a day. This improved the chances of the starving people in Torus-2 since the ship had calculated the arrival based on their uncorrected course. This made Camber a little happier, not much, but a little. Still, there would be no slacking between now and then, and a climb in Shivi Desh would be the ultimate boondoggle. But before they left, Lemkos wanted to pay a visit to Martine Sommer.

It surprised him that Martine had attended the New Skin investment meeting at all. Her reputation as a champion of refugee rights had landed her in more than one lawsuit against Rishi Corp. It was Martine who was the first to recognize the effects of long-term virtual immersion on mindware. Fantasy fulfillment and full-service pleasure stims ultimately led to depression and a longing for true death. Not only had she identified the problem, but she had also created a brilliant solution.

Martine Sommer was a recluse, hidden away in her self-made virtual realm. She'd built this world, Occitania, and made it available to anyone free of charge. This had raised a shitstorm with the other Vested. They deemed her action a "dangerous precedent," an undermining of the monopoly Rishi had on virtual reality tech, because Martine's system was totally independent of the Black Stack.

Like the Black Stack, Martine's quantum stacks were buried deep in the crust of Varanasi at unknown locations. Some even said her systems were more powerful than the Black Stack, but Lemkos knew her resources were nowhere near as vast. How much money could she have possibly made on shoes?

Occitania was a free realm, so all her income had to be generated by her product, "The Samara Experience." What had started as research had become the premier virtual immersion experience.

Martine's clients chose to store their original, biological memories, their mindware, in Samsara, rather than in the Black Stack. They were then born into one of her Samsara realms as infants, totally blank slates. They lived a new reality, complete with pain, suffering, and death. It was so real that it had made Lemkos question if his life on Earth had just been a different iteration of a virtual life experience. Of course, Samsara was no cheaper than any of Rishi's alternate worlds. You had to be a rich prick for any of them.

Being a rich prick himself, Lemkos had tried Samsara more than once. He'd lived an entire life during the Bolshevik revolution, even led a decisive victory in the Battle of Novo Litovoskaya. In another life he was a gladiator in Imperial Rome. In both cases, when he returned to the reality of his bodiless existence, he felt like he'd opened god's eyes and looked out upon the universe—if only for a moment. But in that moment, he was all people and none, everything and nothing.

Humanity had for millennia dug in the earth from dawn 'til dusk in search of food, metals to shape into weapons, and resources to build their shelters. Their very existence was spent keeping their biomass alive. Their sole purpose was to eat, procreate, and die in good stead with their gods. With no such burden upon the bodiless minds on Varanasi, the deepest kind of longing and psychosis had destroyed many of them. To some degree or another, the drifting sense of purposelessness had infected them all. Even Camber Maypole, though she'd fought it better than most.

It took Lemkos longer than expected to get to Occitania. Portal after portal made him feel like he'd spent days traveling, which was all intentional. "Things should not be easy," Martine had once told him, "because the human mind needs challenges and trials to grow. Without growth, it cannot survive."

Martine's castle was in keeping with the thirteenth-century culture of Occitania and overlooked a bustling medieval city. Lemkos would have preferred a simple vid call, but he made his way through the streets on a horse he'd rented from the livery at the gate. The streets were crowded with market stalls selling everything from leather to live chickens. The smell of shit and blood could not be overridden by the fruit stand.

Martine's servants all had the same burly look and matching armor—all but the seneschal, a squat, monkish-looking man with a silver brooch on his shoulder. He led Lemkos through the great hall and out to the central garden.

Martine no longer wore the adventurously hot avatar Lemkos had known years ago, sadly. Her days of orgies and thrill-seeking were long gone. When she was alone, she chose an avatar fashioned of light and air. A "gossamer," people called them. Her virtual flesh was an energy field of color, a scintillating, fluid shape. With galaxies for eyes, her nebular tresses of spun light made a cloud above her head.

Her heart was a red bird that fluttered its wings like a pulse inside her transparent ribcage.

She was barefoot. Interesting for one who had once designed shoes on Earth.

"Martine." Lemkos took the extended hands and kissed both of her glowing cheeks.

"I assume you've come to chastise me for bringing your friend, Dr. Maypole, into this?" Her Danish accent was as sexy as ever.

Lemkos shrugged and clasped his hands behind his back. "To be honest, I'm not sure what it is you're bringing her into. You've got her whipped up about something she was involved with as part of the launch crew. How did you find out about that?"

Martine smiled mischievously and nodded. "It's no secret. Those memories are available for little money at the Memory Arcade."

"But . . . who cares?" he asked bluntly. "What does Camber Maypole have to do with *your* war with Rishi?"

"Possibly everything. I've been able to access a few of the historical files from the ship. Downloading has begun, as I'm sure you know. Two hundred and forty some years of data."

"And?"

"*And* there are records of multiple transmissions between Maypole and John Lauretta before the ship left the Sol system."

"Well, yeah. They were lovers. Why would they not talk?" Saying it aloud brought all that long-buried resentment with it. Lemkos, Camber, and John had been the three amigos, yet Lemkos had suffered the fate of all third wheels—a love triangle worthy of Shakespeare.

"What I saw were not love letters," she said. "They both held up handwritten notes before the camera with ideograms untranslatable without a key. Recall the Rosetta Stone. Neither my system nor the Black Stack can parse it."

"She had secrets to tell John?"

"It appears so."

"Written in code?" Lemkos found that hard to believe. "So you knew Camber would be at the skin meeting and you tried to ambush her."

Martine nodded. "Ambush is not exactly accurate, but she is unwilling to talk to me. I understand this. I represent everything she loathes. But you she trusts."

"I've told you what I know."

"Why is she here, Kolya?"

Lemkos was not about to answer that. He had tried to explain it to himself far too many times. He sighed and pursed his lips.

Martine went on, "She was discharged from NASA for insubordination, and yet, here she is, in their employ once again. How?"

"She won the lottery."

"So she's simply a refugee like most of those here?"

He nodded. Martine didn't need to know anything about Maypole's salvage.

"Maypole drew the right number and hit the uploader," Lemkos said. "Kaja Singh, the Flight Director, wasn't going to let her training go to waste. Not with a ship full of humans on the way. She's a surgeon. Bots can do the basics, but sometimes it takes experience."

Those galaxy eyes could see the lie plainly. "There are surgeons aboard the ship."

"I'm going climbing with her today," Lemkos said. "I'll find out more if I can, but, Martine, I'm not sure what this has to do with Rishi."

"I am not sure either." She ran glowing fingers down his arm and clasped his hand briefly. What was that supposed to mean? Her voice was a crystalline chime. "I once read, 'The forge of the soul is evolution. Without it, we are recursive machines.' And here we are. A population of hundreds of thousands of minds—stagnant, unenlightened machines. There are plenty who would trade it all to return to biology."

"And some of us wouldn't."

"Kolya, when you awoke after living a lifetime as a gladiator, you remember that feeling? That was something called 'involution.' The soul's journey back to its origin," Martine explained. The red bird fluttered in her ribcage. "Our journey to become that which we already are. I want you to find out what Maypole transmitted in her coded letters." She added, "You *do* value the freedom and safety of the people aboard that ship, do you not?"

The colonists represented a distant Earth, a way of existence that had died with Lemkos's body. Did he really care what happened to a ship full of disease-ridden, eating, shitting, neurotic human beings?

"No," he said at last. "But I care about Maypole."

LEMKOS OPENED the eyes of his holo-print. He was in his office at Mission Control, crazy with the bustle of his assistants and multiple readouts of the nav systems aboard the *Vera Rubin*. He'd issued three correction commands to Vera's primary controls. Overrides to her outdated logistics. That should keep the flight director happy for a little while.

After fielding a few questions from assistants, he met Camber on the roof. The long night was giving way to the sun, and the eastern sky blushed a deep crimson. Sunrise and sunset lasted minutes on Earth, but here they lasted a day and a half.

"Late again." She scowled at him and mounted the step into the waiting flyer.

"Yeah. Sorry, Cupcake. Some last-minute problems."

He debated sharing the conversation he'd had with Martine. But Maypole would not be happy that memories of her as a launch crew member were for sale in the Memory Arcade, and even more unhappy that Martine had been analyzing them for some cryptic information.

"Let's go, then," he finally said.

Even by the feeble dawn light, the green cliffs of the highlands were visible, rising steeply toward the eroded canyon called Shivi Desh, still shrouded in darkness. Lemkos hadn't been up this way in decades and was surprised to see islands of light dotting the cliffs. There were more mines than he remembered. Still, the wildness of this place filled him with a primal wonder, like nothing he'd ever experienced on an overpopulated, disease-ridden Earth. This place was still pristine and raw. No wonder Camber spent so much time out here. But today, she was chasing a rumor. Some guy at the Rishi venture capital meeting had mentioned an experiment in Shivi Desh and Martine had doubled down on it.

Camber was pointing at the peaks in the distance, the snow gleaming pink in the dawn light.

"Do you know why they call them the bloody peaks?" she asked over the sound of the flyer's blades.

"No, but I have a feeling you're going to tell me."

"In the summer, red lichen stains the snow at high altitudes. With the spring thaw coming, we should start to see the red appear soon."

"Cool," he said flatly, and she punched him.

Majriti, and hence Varanasi, took three-and-a-half Earth years to orbit its star. During one of those three years, the planet traveled far enough from the star to leave the habitable zone and plunge the land into a long winter. Only the floor of the vast network of gorges remained hospitable then, and when the planet headed back into the warmth of its star, everything thawed quickly. Spring thaw. It had taken some civil engineers' minds to find a safe place to build Colony Village, which turned out to be in the foothills above the Ganges's floodplain.

"Climbing in a gorge with a thaw coming. Smart, Cupcake."

"We won't be there long," she said.

"The Ganges is already thawed. The estuary is greening."

Camber sighed. "You'll be fine."

On a rise above the flood plain, the refugees had built their Shrine of the Dead. The dawn light was enhanced by the ghostly luminescence of the monuments. These lights were joined by those from an outpost where robots mined elements that had been rare on Earth but weren't so rare here.

The flyer touched down, kicking up dirt and leaves into a cyclone. Lemkos and Camber gathered their climbing gear and stepped out. She liked to make-believe they were still thirty-something NASA jocks who spent weekends climbing whatever mountain they could fly to and be back in time for work the next day. Now, the ropes were a kind of psychological prop for her.

A disorganized forest of crooked obelisks, crosses, and weeping angels littered the meadow. In those first years, as digital refugees had poured through the micro-wormhole, people had built this shrine as a remembrance to those lost to the carrion virus on Earth. A jumble of miniature temples dotted the place, though the wind and weather of two centuries had dulled the inscriptions.

Lemkos wondered why Camber hadn't built one for John, but realized her shrine to John was the gorge itself, and the hours she spent climbing it was her ritual, her way of honoring a man she loved deeply, a man Lemkos could never compete with.

Most of the holo images the shrines had once projected were now either glitched or busted altogether. The rags of more recent prayer flags had lost all color.

"I wonder if the wind still carries people's prayers up here?" Camber said, hitching a coil of rope over her shoulder.

"What's left to pray for?" Lemkos answered.

"How about the safe arrival of humanity to this rock?"

He laughed. "*We* are the gods who will bring them safely to ground, Camber. It's what we're here for, right?"

She gave him that smirk, the one where only one corner of her mouth quirked in unison with her Frida Kahlo eyebrows.

Camber lingered over one of the shrines, reading the lengthy inscription immortalizing the family of one refugee named Hung Pellow. Weeds had climbed up the carved stone image of a tree. Their prehensile roots were tapping the small current that ran the holograms. In the center of a Star of David, Maypole pointed out a plant she called a pincer poppy, a carnivorous beast with chitinous spikes as sharp as the teeth of a piranha, all encased in velvety red petals.

"What are we looking for up here exactly?" Lemkos asked.

"Did you go to my funeral?" She asked the question without looking at him.

"What? Oh, come on, Cupcake, you've got to be kidding me? Your funeral?"

"Don't call me Cupcake," she replied, gazing back at the pincer poppy. "Now did you go to my funeral? Yes or no."

"Don't be ridiculous—"

"Yes or no."

Lemkos gave a long sigh and pursed his lips, calculating how to put it. "You didn't have one."

The look she gave him must have required all the functionality of her emotion simulator.

"Let me explain." Lemkos held out his hands as if trying to calm an attack dog. "Your family was already dead, and the ship launched and-and do you know how much money it took to bribe some rent-a-minister to say something generic about yet another victim of the fucking virus? Camberrrr." He gave her his most serious look. "I took some of your ashes to the launch pad. Sprinkled you over the burn marks."

After a long silence, she asked, "Did you say any words?"

"Yes."

"What were they?"

It was his turn to be silent, then he said, "Let me call you Cupcake and maybe I'll tell you."

"Asshole." She tossed him a coil of rope and led the way to the dark mouth of a slot canyon.

He had no desire to relive that part of his life. Being left by his best friends, one on a starship and one squirted through space on a beam of low infrared. If it weren't for Camber, he'd have just puked up his guts and bled out his eyes like the rest of the world and floated off into the wasteland of death.

The cool dawn air between the wind-scoured walls registered in his sensors as a crisp, highly oxygenated embrace. Following Maypole's lead, Lemkos dragged his fingers over a cushion of mossy sponge patapa covering the side of a boulder. It reminded him of cat fur or as close as his sensors could get to that. They waded through a meadow of sprouting plumage. The featherlike plants were coiled like fiddlehead ferns back in the Carpathian Mountains where he'd grown up. But these creatures, once fully open, would take flight and find a host.

Maypole attacked a rock face, setting pitons as if her life depended on them. All she had to do was extend the graspers of her holo-print skeleton and pull herself up. But he wouldn't dispel the fantasy for her. She had always been the best free climber of the three of them.

The last grip of the long winter held the highlands hostage. At this altitude, he expected everything to be frozen, even in the gorge-lands, but the Alaknanda River traced a trickle of milky blue water from the canyon called Shivi Desh. The glaciers had started to warm already, and soon it would be a torrent all the way into the Ganges Valley eighty kilometers away.

He and Camber discussed the tasks required to assist the ship into orbit, but Lemkos guided their talk back to the past, to their friendship with John Lauretta. They topped one rock face and found themselves in a small meadow that led to the main gorge, still steeped in darkness. The sun had not risen high enough to reach into the vertical depths of this canyon.

Lemkos said, "Remember that time John jumped out of the cargo hold wearing a gorilla suit?"

"What's the deal with the John questions?" Maypole asked.

"He's just on my mind. That's all."

"Listen," Maypole said. She stopped in the middle of a field of star flowers and spun to face him. "The last message I got from John was just before the ship left system. He blamed *me* for fucking up. Doing my job, that's all I was doing. Asking the right questions."

"What kind of questions?" Lemkos pushed.

"I already told you. A late shipment of embryos was sent to the ship. I asked where they came from. That's it. They fucking canned me." She took two steps closer, so her eyes were visible in the dim dawn light, white with anger. "Is that what Martine wants to know? You only came along so you can grill me about how I got kicked off the mission?"

He came along because he loved her. And if Martine thought Camber knew something that could put her in danger, Lemkos would find out what it was.

Instead he said, "She wants to know what you know about those embryos."

"Nothing. Absolutely nothing. Okay?"

"Okay," he agreed. "But I don't actually know why the hell we're out here except you'll take any excuse to do some pretend climbing."

"Your friend, Martine, thinks Rishi is doing illegal experimentation up here. Remember?" She hitched the rope coil onto her shoulder and waded through the white flowers toward the yawning darkness of the gorge's mouth.

"Let's go back," he said.

"Back? We're almost to the valley floor."

"I've got work to do," he said. "I shouldn't be out here in the first place."

"Then go. You got what you came for. Nothing."

Lemkos sighed and prepped his onboard arsenal.

It was a short hike to the floor of the gorge. Hundreds of feet up on the rim, dawn lit the frosting of snow and glaciers. But no early morning light could reach the narrow depths of this canyon, so their night vision was a distinct requirement. A few bioluminescent insects moved in swarms, like fireflies. The rest of the beasts were hidden or sleeping.

They paused, bringing up visual magnification to scan the cliffs for lights. The sandstone here was nearly vertical, except for some outcroppings furred with plants.

"If there's a lab here, it ought to be lit. Or at least have a heat signature," Camber said. "Can't run a bunch of mechs without power."

"Unless it's so deep in these walls that it doesn't show. If I were hiding something, that'd be what I'd do." In night vision, the walls of scoured sandstone shone in false color with an occasional blob of brightness. Flying predators called windeaters lived only in the canyons and roosted on the cliffs. Windeaters were nothing to mess with, even in a weaponized holo-print. They had talons like scythes, and their spit was corrosive.

Camber sighed. "Maybe that blue guy at the meeting was full of—"

The blow came from above Lemkos, knocking him to the ground. His night vision was on magnify, rendering the body before him as nothing more than a wall of green flesh and feathers.

As he pulled his magnification back, he saw Camber lasso the thing with her rope. She gave it a yank, pulling the creature off Lemkos and dropping it. It had a neck like the Loch Ness Monster and teeth to match. It lunged, biting the air, flapping its massive, membranous wings as if trying to fly away. In a millisecond, Camber's arm shot out, and she had the snaking neck clamped to the ground. Like a feathered dragon with six limbs, the beast opened a clawed fist and surrendered its spiked cudgel.

In the false color of his night vision, Lemkos saw layers of plumage and snapping teeth, needles of hardened chitin, and the iridescent flash of nocturnal eyes. This thing was five times the size of a windeater. More like the size of a small horse. A hellion.

"Camber, just kill it!" Lemkos cried.

But upon hearing his voice, the beast stopped struggling and stared intently at Lemkos.

From beneath the hellion's fluff of plumage, just below the spot where its long neck sprouted from its torso, a cheap modulator blinked with a dull light.

A synth voice issued from the device; it said, "Kolyaa Lemkus?"

6

THE GOOD OF THE MANY

2345-02-12, *Earth Standard, aboard the* Vera Rubin

SERAPH ARRIVED EARLY on the Command Deck for the officers debrief. All attempts at convincing TJ to allow a delivery of food to the hub had failed. It was time to try another approach. But before he got himself thrown in the brig, Seraph figured he should try one last time to get the data for Camber Maypole.

He had made some failed attempts at accessing the medical database using his officer status but, of course, genetic data was confidential. He wasn't sure he knew what he was looking for, or even if he should be helping this relic from the launch. The only assurance he had that he could trust Maypole was the word of a dead ag specialist. The embryos in question would have been incorporated into the genetic diversity protocol and were in some way attached to Rishi Corporation. Would that be indicated in the records?

Seraph had barely passed his exams on plant genetics, let alone this.

But he owed Maypole. If she was right and John Lauretta's "legacy" was in the hub, Seraph would find a way to get to it.

The Command Deck filled slowly with the sound of whispers and laughter. Sitting in his usual seat, Seraph felt like a stalker, knowing Dr. Zahn was always the first one to these debriefs. He had rehearsed what he would say but knew there was little that would convince a doctor to reveal patient information.

Eighteen seats rose in a semicircle around the podium, beyond which a wall of glass separated them from a field of stars. One, a brilliant golden jewel, was larger than it had been two days before. Upsilon Andromedae.

"Beautiful, isn't it?" Dr. Zahn took her assigned seat beside Seraph.

"I suppose."

"You're early," she noted with a look of surprise. Was he late that often?

He jumped right in, before he forgot what he had planned to say. "Actually, I have a question for you."

She stiffened, probably thinking he would ask for some off-the-cuff medical advice.

"I am a biobank baby," he said. "One hundred percent. Mother and father both residents of Earth." That would be obvious to anyone by his build and looks. "But I am interested in finding out more about my daughter's genetic profile. I know she must have other banked people in her lineage. Now that we're starting a new life on Varanasi, it would be good to carry the people from the past with us, if just in name. Is there a database where I can check into this? A genealogy?"

"Well," Zahn mused. "Everyone has access to their own hereditary lines. If the captain approves, seeing that she is Rain's biological mother, you could search her lines, or she can share them with you."

"I see." That wasn't the answer he was hoping for. His own heredity was unremarkable. He had found nothing but the lineage of the two long-dead individuals who had donated sperm and egg to make him. But TJ must have some biobank inclusions in her background, and he was hoping he'd find one of these Rishi embryos there.

"Okay, great," he said. "Thanks."

A pat on his shoulder announced Mansour from propulsion. He took his seat on the other side of Seraph, sniffed, and gave Seraph a look of disappointment. His wild froth of black hair matched his beard, and he crossed his arms over his growing paunch. He had no room for criticism.

"It can't be that bad," Mansour said, indicating the spiked coffee.

"You don't know anything about it, keso."

"Okay, okay. Just take it easy, Ser."

He owed Mansour no explanations. He owed nobody an explanation. He took a sip of his coffee.

TJ hadn't even been home in days. Seraph had his suspicions about where she was, had for a while. He'd even planted a modified pollibot in the lemon tree in her office, equipped with a camera. But he'd never looked at the feed, because he was a coward. Once he knew for sure what was going on, there would be no way to pretend it wasn't.

With the other seats filled, TJ appeared, her uniform clean and pressed, her silky, untamable hair pulled into that austere black knot Seraph hated. Her eyes met his and held them. She raised one eyebrow as if in challenge then smiled smugly. Did she want him to fight for her? Was that what this was about? Did she want him to lose what little control he had, get thrown in the brig, just to make the point that she was hurting not just him but Rain?

Those officers slated to give presentations sat behind her. Niall Bora was one of them. He leaned forward to whisper to her more than once. Whatever he said turned the corners of her mouth into a conspiratorial smile. She licked her lips. That spack-bender. Bora's pale hair and red beard were trimmed to the same length. He had mitigated the lengthening and thinning of his own limbs by working out with weights since he'd hit puberty, building thick arms and legs and a broad chest.

As security chief, Bora believed he commanded the security mechs, but everyone knew Vera was the one in control. Of everything. Allegedly, that was to ensure no one could commandeer the security mechs for nefarious purposes, like carry food to the hub or pick up a dead crew member's bag.

Seraph analyzed every glance, every gesture, that passed between Bora and TJ. At one point, TJ caught Seraph staring, so he looked at his mug and took a drink.

All these people trusted Vera. They had been chosen by the ship for leadership positions, not necessarily because they were best suited to lead, but because they never questioned the ship's directives. Seraph would never have been promoted to first agricultural officer if his mentor had not died of a stroke with no one else prepared to step into the job. He wasn't top of his class, not even the top half, as TJ liked to remind him.

All psych evals, occ evals, even education, everything was delivered to the colonists through Vera. The people aboard the ship knew and understood nothing beyond what she had fed them from the day they were born.

Vera had engineered their reality, and no one seemed to care.

But Vera was an instrument built by people with an unknown agenda, the designers of the ship, the people who had made money by downloading human minds and sending them to Varanasi. Seraph now knew the meaning of the swirling logo plastered all over the ship and the patch on TJ's jacket. No one had ever mentioned that it represented the builders, a "corporation," they called it. Because no one understood what a corporation was.

Why had Rishi's neural salvage system never been placed aboard the *Vera Rubin*? Because there was no money to be made from colonists. They were nothing but a payload.

TJ opened the meeting and gave the floor to the drive engineer who droned on about corrections to the navigation system that were initiated from the ground. Seraph was thinking about an artist from Retro. Back in the twenties, she did a whole series of Vera portraits—

Vera as a child, holding the hands of the NASA director and a beautiful woman in a silk gown, a woman Vera had named as the head of Rishi Corp. Ru Shi Zhu was her name.

Seraph called up that image on his palmcomm. It gave him pause now, after Maypole had started questioning Rishi. He swiped to the other portraits done by the same artist—Vera as a dominatrix, with a whip made of stars, and Vera as a wizened old woman knitting people's lives together on her needles.

None were censored, oddly. Maybe Vera never recognized herself in those images.

The commander of Retro Torus was attending the meeting on holo. He waited patiently to give his report, which TJ held until the end. She had to expect he would challenge her position.

When given the floor, Commander Dansa said, "I understand that Retro is nothing more than a backup for Command Torus, but if we worship at the feet of protocol, we shall reap death. I beg you to consider some options. My people are hungry. Three have died from malnutrition in the past week."

Seraph wondered if Dansa was a follower of the Harbinger.

"Commander Dansa," TJ said, clasping her hands and leaning on the podium. "You do understand that even if we voted now to send food to the hub, we would be stopped."

His reply was cautious. "We are prepared to . . . confront the forces that would seek to stop you."

"And risk human lives in the process. We are only weeks from our destination."

"Retro lives are already at risk, Captain."

The exchange was carefully crafted by both officers to avoid censorship by Vera. It was a skill that had been developed over centuries—to say what you meant without saying it.

"I want to ask you directly, Commander Dansa. If we decline, can we expect a conflict?"

His response was non-verbal but affirmative.

TJ was struggling to keep her voice even. "At which point, the isolation protocol will be violated."

Again, Dansa gave a subtle raise of his dark eyebrows and a tip of his chin. "The safety of your colonists should be considered." Then his image blinked out.

"A clear threat," Bora said. He was leaning back in his chair, one hand resting on his sidearm, a weapon that had likely never been fired. His lips pursed as if he was restraining himself from saying more. He failed. "We are prepared. And legal action will be taken against the leadership of Torus-2 upon arrival."

"At what cost?" Seraph asked loudly.

The other seventeen turned to look at him.

"A few security mechs and minor repairs," Bora said.

"For us, maybe. What about them? Do we even know what kind of tech they've developed?" Seraph's voice climbed enough to alert Vera to a conflict. A security mech moved behind him, a multi-armed arsenal of violence mitigation. Seraph went on. "The damage was far more extensive than we have been allowed to know. I've seen pictures."

"Why would Vera keep it from us, Lieutenant?" Bora's forehead was bunched in confusion as if Seraph was talking complete nonsense.

"So we won't know when they die; so we won't feel guilty for not saving them."

There was a rustle of murmurs from the others.

"You think they've built this army everyone is talking about?" Bora asked.

"What if they have? And you're going to just let them come?"

"I'll handle it," Bora said forcefully.

"You mean Vera will handle it."

"We'll meet again in three days." TJ stood. The others followed her signal that the meeting was over. She whispered to Bora, who called off his sec-mech from confronting Seraph.

"In three days," Seraph said, "more people will be dead."

Bora strode over to Seraph and picked up the cup on the table and sniffed it. "Hootch in the meeting, Lieutenant? Unprofessional."

Mansour's hand gripped Seraph's shoulder, but Seraph knocked it off.

The others stopped talking and stared as Seraph strode from the Command Deck. He found the concourse outside blocked by protesters. TJ immediately issued a warning that civil unrest would be regarded as a threat to the ship.

Seraph sent a message to Baakos in Retro explaining everything, but by the time he'd hit send, mechs from Retro were at war with Bora's security mechs in the hub. Shots had been fired.

Vera's alarms sounded, and people hastened to return to their units as instructed.

Seraph was waiting when Rain left school. Holding her hand, he led her back to their unit.

"What's happening, Dad?"

"It'll be over quickly. A breach of protocol."

She didn't ask anything else, so he distracted her with a game of chess. They'd made the game pieces out of wood pruned from branches of the old tree in front of the house. Rain had painted faces on the wooden disks—the queen had a captain's epaulets. The king wore a blue jumpsuit with the sprouting farm logo over the left breast, like Seraph's work suit.

Seraph turned over a captured pawn, painted with a smiling child's face. Twenty rings, just in this branch alone. The tree was maybe ten times that old. It had lived longer than anyone aboard. Trees weren't much different than people, laying down layers of life like coats of paint. Seraph was about to add another layer to his own.

"Dad, your move."

He pushed his wheelie-mounted knight to pressure her bishop. "We're only a few weeks from landing on Varanasi."

"I know. We're getting ready in school."

"It's not that far away," he tried to convince himself. But if he succeeded in what he was about to do, he'd end up in the brig. He stroked her hair and pulled her close, touching his forehead to hers. "We'll be together on Varanasi, Chicklet."

Her face bunched up in confusion. "We're always together, Dad."

AFTER CALLING Pearl to stay with Rain, Seraph met Carl on the storage deck. With all security mechs employed to guard the spokes, filling a carry-all with sacks of rice, soy, and chickpeas was easier than he'd anticipated.

"You sure about this, LT?" Carl asked. Fear flashed in the kid's starburst eyes, and Seraph wondered if he could trust Carl to pull this off. This wasn't some routine farm job.

"Carl, if things don't go just as we planned—"

"I know. It's on me." He set his jaw and repeated, "I got you, keso."

Getting inside the carry-all wasn't easy, especially in a pressure suit. This bin looked like it had come from the recycling deck and probably smelled like it too. But Seraph breathed his suit's air supply, thankfully.

The lid closed, and he was in darkness. He shut down his visor display in case any stray light escaped. Carl pushed the cart, and they rolled through corridor after corridor. Seraph's helmet rattled against the sides of the receptacle.

Mansour, the shift leader for the propulsion unit, had been clear that as soon as the incursion was put down, the engineers would return to the hub to work on the damaged drive. They would need the goods contained in the carry-all, or at least, the items listed on the contents.

From the darkness of the cart, Seraph heard the exchange between Carl and a guard, but he couldn't understand what they were saying. They must be at the lift bay. After a minute, they rolled away.

"What do I do now?" Carl asked via comm. "No entry."

Seraph guessed the problem was Carl should not be the one transporting these materials. He was afraid that would happen. "What did Mansour say about the delivery?"

"It has high priority. You said he'd be here. I don't see him."

"He'll be here."

"I think this is crazy, keso."

Carl pushed the carry-all up and down the corridor a few more times. Sooner or later, Vera would catch on.

"There he is." Carl's voice came through Seraph's onboard comm.

Outside, Seraph could hear nothing but the sound of the wheels and some muffled voices. Then the *ping* of a lift call button.

The sound of the doors opening was followed by movement. The carry-all rolled inside. Someone tapped the lid three times, and the door closed with another *ping*. That was the signal that Carl had loaded him into the lift and left him. That was as far as the kid would and should go. This was Seraph's gambit. If he found this legacy bag with the secret object Lauretta had hidden, he had no idea what he would do with it. He'd probably end up in the brig.

Seraph started up lift four inside the carry-all, alone, as planned. The hub was still 0.8 kilometers away. As it climbed away from the spin of the wheel's outer rim, gravity began to release its hold. Seraph had never been in the hub, never been in microgravity. His stomach floated up with everything else. He turned on his headlamp. A bag of something floated up and smacked him in the visor.

As the elevator car moved deeper into weightlessness, he opened his heads-up display. No reply from Baakos.

Sacks of food floated around him like pillows, gently jostling with his body toward the downspin side of the carry-all.

When the door opened, he pushed the lid up, grabbed the rim, and launched himself from the container, hitting the roof of the lift hard enough to ricochet back. The sacks of food floated out behind him. He stuffed them back in and shut the lid.

Feces.

He braced himself against the lift wall, which had handholds, and gently propelled the weightless carry-all into the airlock. As he followed, he could see that the hatch doors leading to the hub had been cut open with torches. The hatch was inoperable. Seraph had thought only Spoke Three was compromised.

A couple of repair mechs floated amid the wreckage of several decimated sec-mechs. They moved aside as he approached.

"Hey," he said to them. "I need to get through the doors."

"This mechanism is not operational," one said in a synth voice.

Through the hole in the bay hatch, he watched the interior of the hub rotate slowly before him.

"I have to get these goods to the reactors," he told the mechs.

They ignored him and went back to their welding.

The carry-all was too big to go through the hole in the door, so he left it. But the items inside were not.

The twenty-five-kilogram bags weighed nothing here, so Seraph propelled sacks of food through the hole, hoping the repair mechs had no ability to identify what they were. Soon, the entire hub was cluttered with spinning, tumbling sacks. He just hoped they wouldn't open and spew rice everywhere. The mech drones that were instructed to retrieve the "tools" Seraph was supposedly delivering had arrived. They were hit by sacks which sent them caroming out of control.

"Mansour," Seraph said through his commlink. "Shut down your mechs. I don't want to bust them with all this stuff."

"Copy."

The mechs powered down and stuck to the wall with their mag holds.

Seraph tried to move forward but ended up swimming in place. He'd have to ease through the hole in the hatch without tearing his pressure suit. Like a diver at the community pool, he pushed off gently. Once through, handholds waited in strategic locations, allowing him to ease into the cylindrical hub chamber among the storm of unsecured sacks.

Inside, the hub became the stationary element and the spoke bays rotated slowly around it. He felt like he was inside a dryer drum and had to fight nausea. About a hundred meters away, the four spokes of Retro Torus rotated in the opposite direction, off-setting the torque generated by the spin of Torus-1.

Seraph moved along the wall in that direction, where the handholds allowed him to propel himself. The legacy bags, left by the launch crew, were down here somewhere. Aft, Maypole had said.

Using a dowel of hardened plastic feedstock, Seraph shepherded the floating food toward the spoke bays of Retro. Then he saw them, aft near the reactor access bay. Yellowed knapsacks fastened to the walls in alphabetical rows—time capsules that looked like peas nestled in a pod waiting to carry the memories of the first crew to the new world.

He found the row of "L" names. Lamb, La Palma . . . Lauretta.

There it was.

He took the straps and pulled, bracing himself against the bags around it. It came free with the scritch of the tacking tape and floated before him. He tucked the straps over one arm and pulled himself by the handholds toward the spokes of Retro.

"Stone?" A voice came over the local comm channel. "You here?"

"Copy, stay in the lift bay until I can get this stuff closer to you," Seraph replied.

For two hundred and forty-two years, the only thing that had passed between the two wheels was censored information.

Seraph was about to change that.

A hatch leading to Retro must have opened because alarms sounded.

"Ah, feces," he muttered.

Seraph began propelling the last sacks of food, one at a time, toward the Retro bay. The action sent him in the opposite direction.

The containers hit the far wall and bounced back, forcing him to repeat it with less force.

Alarms screamed.

The hatch of a Retro lift bay dilated open, and a person in a red pressure suit drifted in, fending off the floating sacks.

"Nice work, friend," she said through the local comm. The illuminated ID over her visor read *Huang*.

She extended a tether that drifted toward him. He grabbed it. Together, they shepherded the containers of food into the open bay as alarms continued to wail.

With only half of them loaded, Seraph turned to look down the hub toward T-1. Multiple sec-mechs spidered from the handholds faster than he thought possible. To cross the center of the hub, they shot cables forward and attached to the walls of the hub cylinder, then rocketed across, all six appendages splayed and pointed at him.

Before Seraph could reach the Retro bay, the mechs fired weapons.

Something whirred past him. His back was on fire. One had hit his shoulder, the other, his lower back. The taser shock blasted through his nerves and his onboard system. Everything flickered, then went dark.

His bladder gave way, and every muscle in his body contracted. He couldn't breathe.

His heart raced.

His vision returned to partial focus as the relentless jolt of current became a distant pulse in his body. He was spinning slowly, convulsing. He could hear the slow leak of air bleeding from the taser darts that had punctured his suit. His onboard system sputtered back to life. Backup power.

In one revolution, he saw Huang fire a device. Then again.

The sec-mechs behind him went dark, their legs clattering together. Drifting, they bounced harmlessly against him until Huang kicked them away. She grabbed him by one arm and then pressed him against the bulkhead with her foot as she yanked the darts out of his back.

Seraph screamed. His visor fogged.

Huang brushed a taser dart from her own arm as if it were a piece of lint. Then she gave Seraph a gentle push toward the open bay door leading to a Retro lift. He didn't fight it. It was either Retro or the brig. He saw the rusty red of Huang's pressure suit pass before his dim vision. Then he was bouncing among the sacks of food in the microgravity of the bay, the inertial tug of Lauretta's bag dragging at his injured shoulder.

"Air," he croaked weakly, his comm crackling. He motioned to the holes in his pressure suit.

"We'll be under pressure in a sec, friend. You'll be fine." Huang shepherded the bags of food into the open lift, then pulled Seraph along like an afterthought.

"You guys don't have armored suits?" Her voice competed with the ringing in his ears and the hissing of the air leak.

He heard the *ping* of the lift doors and the *whoosh* of pressurization coming on. He let his eyes close with the door and didn't even try to answer her.

7

NIGHT VISION

2345-02-12, *Earth Standard, Shivi Desh, Varanasi*

MAYPOLE'S CLAW was clamped firmly around the snaking neck of the hellion. The creature's nocturnal eyes blazed demonic red amongst a bristling forest of dark spines. The beast struggled, dislodging a cloud of plumage with its wildly flapping wings. Given an opportunity, the jaws of this thing could snap off any exposed machinery on Maypole's chassis, or at least damage her circuitry. The fleeing plumage brushed by her face as they drifted away—undulating lime-green leaves in the false-color of her night vision.

The hellion made noises. Not from its gaping mouth, but from a blinking box on its chest. Were those words? It repeated them in a generic robo voice that mispronounced Lemkos's name.

"Kolyaa Lemkus?" it asked again.

"What the hell." Maypole had come upon a dead hellion once and dissected it. Six-limbed like all chordates on Varanasi, they were considered sentient. They lived in clan units and built cliff-dwellings not unlike the ones in the American southwest. Technically, they couldn't fly but used their great wings to glide between cliffs in the gorgelands. Their internal morphology matched the asymmetry of all the species on this planet, with a single lung, and two hearts. But alive, it was scarier than shit with its throwing spears and "bashers" made of knotted wood with animal teeth as spikes. But speaking in English . . . that was something else entirely. Could it understand as well?

She said, "You make a move, and I'll gut you."

It nodded its feathered head three times.

Slowly, Maypole released her grip. The beast's jaws worked to make a throaty rumble, a growl-screech, while a voice emanated from the translator blinking on its chest.

"God damn, Kolyaa Lemkus!" the thing cried. "If you had a throat, I'd gladly rip it out."

"If anyone's getting their throat ripped out, it's you." Maypole reached for it again with her claw, but it held up its forelimbs as if in surrender.

"It's cool," it said. "You can kill me. Got it. I got no beef with you. Just him." It nodded to Lemkos, now standing at Maypole's shoulder with a pulse weapon trained on the hellion.

The creature adjusted its collection of limbs and got back to its feet. It was coiling as if to leap at Lemkos.

Maypole launched her claw and clamped onto the hellion's throat again and squeezed the gristly flesh just below the creature's jaw, dislodging another cloud of plumage.

"Explain yourself," Maypole demanded, tightening her grip.

"Now, now," the thing croaked. "No need to get hostile."

"You threatened him." She nodded to Lemkos. "I squeeze hard, and *pop!* Your head explodes like a berry."

"Nice guard dog you got there, Lemkus," the creature said. "Last I recall, *you* were the gladiator."

"Who are you?" Lemkos asked.

"You don't remember your highest profile fight ever? Lemkus versus the terrorist?"

"Elijah Mc-something?" Lemkos was clearly guessing at a name.

"You were supposed to leave me dead in that arena. But that's not what you did, was it?"

"You can let him go," Lemkos told Maypole, lowering his pulse weapon but not storing it. "I think. If he's really alive, then he'll want to avoid dying."

"Damn right," the hellion said. "It hurts."

Maypole released her grip, and the creature slid backward, hunkering on its thick haunches, its neck writhing as if to find a comfortable resting place against the long gliding wings that were tucked on its back.

His name was Elijah McCaskill, he told them with the synth voice. And despite repeated questions from Maypole, he had no idea how his mindware had been downloaded into a hellion.

"Last I remember, I was standing in the middle of the colosseum trying to deflect the blows of that asshole." He motioned to Lemkos with a clawed hand. With his synth monotone, he said, "They wouldn't even give me a gladiator to fight for me. Had to do it myself, against that." He motioned again to Lemkos. "Next thing I know, I got a spear through the chest. He gave me the old in-and-out with the pointy end until I was gone. Blinked out. Corruption code transfer. Bam . . . I wake up in this," he indicated the hellion body.

Maypole turned to Lemkos, his holo-print looking ghostly in the false-color of her night vision.

"What's he talking about?" Maypole asked.

Lemkos sighed. "Look, wiping people's mindware is completely barbaric—"

"Barbaric?" Maypole cried. "I know this guy. He's that *terrorist*, Lemkos. Elijah the Hairless. He took out three realm servers with a sonic charge he propagated into the Black Stack. Wiped a few Vested backups if I remember right."

"And I won't rest until I wipe them all," Elijah added. "And you'll thank me, Lemkus."

"It's Lemkos."

"You'll always be Lemkus to me, asshole."

"Wait," Maypole held out both hands, one to each of them. "You're telling me there are terrorists running around here wearing the skins of hellions?"

"Not just the skin, sweetie," Elijah said. He spread his wings for display. "We got guts and all. The whole enchilada."

How did this make sense?

"Rishi's the terrorist," Elijah added. "Systematically culling the refugees by withholding treatment. You know that yearly patch you download? The one that plugs the holes in your backups?"

"Yeah," Maypole said. "What about it?" To prevent the inevitable data corruption caused by time and entropy, patches had been prescribed as a yearly requirement for mental health. But not everyone got them. Some people thought the patches were mind control software. But without patching their files, time would do damage, causing the data to decohere. They called it bit rot, and the effects mimicked psychosis in physical humans.

"Rishi is planting whatever it wants into our files," Elijah said. "Now *there's* the terrorism. They can build us into whatever they want. And your friend here," he pointed at Lemkos, "is in good with those thieving bastards."

"Okay, okay," Lemkos said defensively. "I made a deal with a guy. I tried to keep you alive, Elijah. That's all."

This stank of false altruism to Maypole. It had nothing to do with wanting to save Elijah from wiping. It was about the money. Lemkos turned to Maypole. "The corruption code I delivered in the arena created a second backup before it blew out this guy's files. The backup was transferred to a client. That way, I could save some of these guys who were sentenced to wiping."

"How *noble*," Maypole mocked.

"I'm sure he paid well," Elijah said, making a snarling noise to emphasize his displeasure. "Was the guy's name Judah Krane?"

"Yeah, okay, so I made a few bucks," Lemkos said, turning to Maypole again. "Krane told me he was a mining foreman. Wanted mindware, not AI to run his operation. I assumed he dumped them into mechs, you know?"

"Slaves?" Maypole was incredulous. Lemkos had been selling mindware on the black market to work as slaves?

"He's no 'guy' first of all, you asswipe," Elijah said. "Judah's an amalgam."

"What the fuck is an amalgam?" Lemkos asked.

"You're the engineer, buddy. He's not a single mind, not one download. He's been engineered."

"You mean, he's AI," Maypole said.

"No. His mind is built of selected minds harvested from the Black Stack. They found a bunch of neuropsych/geoengineer scientist types in the population and stitched him together to make a super scientist. The best of the best, or some such shit."

"That's a privacy violation," Maypole said.

"And selling mindware ain't?" Elijah replied.

Lemkos started pacing, clearly confused. "This was not my intention. Not at all."

"Well, you made money. Gobs of it, you shifty bastard." Elijah's long tail curled over his back.

Maypole turned on Lemkos. "No wonder you have the money to buy into a venture capital deal."

"Now, Cupcake, you don't understand."

"Oh, I understand. What I need to understand better is how the hell this Judah Krane guy can download digital to biomass. That's what I need to know, and *you*"—she pointed to the hellion—"are going to tell me."

"Shhh," Elijah said. His neck snaked about, his large nocturnal eyes rolling to look up. "Oh, fuck me."

In the next second, Maypole was on the ground. As she fell, her sensors picked up the smell of wet plumage and skin dander.

She launched a defense pulse that knocked the intruder away. Then she shot her claw at the convulsing mass but grasped only plumage. It fluttered away in a cloud, obscuring her visual sensors. She didn't see the next hellion and could do nothing to stop it. Her pulse charge wasn't ready.

Her right arm went first, torn from its socket with a sizzling spark. Flashes of night vision came and went as she tried to initiate the claw on her left arm, but that was immobilized as well. Alerts flashed and howled in her auditory sensors. *Exit holo-print, exit holo-print, exit holo-print.*

She heard Elijah's robo-voice yell, "Allison, get the fuck off these people."

Then Maypole's other arm was separated from her torso. With the residual power left in it, she managed to clamp the claw end onto a hellion's leg. The creature tried to shake it loose but failed.

A flash from Lemkos's pulse weapon struck a biomass body behind Elijah. It lit up blue as the EM pulse coursed through it. But there was another one behind it. And before Lemkos could get off another shot, he'd lost the arm that housed the weapon.

"Don't shut down!" Maypole yelled. "I'm not done here."

"Are you nuts?" Lemkos replied.

Elijah said, "Looks like you'll be able to ask Judah all these questions in person."

The blue guy from the skin meeting knew what he was talking about. But actual downloads into biomass? How was this Judah Krane associated with Rishi Corp? As soon as Maypole could corner Lemkos, she'd get the whole story from him. Probably some other time, however, what with the dismemberment.

It wasn't just Allison, but a whole band of modified hellions that had attacked. Two of them carried pieces of Lemkos, dragging his holo-print's armless torso by one remaining leg. Maypole assumed she was in a similar state. For a fleeting moment, she thought she felt pain. Phantom limb.

It was a long way to wherever they were going. Parts and pieces fell off their broken chassis as they bounced over the rough terrain.

She couldn't move anything, not even her visual sensors. They stared straight ahead. With her holo-print nonfunctional, she and Lemkos were nothing more than a bunch of busted solenoids, processors, and nanowires. The hellions had left their main CPUs intact at Elijah's urging. She assumed it was so they could meet their amalgam master, this Judah Krane. Vacating her print was an option, but the temptation to meet this guy outweighed her urge to dive back into the safety of Virtual. Besides, what was the worst that could happen? Normally, she'd say a nasty rebound back to her virtual avatar.

"Allison, I had this under control," Elijah was saying for the fifth time.

"You just chatting these dudes up." The hellion dragging Lemkos had the same standard asexual robo-voice. "You had nothing, nothing, nothing under. Nothing under. Nothing under."

"Fuckin' rotter," Elijah said, emotionless. He pranced beside the remains of Lemkos, glancing down at him now and then as if worried.

Maypole heard the rustle of plumage above her head caused by the hellion who was dragging her along. She said, "So is Judah Krane able to stop their bit rot? Repair them?"

The hellion's head swiveled to look at her, the globes of its nocturnal eyes reflecting red light. "Does Allison there seem repaired to you?"

Maypole messaged Lemkos on a backchannel. *Stay long enough to see what's what?*

He replied, *What if he locks our mindware?*

He'd have to have our personnel codes. Like you had Elijah's when you sold his DB.

Of course. I had his code.

You sold the guy's personnel code.

Now's not the time, Camber. And if I didn't, he'd have died real death, corruption code fried.

We'll dive out of our prints at the first sign of any real trouble, she messaged.

You mean when we wake up in the bodies of ostrich-dragons?

The first explorers had called hellions "ostrich-dragons." Long-necked velociraptors was more apt.

Who knows, you might like it, he messaged.

Asshole.

Lemkos was not the person she thought she knew. Yes, he was a famous legal gladiator, his hobby job that over the centuries had become not only his primary entertainment but a lucrative one at that. Now she knew why. He'd been brokering deals with some guy named Judah Krane, an engineered guy, amalgam. Selling mindware that had been slated for erasure.

I honestly did not know about the hellion thing, Lemkos messaged. *I had a contract for Elijah. Krane's honored them all.*

How many?

A few.

I see more than a few hellions here.

Not all mine. Okay, maybe four or five.

Fingers of the morning sun were finding their way into the gorge by the time they arrived at what looked like a military compound. From her flickering visual sensors, Maypole could see high concrete walls that showed the striations left by building fabbers. Topped with razor wire and gun turrets, it looked like Krane expected living things to assault his compound. Unlike most mines, it lay on the floor of the canyon rather than the cliffs. According to her onboard map, it was across the river from the rock formations known as the Spiral Towers, a favorite of climbers, herself included.

The concrete security wall that encased the mine showed black stains left by the floodwaters from many spring thaws. The gates swung open, and the hellions dragged what was left of Lemkos and Maypole through an outer yard full of idle mechs. The hellion named

Allison wore Maypole's left arm like an anklet. It made an odd thunking sound as she walked.

Maypole heard automated bolts slide open, then they were in a tunnel, sealed from the outside by a series of airlocks. Maypole assumed the hellions had coded transponders under their skin that allowed them entry.

At last, her hardware was deposited without ceremony on the floor of a low, broad room with slick walls of sandstone. There was no visible cabinetry or lab benches, only a central pedestal upon which sat an urn filled with a spray of cut flowers.

"You call Judah?" Allison asked. She repeatedly tipped her armored snout in rapid nods. A tick. A common thing for a rotter.

"What do you think?" Elijah replied.

If Allison was indeed a rotter, it meant that Elijah could be telling the truth. Rather than wipe those most severely affected by bit rot, maybe Judah Krane shipped the remains of their mindware here to test his biomass download process.

A holo-print appeared from an unseen doorway. The holo image he presented looked like he'd stepped out of a business meeting: neat black suit, buzzed hair, manicured hands. When he smiled, he revealed one gold tooth in the front. His face was broad with high cheekbones and a perfectly straight, prominent nose. Set in ebony skin, the piercing blue eyes were hooded by thick straight eyebrows. His chin was tipped with a scarlet goatee. If this guy was an amalgam of the Black Stack, it made Maypole wonder what combination of mindware it had modeled and augmented. Maybe a partial mind clone of that other dick, Noah Dutro.

"Welcome," he said in a vaguely French accent. "Two wanderers into the wilds of Shivi Desh."

"Yes," Lemkos answered, "I'm Kolya Lemkos. We did some business a while back if you recall." His voice crackled with static. Their hardware had taken a beating.

"I *do* recall," Krane said, squatting beside the heap that was Lemkos. "Yes. The gladiator. So you were seeking me out?"

"Well, ultimately, yes, that's correct."

"I'm sorry about Allison," Krane said.

"No problem," Lemkos said. "We've got insurance."

"Well, you see, there is a problem." Krane stood and began to pace, his hands clasped behind his back. His polished wingtips echoed in the subterranean chamber. "The work I do here is classified. And you, I'm afraid, have fallen into it."

Oh shit, Camber messaged Lemkos. *He doesn't need our personnel codes. Or he has them. Of course he fucking has them, he is the Black Stack.*

"Of course, I have your codes," Krane replied.

"You work for Rishi?" Maypole asked. "For Noah Dutro?"

As she talked, Maypole initiated the code required to dump her mech holo-print, or what was left of it. She kept talking, stalling. Any attempt at communicating with Lemkos would be intercepted. That was clear.

She said, "No one has been successful at downloading digital into biomass. There's no interface. The nanobot imaging of the mind can only translate to digital, not to neuronal synapses."

"That, too, is classified," Krane said.

"Swarms? Genetics?" Maypole went on, her exit was seconds away. "Because it would have to be one or both techs to set the digital teeth into a biological brain, right? And only Rishi could do it."

"Who else could fund something like this?" Krane shrugged. The hellions paced and shuffled by the door like trapped animals. "Now let's get on with it."

Maypole sensed a low infrared beam broadcasting from the urn of flowers. An invasive code, it had already located her RAM. She firewalled it and pulled the plug on her holo-print. She could only hope Lemkos had done the same.

8

RIGOLETTO

2345-02-12, Earth Standard, Torus-2, aboard the Vera Rubin

THE DESCENDING ELEVATOR cab gradually plunged Seraph's battered body back into spin gravity as it dropped the kilometer from the hub toward the ring of Torus-2. He floated in the fetal position among drifting sacks of food that gradually moved toward the floor with him. With no way to stop the rising nausea, he opened his visor and vomited. His hands had stopped shaking, and the piss in his suit was starting to feel cold. But the wounds from the taser prongs in his shoulder and lower back throbbed mercilessly. Finally settling with his back to the cab wall, he looked up at Huang. Her visor was still down. Anchored to a handhold, she was talking into her comms. Seraph didn't bother to listen.

The events of the last hour seemed to have happened in slow motion, to someone else. Whether it was the effects of the micro g or his tasered body, he wasn't sure, but it felt good to go limp and let this woman take him wherever she wanted. One thing was certain, after taking food to the hub against orders, he could never return to Torus-1. If the braking system worked as planned and the course corrections did the same, they might reach Varanasi before they had anticipated. It would still be weeks. Without Rain.

"What was that thing?" he asked Huang weakly.

"What thing?" She looked down her chest at him.

"The gun. You stopped sec-mechs." She had fired one blast of the thing and the armored and weaponized security mechs had frozen, spinning helplessly in space.

"You don't have high freq interrupts in T-1?" she asked.

"No. And no armored pressure suits either." He assumed that was what had stopped the taser from penetrating Huang's suit. "What else have you guys not been sharing?"

She popped the visor on her helmet and grinned at him. "Wouldn't you like to know, friend."

"Yes, I would. Now that I'm one of you, you can tell me."

She gave him a yeah-right look.

"I guess we never needed them in T-1," he offered. It made him wonder what kind of place he was going to. "But why didn't you fire it *before* I got shot?"

She laughed, a round, resonant chuckle. "Had to charge full. Takes a few to fully arm."

He clutched tightly to the yellow bag he had retrieved from the possessions of the first crew, hiding the faded name Lauretta. The objects inside clattered and clinkered as the increasing g settled them. Seraph didn't need any questions from Huang about this thing. Let her believe he had packed for the trip.

Sacks of food clustered around him. Two bags of soybeans became increasingly heavy on his lap. He tried to lift his arms against the new gravity but failed.

Huang offered him a hand. He took it and stood after a struggle. The bulk of Lauretta's bag threatened to stop him, light as it was.

The lift doors opened.

Huang took off her helmet and hung it on the grip of a handcart that was waiting in the bay. Even the pink tips of her spiked faux-hawk didn't hide the threads of gray that shimmered at her temples. She fluffed up the hair that had been squished inside her helmet. He didn't know why he was surprised to see that she was a good fifteen to twenty years older than him. She had smooth skin and laugh lines at the corners of her eyes promising she wasn't as reserved as she looked.

"Give me a hand, huh," she said and started loading the food sacks onto the cart.

Give her a hand? He could barely stand up. But he hefted a sack of rice to his knee and stacked it with the others on the handcart.

"So you guys have no way to down a sec-mech?" She sounded incredulous.

"I doubt we've ever even thought of it."

"Huh." She tossed two bags of beans as if they were nothing. "I mean, if you have no interrupts, then how did you even get into the hub?"

"Luck," he replied weakly. "Dumb luck."

"Not so dumb, friend. We knew from the start that TJ Dela Cruz couldn't help us even if she wanted to. Someone would have to have the balls to come with the food."

"Well," Seraph said, "right now they're numb, but I think they're still there."

She laughed again. "We'll get you fixed up. Welcome to the land of the hungry."

Retro wheel smelled completely different. The way a friend's unit smells like their family—the foods they cook, the pheromones of familial lines left on furniture and walls, all stewed together to create a fragrance of their collective epigenome.

Though they passed dozens of people as they dragged the handcart through A-concourse, Seraph didn't know a single face. It was like a dream. They were complete strangers. Sure, he'd talked to a few people on social media or for work, but he didn't recognize one person he passed. By the way they were looking at him, they felt the same out-of-body feeling he did.

The concourses of T-2 had a woody smell, like the bark of the trees in the commons mixed with the smell of new air filters with a hint of hydraulic fluid, which might have come from the herds of wheelies that sped by. They carried people in brightly colored clothes. They wore shirts with billowing sleeves and iridescent fabric that seemed to sail behind them, fluttering with ribbons. He couldn't help the smile that crept to his face.

When Seraph looked up her bio, he discovered this lady with pink hair, Erica Huang, held the rank of lieutenant, just as he did.

"Software engineering," she said, when he asked about her position.

"Looks like you've got some things to share with T-1 in that regard."

"T-1 has got no shielding, friend. I'm guessing you kesos can't build anything without Vera breathing down your neck, at least that's what I heard."

"Shielding? From Vera?"

She gave him a look, like he had just stepped through a time portal from the distant past. Jesus, was T-1 stuck in the past? He added, "You couldn't share your stuff with us?"

"Not a chance. And risk Vera breaking our firewall?"

If they were so technologically advanced, why were they all starving? He'd have to answer that question when he saw their farms.

Huang towed the handcart, overflowing with sacks of beans and rice. Their first stop was the distribution center where she delivered over a hundred kilos of food staples. The workers were waiting for her return from the hub, and a crowd had already gathered outside the center. Cheers and hugs met Huang. She returned them, giving each person a lengthy squeeze and a motherly rub on the back.

They eyed Seraph with obvious suspicion. He was still wearing a T-1 blue pressure suit with the helm under one arm.

Huang did not introduce him, which was fine by him.

He met the strangers' stares and smiled.

Huang lived in the Canterbury units. As they climbed the stairs to the upper level, he realized they had more trees in the medians here. They were all hung with small white lights that flashed on as dusk settled. But the sky program was the same as it was in T-1, and tonight it was Vera's dramatic fall sunset he knew so well.

Once inside, Huang unzipped her suit, which must have been as stifling as his own.

"Head," she pointed to the narrow hallway, as if Seraph wouldn't know where to find it. "I'll throw some of Alexandre's clothes in for you."

Alexandre? Wasn't that Baakos's name? The Harbinger. Of course Baakos would send someone he trusted to get the food. Huang had to be his partner.

Finally alone, Seraph had to know what was in this bag that he'd risked everything to retrieve. He locked the bathroom door and tried the zipper on it. After two hundred years, radiation had degraded the plastic teeth so that it crumbled as Seraph tugged on it. He finally tore it open.

Inside, he found a collection of seed vials, like the ones they used to bank future crops. They had been marked by hand and the lettering was faint and strange. Archaic twenty-first century.

Three photos printed on paper were loose in the bottom among other containers. Faded and discolored, the subjects had helmets and ropes. Snowy mountains marched out behind them. He could still recognize a much younger version of John Lauretta, but he didn't recognize the woman or the other man. There were no names on the backs. The last picture was of an animal. Maybe a dog?

At least two dozen clear plastic vials chattered together. They were responsible for the noise the bag had made all the way from the hub. Seraph was afraid to open them. One was marked, *Mount Elbrus*, and another, *Cloudy, OK*. Through the clear plastic, he saw dirt and sand, some thick with organics, others nothing more than pebbles. Different colors of dirt, from many different places.

He stopped breathing. He was looking at dirt from Earth. Not even the trees grew in dirt on this ship. Too risky. Too many spores.

Lauretta's legacy item was a bunch of soil? Feces.

Huang knocked.

Seraph jumped and almost dropped the vials. After taking a calming breath, he opened the door a crack and a pair of trousers appeared, followed by a flowing, multi-colored shirt like he'd seen the others wearing. They fell to the floor.

"Thanks."

He went back to the bag and felt around the inside. His hand met something rigid that had been zipped inside an interior pocket. This zipper was equally degraded. It wouldn't budge.

He pulled the multi-tool from the belt of his pressure suit and found a small blade. With it, he carefully sliced around the object, making sure he didn't cut it.

Then he lifted it out.

It looked like images he'd seen of a book, like the kind they used in the early twenty-first century. He turned it over reverently. The cover was plastic that had yellowed and checked with age. There was an image on the front of a faded cartoon figure, a white animal with pointed ears, whiskers, and a faded red bow on its head. Maybe a cat. He couldn't read the words printed there.

As he slowly opened the book, the cover cracked even more, dropping flakes of yellowed, brittle plastic. He would have to do this in a better place than in the head.

Huang's voice came from the hallway. "You okay in there?"

"Fine. Just cleaning up."

He put everything back in the bag but couldn't close the broken zipper. He stripped off his stinking pressure suit and ag jumpsuit. In the mirror, he could see the angry holes in his back where the taser darts had bit him. They throbbed like hell.

He washed, then pulled on the spare clothes which were far too big for him. As he passed by the mirror, he thought he looked like a clown. The sleeves were like sails, and the fabric was a patchwork of colors.

He made his way to the common room with Lauretta's bag wrapped in his stinky jumpsuit.

"Where is . . . Alexandre?" He'd almost called him *the Harbinger* and didn't know if that was a term of endearment.

Huang met him with drinks. "He'll be along. He was going to see to the proper distribution of your gift."

Seraph took the offered glass. He almost spilled it when Huang encased him in a hug as she had done with the people in the distribution center. He inhaled as her skin passed his nose. She smelled like flowers and sweat. A leather thong around her neck held a large seedpod. The shiny outer husk was etched with unfamiliar symbols that shone creamy through the dark enamel of the pericarp.

"You grow macadamias?" he asked.

"This?" Huang touched the seed reverently. "Once a macadamia, now my fireseed. A reminder that I am a spark from the One, the True Fire that burns at the heart of creation. As are you, friend."

He nodded, pretending to understand.

"You can put your stuff in the spare room." She indicated the correspondent of Rain's room in his own unit. Every unit was the same—two bedrooms, a head, and living area.

He had to put the bag down sometime. He stuffed it in the closet, still wrapped in the stinking jumpsuit.

He emerged from the bedroom, feeling awkward in the flowing sleeves.

"Interesting style," he said, waving his arms.

"Well, that suit you were wearing looked like something from the history books. They used to wear those things on the first crew. Same sprouting leaf patch and all." She smiled.

"Yeah, I guess we have no sense of style in T-1."

The first pang of missing Rain crept in. He'd been gone less than two hours, yet the days ahead loomed like a desolate wasteland.

He took a sip of the drink. They may not have much food here, but they sure knew how to distill hootch. Smoother than anything he'd had in T-1, even the high-end grain distillates. He swallowed, feeling it loosen the knots in his body and mind.

"Sit." She indicated a sofa covered in multi-colored fabric, not unlike his shirt. "You have a place to stay here, Stone," Huang said. "Your delivery of food will bridge the gap. We're only a few weeks out. But, hey, there are people here who want to meet you."

"I'm looking forward to it." Looking forward to getting to Varanasi and back to Rain.

"There are plans to be made, and we know some of the residents of Command Torus feel as we do."

"How's that?" Seraph asked.

"Alexandre will explain."

Huang's quarters were as colorful as she was. Mobiles of mylar, titanium fittings, and cast-off gadgets were suspended from the light panels of the living room ceiling.

Seraph's eye was caught by a bauble that looked like the skull of a chicken plated with shiny red copper. It hung among a jungle of twigs and dried flowers.

Like many of the spaces in the commons of T-1, the walls of Huang's quarters were covered in murals giving the illusion of broad orchards and mountains marching off into a false distance. It was like the landscape holograms of some of the restaurants on the galleria level, but these had been painted by hand.

She was talking about distribution plans and the coming cricket crop as she crossed her legs and took a reverential sip of her drink.

"Did you do these?" Seraph asked, indicating the wall murals.

"Me?" she asked incredulously. "Oh my, no. These are master-works. At least a hundred years old. This place belongs to Alexandre's family, his hereditary home. His ghosts are all here."

"Ghosts?" Seraph noted the coffee table was covered in a portrait of an animal that might be a cow. He'd only seen them in virtual. A thick sheen of resin covered the painting to protect it from the wear of using the table. The cow's big, expressive eyes watched him as he retrieved his glass from the animal's backside.

"Yeah, you know," Huang said, "the people who lived here before us. Each home has its spirits. Its genius. According to our belief, whatever and whoever a fireseed touches in life, a web of fire is ignited. They are always part of a place and the people they touch. They never leave us."

"Genius?" He'd never heard that word used like this.

"The soul of a place or thing, you know?"

"No, I don't."

She seemed honestly perplexed at his ignorance. "This place has been in Alexandre's family since the first crew."

"So, if there are ghosts . . . do you contact them?" He smiled, hoping she would take it as a joke.

Huang laughed that resonant laugh. "We don't have seances, if that's what you mean. Everyone who's ever lived on this ship is still here." She was dead serious. "Their destiny is ours."

"Well, yeah, in a way," Seraph replied. "Their atoms are still circulating in the great cycle. In *us*," he lifted his glass and clinked it to hers. "This drink might be your second cousin. But I try not to think about that."

"Well, you *should* think about it. It's what you *do*, friend. As the chief agricultural officer, you bring life out of death. You're like an ancient shaman."

"What's a shaman?"

She just laughed.

He'd never thought of it that way before, but she was right. Growing food was just that. Conjuring life from death.

Huang's hand was on his. "The atoms and energy of our universe are immortal; therefore, so are we. Let's pray," she said, her eyes alight with religious fervor. That misguided trust in the unseen, no matter what name you give it.

"Sure, okay," he said.

Seraph had attended plenty of religious services. Pearl had seen to that. As a teen, he'd been looking for meaning, looking for salvation from the inevitability of his existence, looking for the hand of someone's god to touch him and give him purpose. He'd never found anything but the insistence that he needed to be forgiven for nothing more than living.

"We thank seed, stem, and fruit," Huang prayed. "We thank the fireseed of Seraph Stone by whose hand we are nourished."

He had to admit, this was more heartfelt than anything he'd ever heard from the preachers in T-1.

She hadn't gotten to the amen when the front door opened, and a large man stood against the red sunset projected on the sky behind him. His entrance was in keeping with the legend. The Harbinger.

Alexandre Baakos stepped into the room. Seraph immediately judged him to be a religious charlatan. He had the look, the outfit, the posture, the aura.

Seraph stood, setting his drink aside.

Baakos straightened his exotic robes, a layered garment of varying fabric types, all stitched together into colorful stripes. Here and there, embroidered geometric designs danced. Baubles were sewn onto it like the mobiles in their house. Random parts and fittings, some pieces of glass and painted objects.

"Seraphim Stone," he proclaimed with arms held wide.

Seraph hated that name. He always pictured chubby, winged babies. "It's Seraph."

He clasped his hands behind his back in a military stance, but Baakos had him in a bear hug, rocking him back and forth. Seraph's eyes came to the middle of the big man's chest. Baakos was obviously the product of crew unions from way back. Exceedingly tall and thin, his long bones were stretched by low g over five generations. A spacefarer.

Encased in the hug, Seraph was staring at a bauble on Baakos's chest: a metallic eye. It hung over his heart. The iris of the eye was a mandala of fractals that mimicked the starburst mutation in bright colors, and inside the pupil . . . Seraph thought he saw himself, like a tiny, holographic mirror.

He took a step back. Baakos's bony, seed-brown face was folded into a genuine smile showing gleaming white teeth. The man had the starburst mutation himself, a rusty-red bloom of color around his pupils. How had this eye mutation affected populations in *both* wheels? A mutation is, by definition, a random event.

Baakos said, "Your delivery of food has been assessed and the distributions calculated, Seraphim. It is enough to see us through until our first crops mature in the next few weeks."

"I'm glad."

"You've given up much, and we understand this. You have a daughter whom you will not see until we reach Varanasi. *If* we reach Varanasi."

"I'm sure Vera has no intention of failing in this mission," Seraph said.

Baakos nodded absently, taking an offered drink from Huang.

"You will dine with us, Seraphim," Baakos said.

"Oh, he'll do more than dine," Huang said. "He's moving in."

Huang set three bowls on the small table and motioned for them to come.

Though little more than broth with a few lentils, the soup was spiced with herbs Seraph was unfamiliar with. Could their herbs have mutated over the centuries? Whatever the reason, it was delicious, if not filling.

"Tell us," Baakos said, "how have our commanding officers prepared to engage the minds who await us on Varanasi?"

"Engage? They have responded as expected, as I understand it."

Baakos was shaking his head. "They are neither mechs nor human minds. They are not like anything you know. Our mechs are digital slaves to Vera. The joboxes on that planet were human once. Humans are full of desire, hunger for power, need for control. Have you really never thought about such a thing, friend?"

He hadn't, not until he'd gotten that message from John Lauretta. He had never studied the history of Earth, the catastrophic changes that might have ruined civilization. All he knew was that the ship had stopped receiving messages somewhere after the first year, so the fate of Earth was essentially unknown, or so they were told.

Seraph said, "How could they be much different than us?"

"They've been on Varanasi for over two centuries." Baakos was in preacher mode now. "Their minds are old Earth minds, full of hate and division. They have undergone no spiritual change in those centuries. They are static, divorced from the flesh."

"Are you afraid of them?" Seraph asked. He wondered what Baakos would say if he knew Seraph had already been in contact with Maypole, a "jobox."

"We should all fear them. We should be prepared to fight."

"Fight?" Seraph found the idea insane. "You said yourself, we're outnumbered over a hundred to one. If they choose to kill us—why I have no idea—I doubt we could stop it."

"Precisely."

Seraph suddenly realized that none of them had been using the oblique discussion techniques developed to avoid Vera's understanding. He said, "You speak frankly here. How?"

"Oh, noise," Huang said. "We broadcast it in the right frequency when we wish to speak. It feeds directly into the audio sensors in the room, so we don't have to hear it."

"Huh." Why had they never thought of that in T-1?

Baakos smiled broadly.

Seraph could think of nothing but the bag waiting for him in his room. The message from Lauretta, the crucial information. He had to know what it was and what he was supposed to do with it.

He made excuses, the pain in his back, the need to rest. More hugs were distributed before he was allowed to retire. When he was alone in his room, he lay down on the bunk, listening to the hum of the air handlers and a distant tune playing in a neighboring unit. He held the little book to the bedside light and carefully turned the pages.

He was finally able to read the faded script on the front. It said,

Hello Kitten. On the inside cover, he found faded writing in pen. He struggled to read it.

To Aunt Camber. From your favorite niece Brigid.

The book belonged to Camber Maypole?

He pulled out his palmcomm and searched Vera's records for Camber Maypole.

Position: T-1 Medical Officer. Graduate of UC San Diego medical school, third in her class, flight surgeon on multiple cargo missions before being appointed flight surgeon on the launch crew of the *Vera Rubin*. Then what was she doing on Varanasi? If she had launched with the ship, she should have died on the ship.

None of this made sense.

He gently turned to the next page of the little book. In a rounded hand of faded ink, a date topped the page: 6 Feb 2097.

Seraph struggled with the writing. It looked nothing like the handwritten notes he'd seen.

Brigid,

You'll be glad to know we made it safely to the ship. There has been so much to do, I haven't had time to look out at the stars as I promised. Checklists. More checklists. Equipment tests and meetings. I did glimpse the Moon from the lounge one night. The glancing light of the sun striking the mountains and craters as the dark side glowed with research stations and mining operations below. Like jewels. You'd love it. I think of you daily. Stay safe. Stay well.

Two more installments were addressed to Brigid, as if her niece would ever read these. It hurt Seraph deep inside. If he had had to leave Rain, knowing her chance to survive was close to zero . . .

Following the last entry addressed to Brigid was one addressed to John. Her spiky handwriting was even harder to read, like it had been written in a hurry.

I tried to find you on the farm deck, but the shuttle is leaving. I can't explain why right now, but I'm headed back to Earth. There's always a way back home, remember? It just may not be how you expect to get there. I'll explain later in pictures if I can. Touch the stars for me.

It was signed *Cam*, and beside it was a faded drawing of a flower with a bee nestled in the middle.

The following pages were filled with unreadable symbols. They resembled the letters used to form the word that Lauretta had held up in the video he left for Seraph. The word Maypole had said read *Legacy*. Seraph thought they might be Cyrillic. He found examples of old script on his palmcomm, hieroglyphics, cuneiform, and military code. But these matched nothing in the book.

"Vera, can you read this?" He knew full well that she was looking over his shoulder. Her eyes were in every room, every toilet, every office.

"Human-generated ideogrammatic encryption," Vera stated. "Origin and meaning unknown."

"Can you decrypt it?" he asked her.

There was a pause of several seconds, then Vera replied, "There is no known key."

Whatever was written in the book, it had been encrypted in such a way that Vera could not read it. That was the whole purpose of it. To hide the information *from* Vera.

But why?

Seraph looked at the doodles. Some of them looked like snakes, leaves, flowers, little houses.

Who had written this? Maypole?

It was written after she had left the ship. The pages followed her last note to Lauretta. So it couldn't have been her.

He set the book aside and paced the length of the room, startled by his image in the mirror. The multi-colored shirt bedecked with ribbons reminded him of a costume his biological father had worn in one of his opera performances. His father had played a hunchbacked jester, Rigoletto.

When Seraph was Rain's age, Pearl had convinced him that his father's spirit had visited on Christmas Eve and left a file containing a recording of *Rigoletto*. Maybe she thought he was missing out on having a male father figure in his life. Maybe she was right. Whatever the reason, Seraph watched the production at least a dozen times. Depressingly melodramatic, it was the tale of a court clown dressed somewhat like the people of Retro. It included lots of singing by a small man with a big chest and a heavy beard, his biological father. During a plan to assassinate his lecherous lord, Rigoletto's daughter steps in the way and is killed.

Pearl said the moral of the story was that vengeance will always cut down those who seek it.

To Seraph, it meant something very different—make sure your daughter is safe before you lift the sword to protect her.

He picked up the Hello Kitten book and tucked it into the drawer in the bedside table. He would find a way to send a message to Camber Maypole tomorrow and let her know he had found the book.

He took a photo of one page of the strange writing. He would send that too. Now he just wanted to find some sleep. But first, he sent a message to Rain. He wanted to tell her how much he loved her, that every day they were separated would seem like a year, that their landing on Varanasi was all he could think about.

But he simply typed, *Sweet Dreams, Chicklet.*

9

WHAT WAS LOST

2345-02-13, *Earth Standard, The Monastery, Shivi Desh, Varanasi*

HIGH ABOVE THE vermillion cliffs of Shivi Desh, Tanbo Khando soared in the body of a windeater, delighting in the feel of the morning sun on her wings. The world was awash in colors as the long dawn at last gave way to day. She trusted the muscle memory of the beast and landed in a tree on the edge of the gorge, basking in the slant of morning sunlight creeping slowly into the deep canyon. The windeater's talons clutched a branch that bowed and danced with the incessant wind that blew snow and ice across the upper rim. The great canyon of Shivi Desh, shaped by countless ever-widening tributaries, appeared as a network of runoff that spilled from the frozen high plateau into the distant lowlands of the Ganges Valley. The first rivulets of the spring thaw indicated that winter was leaving them at last.

Tanbo controlled the nervous system of this windeater, every cell and fiber of this flesh, and yet, she could feel its consciousness breathing down her neck, as if someone were standing behind her. Maybe the creature's subconscious was stored in the symbiotic plumage that was embedded in its skin. Did the feather-leaves have minds of their own that linked up with the windeater's mind, like fungi did with trees? This could be a problem she had not foreseen, yet the idea fascinated her—the consciousness of a being fragmented and incorporated into the living things it depends upon for life.

She thought about sending a message to Noah to report it but realized she had no such ability. She was pure biology now.

It sent a thrill of fear through her.

Stretching her long neck toward the sun, she listened to the distant mewling of the beast's own kind. She understood nothing of the high-pitched hoots and whistles of the windeaters. If she could concentrate, perhaps she could understand, but barraged with sensory input, an uncontrollable euphoria overtook her and understanding faded away.

The sensors in her robotic holo-print's hardware were far superior to biology, but only for detection, identification, and information storage. The digital translation of remembered smells and sights was the product of algorithms, not chemistry. The sensations of this windeater were penetrating and reminiscent. But they were also fleeting, with little ability to store the data. The neurons had to choose the most necessary information to save—always the memories that would secure survival.

Its retina captured images in transitory, unsavable snatches of time and place. The olfactory bulb fondled complex organics and translated the orgy of smell in a way no computer could. Then the perfume was gone as the wind carried it off.

Perception is soul, is consciousness, and is shaped by the body as much as the pattern of electrical impulses that shape the mind.

Tanbo *was* a windeater with a human neural net draped over the animal's mind.

She tested her wings. The laminar flow of air over plumage

buoyed her up in the dense atmosphere, and soon she was soaring again, high above the landing pad that marked the entrance to the Monastery and across the great chasm of Shivi Desh. The movement of a spiny hare beside the riverbank caught her eye, and she dove, already imagining the taste of the metallic blood in her mouth—a latent memory stored in the tissue of the beast.

She struck and missed, trimmed her wings, and climbed again. She gained altitude, riding the thermals that twisted from the gorge. Her conscious mind hadn't the instincts of the animal, but the muscle memory instilled in the animal's flesh did the flying. Evolution had schooled this beast just as Tanbo's flesh had once known, and would never forget, how to dance the tango.

Without senses, we are nothing more than gadgetry.

Without the struggle to survive, the species stagnates.

The wind dried her black eyes as she wheeled and turned, heading back.

The Monastery's grand terrace peeked from the sandstone of the gorge like a half-opened eyelid. A gap of no more than four meters, it was a challenge even for a true windeater's reflexes. As Tanbo soared through the opening, she caught the creature's spindly legs on the railing and felt a bone break with exquisite pain. Her body rolled over the smooth stones of the balcony and came to rest in a pile of dislodged plumage.

Mech attendants scurried to her aid and lifted her limp body as if to repair it.

"No," a voice commanded from behind her. "Kill this thing."

It was Noah.

It was done.

Like wringing the neck of a chicken.

Tanbo felt it, a sudden ejaculation of the senses. Her mindware spasmed awake in the waiting robotic holo-print, a stack of neodymium and carbon parts and servos that whirred with her coming.

The windeater lay dead at her feet. A pang of loss welled as her last breath exited its nostrils.

Its plumage took flight, fluttering away in a swarm of downy green feathers into the chasm below.

Tanbo could no longer smell the scent of her flock in the air, see the flowers in ultraviolet. She was back to being a prisoner of chemical sensors and information processing.

The body *is* a computer. She knew that better than anyone. But the design was beyond anything created by humans.

"How was it?" Noah asked.

How to describe her flight to this circuit board of a man? "Better," was all she could say.

"I have something to show you," Noah said. He pushed a strand of blond hair over one ear and headed inside.

Tanbo followed, reestablishing her sensorium inside the holoprint. The maze of the Monastery, carved kilometers deep into the plateau, housed a node of the Black Stack, one that was all but isolated from the central stack halfway around the globe. As a principal designer of the system, Tanbo had seen to the building of this offshoot from the root of the whole. Aggressive use of biological hardware set this system apart from the mainly crystal-based quantum core. Tanbo's system could repair itself, replicate itself, and improve itself. It evolved, like all living things, and its full potential was within reach.

The part she had played as savior of humanity would yield treasures a thousand-fold. For while she worked at building a system to reverse neural net salvage, human beings were putt-putting through the void in a low-tech tin can called the *Vera Rubin*. And now, the time had come to welcome the prize to their new reality, to put an end to mediocrity and help the colonists evolve into their perfect selves.

The path from beast to god was not simple.

She and Noah took a lift to the lower lab. Today's flight was probably the last experiment she'd try before the ship arrived. Broadband channels had opened between the ground and the ship. Downloads were in progress; the files were large, nearly three centuries of ship history and data. Vera's processors were ancient, so accessing the ship's records would take some time.

In the lab, Noah showed her the data he'd collected during her flight.

"How did it feel?" he asked again without looking up from the multitude of graphs he had arranged in the air around him.

"It *felt*," she said with a grin. With the projection of her finger, she traced the tattooed snake along his neck, then slid her hands down his chest. She closed her eyes, trying to hang on to the feeling of touch and smell she had drunk up in the windeater's. "Ah, Noah."

"All in good time."

He nodded and turned back to the projected graphs to point out a more satisfactory ratio of her own brainwaves to that of the windeater. "You're almost there now."

"Soon," she said.

He stood and pulled her holo-print close to his. She groped his crotch, feeling the projection of lumpy silicone, certainly not the cock she remembered so fondly.

They were mannequins. That was all. Imagining life.

Yet, they would continue to try to love each other like beasts.

Sex in Virtual was utterly uninspired. In trying to recreate the act of the flesh, the programmers ignored the part played by the mind. It was something Tanbo had given much thought to in these past centuries but reached no viable solution. It was an act, a ritual, longed for greatly by every disembodied mind on Varanasi. The drive of glands and blood, the smell of a lover's skin. And one day, some of them, the chosen, would know it again. They would know what it was to give birth in pain, to hold a shriveled seed of flesh in their hands, a recombinant soul.

Only this way, could she build a new future.

Only this way, could she save humankind from the rotting fingers of entropy.

Noah met her in her chamber, a suite of rooms that opened onto a private terrace where the sun poured morning light over the stone. Together, they leaned on the railing and watched the dance of a rainbow through the waterfall below. It had awakened only this morning. Another harbinger of spring.

Noah would try again to satisfy the need stirred by her flight in the windeater. The need to join with another in a dance of the flesh. Nothing could be more real. Again, he would fail.

A mech servant appeared at the door.

"I said no interruptions," Noah told it.

"It is an emergency, sir."

"Go on."

"Judah Krane has sent an urgent message. Two employees of NASA stumbled into his research area."

"Does he still have them?"

"No," the servant said. "They exited their prints before he could lock them in."

"That's great." Noah turned to Tanbo. "Contact Singh. She's going to have to round up those two before they talk about this."

Rishi's research into downloading into the local fauna had not been sanctioned by the Council of Five. If discovered, it would raise far too many questions. Questions Tanbo was not yet prepared to answer. Not to mention the fines that would be imposed on them for tampering with native species.

"What do you propose Kaja Singh do with these two?" Tanbo asked.

"Whatever it takes to shut them up."

10

NIRVANA CITY

2345-02-13, *Earth Standard, Nirvana Virtual, Black Stack, Varanasi*

MAYPOLE OPENED her eyes in an avatar that was a copy of the body she had once inhabited on Earth. She glanced at her hands, wearing the ring she'd worn since the climbing trip to Crested Butte with John and Lemkos. John had bought the ring from a rock shop on the way there. A simple sunstone set in a silver band etched with vining leaves.

She pulled her red hoodie over her closely cropped black curls. She had often been judged for "lacking in imagination" and "stuck in the physical." But wearing her own image allowed her to tolerate immersion. Sometimes, she even enjoyed it.

She was in a kitchen. A regiment of professional stovetops extended down a long counter, crowded with students in aprons. The clatter of pans, the laughter of a chef she recognized, the smell of sautéed garlic—she knew this place. The Julia Child Institute. That's right. The last time she'd been in Nirvana Virtual, she'd taken a class in French country cuisine. That was months, no, years ago. She'd left her avatar here.

At least she'd escaped the lock Judah Krane had tried to slap on her, and she hoped Lemkos had done the same.

She breathed in the smells and tried to think through the fog of critical transfer. Seconds ago, she'd left her broken holo-print on the floor of Judah Krane's lab, and it wouldn't be long before he found her in Virtual. He had their personnel codes. She initiated as many firewalls as she had available.

Was that cardamom she smelled?

The smells in this cooking school were amazingly nuanced. A vivid memory assaulted her. Nana, rolling arancini balls between her old arthritic palms before dropping them into hot oil. Nana, whistling that familiar tune as she worked. The memory filled Maypole with longing for life, childhood, and the hunger she had felt as she watched Nana cook.

Hunger. She missed it. And her nana.

There was no time for that now. She launched the map. The cooking school was in the French quarter on the westside. Even though she'd left her holo-print in a pile of parts in Krane's lab, her CPU was still accessible to him, housed in the wreckage. Krane would try to hack past her firewall. If she could send a command to her holo-print and fry the CPU . . .

Lemkos would know how to do it. That was, *if* he'd gotten out. He might be wandering Shivi Desh wearing a hellion for a body.

A stream of alerts came through her access management system. A flood of events had been quarantined. Judah Krane's code was hammering at the door of her primary storage. She could only hope her onboard defenses could keep him out for just a little longer.

"Ah, Dr. Maypole, glad you could join us again." The AI avatar known simply as Julia was holding a spoon in one hand and swilling a glass of wine with the other. "Tell us what this ceviche needs, will you, dear?"

"Another time."

Maypole ducked out onto the busy street. The smell of parsley and simmering scallops followed.

The streets were crowded with people dressed for Carnival. Masks and feathers, sequined G-strings and capes of gilded flowers. Balloons streamed behind floats that were as alive as the avatars that rode them. Women with breasts too large for their bikini tops, or no tops at all. Men with equally large members and exaggerated pecs. Wings and tails, beaks and horns, satyrs and serpents. Balloons with faces and voices. Flowers grew and bloomed, then grew and bloomed again all within the space of time it took for a float to pass. Like a bad dream. But the perfect event to get lost in.

Unlike most people in Virtual, Maypole had a limited inventory of avatars and equipment. Wearing her bio-image avatar would not do if something or someone was scanning visuals.

It probably didn't matter. Even with the ID-blocking apps, it wouldn't take much for Krane to find her. From the explanation Elijah had given them, amalgams were an extension of the Black Stack itself, a slurry of brilliant minds all forged into one.

A prancing zebra with a cat mask threatened to knock her into some shrubs but caught her with a whip made of stars. The zebra lifted its mask and gave her a wink, but the eyes were vacant like those of a blind person, open and eager to see but never seeing. The great majority of people here forgot there ever was a Real or any planet outside of Nirvana Virtual. It was an addiction, this place. When she'd first arrived, she and Lemkos spent the bulk of their time sampling the Realms, searching for the next adrenaline rush. But that was all there was to this place. The over-stimulation eventually dulled everything about existence, at least, for Maypole. She started spending more time in the Real, until she quit Virtual completely. Well, except for cooking classes.

She slipped behind a wall.

In her inventory, she found an avatar named Ryssa Gantu and a wood elf named Skya Pryn. Ryssa Gantu was the higher level, though neither were ranked better than novice.

Dressed in the sand-colored tunic and hooded robe of a Kenzin master, she dropped her Earth image for this fantasy character, a feline humanoid known as a Canteri in the Star Empire universe. Her silky pelt was black and her eyes violet. She checked her weapon inventory and equipped a katana as well as a rungu, but her skill level with the knobbed throwing stick was very low. If one of Judah Krane's NPCs came after her, she might buy some time with the katana.

She left the French Quarter on the back of a standard issue gryphon, her only mount. Everyone else sped past her on fast mounts, but her gryphon beat its wings in a steady, slow rhythm.

After Lemkos spent a lifetime in ancient Rome in the Samsara sim, he built himself a villa in the Roman Quarter. Now she knew how he could afford it.

She soared past the waystation, a ring of nebulas that marked doorways into a multitude of pricy Realms. To enter, one had to pay. A lot. The only Realm available to all was Nirvana City and Martine Sommer's competing realm, Occitania.

Nirvana City had been built with the funds provided by the Vested. This was *their* Nirvana, *their* eternal playground. After signing over their net worth to Rishi upon death, they'd had their consciousness replicated and digitized by nano-swarms. Their mindware were then squirted through a micro-wormhole on a low-infrared beam to the paradise they'd bought: Varanasi. None would have agreed to sharing it with hundreds of thousands of refugees who had won a UN lottery. Sending a random selection of human minds to Varanasi was a last-ditch effort to save civilization as the carrion virus cleansed Earth of its most tenacious parasite, humanity.

As with most obscenely wealthy people, the Vested didn't play well with the great unwashed who had crashed their world. Refugees were allowed limited access to the Realms based on how much they could pay. Most of those refugees resided solely in Nirvana City, which contained, among other adventures, a sprawling simulacrum of Rome, Oz, Neverland, and Future World, all frosted with a hyperreal fantasy gaming feel. The Vested's attempts to drive the refugees to the surface of Varanasi, to the Real, had failed miserably. Nirvana City had proved to be enough for them, and it remained crammed with gophers.

People here bought and sold avatars, designed custom skins, and leveled their abilities in everything from swords and spellcasting to airship piloting and space warfare. They spent decades lost in Fifth Fantasy, Warcraft, Skycloud, and Alien Harvest. Most notably, they forgot they were dead. But there were a few like Maypole, those who understood they were simply shadows of who they'd once been, stagnating here without growth or change, forever young, forever perfect, forever longing to know what comes after.

In many ways, these gophers were as much a projection of the Black Stack as Judah Krane.

As she flew over the streets, she passed conveyances with wheels like cars of Earth, others were constructed from childhood fantasies or old MMO games. Some were ethereal craft assembled from dreams: a flying soap bubble, a mouse with wings, a paper airplane. But everyone had to move from one virtual location to another to do or experience whatever they desired. There were rules to this world, just not the ones that governed reality.

The slow flap of her gryphon's wings carried her over Avalon to the Palatine Hills above Rome. If she couldn't find Lemkos, she would go to Mission Control, tell Kaja Singh what was going on in the labs in the gorgelands.

Was downloading into native species illegal? She was sure selling executed minds was, which would only implicate Lemkos, not Rishi. No, she couldn't tell Singh about this. Not yet.

Landing in the vineyard outside of Lemkos's villa, she slid from the gryphon's back, stroking the tawny coat before it vanished back into her inventory.

Lemkos's house overlooked the river and groves of olives. As a legal gladiator, Lemkos had made some enemies, which warranted a level of security greater than the average citizen. Knowing he was involved in the black-market sale of condemned criminals' mindware, it all began to make sense.

Centurions at the outer door stopped her with crossed pikes. She briefly flashed her ID. Her name was on his approved list, and they let her pass.

A servant led her through carved cedar doors. He informed her that Lemkos was not at home, but Maypole stormed through the atrium of the vast, cold house, all marble and fresh garlands, calling for him. Frescoes of bucolic scenes of nymphs and gods at play covered the walls. Incense fogged the loggia with exotic clouds where a statue of some god battled a snake.

If anyone could get out of Krane's lab, Lemkos could. He must have made it. And he'd be wise to make it look like he wasn't here.

A message pinged her onboard. It was in her cooking school account, the one she'd given to Seraph Stone. Using her NASA comms was not a great idea, and the school account was the only other one she had. After what just happened, even that was probably not secure.

It was from the ship, the *Vera Rubin*. Lt. Stone. He must have found John's hidden legacy. She couldn't open the message here.

Lemkos had an air gap in this place, a room that was completely disconnected from all networks. He'd shown it to her when he'd first built it. She suspected now that it was somehow related to his shady dealings.

She guessed he would put the air gap close to his main bedchamber. She'd only been to this villa once, long enough to deem it tasteless. She imagined it impressed Martine Sommer, though.

The bedroom was a terraced suite swathed in silks and tapestries. If Lemkos had a secret room, it had to be here.

"Hey! Lemkos!"

She felt the edges of a mosaic inlay for an access switch. The servants made multiple attempts at stopping her, but she pushed them away.

"I am a friend," she repeated. "Check your guest list."

"Access to this space is restricted."

One of the thugs placed the point of his sword into the fur of her neck, and Maypole drew her katana.

Her moves were beyond rusty. A few ringing blows against the Roman sword made it clear she could not win. She utilized her Canteri ability to leap and made her way to the top of a high cabinet. Slashing down at the helmeted thug, he caught her katana with his sword and, without effort, snapped the blade. She tossed the hilt away and pressed herself to the wall.

Two more guards appeared.

They rocked the cabinet. Vases and statues crashed to the ground with Maypole. Sitting among the shards of pottery with a sword at her throat, she saw the hidden door open from behind the mosaic.

Lemkos stepped out. With his hands on his hips, he said calmly, "Leave her alone."

He wore his gladiator avatar. Everyone in Nirvana City knew this avatar—a ripped warrior with perpetually oiled pecs and trees for arms.

Lemkos said, "Sorry, Cupcake. Come with me."

The guards stepped aside, and she got to her furry feet. Crunching through broken glass and pottery, she followed.

The air gap was a windowless rectangular room covered in frescoed garden scenes. In the center, a computer sat on a marble desk. Outwardly, it had the appearance of a classic "desktop," as they used to call them in the twenty-first.

"We need to wipe our local CPUs, the ones in Shivi Desh," she said.

"Mine is done. I can get yours blanked out in a few seconds. Type the command here. It will encrypt the instructions and place a false source code in it. Then we can step outside and send it."

He fiddled with his faux ancient console and a holo popped up. He slid some code here and there. "Now step out and initiate this."

"Jesus, Lemkos. You have been up to some shady shit."

He shrugged.

She did as instructed and stepped into his bedchamber to initiate the CPU wipe. Then she returned to the air gap.

"I have a message I need to access," she said. Making sure the door had closed. "From the ship."

"The ship?"

Knowing what Lemkos had been hiding from her, she was hesitant to share the story of John Lauretta's message until she knew more. Her trust in Lemkos had taken a hit.

"From the medical officer. Data for my clinic."

"You need that right now?"

"Actually, yes. And it's confidential, so you need to . . . get out or something."

He chuffed. "I know when you're hiding something from me, Camber."

"Apparently, I can't tell the same about you. Really, Lemkos? Selling criminal mindware?"

"Okay, let's not start with this again. Is this message onboard?"

She nodded.

"Okay, you should be good to open it. But make sure it's dumped before you leave the air gap." Then he stepped out of the room.

Maypole logged into her cooking school account. Sitting on top of hundreds of ads for classes and recipes, she found the one from Seraph Stone.

I have the object. It's a book. I can't read it. Maybe you can.

Attached were two photos. The front cover—it was Brigid's journal, the one Maypole's niece had given her when she left Earth. Brigid had picked it out herself. She'd told Maypole that if she wrote in it every day, she wouldn't miss Earth as much. Maypole had left it behind with a message for John. She'd had no time to say goodbye.

The air gap fell away. All Maypole could see was the image of that book, the tears on her niece's face. She could still feel the weight of it, feel her hand moving across the page as she wrote words to her niece who would be dead before the ship even launched. Maypole felt all the current drain out of her circuits. Her "feels" simulators maxed out, and there was nothing but zeros and ones flowing through her.

The second image was a page of picture words: Camber's shorthand, the alphabet of pictograms she had invented as a kid to help with her dyslexia. She had always taken notes with her pictograms, all through college, even in astronaut training. John had asked to learn it, and left notes . . .

But she didn't write this. John must have used her code and the journal to hide information. He must have gotten the idea from the letters she'd sent him from Earth before the ship left system, before Maypole got sick. But who did he expect would read it? The same person who had translated the word "legacy." Camber Maypole.

She increased the size of the image. It had been so long, it took time to work out the words.

I tried to convince Unger to shelve those embryos, just like you said. But he says they are in the bank for a reason and it's not his place to question them. Whatever is so special about those things—

That was the end of the page. "Shit!"

"Cupcake?" Lemkos called from the other side of the door. "Everything okay?"

"No. I need the rest of this—"

"Of what?" Lemkos asked.

She sighed and began to pace. She wasn't inclined to trust Lemkos after his dealings with Krane. If not him, then who?

"Get back in here," she said.

He did.

"John left notes for me." She told him about Seraph Stone, the vid message about a "legacy" that was crucial to the colonists. "John hid my own journal in *his* legacy bag in the hub. With *his* notes in it."

"In your crazy writing," Lemkos said, looking at the image of the code hovering above the table. "Why the crazy writing?"

"So Vera can't read it," Maypole said.

"Huh." He scanned the little hieroglyphics. "No one has a key to these things? I mean, it's not searchable?"

"No. Not unless Vera has access to my notes from anatomy class. The code is mine. It's in no database, just my head." She tapped her furry cat head.

His face lit up. "Let's be sure."

He had Maypole write a short note in pictograms and send it to him. Then he exited the air gap and retrieved it.

"Looks like you're right. The Stack says it's art done by a child."

"Why use my code?" None of this made sense.

"John has something important to tell you, Cupcake."

Maypole thought back to her weeks on Earth after being grounded and replaced by Rishi's chosen physician, Unger.

"One more thing about Unger. He was an employee of Rishi Corp, their corporate physician before he got chosen for the backup crew."

"What does that have to do with anything? Lots of people on this planet were employees of Rishi."

"I think they were just looking for the chance to bump me and put him in my place."

"But why?"

"Ru Shi Zhu, founder of Rishi, came herself to debrief me," Maypole said. "Lemkos, she was waiting when I stepped off that shuttle. Oh shit." She started pacing, the connections flashing in her mind.

"What?" Lemkos asked.

"That's who Dutro's assistant looks like. The one in the skin meeting who tried to throw me out. She looks exactly like Ru Shi Zhu." But it couldn't be her. According to legend, Zhu was never salvaged. She died on Earth. "Who is wearing her face?"

"Maybe just a fan," Lemkos said. "Let's back up, Cupcake. Slowly."

Maypole's mind raced. She said, "When I got back to Earth, Zhu wanted to know everything I could tell her about the embryos that got me canned. It was like she knew nothing about them."

"And? What did you tell her?"

"Exactly what I told you. They had no provenance, not even a karyotype, but they had originated in Rishi's labs."

"Maybe Zhu lost control of things at Rishi. Maybe some things were going down without her knowledge," Lemkos said. "Did you mention the code?"

"Of course not." She thought for a minute. "But I *did* mention that debrief to John. In a note I sent him aboard the ship using my code."

Lemkos started pacing the small space of the air gap. "Wait, what?"

Maypole was standing now.

"John left an encrypted book hidden in the hub," Lemkos said. "Left it for the senior ag specialist to pick up. What did he expect him to do with it? Find you. He knew you would be here on Varanasi. And he knew Vera could not read it because it's a personal ideogrammatic code. *You* are the key. John left it for you."

Maypole's head was spinning. Two centuries was a long time to dig up old memories. John using her as a decoding device? Could that possibly be true?

Lemkos's gladiator face moved to the other side of the holo image, his arms crossed over his oiled chest. How could John have known that she would be salvaged, that NASA would give her a position here on Varanasi after everything she had done? Unless . . .

"Oh, shit," Maypole groaned, then stepped around the projection and squared up to Lemkos. "You and John. You *planned*, no, you *conspired* for me to be salvaged and squirted through space to this fucking place!"

"Now, Cupcake, think about that—"

"I *am* thinking about it! NASA would never pay for my neural salvage; they have no need for an insubordinate doctor here. How could I have been so fucking naïve? *They* didn't bring me here. *You* did, Lemkos. You did it because John convinced you that I was needed here. For this, this, fucking journal."

Lemkos stared at the ground, then dragged his hands down his face. "I knew nothing about this journal, Camber. I only knew . . . I wanted you here. I needed you here, and when John asked—"

"Bullshit, Kolya."

He blinked from his gladiator avatar to his original physical image, a tall, skinny Ukrainian who needed more sun. There was hurt on his face, or was it confusion?

Maypole exited her black cat avatar and blinked on her own image. She paced the room, her arms crossed. "You knew about this journal all along."

He held up his hands as if to deflect a blow. "I swear to you, Camber, I knew nothing about it. I just-just couldn't be without you."

She searched his eyes and found what she had been running from for so long for reasons she didn't understand. When she had ended their relationship, just before he vanished into the Samsara sim, he acted as if what they had shared was nothing but entertainment for him. He was as responsible for ending it as she was. Being with Lemkos reminded her of living, of friendships and loss. Wasn't that all there was? But she could not deny what she saw in his eyes at this moment, or what she felt in her gut.

She didn't have time for this. Not now. Maybe not ever.

11

THE FIRST FLAME

2345-02-15, Earth Standard, Torus-2, aboard the Vera Rubin

AFTER A DAY SPENT BREAKING his back in the Retro farms, Seraph climbed into bed with the Hello Kitten book. The code made no more sense than it had days ago, but there were doodles here and there. Animals crawling around the edge of the text as if trying to draw his attention to a particular indecipherable word. The drawings made him feel loss and longing the way some music could. They were like Rain's daily messages, complete with doodles.

He'd spent more time talking to TJ in the past few days than he had in the past year. After she'd called him every foul name she knew and threatened imprisonment when they reached Varanasi, she'd cooled down. He simply pointed out that Retro's assaults on Torus-1 had stopped with the food delivery. Predictably. The people of Retro might not be feasting, but they had enough to survive the weeks ahead.

At the least, TJ must have realized that now she had an informer inside Retro. Seraph figured she'd use him to maximum advantage.

He was okay with being used. He was good at it.

Most of her questions were about the weapons Retro had developed. Seraph had been sworn to secrecy by Huang, who had contended that sharing tech with TJ would be an alert to Vera who would shut them all down. Seraph had stalled TJ with mostly honest answers.

This time, she called him late, waking him from a deep sleep.

"Hold on," he said. He got up and initiated the interference as Huang had taught him. "Okay. Have you guys started the signal interrupt on your comms?"

She shook her head. "Too many other things to worry about. With the course corrections our arrival date has moved up."

"To when?"

"Likely within ten days. The braking isn't slowing us as much as calculated. Which means we may overshoot."

"Ten days?"

She nodded.

TJ propped her palmcomm on a pillow which bathed her face in a sterile blue glow. Sitting cross-legged in her underwear and white T-shirt, she worked at loosening her hair. Like him, she was in bed. But she was in *their* bed. A painful longing washed over him.

"Tell me about Baakos," she demanded.

"He has substantial influence. There are many here who see him as the true leader of Retro."

"It sounds like you're one of them." Was that a smirk on her face? But there was something else there in her starburst eyes. Distrust. She was playing it safe. The realization came as a blow. Vera had put her up to this.

"Look, Ser," she started with a sigh. "Vera sent me a comm alert. She says you contacted one Camber Maypole, M.D. on the ground. A jobox."

"Use noise and we can talk," he said. He wanted nothing more than to bring TJ into his confidence about Maypole, the journal, the code.

"Vera needs to know why you contacted Maypole."

"TJ," he said, "use the noise. Then we'll talk."

"Feces."

Her hand moved toward the palmcomm as if to close the connection.

"Wait, wait. Just tell me one thing. How's Rain?" The question just dribbled out. He knew damn well how Rain was, how he had hurt her. How *they* had hurt her.

TJ's eyes narrowed and she drew close to the screen. "She's just a kid, Seraph. How do you think she feels? You left her."

He pursed his lips, nodding.

Her face morphed from a scowl to one of peeved exasperation. "I know you were running from-from *us* with this stunt. But you left her behind."

"I wasn't running from anything, TJ. I was doing my best to keep people alive. Maybe," he stammered, "maybe I'm running *toward* something."

"Your *First Flame?*" She laughed and closed the connection.

Maybe she was right. Maybe he was nothing more than Vera's pawn, no different than TJ. He got up and went to the galley, looking for Huang's hootch.

THE NEXT MORNING, Seraph was supposed to be in Farm D by 0700 to restock the repaired fish tanks. He didn't hear his alarm, only the throbbing of his head brought on by TJ—and all the hootch in Huang's kitchen.

"Feces."

After pulling on his clothes, he couldn't find his palmcomm. He'd been talking to TJ, and maybe it had fallen off the bed. No luck. He opened the drawer on his bedside table. His palmcomm was there—

but the book was gone. He searched the room, his clothes, the head. The answer became obvious.

Seraph left the unit, buttoning up the oversized shirt. The wing-like sleeves rippled behind him as he rode a wheelie. The two-wheeled transport had been modified as only Retro could—four speeds instead of three and a retractable seat for the elderly or infirmed, and an optional third wheel for stability. The place he was headed was a unit in the AD marketplace. In Torus-1, its analog was a popular pub. There were few pubs here in Retro. The sign above the door read *The Temple of Fire.*

Church. Baakos style.

Seraph ditched the wheelie, pushed stray strands of hair behind his ears and walked in.

Chairs, loosely arranged in a semicircle, were filled with people. Close to fifty, he estimated. They all turned to stare at him in unison.

"Ah, the weary one joins us," Baakos said. He stood on a dais wearing his patchwork robes. A jester mystic. Behind him, a looping holo image of a roiling star in time-lapse filled the stage. In the center of the boiling plasma sat the silhouette of a person in cross-legged meditation.

Baakos's baubles chimed as he motioned for Seraph to join him.

Seraph strode to the small stage. Drawing close, he said, "You took something of mine. I want it back."

Baakos leaned closer and whispered, "Something? You mean the book? You traded it to us last night, remember? For the hootch."

"Like hell I did," Seraph said loudly. "What do you think you're going to do with it? You can't read it."

A murmur of discussion broke out among the congregation. So many eyes on Seraph. They were whispering. Baakos placed his big hands on Seraph's shoulders, but Seraph shook him off.

"This man," Baakos proclaimed, putting on his benevolent preacher persona again, "saved us from hunger. This man has opened his eyes to the ways of Retro, to the truth we seek as a people. Here"—

Baakos strode across the stage, his arms wide—"here is the man who challenged our captor."

The crowd exploded into hoots and cheers.

The image of the star burned like a halo around Baakos's head. He grinned at Seraph.

"It was the First Flame, the True Fire, the fire within who saved us, Seraphim Stone. Your fireseed, the will of eternity. Now you have met your shadow and have come to join us in the light." He indicated the flaming star. "In the community of immortals, our trials are shaped and pressed upon us. As we rise to meet them, with each victory, our fireseed changes, our atoms rearrange and we are new, evolved. For you have a secret, Seraphim Stone."

Seraph's bleary eyes met Baakos's. Those starburst eyes were laughing at him. The bastard was going to hold the book ransom. What was he after? Seraph's conversion? Another pawn in his game of controlling these people?

Seraph clenched his fists, ready to punch. But that would just prove Baakos right. He was a hotheaded drunk. Did he really trade the book for the hootch? *Yes*, he thought, he must have. He was swimming in a rising pool, and he knew he'd drown one day.

"You'll give me my book," Seraph said evenly. Then he left the Temple of Fire to the believers.

HUANG CLAIMED to know nothing about his book. She laughed at him. "Paper? Drawings? We have enough drawings here; we don't need to steal yours."

"That book is important."

"Important how?"

Seraph found Huang at work on the fabber deck. The glow of the display exposed the gray around the roots of her pink hair. She'd been programming the 3D printers. She pushed geometric shapes around on a screen, rotated the graphic, and rearranged things.

"Look," he said, "I know you intend to hold the book hostage until I tell you what this is about."

"So tell us," she said.

"Show me the book."

She glanced around the deck at the others working at their consoles. "Tonight. In a safe place."

Seraph left the fabber deck and went back to stocking fish tanks, trying to convince himself there was nothing worth finding in the scribblings of a dead farmer. Probably.

That night, the book was sitting in the middle of the painted cow on the coffee table. Baakos sat on one end of the sofa and Huang on the other. Seraph felt like he had when Pearl had found out he'd been copying Jasmine Lee's homework every night for an entire year.

Huang poured Seraph a glass of hootch and pushed it across the table. He let it sit there. The amber liquid called to him. He recognized the hooks Huang had in him, the weakness she exploited. No more, he vowed to himself. Seraph met Baakos's eyes and pushed the glass back to Huang. She let it sit there until Seraph got up, picked up the glass of amber numbness, and poured it into the recycler. It was time to let all the pain, all the fear, all the loneliness, come to the surface. Time to feel it. All of it. And then let it go.

"What is this book?" Baakos finally asked.

Seraph told them only what they needed to know—the message from Lauretta telling him about a legacy.

"A legacy?" Baakos said. "Most certainly the information contained within this book has been hidden from our captor for just this moment. The cypher is unreadable, even by Vera."

"Yes."

"We must know what it contains if this man, Lauretta, saw fit to reveal it to us—"

"Only one person can read it," Seraph said.

"Who?"

Smugly, Seraph leaned toward them. "A jobox." He told them

about Maypole, about her removal from the launch crew. But he did not confess that he'd already contacted her.

"It's a personal, ideogrammatic writing system," Huang said. "The only way to read it is to have a key." Huang sighed and closed her eyes. Her hands went to the carved nut around her neck. "Someone wanted this message to be read at the right time, by the right person."

"By a jobox named Dr. Camber Maypole," Seraph said.

"She cannot be trusted." Baakos crossed his arms defensively.

"We have no option but to trust her," Seraph said.

"No," Baakos concluded.

"I've already contacted her," Seraph said. "I'm waiting for her response."

Huang said, "Then I will be waiting with you, friend."

THAT NIGHT, Seraph borrowed Huang's VR rig and logged into Rain's Varanasi science project. He'd been in with her a few times in the past and knew they had a group lesson every Tuesday evening. According to the posting in the class lobby, they were in the gorge-lands today, cataloging native species. Seraph's favorite place. The sky here was the thing he wanted to see more than anything—more than the rivers, more than the marching forests. Sapphire blue in the long day, and at night—the specter of Majriti draped across it, a mantle of colorful storms. He would see it. He felt more certain of that every day.

He waited beside a river in a massive gorge called Shivi Desh and watched several kids go by. Axel Finn and Darlene Espinoza, two friends of Rain's, though they were both a few years older.

"Can you tell her I'm here?" he asked them.

They scowled at him. A parent had infiltrated their virtual classroom.

"She's not coming, you know," Darlene said. "She doesn't want to see you."

Seraph nodded, picked up a rock and tossed it into the flow of the milky river.

He looked up at Darlene, squinting against the blinding radiance of the sun. He said, "Tell her I'm going to be here anyway."

He got up and headed out along the river that threaded between two massive cliffs where a meadow of white flowers bloomed. Clouds coursed high above, leaping across the chasm to vanish on the other side. He'd been in this simulation so many times he'd memorized the shapes of the clouds, the cliffs, the waterfalls. As a kid, he'd spent hours lying beside this stream, watching the clouds appear and disappear above the cliffs. He wondered if this place could still exist, or had the joboxes squeezed every bit of metal and nanodiamond from these canyons by now?

The volume capture had been done by robotic explorers not long after the first mechs were up and running on the planet. They had sent petabytes of data through the micro-wormhole that once linked the sol system with the Ups-And system. He'd memorized every turn of this river, had built a fort in a thicket of migrating trees, and dived from the cliffs into the deep pools on hot days. He'd tried to mimic the calls of the windeaters and stalked the hellions who hunted here with crude spears, the skulls of their prey strung around their necks.

The things Vera taught them in the education modules were all programmed on Earth two centuries ago. She could have decided to teach them anything. Seraph wondered if Vera's version of history had any resemblance to reality. And if it didn't, would it matter?

As he walked on, the forest grew dense.

Creatures the early explorers had chosen to call "trees" clung to the red walls of the canyon in a bright emerald band near the chasm floor. It seemed the entire forest watched him with eyespots at the ends of their branches. The trees loosed leaves, which were organisms themselves, symbionts called plumage. Their fluttering reminded him of the doodles that danced in the margins of the Hello Kitten book.

A chorus of unseen creatures hooted and chanted in high rhythmical peels. The sun drove splinters of golden light into the chasm. Seraph could swear he saw the trees moving, marching as one unit along a ridge high above him, but he knew they moved slowly unless it was migration season. A flock of bright blue flying creatures crossed from one side of the canyon to the other, and a plant-like thing plunged bloom-first into the river and brought up a wriggling, tentacled morsel.

"Don't step on that thing." A voice sounded from behind him.

He spun around to find Rain, following at a distance.

"Yeah," he said, trying not to overwhelm her with his need to sweep her into his avatar's arms. "Pincer poppy."

"Atmosphere is mostly nitrogen." Behind Rain, a ghostly image of Vera, wearing her officer's uniform and her hair pulled into that austere bun, lectured. "It is higher in oxygen than Earth with a slightly higher pressure. Combined with the relatively higher trace amounts of—"

"Vera, stop," Rain commanded.

Rain's avatar looked like her in an animated way. Her starburst eyes were as big and timid as a rabbit's. They reminded Seraph that it wasn't her, that he couldn't scoop her up in his arms. They were just shadows of themselves.

Rain walked on ahead of Seraph, her hands clasped behind her back, mimicking Vera. "She was going to say there's a relatively high concentration of xenon in the atmosphere, which can cause a sense of euphoria."

"I don't need xenon to feel euphoric," Seraph said. "I just need you."

She looked back at him and rolled her eyes the way only a ten-year-old can.

"This sky"—he gestured at the expanse of sapphire over their heads—"will be ours soon, Chicklet."

"If," she said.

"If," he repeated. He knew what she meant. He'd been qualifying her dreams with *if* since she was a baby. If all went as planned, if every calculation was correct, if computers and disembodied minds would concern themselves with the fate of a boat-full of humans.

But for now, it was enough to know Rain had chosen to walk with him here.

"Pearl is with you, right?"

"Yeah, but Gran isn't you."

Seraph just nodded. "Tell her, it's important I speak to her. Please."

Rain stopped, got to her knees to take a closer look at sponge patapa moss.

Seraph knelt beside her and took both her hands in his. Vera was strolling over to another student, lecturing about the carnivorous fish in the river. He whispered, "Listen to me, Chicklet. If I could be back in T-1 with you, I would be. But there were kids like you, who were going hungry—"

"I know, Seraph," she said. Using his name rather than *Daddy* was a good indication of how ticked off she was. "You saved the kids over there, I get it. It's time for me to grow up. That's what Gran says. She says I have to share you."

"Not for long. We'll be on the ground soon," he said.

She wiped tears away from those beautiful, starburst eyes. The eye color that had been created by random mutation, according to Vera. The same mutation that randomly affected Torus-2. He had calculated the odds. There was something else at work here.

"Chicklet, I need you to do something for me. Dismiss Vera."

She gave him a puzzled look and glanced back at the avatar of the ship's AI, helping Darlene with an experiment. "Okay. End lesson."

The image of Vera faded.

"Hey," Darlene called, "I wasn't finished."

Seraph whispered, "I want you to ask Dr. Zahn to give you your genetic files. All the names of all the people who made you. All the way back to Earth. Then I want you to send them to me."

"Why, Daddy?" He softened, feeling her need for him surface.

"It could be important. And I'm trusting you."

"Trusting me?"

"You can't tell Mom about it."

She stood, brushing dirt from her hands on her pants. "You don't trust Mom."

Seraph sighed. "I don't trust Vera."

THE RESPONSE from Maypole had been sitting in his inbox for at least a day. But there was no way he would open it unless he felt completely secure.

With minimal effort, he had converted a busted aquaponics tank into a type of Faraday cage by wrapping it in metal mesh and foil. Then he'd insulated it with foam scavenged from the fabber deck.

The tank still smelled like fish turds, and the inside glass was crusted with dried algae and scales.

Seraph started to sweat even before he reached up and pulled the lid over his head. He crimped all the seams of foil, then flipped the light on his palmcomm. Here, his device was isolated from all wireless connections, the ship network, and Vera. He could open the encrypted message he had downloaded, read it, then delete it, all inside the box.

It was a video. The image of a round-faced woman in her thirties filled the small screen. She had the compact build of one who'd developed under full g. Her curly hair was dark and cropped short. Her stern straight brows didn't match the softness Seraph saw in her dark eyes, which were hooded by dense lashes. Her mouth was small and full, and when she spoke, he saw a small gap in her front teeth. Camber Maypole looked more human to him than many people he knew.

She was the woman in the photo he had found at the bottom of the legacy bag. Yet, it was difficult for Seraph to remember this was not a living woman, but a hologram. Behind her was a panorama of hills, groves of trees, and a brilliant blue sky.

"Seraph Stone," she said. "Do you know your ABCs?"

With that she held up a drawing of three straight slashes and a circle through them. It was a symbol he had seen repeatedly in the journal. She sang a forced song, completely off tune, "A is for astronaut, a job I miss so much."

"Feces," he cursed and scrambled to write it down. He had nothing for that purpose, so began writing with his finger in the dried algae that covered the glass.

It was followed by another symbol and the lyrics for B, the "th" sound, "ing," and a string of other common sounds. It was far longer than the ABCs.

Maypole held up a symbol that looked like a sword. "F is for freedom." She drew close to the camera and said, "I trust you will use the utmost caution with this. Destroy this message. Send me photos of every page in that book and the info you find on Rishi in the biobank logs." She drew back and gave him a confident smile, singing, "Now I know my ABCs, tell me what you think of me."

A muffled sound came from outside the tank. Someone was opening the lid, sliding it aside, letting a blast of fresh air into the fish tank.

He quickly closed the message.

"Clever," Erica Huang said. "Move over, friend. I'm watching it too."

Retrieved from *Vera Rubin* database 2347-12-02

Image capture from video dated 2119-11-04

Description: Subject Lt. John Lauretta, judged to be despondent, in a recorded message to unspecified future recipient holds up a sheet of paper with encrypted writing. Translation provided by Dr. Camber Maypole.

John,

Brigid is gone. So is my brother. Lemkos and I are holed up in his house living on food delivery and indoor croquet, but I keep telling him there's no point to this. Someday, the food won't come. We should just run out and give the carrion virus a great big hug. Be done with it. But he says NASA wants to send him to Varanasi. They'd pay for his neural salvage when his time comes. No such offer for me.

There's a rumor a vaccine might be ready soon. But there may be no one left to give it to.

I'm not telling you this to make you feel guilty or sad. I just think you deserve to know.

See you on the other side.

Cam

Beside the name is a cartoon drawing of a wilted flower with most of its petals gone and a bee flying away from it. Determined not to be part of encryption.

12

WAITING FOR NIGHT

2345-02-15, *Earth Standard, Nirvana Virtual, Black Stack, Varanasi*

LEMKOS CHECKED THE TIME. It had been fifty-three standard hours since they'd left Mission Control and headed into the gorgelands. The flight director would be looking for them. After Camber sent the reply to Seraph Stone, they left Nirvana Virtual and were now wandering a medieval village in Martine's Occitania. Maypole was eyeing a rabbit that hung in the butcher's stall as if she wanted to dissect it.

"Can you believe this is virtual?" she asked.

"We can't stay here. Come on." He led the way through a winding alley, out of visual. "We can't bring Martine into this."

"*She* brought *us* into it."

"Oh, no. John did that."

Camber sighed and ran her fingers through her short hair and ruffled it. A tick he knew and loved. She was chewing on a piece of rabbit jerky, analyzing the flavor. "Not bad."

Lemkos was blasted with a memory. The feel of her hair, the taste of her skin. Once upon a time, the Earth had been collapsing into death all around them. He had wanted to tell her how he felt so many times, but knew she still grieved for her lost future . . . and John. There would always be John. He was untouchable, an angel flying away from them at sixty million meters per second. He would find love again, surely. Couldn't Camber?

"Come climbing with me," she'd told Lemkos. It had been almost a year since the *Vera Rubin* had launched. "Why wait for the fucking virus to find us. Let's do what we love."

She chose the keyhole route of Longs Peak, one of her favorites. They sat on the summit laughing and drinking whiskey, remembering their life, their friendship. On their descent, they stopped at the lake at the base of the peak and pitched a tent in a meadow singing with flowers. Beside a fire, they waited for night.

"It'll be hard to leave such beauty," she said, watching the sky blush crimson. Then she took his hand in hers. "We've shared so much, Kolya. Let's cheat death of the pain it has ready for us."

Her hands were rough from climbing, and cold. She pulled a vial from her pocket and put it in his palm. He knew what the pills were.

"Camber, I need you to know—"

"I know." She faced him, and with a fierce look, took his face in her hands. "To say I never felt the same would be a lie. But there's no time for us. Not in this world."

Her kiss was not one of physical passion, but of deep sadness and regret—a longing of the soul. He returned it, and their bodies attempted to share the love they'd tried to hide.

Dawn came, and while she slept, he threw her pills in the lake. To his surprise, all she said was, "You're right. We're not cowards."

Death changes you. He wanted to believe for the better.

He glanced at her, still chewing on the rabbit jerky. He felt a tender kinship, and knew she felt the same. "We go top side," he said.

"Okay, you go check in with the FD. I'll meet you later at the arena."

"I thought we agreed we should both go to Mission Control."

"I have to make a stop," she said.

"Where?"

"Business. I'll see you at the arena. In the meantime, ask your friend Martine to send some security to my house."

"Krane will be on you in no time."

"Exactly." Camber shrugged. "What can he do to me? I'm already dead. But he's not touching my house."

"Cupcake—"

But just like that, her image faded away. He'd forgotten how impulsive she was. Maybe it was the inevitable awkwardness of failed lovers, trying to find a way to be friends. Maybe it was his decision to dive into two lifetimes in Samsara. He'd tried to convince her to come, but she said living a simulated life was no better than living virtual. By the time seventy or eighty years had passed, she was a stranger to him again, a rover of the highlands, a collector of plants, a hermit.

He climbed a narrow stairway to reach the top of the city walls. Beyond lay forest and mountains, pastures and fields, as real as anything he had ever known on Earth. How could he make Camber see that biology didn't matter—it had *never* mattered. *Life is a stream that we all dive into at birth and let it carry us away.*

A storm was brewing over the northern hills. The air smelled of rain.

He activated the tracking code he'd inserted into the files Seraph Stone had sent, now stored in Camber's temp files. If Krane took her, Lemkos would at least know where to look.

13

THE CAGE

2345-02-16, *Earth Standard, Torus-2, aboard the* Vera Rubin

RAIN'S genetic file made no sense to Seraph. Five columns of numbers and letters streamed back three centuries. Birth and death dates were all he could understand. His own ancestors were clearly marked as Earth-born. But TJ's side was completely different. There were several entries that were missing both birth and death dates. How was that possible? Was this what Maypole was looking for? But there was no mention of Rishi anywhere in Rain's profile.

Huang had the Hello Kitten book on the other side of the steel galley table. After their standoff in the fish tank, it had become clear that Seraph could do nothing without sharing information with Huang and Baakos.

"Come with me," she told Seraph, tucking the book into her pocket.

She led him to the fabber floor where printers were at work.

Three storage units lined one wall where he assumed feedstock was stored.

Huang scanned her finger and a door unlocked. Inside, the small unit was lined completely with metal foil, just like Seraph's fish tank. It was a larger Faraday cage. A small table with two chairs sat beneath a light and a mobile of gilded baubles.

"Sit," Huang said.

Seraph sat.

She took the other seat and unfolded a sheet of paper onto the table. She had copied Maypole's alphabet while she was in the fish tank. "We open the book and this key here and only here," she said. "Now let's get busy."

Seraph closed the file on Rain's genome and took the paper and pencil Huang offered him.

"What are you working on there?" she asked him, nodding toward his palmcomm.

"Just some correspondence with my daughter's school." He was a terrible liar.

Huang sucked in her lower lip and nodded. Her trust in him had been shaken when she'd discovered his secret Faraday cage, and he continued to hide Maypole's suspicions about the genome of some of the banked embryos. But Baakos and Huang had minds about as open as Vera's. One was controlled by Rishi; the other was controlled by an imaginary god. Once he knew more, he could present some real information. But he would have to wait for Maypole to look over Rain's profile and read through the journal. Next, he would send her images of every page.

Seraph reached across the table for the book. But Huang's hand came down hard on the cover.

"The book is mine, Huang. What does your First Flame say about stealing?"

She stuck her chin in the air. "I stole nothing. You traded it away, friend."

"You think taking advantage of a drunk constitutes a fair trade? You and Baakos *took it*."

She inhaled deeply. "We're transcribing this together."

"Agreed. *Friend*."

She slid the book across the table.

IT WAS ALMOST as hard to find paper as it was to work through the transcription. Huang had to fab it out of wood pulp.

Within days, the relativistic lag would decrease from hours to minutes as the ship plowed through the magnetic current of the heliopause and entered the star system. Maypole would get all the information she had requested if Seraph had to hold Huang hostage to send it.

The small storeroom got stifling hot. Huang had covered the air vents. Letter by letter, the pages began to make sense.

John Lauretta had approached Maypole's replacement about the embryos, a doctor named Unger. He saw no reason to suspend the implantation plan. Lauretta even contacted Ru Shi Zhu, the founder of Rishi, hoping she could halt the use of the embryos. It was then he learned that the board of directors made all the decisions and had created the embryos without her knowledge. They were under the control of Noah Dutro, chairman of the board and one of Rishi's principal developers. Dutro never replied to Lauretta.

"Who is this Dutro guy?" Huang asked, swabbing her sweaty face.

"No idea. This is something we need to run by Maypole."

"Not without Alexandre's approval," Huang countered.

Seraph said, "I don't need Alexandre's approval."

He continued his own transcriptions, no division of labor. Huang might withhold something important.

"Have you reached page five?" Huang asked.

He hadn't. He flipped ahead and worked out the first sentences. Lauretta wrote:

Zhu sent me a warning. The minds on Varanasi will be affected by decoherence. Unless they have found a way to stop it, the passage of time will punch holes in their data, changing them in unknown ways.

His eyes met Huang's. She said, "Just as Alexandre predicted."

"We don't know if they've found a way to mitigate it—"

"We must prepare for the worst."

He couldn't argue with that. On page six, Seraph worked out an entry dated ten years post-launch:

In exchange for the best of the plum crop, Unger let me know when the first Rishi embryo was put into the population. The child, Orion Ivanov, was born with a strange eye mutation. The iris exhibits a red ring around the pupil, giving it a starburst effect.

Huang scowled. "Starburst eyes. But why?"

"I should have realized it sooner. The same mutation could not have arisen naturally in both T-1 and T-2. It's a visual marker. But for what?"

Seraph could only think of Rain and TJ who both carried this mutation. Carl, his apprentice, Baakos . . . He wanted to warn TJ. But warn her of what?

He read on, "'We keep waiting for these starburst people to have superpowers. But so far, nothing. Just interesting eyes.'"

There were three more entries in the book. A statistical report on the number of people with the mutation over time, and a final, parting note to Camber Maypole. It was personal. As much as Seraph tried not to read it, he couldn't look away. Maypole had to have this, and he doubted Huang could argue. But on the very last page, there was a large drawing of what looked like an angel with a sword in each hand. It was blindfolded, its double pair of wings stretched as if to fly.

"A seraphim," Huang said, running her finger over the image. Her eyes met Seraph's. "Do you still think you have no part to play, Seraphim Stone?"

That night, he played his part. Alone in his room, he

photographed all the pages of Lauretta's journal and attached them to a message to Maypole. He attached Rain's genetic profile, too, hoping she could tell them what awaited them. He was no geneticist, but it looked like Rishi had not only engineered the ship, but the colonists themselves.

SERAPH PUT in more than the required hours in Retro's farms. But sleep was almost impossible. He awoke in sweats, dreaming of Rain. He had drawn up a list of crazy possibilities for those with the eye mutation. Radiation resistance? Disease resistance? Something had to be linked to it. The eye color was just a phenotypic marker.

He contacted Dr. Zahn and asked for Rain to have a full genome sequence performed. Zahn told him there had to be a medical reason.

Baakos had the mutation. Maybe he could get a full sequence performed. Huang understood there was more to that little book than they could parse. They needed Maypole. So she promised not to tell Baakos that Seraph had sent everything to Maypole.

He lay in bed, staring at the ceiling and thinking of hootch. One of those prismatic eyes was plastered there, staring down at him. A big holographic eye reflecting your sad face is a great sleep inducer.

He got up. Checking the time again, it had been eight hours since he'd sent the files to Maypole. The irrigation systems in the farm needed rewiring.

He found himself in Farm G watching the turtle beans grow, the pods rippling with the swell of the black beans inside. He tried to recall whether his need for drink had started before TJ had been promoted to captain or after. He remembered holding Rain, moments after she was born. He had never felt so connected to TJ, had never felt so full of life and hope. He had started hitting the hootch after she was promoted. After they had started growing apart. When someone else started making her smile, when she stopped coming home every night.

He watched the fish in the tank below the beans. They schooled so close, silver flashes in the low light. He dragged a finger along the glass, but they didn't follow it, not like the fish in T-1. Maybe they were just different creatures, evolving here in different ways.

He had forgotten to bring sensors to check the water chemistry. It was on his checklist for tomorrow. There should be some in the inventory. As he moved through the storage lockers, he found feed-stock for the fabbers along with sheets of aluminum, high-density plastics, bags of cement, carbon fiber, and glass. But no chemical testers.

Beyond the storeroom, a locked door beckoned.

Vera's face appeared on the access pad. "Restricted entry. Officers only."

"I *am* an officer."

"Lt. Stone, you defected from your position. Your status as officer has been revoked."

"Surprise, surprise."

No reasons came to mind for the Retro ag specialist to lock water testers away under high security. Even the fertilizer wasn't the old-fashioned compounds once used to blow up buildings, but just the digested guts of fish, chickens, and humans. His curiosity was piqued. But he'd have to get past Vera to see what was inside.

He was surprised TJ answered his call.

"This better be important, Ser," she said. She was beautifully groggy with sleep.

"I need you to open a door for me. I'm looking for fertilizer."

Not even a small interrogation followed.

The light blinked green, and the locks racked back. At least TJ had *some* authority over that bitch Vera.

An interior light came on in response to his entry. It became clear that Huang had experience making Faraday cages.

The back of the door was lined with reflective sheeting as were the ceiling, floor, and walls. The whole storage room was lined. The shelves were neatly stacked, but not with fertilizer. Instead devices identical to the one Erica Huang had used to subdue the security mechs in the hub were lined up in neat rows on full shelves. Printed from hard plastic and aluminum, he recognized them as what she'd called pulse interrupters.

There were hundreds of them, enough to arm half the population of Retro.

He took a gun from the shelf, felt the weight in his hand. A hollow compartment in the grip awaited a battery pack, which he found on the shelf above. He inserted one into the gun. A selector screen lit up. Among the options for ordinance was Laser. It was listed with an asterisk which Seraph decided might mean that it was lethal.

He looked up to find baubles hanging from string. Gilded acorns, small mirrors set inside 3-D cubes. Focus totems, Baakos had called them, used to aid in communion with the First Flame. Seraph had to assume his god was the brains behind this arsenal. If so, he was beginning to feel some respect for the Harbinger's imaginary friend.

In the next room, he found devices that looked more like cannons. Tripods folded up against carbon bodies. If one was planning a war against robots, this was the kind of weapon that might give you a chance.

One thing was abundantly clear. Retro was prepared for war. For the first time, Seraph believed it might be a good idea.

14

INTO THE GREAT GREEN

2345-02-16, Earth Standard, Nirvana Virtual, Black Stack, Varanasi

---

MAYPOLE HEADED for Nirvana City while Lemkos left Virtual for Mission Control. Let him try to explain his nefarious dealings to the Flight Director; Maypole had other things on her mind. Before the trip to Shivi Desh, she'd done some homework on the woman who had assisted Dutro at the skin meeting. Tanbo Khando was her name, but there was no record of a biological past for her. No Earth records. She was a perfect likeness of Ru Shi Zhu and had tried to eject Maypole from the meeting. So not a subservient assistant but someone with some authority. What this might have to do with downloading into hellions . . . She was grasping at straws.

She activated her elven avatar, Skya Pryn. Barely able to cast the most basic spells, it would be impossible to protect herself. But she'd also rarely been seen in this avatar, so data would be scarce. Still, she would have to head straight to the bay, get what she needed, and log out of Virtual.

The Memory Arcade was hidden in a back alley that branched off the boardwalk, nestled in with porn theaters and brothels. A few people came and went through the gilded doorway, scattering seagulls busy picking through trash. The Arcade was sheltered under brightly colored tenting, giving it the look of a bazaar. It served as a clearinghouse for juicy memories, and clips from steamy life events danced above the entrance. People made good money, pay-per-view style, of their best and most twisted life experiences.

Maypole was hoping there might be more stored here, like Earth memories of Noah Dutro and his assistant, Tanbo Khando.

Maypole stepped through a curtain of beads.

"Hey now, babe." Puzzled, Dayo looked up from the archaic tablet in their hands and checked the ID Maypole flashed at them. "Do I know you, Skya Pryn?"

Dayo wore their androgynous elf avatar, eyes glowing with peachy fairy fire. When they smiled, they showed a set of sharpened diamond teeth. Once Dayo had been Cherise Dayamano, lead on the biometrics team for the Varanasi Mission, before they'd contracted the carrion virus. Maypole had forgotten what Dayo's physical body looked like, but their mindware had been among a cache of NASA personnel deemed necessary for success on Varanasi. They'd come through the wormhole with Lemkos and Maypole. The Memory Arcade was their brainchild, and they'd made almost as much as Lemkos in their second career.

"I want a Thanksgiving dinner," Maypole said. "Not one of those Mrs. Cubbison's kind, but one with some real cooks."

Understanding bloomed on Dayo's elvish face as they deciphered the clue. "Maypole? Is that you?"

Maypole put a finger to her lips. Until now, the only reason she visited the arcade was to mine memories of fine meals, smells, tastes, for her sensorium apps.

"Oh, damn. What's up?"

"Research," Maypole said.

"Thanksgiving?"

"No," Maypole said, "a, uh, different kind of cooking."

"Uuuuh-huh." Dayo dragged the word out, a tone of disbelief in their voice.

Another customer wearing a pirate avatar emerged from the endless corridor. He approached Dayo, stiffening as if for a fight. "Look, I've still got my last few days to sell. They gotta be worth s-s-s-s-s-something." His avatar's head whipped back and forth like someone possessed. "I gotta gotta sell them, Dayo."

"Doug, buddy." Dayo sniffed at him, their diamond teeth glinting. "You look like you could use a patch, man. You got money for a patch?"

He shook his head. "That's why I need to sell something."

"We all got the same last days," Dayo said. "Puking and bleeding from our eyes and ears. We'd all like to fucking forget it, not pay to remember. Spend those last bits on an entropic patch, man." Dayo gave his shoulder, complete with naval epaulettes, a firm grasp and pointed him out.

The pirate measured Maypole's sexy elf and licked his lips.

"Sounds like you don't got the credits," Maypole said to him with a smile.

Dejected, Doug headed for the door.

When he had gone, Dayo said to Maypole, "Fucking rotter. Sold every memory he has worth selling and still can't get into Fifth Fantasy. Even if he could, he'd be a decohered mess without any patches."

"Maybe it's time to go topside." Maypole pointed up, indicating the surface of the planet.

A dedicated gopher, Dayo just laughed. "No effing way, girl. Not Doug, and not me. I gave that shit up with NASA. Virtual is the only real I need."

Dayo led Maypole to a booth with faded Oriental rugs hung on all sides. This was just a cheap version of an air gap. Maypole doubted it was as secure as Lemkos's hidden room, but it would have to do.

"Oh yeah," Dayo said as an afterthought. "I found a cooking memory from Italy you're gonna love. I'll put it in your queue." She manipulated the tablet she held, then handed it to Maypole. "You know the drill."

"Yeah, thanks," Maypole said. She took the tablet and pulled the curtains closed.

From the screen, a diaphanous figure that looked a lot like Dayo hovered in the air at the center of the booth.

Maypole queried the system, "Search Noah Dutro and-not-or Tanbo Khando."

No matches.

She broadened the search parameters.

No matches.

She searched just Noah Dutro. Thousands of hits came up.

She narrowed these to Earth memories only. The date on one interested her. It was labeled *Rishi Launch Party* and was dated the day of the launch of the *Vera Rubin*, the day after Maypole had been sacked and sent back to Earth.

She opened this one. The holo bubble grew around her. She was in a mansion, maybe Dutro's house, all glass, steel, and concrete. The point of view was from a servant, maybe even a mech someone had hacked for the memories. But there, striding confidently toward a podium, was the founder of Rishi Corp.

This was the woman who had found Camber Maypole holed up in Lemkos's house in Charlotte one day before this party. This was the woman, the brilliant scientist who had asked question after question about the Rishi embryos. It was Ru Shi Zhu. Or was it?

"Friends," the woman began, "today marks an unprecedented chapter in the history of mankind. Our voyage to another world to build a new and better civilization is underway, and all systems are *go*!"

Cheering.

But the view turned abruptly toward a scuffle at the door. Maypole clearly saw security personnel grab a woman and drag her toward the exit. Another Ru Shi Zhu. Older than the one on the stage. Ground down by worry. The one who had debriefed Maypole the day before.

"This, this amalgam is not me!" Zhu cried.

Amalgam? The Zhu at the podium?

"Shit."

Maypole paused and replayed the segment three more times until she was certain there were two Zhu's there, and only one was real.

Khando was no assistant. It was an amalgam. Like Judah Krane. A super mind wearing the image of Ru Shi Zhu, maybe even housing part of her mind.

As the real Zhu railed against Noah Dutro, accusing him of stealing her company, the memory broke as if it had been edited. But Maypole had found what she'd come for.

MAYPOLE SENT Noah Dutro an invitation to meet at her house on the Gandikota coast. Let him think what he liked about her reason for it. But she hoped Tanbo would come with him. Maypole didn't have the time to finesse this plan which was, admittedly, half-baked, but what was that old saying about the best defense?

With the little time she had, she reprogrammed her home security system to transmit events directly to the Flight Director, Kaja Singh, and Martine Sommer. She instructed Kiki, her mech servant, not to speak unless spoken to, and then Maypole waited.

With her print demolished by hellions, she was forced to wear a basic rental unit. The blank bot lacked all sophisticated gadgetry and had an annoying gear noise that accompanied the movement of her left leg. With its basic sensorium the sea breeze smelled like formaldehyde and Puppy's coat of downy photosynthetic fuzz felt like a hairbrush. The visual sensors lacked anything beyond visible light. She had no magnification, and no defenses. It would have to do.

She sat at her patio table trying to convince Puppy it was her inside this bot. With her back to the cliff that fell away to the sea, she had a clear view of the house and the hills beyond. Dutro had not replied, but she would give him time.

Puppy finally decided she was okay and crouched beside her but watched with suspicion.

An hour had passed when Noah Dutro came in a private Rishi flyer. Thankfully, his perpetual shadow was with him.

Tanbo looked like a mythical goddess with the wind in her hair and her radiant cheongsam projecting a frothing river of emerald-green silk behind her. Tiny holographic birds circled her head like something out of a fairy tale. She was the picture of Ru Shi Zhu with all the pressure and stresses of life erased. Remade, reborn in the prime of life.

"Ah, Dr. Dutro and Ms. Khando, is it?" Maypole said, offering chairs. Sitting was an act of body language to those without bodies. A remnant of culture more than biology.

"Dr. Maypole, we meet again." Dutro took the chair, shooting the cuffs of his leather jacket. The sea breeze played realistically at his blonde hair. "Somehow I doubt this meeting has anything to do with the skin proposal."

Tanbo stood behind him, her manicured hands on his shoulders like a sex-bot. The real Zhu would have strangled Dutro from such a position.

Maypole opened the secure commlink to Kaja Singh and Martine Sommer and began sending.

When Dutro spoke, the snakes on his neck rippled with his throat. Pricey hologram, that.

He said, "You've brought me here why exactly?"

"You've come why exactly?" Maypole replied. "Did you think I'd try to blackmail you with a threat to tell the world about your hellions in Shivi Desh?"

"It had crossed my mind," he said. He forced a chuckle as Kiki arrived with a tray of pretty drinks coded with pleasure stims.

Maypole took the martini glass and raised it in a toast. She sipped and felt the euphoria code calm her nerves.

"I don't care what you're doing out there, doctor. What I want to know is"—she leaned on the table, looking directly at Tanbo—"do you remember coming to see me after I was bumped from the launch crew?"

Tanbo's face folded in confusion.

"Tanbo would have no reason for such a visit," Dutro said.

"Ah, but Ru Shi Zhu did have a reason. I thought Ms. Khando would have some of those memories too."

"What memories?" Tanbo asked, finally taking a seat beside Dutro.

The bait was taken. Maypole said, "I met your friend Judah Krane. It would seem that he was shaped in a most unethical way. In a way, not unlike Ms. Khando."

"He's an AI," Dutro said. "There's nothing unethical about him."

"Except he tried to lock my mindware. Something I doubt the Flight Director would be happy about."

"Oh, the *Flight Director*." Dutro laughed. "Singh has already been notified that you and Dr. Lemkos were apprehended trespassing at a Rishi mine."

"Trespassing?" Maypole snorted. "Beaten and kidnapped and brought before a being assembled from many prominent minds in the Black Stack database. Judah Krane is an amalgam. Isn't that what you call them? Built from a carefully curated skill set from what? Ten? Twenty? A hundred minds all stored in the Black Stack? If that isn't an ethics violation—"

"Then bring a charge against me in court," Dutro said, getting to his feet. "You've wasted enough of my time, Dr. Maypole."

She shot a glance at Tanbo, measured her response. There were a hundred questions seething behind that perfect face. If Maypole was wrong about her . . .

It was time to lay down her cards.

"How much of Tanbo is Ru Shi's mind?" Maypole said.

Tanbo's palms were pressed to the table, her eyes boring into Dutro.

"None, plenty of people wear the faces of those they admired on Earth. The Flight Director is one of them, no?"

Maypole pressed on. "Ru Shi Zhu refused neural net salvage. How did you steal it from her? On her deathbed? Just one more genius to add to the mix that makes up Tanbo Khando."

"Stop this charade—"

"Zhu chose death rather than follow you to Varanasi, Dr. Dutro. After you stole her company, her creations, you stole her mind. Or the part of it you wanted. Her genius. Her vision."

"What a pathetic attempt at coercion," Dutro chuffed.

Maypole leaned across the table toward Tanbo. "Do *you* remember? Ru Shi Zhu came to me. She wanted to know about the embryos that got me scrubbed, the embryos made in your own labs—"

"That is quite enough!" Dutro was on his feet, his hand on Tanbo's arm.

Maypole smiled. A direct hit. She was right, and it appeared that Tanbo was confused. Could she not know what she was? Was that possible?

Tanbo shook off Dutro's grip. "What is she saying?"

"She's firing blind, love. She's making this up."

"Dutro manipulated Zhu's mindware," Maypole went on. "He created a holo-print receptacle and gave her another name. He filled in Zhu's memories the way he wanted Ru Shi to be—a fantasy lover and business partner. He rebuilt her, just like he built Judah Krane."

Maypole watched Tanbo's holo-print carefully. From her stricken face, it was clear she didn't know. This was exactly as Maypole had hoped.

Puppy stood and moved toward Khando as if sensing something, but Maypole called him back. He rumbled a guttural hoot of displeasure.

Dutro laughed, his fingers laced so the silver rings touched. "Tanbo has been in my employ since long before Ru Shi passed. Nice try. What is this really all about Dr. Maypole?"

"I want to know why those embryos were so important," Maypole said evenly. "I want to know why they cost me my career and my life."

Tanbo was on her feet and backing away toward the house, a stricken look on her face.

Dutro got up and took a few steps toward her. "You can't really believe you are an amalgam, love. You were the principal researcher on that project. You built the first one. This is ludicrous."

Maypole was standing now too. She said, "Tanbo, when you're ready to talk to me about those embryos, I'm ready to listen. Because this guy"—she motioned to Dutro—"thinks he owns you, just like he owns Judah Krane."

"Enough!" Dutro spat.

Tanbo had backed all the way to the patio doors. Her lovely face was twisted in pain.

Maypole took a few steps toward Dutro. "And you are using Ru Shi's genius even now to download mindware into hellions."

Tanbo stood in the open doorway to the house. The look on the woman's face was an attempt by her emote programs to cope with the truth.

Dutro was frozen between Maypole and Tanbo.

"No," Tanbo cried. "No!"

She held her hands to her ears like a terrorized child. Her primal scream drove her fluttering birds away.

Agitated, Puppy yapped and circled between them all.

How could an amalgam not know what they were? Maypole felt a stab of guilt for pulling the blindfold from Tanbo's eyes, and yet she had been right. She could not feel sorry for this creature who was as much or maybe more responsible for the experimentation on the hellions in Shivi Desh. She hoped the Flight Director and Martine were seeing this clearly.

Dutro's print had frozen momentarily, like a glitch. He began gesturing in the air, as if he worked a projected screen.

Here came the corruption code. Time to bail out of the rent-a-print.

Maypole turned to see a battle drone, black, sleek, and armed with cannons, rise from behind the house. Without hesitation, it fired, first one then another sonic pulse. It struck the house. A cloud of flying glass and metal moved outward with concussive force. It flung Maypole backward until her print struck a boulder at the edge of the cliff and collapsed to the ground.

She got back to her feet, shielding her visual sensors from the heat of the burning house. Shrapnel had struck Tanbo and Dutro. Their prints had landed on the patio in a rain of convulsing servos and shredded wiring.

He wasn't trying to wipe Maypole, but himself and Tanbo.

Kiki stepped from the house, engulfed in flames. Shards of glass were embedded in Maypole's silicone skin, and Puppy . . .

The drone, still hovering over the scene, took a bead on Maypole. She was already running for the cliff when she heard the unmistakable sound of projectile fire. She glanced over her shoulder to see two battle mechs round the corner of the smoldering house. They were firing at the drone. They had to be Martine's mechs.

Hit, the drone spun wildly toward Maypole.

With a last glance at the still body of Puppy, Maypole moved at full speed toward the cliff edge ten meters away.

Lacking three-sixty visual, she only heard the drone impact the ground behind her, heard the smash of the table and chairs. Then the smell of burning flesh hit her receptors.

The cliff was less the five meters away. The fallen drone burst into flames right on top of the remains of Dutro and Khando.

Maypole had taken a hit in the thigh that fried the silicone and took out the wiring underneath. She staggered, fell, and rolled toward the cliff edge. Her momentum took her over, rocks, and sod coming too. The drop was punctuated by jagged outcroppings white with bird droppings.

It was a long fall, two-point-three seconds according to her spatial sensors. Maybe long enough to initiate login to Virtual. Her last thought was to wonder if Dutro would be there waiting for her. In milliseconds, her mind had exited the one-way gate of circuitry from her blank bot into the software of her avatar.

She never saw her blank bot hit the rocks and her parts sink into the Great Green.

MAYPOLE OPENED HER EYES. The feel of falling was still cycling through her sensorium. She inhaled a false breath.

She had left her home blasted to pieces and yet here she was, in a tiny, yellow kitchen with an old gas stove and a shelf above the burners crammed with greasy tins of spices—bay, thyme, cardamom. Through the illusion, she could vaguely make out the rugs that surrounded the booth. She was in the Memory Arcade. This is where she'd logged from.

That's right, Dayo had queued a memory for her. It was before her and around her. An old woman, a grandmother, *her* grandmother, the one she always knew as Nana—she was rolling arancini between her arthritic palms and whistling a breathy tune, the one Maypole always remembered. The little kitchen smelled of rosemary and garlic cooking in olive oil. The modest room opened onto a creaking wooden staircase. Maypole had been down those stairs a hundred times and climbed the ancient fig tree in the back. She knew there was a shed lined with shelves of canned fruit and vegetables and plum brandy. Out the kitchen window, the sky was heavy with clouds. The laundry danced on the line and seagulls trilled from the roof next door.

"Thought you'd dig this one." It was Dayo's voice.

Maypole turned her attention outside the holographic bubble.

Dayo was standing at the parting of the rugs, peeking into the booth with those blazing eyes and diamond teeth.

Dayo said with pride, "This has been in the system for a while, how'd you miss this one? Something called arancini?"

Maypole had never sold a single memory to Dayo, never shared this story with anyone, even in passing. Which meant this memory was never hers in the first place. It was someone else's, and her mind-ware had been patched with it.

15

SAMSARA

2345-02-16, Earth Standard, Mission Control, Varanasi

LEMKOS ENTERED the foyer of Mission Control and was stopped by an army of security mechs. He wasn't sure if this confrontation had been triggered by his unusual attire (he was wearing a gladiator mech he used for arena fighting in the Real) or maybe it was his altercation in Shivi Desh. Maybe both.

His shoulders were so broad he barely fit through the corridor, a hulking mech built for hand-to-hand combat and a good show. But with his holo-print smashed to bits somewhere in Shivi Desh, this was the best he could do on short notice. The reason for the hostility appeared to be his attire, equipped as it was with some badass weaponry. The sec-mechs needed proof of disarming before allowing him to pass. He offered up his ID, the high-security password, and still they wanted him completely disarmed.

He grudgingly conceded. If he needed a weapon, it would take several minutes to initiate. But he wasn't planning on a fight at Mission Control. He'd check in, then catch up to Camber, whose tracker showed her at her house out on the coast. He had asked Martine to send a few Samsara security mechs to tail her just in case someone was waiting for her.

Lemkos found Kaja Singh in the logistics lab. The flight director wore her Gene Kranz holo, complete with sweaty face, which was never a good sign. She paced behind the row of 3-D projections where Lemkos's team worked, tapping and dragging data that scrolled past.

"Out of contact is unacceptable, Dr. Lemkos," Singh said. She scowled at his silicone-skinned attire. "Playing games again?"

"I'm sorry, sir," Lemkos said. "My print's out of commission."

His team of AIs and human minds were too busy working through the information that had been sent from the ship to ask him why.

"Status?" Lemkos asked Chloe, his primary assistant.

"The triangulation to our pulsars does not match the numbers aboard the ship." The intern pointed out the difference of 2.6 arc seconds to GX-301-2.

"You sent a correction," Lemkos said.

"Yes."

"Then what's the problem?"

"It appears someone has attempted to block our corrections, sir." Chloe turned to face him.

"Override? From where? Who?"

Maybe someone on the ship had already decoded the book and knew something Maypole and Lemkos did not. Maybe they had advanced their tech enough that they could override the navigation system and change course. "Has Captain Dela Cruz been notified?"

"Yes, sir."

Lemkos stared at the telemetry. "Well, it doesn't look like they succeeded."

"No, sir," Choe answered. "Vera sent an alert to the captain to inform her that attempts were being made to override ground instructions. The overrides were successfully blocked."

Kaja Singh looked small beside Lemkos's hulking battle-bot. Her arms were crossed over her sequined vest. "This has all the earmarks of a mutiny, don't you think, Dr. Lemkos? As if the colonists *feared* something here."

The blue Gene Kranz eyes turned up to meet Lemkos's. She was saying something with those eyes. An accusation. An incrimination. Had his little trip to Shivi Desh caused all of this? Or had Seraph Stone decoded the Hello Kitten journal and the information left by the launch crew warned them off landing here. But why?

"What could they possibly fear on Varanasi, sir," Lemkos asked with all the seriousness he could muster.

"Why were you in Shivi Desh?" Singh asked, clasping her hands behind her back.

"Checking up on some rumors, sir."

"What kind of rumors?"

"Sir, Rishi is downloading human mindware into hellions." He decided not to mention the amalgam, Judah Krane. He wanted her to earn that information.

Everyone in the room turned to look at Lemkos.

Singh grabbed at the stiff, silicone trunk that was his arm. "Lemkos, let's talk in my office."

His team shot nervous stares his way.

He followed the flight director down the hall and into her office. As the door closed, the Kranz image faded from Singh's print and was replaced by her own. The dark, buttery skin of a middle-aged Punjabi woman wore a painted smile to cover secrets Lemkos could only guess at.

She said nothing, just cast a holo image of Maypole's house on the Gandikota coast. The capture showed a drone hovering above it. In the next moment, the house was blown to pieces. A cloud of shattered glass and aluminum engulfed the viewer. Maypole?

"What happened?" he asked.

"Dr. Maypole sent an open comm to me during a meeting she initiated with Noah Dutro."

Singh played the message from the beginning. Maypole accused Tanbo Khando of being an amalgam of Ru Shi Zhu's stolen mindware. And it looked like she was right.

"Tell me where Maypole has gone," Singh demanded, "and I'll see you are treated fairly."

"Fairly? For doing what? For getting beaten and kidnapped by Rishi?"

"Without Rishi, NASA would have no chance to establish a colony on this planet." Singh's eyes blazed in warning. "We are in a partnership, Lemkos. Binding covenants. You will not interfere with the agreements made centuries ago."

She didn't need to say more. Her dark liquid eyes said the rest. She knew exactly what was going on in Shivi Desh, and she knew why the colonists aboard the ship were trying to change course.

Singh said in an even tone, "You will find Maypole and deliver her to me. If you fail in this, your time here on Varanasi will come to an end."

ONCE IN VIRTUAL, Lemkos made his way to the Colosseum where he had agreed to meet Camber. Singh's security certainly wouldn't be far away. If he sent Camber a message, it would be intercepted. There were enough people here that it might be possible to meet long enough to warn her away, that is, if she had escaped a full wipe from Dutro.

He pinged the tracking code he had placed in Maypole's files back in the air gap. No location found.

The Hall of Justice was modeled after the temple of Jupiter on the Capitoline Hill in Rome. Beside it stood a perfect recreation of the Flavian Amphitheater, the Colosseum. This was Rishi's idea of making the law entertaining. Trial by combat revealed the will of the gods, or in the case of Varanasi, the will of the justice algorithms.

The piazza outside was crowded with spectators, pushing their way in to get the best seats. There must be a high-profile trial on the docket today.

Half the crowd was looking at him and pointing. He had forgotten to dig up another avatar and was wearing his gladiator.

"Shit." He pushed his way through the mob.

"Will you fight Bently today?" someone asked.

He ignored them and headed toward the combatants entrance. Once inside, he was stopped by the arena NPCs. "What's your case number?" it asked.

"I haven't picked it up yet."

"Unassigned gladiators are not allowed in the combatants quarters."

"Okay, okay." He called up the day's docket and entered the queue for a case assignment. At least Camber might see his name on the court docket.

He made his way deeper into the tunnels. Lions paced and circled, and a bear was curled in the corner of his cage, his head tucked under his paws. He doubted even NASA security could find a way in here. But then, neither could Camber. He'd be safe until the contest. In the meantime, he contacted Martine via her server.

"Do you know where she is?" he asked Martine.

"She bailed, went off the cliff," Martine said. "She's in Virtual. But I don't know where."

"Shit."

Lemkos wasn't going anywhere until he finished this fight. He was assigned to represent a writer accused of inciting civil unrest. He liked revolutionaries. This must be what the crowd had come for.

Lemkos had been fighting in the arena for so long that prepping for it was an unconscious series of armor checks now. He found his way down the narrow staircase to the maze of cages and small rooms. His locker was among them.

Prowess in the arena had nothing to do with the outcome, but Lemkos liked to make-believe. The verdict was decided by an algorithm. The Black Stack weighed all the evidence and delivered a decision by way of the two combatants. But most of the spectators had forgotten that centuries ago.

He chose a retarius gear set: a net, trident, and short sword in case they got that close. The minimalists of the gladiatorial world, the retarius was underrated. Quick, clever, and versatile, he had put down two metal-encumbered secutors swiftly the last time he'd fought. In doing so, he'd won a favorable judgment for a refugee who had suffered irreparable data loss at the hands of a sham patching service.

Today, his opponent would be Bull Balls Bently. He'd beaten Lemkos at their last meeting. In that contest, Lemkos had repped a madam who had designed a puppet porn star after the likeness of Melody Helios, once superstar of the music world on Earth. That puppet had earned a boatload of money. It was a big loss for Lemkos.

The Colosseum was aflutter with scarlet pennants and loud with the crowd. The naked marble statues of the gods watched from archways high above, framed by a perfect blue sky.

The oval arena smelled of roasted sand, and the crowd erupted into a deafening roar as Lemkos strode upon it, the heat seeping through his sandals. He raised his arms and inhaled their praise, hoping Camber was in the crowd.

Bently had armed himself with a sword and a device known as a scissor, a cuff of bronze with a curved blade on the end.

Unencumbered by heavy armor, Lemkos evaded Bently's attacks easily.

Bently was a brown-skinned bull of a man, his eyes glowing red from behind the faceplate of his helmet.

"Slow down, Lemkos," he said. "Let's dance a bit."

"What do you think I'm doing, man?"

Lemkos aimed for that scissor, which was a poor choice against a retarius. He caught the curved blade in his net and gave it a twist. As

Bently slashed with the sword in his off-hand, Lemkos yanked Bently off balance and quickly had the trident pressed to the man's throat. Far too fast. If it was over too quick, the crowd couldn't bet enough for a good pot, and it would look suspicious. But Lemkos was in a hurry.

He let Bently up, raising the trident to his own forehead in salute.

As Bently struggled to his feet under all that metal, Lemkos urged the crowd on, waving his arms as if beckoning them to shower him with their money, which they did. A quick check on the pot balance showed they were heavily betting on Lemkos.

Bently was ready the next time, but after a few thrusts and parries with the trident, Lemkos had him down again. He pressed the trident against the man's throat and deferred to the crowd. They issued the predictable thumbs down.

"Sorry, man," Lemkos said. "Payback's a bitch."

It would take Bently half of his pay to buy his way to resurrection.

NPCs cleared the body from the arena as Lemkos made his way to a tunnel leading back to the cages and armories. He scanned the faces in the crowd for Camber.

He waited for as long as he dared.

When she didn't appear, he logged out and back into the cumbersome gladiator mech he'd left in the Logistics Lab at Mission Control. If Camber was right about Khando being an amalgam of Ru Shi Zhu, then there might be some usable pieces of that mindware strewn about the patio. If Lemkos could recover it, he might have some bargaining power.

He took a flyer out to Camber's house on the cliff.

The afternoon sun hung over the distant highlands of Sindhu Kush; the ever-present cloud bank was silvered with late afternoon. The broad expanse of the Ganges valley lay in a puddle after what seemed to have been a heavy rain. Clouds of plumage rode updrafts in search of hosts for another day, reminding Lemkos of flocks of starlings back on Earth. No wonder Camber preferred the Real. It was untainted by the hand of humankind—at least, so far.

Camber believed John had planned her neural net salvage and sent her to Varanasi for one reason: to decrypt the journal. But Lemkos already had the winning lottery ticket in hand before John contacted him. Lemkos had already planned that he and Camber would live happily ever after while John sailed away into old age and death. He had told John so. He had admitted to John that he loved her, and that there was a chance they could build something together on Varanasi. Lemkos felt like he was stabbing John in the back. But seeing the whole story now, from so far away, he knew the truth. As much as Lemkos wanted to believe that John simply wanted her here to decrypt the damn book, he knew better. Lemkos had watched those two together.

It had been a long time since Lemkos had bothered to remember death—since he had lain in a hospital in Charlotte and bled out of every orifice in his body. Before that, it was Camber. He had the ticket and had arranged for the neural salvage to be done as an emergency procedure while she lay unconscious in an overcrowded triage center.

But what he remembered most about it was the man who'd sold him that lottery ticket.

After cashing in his house, Lemkos had traveled to India to purchase the ticket from a monk who had no intention of leaving Earth, pandemic or no. Lemkos had found him tending the dying that were housed in tent-cities outside of Benares. Row upon endless row of cots. The stench was like being inside the bowels of a corpse. The pyres burned day and night on the banks of the Ganges, the original one, where the ancient ghats were filled to overflowing with the dead and the few who remained to burn them. This was the Varanasi Lemkos had known. The old city of the dead, redolent with the stench of burning flesh. Why had they named this wild, beautiful planet for such a place?

The monk had looked at Lemkos as if he were measuring an unevolved slug. His saffron robe was stained with blood and pus.

Lemkos held a cloth over his nose as he asked, "How much for your ticket?"

"You want to live with yourself forever?" the monk scoffed. "You want to cheat yourself of enlightenment, of breaking free of rebirth?"

"That's all a bunch of mumbo jumbo, man." Lemkos didn't like the way the guy judged him with his froggy eyes. He said heatedly, "You have a free ticket to live forever, and you're selling it to *me*." He had not come to talk the guy out of the sale. What was he doing? "It's for a friend. Don't I get brownie points in heaven for that?"

"You presume to know that your friend's destiny lies in the stagnant backwater of a distant world?" the monk asked.

Yes, he did presume to know that. In all these centuries, he'd never confessed to Camber what he'd done. He'd forged her consent to neural salvage out of selfishness. He would never have left her behind, John or no. But it was not her choice to come.

Now, as Lemkos flew toward the vast phosphorescent sea, he wanted to think he understood what the monk tried to tell him so many centuries ago. Even with an eternity open before him, his failings would never be righted. The Black Stack might patch him until he didn't remember who he was anymore, and would it really matter? He had never told Camber that part of the truth—that patching was done with memories taken from the collective, that they might not be their own. He never wanted to lose the memories of those last months with Camber.

But what balm could death possibly hold that might redeem him? The balm of forgetfulness? Of starting over as someone else? He'd already tried that in Martine's simulated worlds, born as a babe without memories of being Kolya Lemkos.

But returning here to the Real made everything clear. *We can never be someone else. We will always make the same mistakes.*

The flyer crested the russet-colored uplands called the Cardamom Hills.

Once landed, he armed his arsenal of weapons and made his way around the smoldering remains of Camber's beloved house to what had been the patio.

Glass and metal beams were scattered in a wide arc toward the cliff. Little remained of two holo-prints and three mechs. The charred corpse of a seahound lay shredded by glass, its plumage having long fled.

"Oh, Puppy," Lemkos said.

Half of the hound lay pinned beneath the wreckage of a battle drone.

He searched through the twisted pieces of carbon fiber and metal. With his toe, he kicked over a sheet of paneling. Painted on the side was the ID number for the drone. Just above the number was the symbol for Samsara—flames forming an "S" with a red bird rising from it. There was no way this was one of Martine's drones. The stream Singh had shown to Lemkos made it clear that Dutro had summoned the drone. His drone had vaporized the house along with himself and Tanbo. But he was implicating Martine, covering his ass.

"Fucker."

It took some time to dig through the rubble, but crystal-encased CPUs were resilient. If it hadn't been remotely wiped yet, it might still have useable data. Lemkos must have moved a ton of steel and melted glass before he found what he was looking for. It was hidden in a bubble of charred plastic.

He scraped it clean and was trying to access the data with his reader when he heard a flyer cresting the hills to the west.

A stand of boulders provided a good hiding place. Plovers rode updrafts from the sea below, their squawks so loud he couldn't hear the engine on the flyer any longer. A few minutes later, Tanbo Khando in a brand new holo-print rounded the smoking wreckage of the house.

Lemkos expected Dutro to follow, but Khando was alone. She picked through the debris, just as Lemkos had been doing. Clearly, she had the same idea: find her CPU. She didn't need all the memories stored there; she had those preserved in her backup. Then what was she doing here? Was she trying to keep those memories from scavengers like Lemkos?

Whatever the reason, that CPU had value.

He stepped out from behind the boulder, his hands held wide to assure Khando of his peaceful intentions.

"Are you looking for this?" Lemkos asked, holding out the CPU.

"Stay where you are."

"Excuse my appearance," he said, "but your hellions fucked up my holo-print."

"Kolya Lemkos?" She grinned at him broadly. "Navigation engineer and supplier of executed mindware for our research."

"I believe this is yours." He again held out the crystal to her. "It's why you're here. You were told that your last print was blown to hell by Samsara, that your temporary files were lost, the meeting with Camber Maypole. What she told you. You don't remember what happened here, do you?"

He held up the CPU. "This is what you've come for."

"Yes." She laughed. "What's your game, Dr. Lemkos?"

"No game. Just the truth."

He extended his hand again.

"What's your price, gladiator?" she asked.

"Guarantee that Camber Maypole will be unharmed. Call off Kaja Singh. In exchange, I will give you the CPU. We've helped each other before," Lemkos said. "Without the mindware I supplied to Judah Krane, your experiments would still be theoretical. I'm just calling in what's owed me."

"I can't speak for Noah Dutro. He's the one hunting your . . . friend."

"But you are resourceful. I trust you will keep Maypole safe, because she delivered the truth to you. Here in this CPU," he said with finality. Kaja Singh had made it clear that she would hand Camber over to Dutro to fulfill some agreement between NASA and

Rishi. Lemkos had to trust Khando now. There were no other options.

A wind picked up from the Great Green, bringing the scent of salt and fish, and stirring eddies of white ash from the remains of Camber's home. Spiraling upward were the few remaining plumage that had abandoned her seahound.

Tanbo reached out and took the crystal housing of her CPU. "Maypole will be unharmed. I will see to it."

16

OUT OF BODY

SERAPH WAS AWAKENED FROM A RARE, deep sleep. Against the glare of his bedside light, he saw Baakos and Huang with both fists wrapped around the butt of a gun, the business end pointed at Seraph.

He raised his hands slowly, like they did in the movies.

"You got into the storeroom," Baakos said.

Seraph should have told them he'd found their guns, now they were suspecting him of . . . What?

"I was looking for fertilizer—"

"You were prying into our business." Baakos took a step closer.

"*Your* business? This is everyone's business."

"Is it?" Baakos asked. "Is it Captain TJ Dela Cruz's business? I think not. I think she would confiscate every weapon we have produced, and you know this, Seraphim Stone."

He did know it. TJ would do exactly what Vera commanded, and the ship would not allow weapons in the hands of the people. Only her security bots.

"I believe you now, Baakos. The book." Seraph nodded to the little volume sitting on his bedside table. "It says we may have a fight on our hands when we land. And I agree, TJ should not know. Not yet. Now can I put my hands down?"

Baakos gave Huang a reluctant nod, and she lowered her gun. But her eyes were locked on Seraph.

He asked Huang, "Have you told him?"

The look on her face said she had not. It was time to talk.

The three of them huddled over their galley table, hands warming on cups of coffee. Huang told Baakos everything she and Seraph had transcribed—the warning Ru Shi Zhu gave to Lauretta about decoherence, bit rot, everything but the part about the starburst eyes. Was she afraid of his reaction?

Seraph leaned closer to Baakos and said, "Your eyes." Huang got to her feet and began pacing. "They are a planned mutation. People in T-1 have eyes like yours. It is statistically impossible that a random mutation would appear in two isolated populations. But my wife, my daughter, they have them." He placed his palmcomm on the table with Rain's genetic data open on the screen. "Somewhere in this mess of codes I am betting is one or more of the Rishi embryos."

"Rishi embryos?" Baakos asked.

"Maypole, the doctor on the ground, she was on the flight crew and got canned for questioning some embryos brought aboard the ship. She's asked me to find people who have those embryos in their genome. I think it has something to do with the eye mutation."

"But why change eye color?" Baakos asked.

"It's not about the eyes. The eye color is linked to some other change. To find out what, we have to trust Camber Maypole."

Baakos dragged his hands down his face. "Yes. Yes, you are right. But you are also a threat to us, Seraphim Stone. We must keep you somewhere safe."

"What?" Seraph couldn't believe what he was hearing.

"You will know sooner or later," Huang explained. "We are hacking the navigation system."

"What are you talking about?"

Huang put a hand on Seraph's arm.

Did this mean they were trying to change course? To bypass Varanasi? "No, no, no," Seraph pleaded. "We can't give up Varanasi. Are you crazy?"

"It's the will of the First Flame. My fireseed has shown me a future of violence, and it is proven by your book." He tapped a long brown finger on the brittle cover. "Varanasi will destroy us. We must keep going."

Seraph shouted, "It's the will of *my* fucking fireseed to see the world I've been living for. To see my daughter raise a family there. To plant crops and harvest in soil."

"We're eight days from orbital insertion around Varanasi." Huang's face was impassive. "We'll use Majriti for a gravity-assist and leave the system."

"If she can evade the corrections made by Mission Control," Baakos added.

"I will," Huang said with confidence.

Seraph tried to stand, but Baakos held him in his chair. Seraph said, "And give up everything we've worked for?"

"There's a habitable star system twenty light years from here," Huang said. The pink tips of her fauxhawk looked silver in the low light. "No joboxes with decohered mindware."

"Twenty light years? That's what? A hundred-plus years of travel? Are you kidding?"

"I don't kid," Huang said. "Come, we have new accommodations for you, friend. You'll be safe." She stood and drew the gun from where she had rested it on her lap.

Accommodations? He knew instantly what she meant.

Seraph was on his feet. Before he could change his mind, he had one arm around Baakos's throat as he dragged the big man from his chair. The other hand found the gun he hoped would be in Baakos's pocket. With a fear-palsied hand, Seraph pointed it at Baakos's head and dragged him toward the door.

"We're going to talk to TJ," he said to Huang.

He backed out the front door with the gun stuffed into Baakos's back.

He was halfway down the stairs when he took his eyes off Huang for a moment to check his footing.

She fired.

A jolt coursed through him. He felt his heart stop, felt himself hovering above his body—a thing that wasn't him, but a piece of himself, as if he'd been cut from a great tree that grew . . . Where? He fell down the stairs and came to rest in the empty concourse.

***

THE SOUND of bleating goats woke him. That, and the pain caused by his shirt resting against the skin of his back. Facedown, Seraph ran quaking fingers over the corrugated flooring, but he couldn't feel it. His lips were equally numb.

He rolled over and wished his back was numb. Whatever Huang had shot him with, it had fried the skin on his shoulder. The pain radiated in a web-like system that crept over his shoulder and down his chest.

In the dim light, he stared into a pile of fluffy material. The smell confirmed his guess. He was in a stall in the goat farm.

He managed to get to a sitting position and felt his shoulder with quaking fingers. It was wet, and he smelled burnt flesh. His fingers came away covered in blood with bits of goat bedding stuck to them. Had she shot him with the lethal setting? No, she'd have made sure he was dead if that was her intention.

The walls of his cage were made of aluminum panels covered in chipped green paint. Dark stains marked spots where previous residents had rubbed, most likely, their asses. Goats did that. A gate of steel with mesh at the top was the only exit from the stall. It was undoubtedly locked—not that he could get up and check. His palm-comm was gone, of course. He wondered if Baakos would destroy the Hello Kitten book or use it as proof that they must change course.

He groaned. He had to get to TJ.

"Hey!" he called.

He was answered by a chorus of bleating from pens across the narrow aisle. He guessed it was still night by the low corridor lights. But the rhythmic bleating told him it must be close to morning and feeding time.

He'd been sitting in the corner for at least an hour, listening to a fan blade brush its housing when a young man's face appeared at the mesh of the door.

"I brought breakfast."

"That's really nice, but," Seraph said, "I've been shot, and I think I deserve some medical attention."

"I'll ask."

The goat keeper's name was Ever Walsh, and he was a follower of the Harbinger. He had orders, of course, to keep everyone away from Seraph.

"What if I bleed to death?"

Ever eyed the black stain on Seraph's shirt, then said, "I don't think so." He slid a bowl of cooked cereal through a small flap in the wall, then headed to the trolley where feed buckets waited to be distributed.

Seraph managed to get off the floor and stand. He held himself up with his fingers locked in the mesh. The chorus of hungry goats drowned out anything he might hope to say to Ever. So he waited until the guy was done with his rounds, then he called the kid over to the door.

"I just want to talk, nothing else."

The young man approached cautiously, leaving his buckets on the trolley. He laced his arms over his chest. He was strangely pudgy for someone who had suffered the food shortages of Retro. Maybe some of the goat milk never have made it to distribution.

Seraph summoned a diplomatic voice. "I know the Harbinger thinks he's protecting you and everyone on this ship. But he's going to try to take your future from you. If I stay in this cage, there's a good chance you'll never see Varanasi."

"How?" Ever asked.

That was the opening Seraph needed.

From their conversation, it became clear that Vera had accurately placed Ever in this job based on skill. But he was no less invested in their journey than anyone else on this ship. Seraph would make him understand that.

After explaining in detail that Huang was going to hack the navigation system, Seraph said, "Ever, they want to change course to another star system twenty light years away."

"Is that far?"

"Yes, very, very far. And not only that, there is no way to slow us down when we get there. We need the ground crew on Varanasi. They are slowing us down so we can enter orbit around Varanasi. Even if we made it to this other star system, we would sail right by with no braking."

"Huh," Ever said, his face screwed up as if trying to unravel all that. "But why are they changing course?"

The explanation for that did not come out as Seraph had intended. It made the course change sound like the only smart move that could be made considering there were decohered, unpredictable machines waiting for them. He found no way to soften that fact.

"So, let me see if this is right," Ever said. "If we land, we are going to be attacked by joboxes."

"We don't know that. We don't really know anything about the effects of decoherence. There's a good chance they have fixed their problems."

"Huh," Ever snorted and walked away.

Seraph slid back to the floor of the stinking stall.

"At least tell the captain!" Seraph called after him.

Seraph thought about the prospects of life in Retro for the rest of his days. He'd never hold Rain again, a prisoner on a hundred-year journey to a new star.

He wanted Rain to grow up with her feet on the new world. He wanted her to explore Varanasi and build her legacy there, not on this damn ship. But what Seraph wanted didn't matter. It had to be a collective decision. Not Baakos, not Huang's.

The clanking of steel buckets echoed down the stall corridor.

"Ever?" Seraph called loudly through the mesh door. "Ever, you can tell the captain. Just send her a message. No one has to know it was you."

There was no reply.

Seraph slammed his good fist into the mesh repeatedly until that arm also dangled uselessly at his side.

"Vera, damn it. Do something!" Seraph screamed. No way Huang would leave him in a place without the white noise Vera scrambler. There was only Seraph, Ever, and the goats.

"You'll die in this cage if we don't land, Ever! You'll die an old man still raking goat shit and longing for an endless horizon. Do you want that, Ever?"

A day passed of milking and raking and baa-ing.

With one finger thrust through the mesh, Seraph tried hitting all the combinations of numbers on the lock pad. But he couldn't reach the three, six, or nine. Useless.

That night, Seraph upended his piss bucket and stood on it to reach the tracks that held the door. He discovered that he was still half a meter from the mechanism. But he could see down the corridor from that vantage. In the stall across from him, he could see a nanny goat and her two kids, their golden eyes wide as they watched his acrobatics.

It didn't take long to conclude he stood no better chance of getting out than the goats did.

Cradling his numb arm, he stepped down from the bucket, pressed his back to the cool metal of the wall, and slid back to the floor.

He would live out his life in this wheel. Rain would grow up, grow old, maybe raise a child of her own, but safe from the unknown dangers on Varanasi. She would die without ever knowing the wonders of a world they had been promised. All because he had found that goddamn book.

17

COSMIC VISCOSITY

2345-02-18 Earth Standard, Nirvana Virtual, Black Stack, Varanasi

MAYPOLE FOUND herself far from the Memory Arcade in a place that looked like Victorian London. She had been wandering for hours from one sector to the next, past residential neighborhoods where gophers pretended to live in fantastic houses with floating pools. Past bistros and coffee houses, theaters, and sporting fields. Maypole was lost and she wanted to stay that way.

But no matter how far she walked it couldn't change the fact that the memories of her grandmother belonged to someone else. Her *Nana* belonged to someone else. She was no more a unique being than Tanbo Khando. She remembered her time on the launch crew. That had been real. John's message had proven it. Entropy had not claimed that part of her life. Yet.

That knowledge may be all she had left.

She pulled up the hood of her cloak and headed down the street to a metro stop. She would return to Rome and find Lemkos at the arena as planned. Let Judah Krane find her; she was tired of waiting for him.

A message from Seraph Stone pinged in her peripheral. It was the third reminder that his message was waiting.

She couldn't open any message out on the street, especially this one.

Her onboard map led her back to the Memory Arcade.

Dayo was surprised to see her back. "Camber, are you okay? It's raining out there, girl. Need a change?"

"I need a booth again. Short stay."

Dayo sent her to the same carpeted cubicle she'd left six hours earlier. Inside the technical cocoon, Maypole opened Stone's message which included images of eight pages from John's journal and a genetic profile. He'd finally found something.

Her hieroglyphs raced across yellowed paper. The margins were decorated with John's doodles of plants and animals. Memories washed over, memories that were hers alone. Memories of their messages, always handwritten in her homemade code and always embellished with drawings. Victor the raven, Belladona the jonquil, Robin the badger. They had made up stories about these characters.

She released a virtual breath of gratitude. These memories were real. And hers.

John wasted no words, and it didn't take long to understand what was happening aboard the ship. The embryos Maypole had once questioned were implanted within months of leaving the Sol system. Not long after, John described the rise of the eye mutation that Stone called "starburst eyes" and noted it had arisen in both T-1 and T-2. John had figured out that this eye mutation was a phenotypic marker, but he didn't know for what.

And neither did Maypole.

Researchers often bred mice of particular colors to indicate the presence of a desired gene whether natural or artificial. The gene for color, the phenotype, was linked to the desired gene. That way the researcher only had to look at the color of the mouse to know it possessed the target gene sequence. The gene that coded for "starburst" eyes might be like mouse color. It was marking a gene sequence. If this was the case, it would be easy to find in the genomic profile Seraph had sent. It was his daughter's.

The biobank embryo XVR04467 was in Rain's lineage five generations back. Maypole recalled that all the embryos in question had been coded with XVR prefixes. She brought up Rain's entire genome. Once outside the booth, she sent the genome into the medical database at her lab in Colony Village. She inserted a query asking the system to compare Rain's genome to Maypole's on record. An overlay of blueprints. Maypole had never undergone genetic therapy of any kind, unlike most of the population. So her DNA would be representative of one from a natural population.

The differences lit up quickly. Rain had some remnants of gene insertions for cosmetics in one of her ancestors way back on Earth, one to control weight gain and one to prevent lymphoma. But there was something else. The gene for starburst eyes was easy to find. It was attached to an artificial chromosomal fragment encoded with a known palindrome. This marked it as a master switch region, an inserted receptor for whatever protein matched the transcription. If that protein was present, it would turn on the gene attached to it. It was like a lock waiting for a key. But it didn't tell Maypole what that gene would do if it was turned on.

She startled at the sound of Dayo's voice. Maypole had forgotten where she was.

"Let yourself out, honey," Dayo called to her. "I have a party to start somewhere."

"Yeah, will do."

Maypole stepped out of the booth and messaged her AI technician at the lab instructing it to reverse engineer this protein, build the mRNA that would fit the artificial sequence. Then it could build the protein itself.

While she waited, she read the rest of the journal. John said that

Ru Shi Zhu had contacted him directly, something he had never told Maypole. Or maybe she had died before he had the chance. Zhu had sent John information about the probability of entropic decoherence in the digital population on Varanasi. Bit rot. Zhu had predicted that some intervention would be required to maintain mindware indefinitely.

The journal confirmed the reason Zhu had not joined the other Rishi execs on Varanasi. She knew that without constant patching and correction, the minds that believed they would live for an eternity would slowly turn into entities like Allison, the crazed hellion Maypole had encountered in Shivi Desh, or they would be patched so frequently that nothing of their original memories remained.

If Martine had found the solution to bit rot with her Samsara system of rebirth, why wasn't Rishi following her lead? Why weren't they building another system like Samsara for their Vested clients?

One more page of the journal remained. She opened it to see one of John's doodle arts that covered a whole page. An angel. It carried a sword in each hand and was blind-folded. What the hell was that supposed to mean? The margins were filled in with geometrics and racing rabbit doodles, like a medieval illumination. Across the bottom, in Maypole's code, it read, *a dream.*

"Huh," she said to herself.

Maypole sent a reply to Stone, explaining what she had found and that she was attempting to determine what the artificial gene fragment did, if anything. She said there was nothing she could see that would threaten Rain's life by having the artificial fragment. Maybe that would reassure him.

The results from the lab came in. The protein matched nothing in her database, either from Earth or Varanasi. It had all the earmarks of a synthetic. It would take time to test it on living substrates to see how it functioned.

She scrolled through the images of the journal again. She had thought the angel drawing was the end, but she found a short message farther down the page. She read:

I know neural net salvage is the last thing you would choose, Camber. But we need you there on Varanasi. If anyone can figure this out, it's you. I hope you will forgive me one day. John

Beside his name was a drawing of a bee with a sad face and tears dripping from its eyes.

A half laugh, half cry escaped Maypole. "Not a chance."

MAYPOLE LOCKED up the Memory Arcade by hitting "lock" on Dayo's tablet controller, but not before she'd sent a message to Martine Sommer.

Meet me at the Medical Center in Colony Village.

She stepped out onto the street. A storm brewed over the bay, and boats tossed at their docks. She pulled up her damp hood against the wind.

The problem was getting into the Real. Maypole had wrecked two holo-prints in the past week. The rental companies had black-listed her until her insurance paid for the one she'd thrown off the cliff.

Maypole unblocked her comms.

Singh had left four messages demanding that Maypole return to Mission Control ASAP.

"Sir, I can't exit Virtual," she messaged Singh. "My print is destroyed and a rental is . . . not available."

That might buy her enough time to meet with Martine Sommer.

She found a tissue culture mech in the Medical Center that had been returned after some repairs. Built purely for filling and spreading culture media to grow a variety of cells in plates and tubes, this little mech had tracks instead of leg appendages. It rolled slowly, able to spin 360 degrees at the midsection to change the orientation of its six graspers and injectors. It had a voice synthesizer. But that was about it. Commandeering such a basic mech would allow her to communicate with Martine, though not much more.

By the time Maypole had updated drivers and jury-rigged control over motion and voice commands, a little red bird appeared on the security cam outside the Medical Center door. When the door opened, Martine flew in, right past Maypole's nondescript worker mech.

"I'm here," she told Martine in a high-pitched munchkin voice. "Come into the lab."

The bird flew after her.

It took some time to tell Martine all she had learned about the Rishi embryos. The master switch that coded for a new protein that, when present, would switch on a piece of artificial code.

"To do what?" Martine asked.

The bird had perched on the back of a desk chair. It began preening itself too convincingly.

"That's what I was hoping you'd help me with. You claim to have prevented bit rot in all the minds who have chosen to live in your Samsara system, in rebirth."

"I don't claim," Martine said. "I have proven it."

"Okay, so why isn't Rishi following your lead? If they are looking to cure bit rot, why not use a similar system and take part of your pie?"

"That's why I told you about Shivi Desh," Martine said. "I suspected they were downloading into living creatures, something no one thought possible. It has long been theorized that minds do not decohere in a living system. It has the same effect as my Samsara."

Maypole's mech voice lacked the urgency she felt. She said, "So you're telling me they are going to download a bunch of Vested minds into hellions?"

Martine took flight, circled the lab, and landed on Maypole's carapace.

"I went to Shivi Desh, exactly where you and Lemkos met Elijah," Martine whispered. "I found one of these modified hellions. My battle bots incapacitated it. I was able to draw blood."

"I could kiss you," Maypole said. "Where is it?"

The little bird pressed its feathered head against Maypole's visual sensor in a mock embrace, then, with its beak, it withdrew a tiny tube from under its holo projection.

Maypole gave it to her AI assistant with instructions to map its genome. "Compare it to known hellion genomes."

During the skin venture capital meeting, Maypole remembered that blue guy saying, "What about the work in Shivi Desh? Wouldn't that be better than skin?"

How could being a hellion be better than skin?

"Hold on," Maypole said to the AI. It turned back to her. It wore the image of a middle-aged woman in possession of absolutely no sense of humor. Maypole added, "Also compare this genome to that of Rain Stone."

THE TRANSCRIPTION of the hellion genome was almost complete when the security alarm sounded. Maypole's time was up. It was either Judah Krane or Noah Dutro, come for their pound of flesh, so to speak. Maybe she could convince them she was nothing more than a tissue culture mech.

Maypole messaged Lemkos. *At Med Center. Have been located.*

But the exterior cameras showed a short, middle-aged Punjabi woman in a sari.

"Shit, the FD. Martine, you should go."

The bird fluttered to the top of a bank of incubators and went still, the holo print fading until there was nothing but hardware left.

Maypole went to the entrance, unlocked the door and looked up at Kaja Singh's unsmiling face. "Sir, as you can see, I've had some trouble finding a print—"

"Doctor Maypole, I tire of your theatrics." Singh pushed past her little mech and started down the hallway.

Singh stopped at each successive room to scan it. What was she looking for?

Maypole followed, rolling at max speed. She banged into door-jambs and walls, unused to the rough maneuverability. In the short time she'd spent in virtual, it was enough to make reality feel heavy. She was at the mercy of physics here, cosmic viscosity, the syrupy slowness of moving through four dimensions without the comfort of a body she'd grown into.

"Sir," Maypole began, "I was on my way to Mission Control—"

"I understand. We have things to discuss."

"Can I help you find something, sir?"

Singh stopped in the middle of the lab and turned to Maypole. "You have been in communication with an officer aboard the ship. I want to know why."

"I-I was scanning the medical records of the current population."

"And you thought an agricultural officer could help you with that? Doctor Maypole, your actions in Shivi Desh are outside your job description. Rishi has registered a complaint of trespassing and theft."

"Theft? What was it they claim I stole?"

"Information. Of the most delicate sort."

"Sir, you saw the encounter with Dutro at my house. He came to wipe me."

"I saw a Samsara drone take down both him and his assistant. That's what I saw, Doctor Maypole."

"Samsara? No, *he* called that drone. Why would I open a feed to you if I was trying to kill him?"

"Why did that drone not blow your print to bits?"

As if on cue, Singh turned and scanned the tops of the incubators. She reached up and brought down the tiny mechanical chassis of a bird.

"I'm afraid, Doctor Maypole, that bringing you to Varanasi was a serious error."

Two NASA security mechs appeared at the door. Singh ordered, "Take her in."

At that moment, the genomic comparison report flashed in

Maypole's peripheral. The conclusion was a single line. *Hellion DNA from Shivi Desh possesses the same master switch and artificial genes as Rain Stone.*

Holy shit. That's how they did it. They engineered a gene to give the downloader an anchor. It allowed Rishi to do to the colonists what they were doing to the hellions. Download into them.

"Sir," Maypole said, holding up all six appendages, "Rishi intends to use humans as hosts for Vested minds."

"Without Rishi, there would be no colonists, no refugees from Earth."

"Are you saying you *knew* about this?"

"More than *knew*. Agreed to it in writing before the ship launched."

Before the security mechs could lock her mindware, Maypole shot a message to Seraph Stone. *Starburst eyes mark colonists for download, neural net overlay. Death.*

Singh went on, "Your meddling may cost the colonists their future."

"Not if you choose to defend them."

"I have agreed to this exchange, Doctor, as you have pointed out." Singh strode about the lab, eyeing every piece of equipment. "I am bound by contract. How do you think we negotiated the use of the Black Stack? Of all this infrastructure? The colonists have a city awaiting them, built by Rishi. A paradise."

"All they have to do is hand over part of their population to be killed."

"They will not be killed. They will be downloaded, like us, into the Black Stack. Live virtually or topside."

"Lucky them. We *are* human beings, sir," Maypole said. "We were sent to protect humanity, not use them like puppets."

Singh motioned for the security mechs to hurry up. "I'm afraid there is nothing you can do about negotiations made two centuries ago. We are in debt to Rishi."

"Sir, I appeal to your humanity."

"What is it you expect to hear from me, Dr. Maypole? I am here to do my job, just as are you and Dr. Lemkos."

"Do the right thing. Protect these people."

Singh said, "I want to know what countermeasures you have recommended to your contacts aboard the ship. In what way do you intend to thwart this exchange?"

"I would hardly call handing human beings over to be subsumed by other people's mindware an *exchange*."

"Which brings me to my next task." Singh sighed audibly.

A light blinked in Maypole's peripheral. It went from green to red. Singh had initiated a login freeze, locking Maypole into the tissue culture mech. No diving into Virtual.

"Dr. Dutro asked me to sequester your mindware," Singh said. "As you know, he has evidence to show that you attempted to wipe him. At your house."

Exiting the mech was impossible.

Singh stood in front of Maypole, looking down the brilliant blue folds of her sari into Maypole's illuminated carapace. "A warrant has been issued for the arrest of Camber Maypole. We'll let the Justice Department determine what happened at your home, Doctor."

The two mechs moved forward to take hold of Maypole.

She thrust out two of her graspers, striking them. They were twice her mech's size and she failed to move them. Using her long stabilizing arms, she attempted to crawl on top of one but was swiftly pulled down by the other. She landed with a crash.

A query popped on her display, a command from one of the bots, *Stand down, Dr. Maypole, and come with us.*

The lab door burst open.

It was Lemkos in his beat-up gladiator mech. He threw the first NASA bot against the bank of incubators. When the other came at him, he wedged a short dagger into the housing of its main sensorium. It fired its pulse weapon, shooting randomly.

Glassware shattered and rained down. Reagents poured over the lab benches.

"Go!" he said to Maypole. His eyes were fixed on Singh who stood, unmoving at the back of the room. She had undoubtedly called in more security.

Maypole rolled toward the hallway. She turned to look back in time to see a snaking probe issue from Lemkos's forearm. It inserted itself into Singh's access panel. Singh went dark, her holo collapsed, and she was nothing but a carbyne and neodymium chassis.

"Sorry, sir," Lemkos said, releasing Singh's skeleton. It fell to the floor amid a sea of broken glass and chemicals.

Lemkos followed Maypole out the door and into the hall.

The AI pilot of the waiting cargo flyer refused them entry, so Lemkos smashed the window and dragged the bot from the vehicle.

He climbed into the pilot's seat. Black streaks had burned through the silicone skin of his arm. He'd been hit. But his oiled chest and leather harness made him look like something out of an old Earth action movie.

He turned his chiseled and scarred silicone face to her and extended his fried hand. She grabbed on, and he lifted her little mech into the passenger seat.

Lemkos grinned at her. "You're right, Cupcake. The Real is more fun."

18

OUT THERE

2345-02-18 Earth Standard, The Shrine of the Dead, Varanasi

THE SHRINE of the Dead was as good a place as any to hide, at least long enough for Lemkos to pry Camber out of that lab mech. He hoped Tanbo might turn on Dutro, since it would be news to her that she was cobbled together from many minds. She might harbor some bitterness, if that was in an amalgam's nature, and maybe, just maybe she'd find a way to save Camber. But at this point, with a warrant for Cupcake's arrest, they could do nothing but run.

A warm wind had picked up from the west and ruffled the faded prayer flags. The sun hung low over the Great Green. Night would be upon them soon.

It wouldn't be long before Singh rebooted and came after them. Lemkos could only hope she'd forget to reset the security passwords he had pinched when he shut her down. One of them had to release the lock she'd put on Camber's mindware.

If he could get Camber back to Virtual, they could make their way to Martine's Occitania. He'd have to do some talking to get her protection. Martine was a sworn member of the Council of Five. Justice and truth were all part of their ersatz mission. But it was the only place Lemkos felt was safe enough for Camber. Dutro had framed her, and the outcome of a trial by combat was guaranteed to be a complete wipe.

In a quick scan of pending court cases, Lemkos noted that Dutro had already submitted "evidence," a corruption code he claimed had been laced in the drinks Maypole had served him.

Lemkos could only hope Tanbo Khando would stand by their agreement.

Right now, he had to get Maypole out of that mech. She had gone for a walk among the shrines—a roll really. Her wheels failed to navigate rocks well and almost fell over into the shrubs. Obelisks and statues of weeping angels projected holo images of long-dead people from Earth. Most of the shrines had shut down decades before, but some sensed their motion and flickered on. The dead spoke or sang a few words, then blinked off.

Maypole's grapefruit-sized carapace was pointed at the hologram of a little boy singing "Jesus Loves Me."

"Let me take a look at your system," Lemkos told her.

Maypole's mech turned away from the translucent image of the boy and faced Lemkos, the red sensor of her visual scan more like a cyclops eye as it rotated in its housing.

He used a dagger to pry open the access port that was concealed in the torso. From his forearm, he initiated the link cables and fed them into the ports.

"Did you know Singh was going to arrest me?" Maypole asked in her chipmunk voice.

"It was on my list of possibilities, but . . ." He had hoped his deal with Tanbo would protect Maypole. Clearly, he was wrong.

"But what?"

"I didn't think she would turn over one of her own," he said. "I went to your house. Right after your meeting with Dutro. I found a CPU. Khando's."

Maypole's sensors rotated back to the image of the singing boy.

"Then you know Tanbo's an amalgam. Just like Judah Krane."

"Yep."

"And Noah Dutro is ready to kill me for plenty of reasons." She gave a synthetic laugh. "Or wipe my backups anyway. Lemkos"—her red eye pinned him—"Dutro plans to download digital mindware into human beings. The colonists with the starburst eye mutation—"

"What?"

Everything she told him next should have come as no surprise, but hijacking a human body?

"This can't happen," she said. Camber turned her garnet-red eye back to the boy and his repetitious verse. Lemkos drew his EM weapon and fired, taking out the projector. The little boy evaporated into data and blew away on the wind.

"Jesus, Lemkos."

"Loves me, yes, I know. First, I got to get you out of this thing. Then we need to get to Martine. I need to be able to monitor the ship's nav system. Whoever hacked it will likely try again. Maybe it's your friend, Stone."

"Maybe you should let them," Maypole said, turning her eye back to him.

Lemkos shook his head. "If that's what they want, then sure. We need to know it's not just some rogue faction."

He had no desire to be a martyr, and Singh would make sure he paid if that ship didn't come in.

A string of failed logins scrolled by his visuals.

Camber's red eye turned back to the view, to greening hills and the valley far below.

"The charge Dutro is slapping on you is no light thing, Camber." He initiated a second string of possible passcodes.

"I should have been dead two hundred years ago." Even with the bad speech emulator, Lemkos could hear her voice tremble. "I've done what John and you planned for me to do. I've told Seraph Stone everything I know. Mission accomplished."

"Look, Camber. Tanbo was curious enough to find her way back to your house the next day, looking for evidence of what happened. She's in a logic loop. Not allowing herself to move forward but trying to find the answer. Round and round."

Maypole made a noise almost like a laugh. "I know how that feels. Lemkos, what if we're all amalgams trapped in logic loops? How do you know that we haven't *all* succumbed to bit rot a century ago and we're nothing but a bunch of data patches generated by the Black Stack?"

"Because you remember your encryption, you remember John, the embryos, our life together on Earth." He wanted to say, *you remember us.*

"How long did you think we'd have before bit rot replaced every-thing we are?" she asked.

"Come on, Camber. No one knew about it until we'd been here for fifty years."

"And you chose not to tell me then. Or *now*, even."

"I tried," he said, "I tried to convince you to come with me into Samsara where bit rot is suspended. I told you—"

"You told me that Samsara would let us start again. We could forget who we are and become someone else for a century. Well, I never wanted to forget who I am. I want to just *be* who I am, Kolya."

She waved him off with two pincer appendages. "I get it, Lemkos. I do. You thought you were doing the right thing because John asked you to bring me here."

"Are you angry that you were able to warn the people on that ship of Rishi's plan? Isn't *that* worth the trip?"

She was silent for a long time, her sensorium seeming to gaze off in a thousand mile stare. "Yes," she finally said. "But is it so wrong to wonder what's out there?"

"What's *out there*? Where?"

She waved her primary grasper at the sky. "You know," she said with that passionless voice, "people used to die because it was the natural order of things. Now we have no time limit on our achievements. We have no limits at all to pleasure or depravity. Pain and pleasure are *selected*, they're not *consequences* of life choices. But have you ever considered . . . maybe that's why we decohere? We know deep down that this isn't all there is. Some part of us awakens in the stacks, our eyes open. When we do, we collapse the quantum state of our mindware, one qubit at a time."

"Well, if Noah Dutro wins his case against you, you'll be finding out what's 'out there' sooner than you expected."

She paused, spun her sensorium in a full three-sixty as if taking in the immensity of the view across the Ganges far below. Sunset was coming, and the six standard days of warmth had begun to melt the ice packs high in the mountains. Streams surged toward the river in the distance, cascading down the cliff walls around them. The spring thaw was coming.

"I'm not afraid," she finally said.

Access granted flashed across Lemkos's visual.

Maypole's red eye rotated back to face him.

"Time to go," he said, talking fast. "Here's the address for a blank avatar I've got stashed at the villa. I'll meet you there."

"Then where?"

"Martine's. We can lose ourselves there."

He paused as he worked at closing the access port and looked at the transparent casing of her mech's carapace. He wanted to see her face, hear her voice. Because he wasn't sure how long he could protect her from Dutro, or if she even wanted him to try.

LEMKOS WAITED for Camber in the loggia of his villa. It opened onto the garden and reflecting pool. What was taking her so long?

At last, she appeared through a flaming door and stepped onto the mosaic floor with delicate sandaled feet. Her avatar was fashioned after a girl he'd known during his life as a gladiator in Martine's Samsara realm. A girl he would have died for many times over, in fact he did, in the end.

Lemkos would have preferred Camber's bio image, the one he'd fallen in love with so long ago, but this one suited her. Her ivory toga was belted with gems, and the brooches at her shoulders were shaped like golden leafy vines. A goddess of the wild, maybe. Her long light-brown hair was piled in an intricate plait and held with blooming flowers. Her face was as innocent and placid as Camber's was fiery and willful.

A jeweled dagger appeared at her belt. She'd found her inventory.

"I can't find an ID page for this girl," she said in Camber's own voice. She'd already made a few changes to the settings.

"You can make one. That's why it's called a blank, Cupcake." He grinned at her, his gladiator arms crossed over his chest.

"I'm nobody's cupcake. And you agreed to stop calling me that, Kolya."

"Ah, Kolya. Not Lemkos? No more NASA speak? I like."
She scowled.

"We need to get out of the Roman threads anyway," he explained. "Could give us away."

"If you're going for inconspicuous," she said, "you're not going to be wearing that." She indicated his famous gladiator avatar.

"It was handy. I'll switch it out."

By the time they had mounted Lemkos's favorite dragon and launched for the waystations, Camber had found a medieval archer's set at auction along with a leather kirtle and trousers, high boots, quiver, and bow.

Lemkos had looked for something similarly well-suited to the period and settled for the simple sackcloth of an itinerant preacher. Not wanting to give up his stats for a blank, he used a dark-skinned warrior from the deserts of Kush he had leveled a long time ago in the arena. No one would remember him.

The staff he carried had maxed damage points. He'd leveled every weapon and didn't hold back in filling his inventory with his favorites, just in case.

"You're assuming I'll be arrested," she said, as if testing the truth.

"Yes, I'm assuming. Eventually. But Martine may be able to put you in touch with Stone. See what's happening aboard the ship."

The rhythmic beat of the dragon's wings made it seem like they were rolling over waves of air. The land below was a patchwork of sunlight that peeked from behind the broken clouds.

She asked, "How did you get involved in all this legal gladiator stuff?"

"I wish I could admit to an altruistic drive. But the reality is, there hasn't been much navigation programming to be done around here for the last few centuries. A guy gets bored. Martine presented me with an opportunity to make some money."

"So you took up law. You know the difference between a lawyer and a vampire, right?"

He laughed and they answered in unison, "Vampires only suck blood at night."

Calling what he did "law" was like calling a butcher a brain surgeon. "All I do is fight," he said. "It works out all that existential bullshit that bothers you so much. You go climbing and hunting for new smells and tastes. A little pain taken and inflicted makes me feel alive. I know you know what I mean."

Though she didn't look back at him, he could feel her smile.

The waystation to Martine's Occitania slammed shut as they approached, a blinding white wall of light flashing across their path.

"It's Felix," Lemkos said, bringing the dragon to a soft landing on a grassy hillock.

"Felix?"

"My dragon," Lemkos said, stroking the feathered neck. "They have his ID. They know he belongs to me."

"So this is it?" she said weakly. "Time for arrest."

"Not necessarily. Let's try walking through."

Leaving the dragon on the hill, they headed through wildflowers that grew as high as their knees. The road was empty but for a road sign reading *Occitania* and a Realm to the west called *The Bitter Expanse* offering free entry to all.

As Lemkos figured, their false IDs and bios were impeccably crafted, thanks to Martine's engineers. She'd linked them to real mindware active in Nirvana Virtual. The only problem might be if the gatekeepers noted these minds were occupying two avatars at the same time. But the gatekeepers let them pass.

They stepped through the flaming hole punched through virtual space and into the bucolic farmland that lay outside the walls of the great medieval city.

The land of Occitania smelled of dung and woodsmoke. Once inside the city walls, night soil required that they step on the elevated stones set for that purpose. They wound through a maze of streets and alleys, past coopers and smiths and tanners stooped over their work.

Across a moat filled with water boiling with fish, rose the fairytale castle. He recalled it smelled better in there.

Martine was waiting for them. She wore her biological image, a short, stout Danish woman in her forties, blond hair embellished with a headdress of the period studded with seed pearls and gold. She wore a period dress with long sleeves that nearly reached the floor.

"Come," she said. "We haven't much time." She linked arms with them both and led the way down a long, vaulted corridor. They must have looked like the three musketeers. "The ship is merely six days from orbital insertion around Varanasi. Once this occurs, there will be no chance to change their trajectory."

They passed through vaulted corridors hung with tapestries and weaponry.

"Are there any laws in Occitania that might be used to protect Camber?" Lemkos asked.

Martine said bluntly, "We will conceal Dr. Maypole as long as possible. Beyond that, I can make no promises."

He glanced at Camber. "You know Camber didn't do it," he said to Martine. "This is all fiction."

"Of course she didn't do it," Martine said evenly. "She did something far worse." She motioned to the ornate doors leading to the expanse of the great hall. Here, she paused and held both of their arms tightly as if she could bind them together. Then she said, "Camber is trying to save the colonists. Now come. There is someone here you must meet."

She led them into a room where red birds roosted among the high vaulting of the roof. Dagger-like windows of stained glass colored the tables and floors with the afternoon sun. A feast had been laid out on long trestle tables, including roast goose, poached apples, pies, and goblets brimming with wine. The smell of burning candles and the sweet, cut-grass scent of the rushes on the floor mixed with the heavenly smell of food. Courtiers rose at the sight of Martine and bowed. Lemkos guessed they were NPCs, but there was no way to know in this Realm. No tags, no backchannel inspections. Just like life.

Everyone wore the customary clothing of the period, except for one tall woman with dark hair. She wore trousers and a blue jacket with gold epaulets. Her avatar was not rendered in high def, in fact, the opacity was rather low. When she moved, there was a strange lag.

Martine stood beside her, and said, "May I introduce the captain of the *Vera Rubin*, Terra Jean Dela Cruz."

19

THE LONG TABLE

2345-02-18 *Earth Standard, aboard the* Vera Rubin

SERAPH WOKE to the sound of the steel gate rolling in its tracks. The door hit the bumper with a *thud*. The control panel chimed to indicate the goat pen was open, but no one was there. No Ever Walsh or his day shift counterpart.

Seraph stepped into the dimly lit corridor, waking the nanny goat across the aisle. The animal got to her feet, tail spinning. She bleated at Seraph as if he was there to feed her. Soon a great goat chorus erupted, echoing down the long corridor.

"Feces."

Apparently, Vera had no interest in him. No alarms went off. No security mechs appeared. So he headed for the exit.

Who had let him out? Ever Walsh? Unlikely.

The exit stood open onto the main farm concourse. He hesitated. This wasn't right. It had all the signs of being a setup. But for what?

He cradled his bad arm and moved fast. The pain had been

replaced by immobility and total numbness. Anything was better than the throbbing.

He had to find a comm system.

After a few wrong turns, the double doors that led into the lift bay appeared and slid open upon his approach.

He couldn't go to the aquaponics section, even the night shift would know him. Baakos had a lot of pull among workers there, which meant they'd throw him right back in the brig.

He was in the A lift bay. One floor up was the Fabber deck. He hit the call button. The doors opened, and he stepped in. Still no security.

The Fabber floor was busy. Crews were running the small printers, making parts for something, aluminum O-rings and plastic gaskets.

A girl idly watched a printer lay down threads of liquid plastic.

"Hey, friend," he said, as casually as possible.

"Heyo." When she finally looked at him, she said, "Hey, I know you. You're the guy who brought the food."

"Yeah, that's right. I hurt my arm in the temp farm." He pointed to the useless limb. "I need to make a call. Can I borrow your palm-comm for just a minute? Mine's broke."

"I can call you a medic—"

"No, no. I just need to call a friend."

"Sure." She handed over the device, wrinkling her nose as if she'd gotten a whiff of him.

"I'll bring it right back," he said, then headed to a quiet corner behind a stack of boxes and called TJ.

Vera's face appeared. "The captain is unavailable. If you'd like to leave a—"

"Feces."

He started recording a message, spilling everything he knew as fast as possible. Baakos's plan to hijack the nav system, Rishi, the journal, and Camber Maypole. It sounded like the ravings of a crazy person. He hit send.

Then he opened his messages. Maypole's reply was there. As he read, blood drained from his head. He felt the warm, moist press of stale air, the sweat that beaded on his face. *Starburst eyes mark colonists for download, neural net overlay. Death.*

Death. His back struck the cold metal of the wall. He slid to the floor.

The population had been manipulated from the start. This was planned before the ship launched and if Maypole had successfully raised the alarm . . . NASA knew. That's why they canned her. They *planned* to sacrifice a percentage of the colonists to Rishi and their rich backers. Now the *Vera Rubin* was delivering on a promise made hundreds of years ago, delivering a ship full of human bodies for the taking.

Baakos and Huang were right. They needed to leave the system, override the nav.

But he had to get to TJ first.

He swabbed his sweaty face with his sleeve and called Rain.

She answered, her eyes barely open, her hair a tousled cloud. "Dad?"

"Hey, Chicklet." He swallowed tears. Not now. "I'm sorry to wake you, but it's important. I need to talk to your mom."

"She's not here. You want to talk to Gran?" Rain yawned.

Feces. This was not the time for TJ to be humping that bastard Niall Bora.

He replied, "No, no. Yes. Yes, let me talk to Pearl."

"Hey, friend!" The girl at the fabber called. "You done there?"

Seraph held a hand up and walked slowly back toward her. Pearl's face reappeared, looking about as awake as Rain.

"Seraph, what's happening?"

"Pearl, I need you to find TJ and tell her to check her messages—"

"She told me you might call." Pearl ran fingers through her short hair. "She has a message for you. She says she knows what's going on in Retro." She must mean the nav system hack. Pearl went on, "TJ wants to meet you in VR. Go to . . . Let's see, I have it here." She fumbled through her notes on her palmcomm, holding it far away and squinting. Then she sent it. It blipped up on his screen. "This IP address."

Seraph returned to the girl at the fabber. "Hey, do you have anything to write with?"

"Write?" This time she sounded peeved.

"Yeah, chalk markers or something. Anything."

She produced a fat-tipped pen. Seraph pulled up the sleeve on his dead arm and copied the numbers onto it.

"Got it. Thanks, Pearl. Tell Rain I love her."

He handed the palmcomm back to the girl and headed for the lift bay.

THE GAMING ARCADE in Retro was disgusting. No bigger than a meeting room, it was wedged between the school and a clothing shop. Getting Vera to open the door during off hours required some good lying. Seraph told her Baakos wanted him to check on an educational sim he had installed in their system. The delay told him that Vera was likely checking on it. But checking with who?

But the door unlocked.

Once inside, he chose the VR pod that looked the best. The padded seat was sticky, and the air smelled faintly of farts.

Seraph missed Huang's VR rig almost as much as he missed her top-shelf hootch. At the same time, he was fairly certain she would set her gun to the asterisk setting the next time he crossed her path.

Vera surely saw Maypole's message and could have alerted Baakos, but more likely she'd go to TJ. Seraph wouldn't hear anyone coming in the VR rig, and there were no locks on the door of the pod. He found a piece of plastic and wedged it into the space between the door and the jamb. If it was pushed from the outside, it might stick and hold the door closed long enough to alert him.

Glancing at the scrawl on his arm, he keyed in the IP address and initiated login.

He pulled on the stinky headset. The skin sensors positioned themselves quickly and made a seal at his temples, neck, and the back of his hands. An infrared beam calibrated his vision reader and sender, and then the visual connections blossomed before his eyes.

His avatar spun up from his stored data, which meant he'd never been in this particular sim before. Where was he going?

The rendering took several minutes in which he couldn't move the avatar. Without warning, his stomach dropped as he fell into the simulation. He passed a portal composed of standard nebulosity and swirls, and then he was inside of something with stone walls and windows of colored glass. Light streamed through and painted the stone floor with a river of color. Dust motes floated through the light shafts along with something that looked like smoke.

Gradually, he smelled food. That couldn't be right—he didn't have a smell synthesizer. Not in the gaming arcade. But it was distinctly roasted meat.

He stifled the urge to call out for TJ. The corridor before him led toward a room lit brightly with a warm golden glow. The ceiling of the vast hall was higher than two decks of the ship. Despite the sunlight that sent shafts of daylight into the room, torches burned on the walls. A long table, or several tables that had been pushed end to end, filled the center of the space, making a T shape. Candles speckled the table with pure light. It was crowded with people— women in flowing gowns and men in silk vests and hats with feathers. Avatars surely, but they looked so real, he couldn't help but stare.

This was not the uncannily hyperreal VR he was used to. This was like another existence altogether. No telltale crispness of the objects, no overly vibrant colors. The skin tones were imperfect, real, the faces imperfectly asymmetrical, like real faces. This could not be housed inside Vera's system. He felt a rising panic. He must be inside the Black Stack itself. He had to be.

Not only were all his senses engaged, but he was overcome by a strange emotion, the feeling of returning home after some impossibly harrowing journey. It was as if he had stepped into a movie as a character.

Who were these people? *What* were they? And where was TJ?

The table was overflowing with food, much of it unrecognizable to Seraph. But it smelled incredible. The people reached from plate to plate with their fingers, tasting everything, talking, laughing, flirting, touching. None glanced at him or said a word to him. Was he invisible?

He looked at his avatar's primitively rendered hands. How could they not see him?

The people who sat at the head of the table had their backs to a fireplace that ran the length of the wall. The flames cast strange shadows around them and filled the air with the fragrance of woodsmoke.

At the center of the long table, five people were huddled in close conversation. In the middle of them sat TJ.

Like him, she was clothed in the ship's uniform. She turned her avatar's starburst eyes to him and smiled. Seeing those eyes brought a burning to his chest that he felt back in the VR couch.

"TJ," he said. "Where are we?"

"Seraph." She gave him a smile that was clearly fake, even on the face of her avatar.

A blonde woman with a red bird on her shoulder sat beside TJ as if they'd been deep in conversation. To her other side was a man with skin darker than any Seraph had ever seen. He was dressed in an equally dark robe that reminded him of Baakos's robe, but without the baubles. Beside him, was a young woman with an angelic face. She was dressed in leather and a crimson cloak that was pinned at her shoulders with two silver brooches. At her belt was a jeweled dagger. They all wore looks that said he'd interrupted something important.

TJ got up from the table and gathered Seraph into an abbreviated embrace, whispering. "Not sure I trust them."

He caught her arm. "TJ, I have to talk to you. Now."

"I know," she said. "When you didn't answer my calls, I had Niall access the security feeds in Retro. We found Ever Walsh leaving a bowl of stew in a goat stall. When I pressed, he told me everything. How do you think you got out?"

TJ had let him out? It was beginning to make sense now. No security had questioned him when he'd wandered through Retro.

A servant placed a metallic flask in Seraph's good hand. "Bienvenue." It smelled like nothing he'd ever had before but tasted like alcohol. How could he taste it? He was in the gaming center's VR pod.

"I have to talk to you. Now," he repeated.

"They brought me here to discuss the navigation hacks your Retro friends have been trying," she explained.

"Look, we need to leave system."

She stared at him blankly. "Leave?"

"We're in danger."

That was all he could get out before the dark-skinned man approached. He put a hand on each of their shoulders. "Join us. You must be Seraph Stone?"

"Yes."

"I'm Kolya Lemkos, and this is Camber Maypole." He indicated the beautiful young woman with the angelic face. This was not the image of the woman who had sent the video messages.

She got to her feet and extended her hand to him. "You got my message."

He nodded and took her hand. It was too real.

"What can we do?" Seraph whispered to her. "To stop this?"

He stepped behind their bench to the fireplace and, finding a thin layer of ash over the flagstones, started marking with his finger. He wrote in the symbols of Maypole's pictoscript, "Trust them?"

Maypole stood beside him, read the words, and smiled. "Absolutely. The people you see here are committed to doing whatever we can to help you."

She made room for him to sit beside her on the bench. The fire felt warm on his back.

"This is Martine Sommer's system," Maypole said. She indicated the woman with the red bird who inclined her head slightly as if in greeting.

"We can speak freely here," Martine said. "I understand your reticence in sharing information with us, but we don't have time for courting. You must trust us."

Lemkos said, "The first thing that must be tackled is the repeated attempts of someone on the ship to hack the navigation system."

TJ responded, "It appears to be coming from Torus-2. Our engineers are looking into it."

"So are mine," Lemkos said. "You may want to keep that option open. If you have the capability."

"Open?" TJ asked.

"If you decide not to stay." He bowed again and sat down.

"Why would we decide not to stay?" TJ asked.

The others shared a look, realizing the captain did not know. Seraph felt it was his place to explain. He started with finding Lauretta's book, his communication with Maypole, and the deciphering of the messages.

"TJ, the starburst eye mutation was planted as a marker," Seraph said. "Rishi intends to download their Vested minds into the bodies of those with the mutation."

Maypole gave her the technical explanation and told them about what she and Lemkos had found in Shivi Desh: hellions with human mindware.

Maypole asked TJ, "Can you access the medical records for the genetic diversity project?"

"I can try." TJ seemed confused by the particulars of Rishi's plan. Her eyes met Seraph's with the look of a cornered animal.

"We can confirm who carries the artificial fragment and figure a way to remove them from the ship early."

"What do you mean? Remove us early?"

"I have shuttle craft docked at the spaceport," Martine offered. "Now that the ship has been slowed sufficiently, I can dock with the *Vera Rubin* and bring the affected colonists to a hidden location."

TJ glanced at Seraph, panic in her starburst eyes. "Then what?" she asked Martine. "We hide for the rest of our lives?"

The table grew silent. They had no answer for that. A lifetime of running from joboxes?

"TJ," he took her arm. "There is another way." She gave him a hopeful look. "Help Erica Huang override the nav system."

"And give it all up?"

He nodded.

TJ got up and began pacing, her arms crossed, her fingers jiggling nervously. "I can't make this decision alone."

"No," Martine said. "Perhaps it is a decision for all the people."

TJ turned back to the table. "Can you help us if that is the decision?"

"We're here to help you," Maypole added.

Lemkos said, "I certainly can. I lead the navigation team at NASA. No course corrections. You just give the word."

Martine Sommer was listening intently, feeding morsels to her red bird as Lemkos offered detailed instructions to TJ on the navigation system hack. "It appears the Retro hackers are able to jam Vera's controls. They feed her logistics that say she is on course—"

"When she's not," TJ said.

"Yes. It's brilliant."

"But does this artificial chromosome even work?" TJ asked, a note of panic in her voice. "If it has been replicating for two hundred years, maybe it has changed."

"From what Lemkos and I have seen in the hellions of Shivi Desh," Maypole said, "the artificial fragments are identical to yours."

Lemkos pinned TJ with his gaze. "Whatever you decide, it must happen before orbital insertion. An override after that would require thrust I'm not sure Vera has, unless you guys have engineered some awesome shit in two hundred years."

Seraph thought of Huang's arsenal and her ability to hack the nav system. He would not underestimate her.

"Let's go," TJ told Seraph. "We need to talk." To the others, she said, "I am grateful for your help. Allow us to consult others aboard the ship, and I will give you a decision."

Lemkos added, "Your slide down the gravity well is underway. You have six days until we initiate the maneuver to reach orbital insertion. Act before then."

TJ nodded.

Camber Maypole lay her hand on top of Seraph's and gave it a reassuring squeeze.

He felt his real body ease back into the cradle of the VR pod. He exhaled the breath he'd been holding in two worlds and inhaled the stagnant stink of the pod.

TJ INSTRUCTED the commander of Retro to give Seraph his freedom. He was under her protection. Baakos and Huang offered no apologies, nor did he expect it. Now a social pariah due to Baakos's sermons, Seraph was forced to appeal to the Retro commander to find a place to stay. He was assigned to an abandoned unit in the Shanghai District. Whoever had lived in the place before had trashed it, and there were rumors of a murder here decades earlier. Rather than place new people here, it was locked up, as if whatever had happened had tainted the place's mojo forever.

The Retro medical center provided Seraph with a palmcomm and a neural evaluation of his useless arm. They cleaned up the wound and wrapped his shoulder in a bulky sling. Within the next few days, he was able to use the arm somewhat. But orbital insertion was only days away. He had to be completely fit. He had to be able to fight if the decision was made to land.

TJ had delayed the vote two days already, allowing people to voice opinions and ideas in open forums, chatrooms, town halls. Egalitarian. The will of the whole. For the good of the whole. Wasn't that what the social order was supposed to be about?

Baakos took every opportunity to campaign for leaving the system. His face was on every cinescreen, his voice sounded through every palmcomm. His premonitions of war now had data to back them up. But even his followers were not willing to give up so easily the planet they had travelled forty-six light years to reach.

They reasoned that such a small percentage of colonists carried the artificial chromosome, it should not outweigh the needs of the larger population.

When the day of the vote came, there were protests in the commons. Clashes resulted in multiple arrests. The goat pens were getting full.

In Retro, Baakos led a group of starburst-eyed people and their supporters, and they barricaded the command center. Baakos might do time in the goat pen too.

Many people seemed willing to fight to protect the affected ones, but there was a large and vocal group who wished to hand over those affected in exchange for a promise of download. Hell, there were even some old folks ready to give themselves up, take the neural net download, and leave ailing and weak bodies behind to the highest bidder.

Daily, Seraph watched from a pub in the commons, sipping whatever his reputation would buy him until the bartender threw him out. The results of voting would be announced that day, leaving them only two days to execute the navigation change. Lemkos had sent Seraph multiple messages, pressing him to hurry the decision. Of course, Seraph had no control over this.

"The vote is in," TJ said to the camera.

A hushed silence came over the crowd in the pub.

TJ's face was drawn, her lip quivered. Seraph could see tears in her eyes, and he already knew the result. She said evenly, "We land on Varanasi."

"Feces."

The pub erupted into screams of joy and pain. Seraph pushed his way out onto the concourse.

He opened his palmcomm and sent a message. "To hell with that, TJ. You can tell Lemkos the decision is to leave system. Tell him not to correct the navigation hacks."

But she never responded.

Over the next two days, everyone aboard the *Vera Rubin* watched the closing image of the tiny white and blue marble. Varanasi was suspended over the pastel storm bands of the giant planet, Majriti, like a water drop at the tip of a leaf. Varanasi moved relentlessly closer. The *Vera Rubin* slowed and made a long parabolic arc as the moon trapped the ship in its gravity well. Below them, a world filled with disembodied minds were gradually degrading into nothing more than sophisticated emulations of once-living people, their backstories and emotions generated by the Black Stack. In another hundred years, they'd be no more complex than the NPCs that had been sitting at the table with them at Martine's castle. At least, that was how Dr. Maypole had explained it to them.

The mindware on that planet had two choices if they wanted to retain their humanity—download into a biological body or enter Martine's Samsara, repeatedly living new, simulated lives.

Orbit stabilized. The status flashed at the bottom of the live view of Varanasi.

Seraph exhaled and blinked through tears. There would be no trajectory change now.

On the big cinescreen in the commons, he watched the brilliant golden sunlight reflect off the puzzle pieces of seas that covered their moon. The white of storm clouds and winter snow blanketed the vast northern continent of Uttar Pradesh, broken by the green veins that marked the network of gorgelands. The thaw had started. The swift melting of the long winter's snowpack would turn the canyonlands into torrential flows. If TJ had negotiated with Martine, if she could remove those with the genetic anomaly, how long would it be before NASA or Rishi found them in that wild land below?

He opened a link and called Rain.

Her sweet face appeared on his palmcomm, her starburst eyes bringing a tightness to his throat.

"We're here, Chicklet," he said to her. "Are you watching?"

"We're here," she repeated. But her voice was weak with fear.

"I want you to know," Seraph said, "there are people on the ground—friends. They're going to help us, help me, keep you safe."

She nodded weakly, tears in her eyes.

"Remember that. Whatever happens, we can fight. I love you."

His palmcomm chimed with an emergency message. It was TJ. He switched to the incoming call. TJ was walking rapidly, her face flashing in and out of view.

Her voice trembled. "A ship is approaching."

"A ship? What do you mean?"

"I mean, a *ship*."

"Martine Sommer?"

"A *Rishi* ship." She stopped walking and stared into the camera. "Seraph, Vera has given me something. To be used only if our lives are at risk."

"What do you mean?"

"It's a failsafe. A crash code."

She held up a piece of paper to the camera. It was a printout in black and white. At first glance, he thought it was a copy from a page in John Lauretta's journal. The one of an angel holding two swords with all the doodling around the edge. But it was overlayed with dots, dashes and chevrons. This picture looked more like a QR code of some kind, and the angel was just barely visible in the design.

"What is that?" he asked.

"Vera says it can be used only as a last resort. This might be the time, Seraph. I have to go." The connection dropped.

"Used how?"

But she was gone.

Vera's AI image appeared in her place, her smile eternal before the field of ever-blooming wildflowers. "Rishi Corporation's shuttle, the *Sandworm,* has hailed us. It has transmitted the appropriate security codes. Prepare for docking."

20

A MEASURE OF FLESH

2345-02-26 *Earth Standard, aboard the* Sandworm

THE MINDS CONTAINED in the Black Stack were nothing more than rats in a Skinner box. Ultimately, they would self-stimulate until nothing else remained of them but the thirst for pleasure, their neural net shot through with holes backfilled by the computer that hosted them. The realization that she, Tanbo Khando, was not one of those minds should have filled her with relief. She was not one mind, but many. The genius of Ru Shi Zhu blended with how many others?

Relief was far from what she felt.

She was not conceived of one man and one woman, but a multitude. She had never gathered mushrooms in the forest with a brother she idolized; someone else had. She had not studied engineering at Oxford or Yale or the hundred other institutions she remembered; yet parts of her had. She wasn't just the founder of Rishi Corporation; she was more. She was so much more than a single human being. She was the best of many.

She had made the trade with Kolya Lemkos, her CPU for Camber Maypole's continued existence. It was proving worth it. For the third time, Tanbo watched the exchange between Noah and Maypole that had taken place on the patio overlooking the Great Green.

She's just a memory given form, that's what Maypole had said of her. *An amalgam like Judah Krane.*

In a mirror, she examined the holo image she'd worn for two centuries, believing she had chosen to look like Ru Shi because they were so close, had worked side by side in the building of the empire that was Rishi. But Tanbo was made in Ru Shi's likeness for a reason. The knowing, eternal eyes, the heavy black veil of hair. Information was the only reality, and Ru Shi's information had returned to the dust from which it was once constructed. Tanbo was shaped as much from Noah's memories and desires as she was from Ru Shi's. All of her brilliance but none of her willfulness. All of her beauty and none of her independence. Noah had sculpted her from the minds of the gifted to create what? A goddess? Certainly a mind that far surpassed his own, or even Ru Shi's.

But Noah Dutro knew far less than he thought about the journey of the soul. He would learn soon.

Countless creators had remade the universe countless times in countless simulations, seeking the algorithm that would lift humanity from the sludge of their savage origins to stand beside those who had written the first code in flesh.

Tanbo understood this. She was never one of them; she'd known that all along, felt it deep in her subconscious. The refugee minds of Earth wallowed in simulations that pandered to senses that had long ago been snuffed by a lack of biology. No, Tanbo would begin the next simulation in the savage wilds of Varanasi where the hand of the first creators continually left their mark, where evolution was real, where change was shaped by desperation and predation, by the infinite pressures of a living world.

Only here was involution possible.

Whether he knew it or not, this was why Noah had created Tanbo. This was what he wanted from her. Now, she would take what *she* wanted.

But to begin, she must have bodies.

THE *VERA RUBIN* had slowed to a speed suitable to maintain a stable orbit around Varanasi. If it had been traveling any faster, Tanbo's shuttle would be unable to dock. The timing had to be perfect to intercept it properly. It would be a good test of her systems.

The *Sandworm* could carry eighty-one colonists comfortably, but it was built for high orbit to ground transitions, nothing beyond. This distance was testing her upgraded fuel capacity. Tanbo had made sure it was outfitted with temperature and pressure regulators for atmospheric control, with seats and locking harnesses, even food and water.

She and Noah often cruised above Varanasi, and had once spent weeks aboard the *Sandworm,* watching the stars and the changing storms on Majriti; they'd watched the dance of the moons and the auroras on the planet below. Tanbo shook the romantic image from her mind. Sentiment, especially false sentiment, wouldn't help her reach her current goal.

By retrieving the subjects herself, she would avoid a nasty public confrontation on the ground. She would deliver her prized cargo directly to the Monastery. Besides, the possibility of Kolya Lemkos initiating a course change was a great risk. She doubted Kaja Singh could even stop him.

Tanbo had ignored Noah's messages. He was pretending at being overprotective. *They have an arsenal,* he messaged her. His real fear was that she'd take control of the project, which of course, she already had.

The *Vera Rubin* looked like the rear axle from a child's tricycle.

The two tori rotated in opposite directions, creating a net-zero torque on the hub. This allowed for easier navigation with less drift. The hub was a cylinder that housed the fusion drives, docking ring, backup storage, and the gold-graphite photon sails, which were fully deployed like the plumage around a windeater's neck.

Tanbo had fond memories of working on the design of this ship. Memories that were created or borrowed from someone else. "Ugly as a platypus, but more functional," Ru Shi had said of it.

Using the technology now available to her, Tanbo might create a ship to take them back to Earth one day, or on to another world. The little *Sandworm* was the first of her designs.

As she drew closer to Vera's hulking mass, it became clear that the ablative casing showed extensive battering by micro-debris. A legion of mechs scrambled over the dark hull like ants on fallen fruit. The NASA logo and UN flag were barely visible.

Twelve dropships were housed within the docking ring, like chicks in a nest. There were two unused docks, purposely left for emergency boarding in case of disaster. Tanbo saw this as a real disaster.

"Captain Dela Cruz," Tanbo hailed over the command comm. "Permission to come aboard."

TJ Dela Cruz needed to believe Tanbo represented a welcoming party, nothing more. If Dela Cruz had been warned of the project, she would resist, certainly. But Tanbo was ready.

The woman's face appeared on Tanbo's commlink. The artificial chromosome was right there in her eyes—an amber starburst that flared around her pupils woven with the color of the irises dictated by her human genome, dark brown. Dela Cruz was a picture of beauty— high cheekbones, dark hair pulled tightly into a knot, full lips . . . Tanbo could already feel her tongue on those lips, on Noah's lips.

But those lips made a firm, unsmiling slash across her face now. They said, "Permission granted, though I retain the right to be accompanied by security personnel, and to restrict our meeting to the hub."

Ultimately, Dela Cruz had no control over the docking bay doors, Tanbo knew. Vera had decided, based on the code Tanbo had sent to the ship's AI, to allow docking and entry. There was nothing Dela Cruz could do about it.

Tanbo offered her most soothing voice. "As an executive of Rishi Corporation, I'm here to see to your immediate needs and make sure you are provided for in Colony Village. I'll see you in the hub, Captain."

Dela Cruz gave a grim nod, then closed the link.

The docking pod doors dilated open, and the *Sandworm* snuggled into the coupling.

Tanbo tethered herself to the bulkhead before pushing off into the expansive belly of the hub. Segmented like the abdomen of a dragonfly, this compartment was the docking bay. Thirteen airlocks circled her, leading to the colonist dropships.

With her war-bots awaiting instruction aboard the *Sandworm*, Tanbo floated alone, her hair and holographic cheongsam unmoved by the micro g. Even her butterflies had come along.

In a blue pressure suit, Dela Cruz floated through a door from the adjoining segment. Beside her were a dozen security mechs, little more developed than they had been when the ship had left Earth.

"Captain Dela Cruz, I am Tanbo Khando. Welcome to Varanasi."

"We're not quite there yet, I'm afraid." Dela Cruz wore a gun of some kind at her belt. Her hand rested on it.

"You're closer than you and your ancestors have been in 247 years. As the liaison from Rishi, I'm here to help."

"Are you? Or are you here to collect your payment?" Dela Cruz said. "I understand NASA owes Rishi a measure of flesh."

"This does not have to be a struggle," Tanbo said. "We offer all affected individuals download into our virtual world with unlimited access to all Realms."

"Is that supposed to be tempting? A free game subscription?"

"If you saw the Realms I am suggesting—"

"So we can decohere? Succumb to bit rot with the rest of you? Is that what we're supposed to choose?"

"Solutions are in place for decoherence problems."

"Like downloading into biological bodies, yes, I've heard."

"The disengagement from your bodies would only be temporary," Tanbo said, "until clones can be raised—"

"I understand what you are, Tanbo Khando, though you may not yourself." Dela Cruz moved closer to Tanbo, who silently summoned her battle-bots. Dela Cruz had the weapon in her hand, pointed at Tanbo. But she also had her left hand tucked behind her back. What did she have there?

"Go ahead," Tanbo urged her. "You can't kill the dead."

"You never lived, so you never died," Dela Cruz said. "You don't think for yourself, you think what Dutro tells you to think. You're nothing but a puppet of the Black Stack."

Tanbo laughed. "My, my, what a negative image Dr. Maypole has painted of amalgams." She instructed her bots, "Don't hurt her."

Dela Cruz fired a weak EM pulse at Tanbo. It was easily deflected by her shields. At the same time, Dela Cruz withdrew her left hand from behind her back. She held the object in her hand at arm's length, flashing it toward Tanbo and then to her bots. It was paper.

She initiated visual sensor shields on herself and all her bots. The view before them was now slightly distorted, filtered for organic targets only. The rest of the hull looked like unrendered wireframe. Only TJ Dela Cruz was visible.

Though her visual shield had blocked it, Tanbo was certain the image on the paper was exactly as she had feared. Ru Shi would not have left the colonists without a weapon against the Black Stack. This woman believed she could shut down everything with a crash code.

Tanbo smiled.

Her bots had the captain subdued in seconds.

Tanbo commanded her bot. "Torch whatever was in that woman's hand."

The smell of burning paper filled the air.

The *Vera Rubin's* security mechs went offline instantly as Tanbo sent a command to Vera's defense system.

"Your lies are clever, Captain. I look forward to stepping into your flesh more than you can imagine." Then Tanbo sent the battle mechs in to gather her treasure.

21

CROSSROADS

2345-02-26 *Earth Standard, Occitania, Samsara Virtual, Varanasi*

EIGHT DAYS HAD PASSED since Maypole, Lemkos, and Martine had met with the captain of the *Vera Rubin* and Seraph Stone, arrayed around the big trestle table in Martine's great hall. The ship was in a stable orbit, from which Lemkos doubted they could escape even if they chose to. The colonists aboard the *Vera Rubin* had voted to land on Varanasi, to sacrifice eighty-one of their own in exchange for a peaceful future for the others.

Maypole's thoughts were never far from Seraph Stone now, and others like him. Those who would be forced to give up spouses, children, to Rishi.

During that meeting, Maypole had found it hard to take her eyes off Stone's avatar. He was off the rack from 2090s VR. Several seconds of lag due to relativistic time and the ship's outdated technology caused the avatars representing Seraph and his captain to blink in and out. Even so, Stone's chiseled, cartoon-ish face with its unshaven, plain features had a sadness about it. He must have known all along that it would come to this.

Lemkos, Maypole, and Martine had a rudimentary defense mapped out, though it sounded crazy. Martine commanded her mech troops like a general, mobilized them above ground where they would muster at their assigned locations—Colony Village, Mission Control, and the spaceport where the dropships were scheduled to dock. She got some pushback from Singh, but pointed out there was no law forbidding the distribution of mechs owned by a private enterprise.

No time frame had been established for the first dropship launch from the *Vera Rubin,* at least, according to Lemkos's sources inside Mission Control.

Still, Dutro had not come for Maypole. She began to believe the deal Lemkos had made with Tanbo Khando might hold. Maybe Khando had taken control of things after Lemkos had restored her memory, maybe seek retribution for being misled all these years. One could only hope.

Lemkos was in contact with Captain Dela Cruz. They had hatched a plan to launch the affected members of their population in a dropship to rendezvous with Samsara security forces at an undisclosed location. Lemkos had devised a way to disable their transponder, but without a cloak of some kind, radar could still track the dropship easily. But if they could beat NASA and Rishi forces to the location, they might stand a chance. Samsara's army of battle mechs rivaled Rishi's.

Maypole was at work on a treatment to expunge the artificial fragments from the colonists' genomes. From her hiding place in Occitania, she gave instructions to her lab techs at the Medical Center. Most attempts at excising the fragment ended up killing the tissue it was tested on. Even if she succeeded, any gene therapy would take months to complete, maybe years.

She was deep in concentration in the virtual mockup of her lab when Martine startled her.

"Camber, my dear, we need to talk."

"They've come," Maypole said.

"An order from the Hall of Justice. They require that I turn you over." The red bird on her shoulder flew to Maypole and settled beside her cheek. Was that supposed to make this easier? Its eye was an unnerving shade of bright yellow, giving it a frantic look.

"Okay, hand my notes over to the ranking medical officer from the ship, but let them know I couldn't—"

"Camber, please hear me out."

Maypole sighed. She knew what was coming.

"If you enter a sim now," Martine reasoned, "when you return this will be over. Your name cleared. We will see to it."

"And while I have amnesia and play at some other life, what happens to the colonists?"

"Lemkos and I will—"

"I was sent here for one purpose, Martine, to see to the safety of those colonists. If I can create a therapy—"

"It won't be fast enough, and you know it," Martine said. "By the time you complete one lifetime in Samsara, everything might be resolved."

"It will certainly be resolved. In days, maybe less. If I leave now—"

"You will be safe in the sim. Camber, we cannot harbor you any longer. I can say I knew nothing of the charges against you before I dropped you into Samsara—"

"But you *do* know," Maypole said. "And so do I."

It was a tempting choice. To live another life in a state of total amnesia, forgetting this existence and building a new one with all the pain and joy of living. Forgetting the colonists, Lemkos, everything she had built here on Varanasi. All may be gone when she returned. *If* she returned.

"Camber." A voice came from the doorway. "Please."

It was Lemkos.

Maypole held his gaze, imagining his true eyes behind the

avatar's. Had she ever seen such a look of utter helplessness in this man before? What did he want from her? Just to exist? Or to do everything she could for those colonists? To bring down Rishi and help build the first human colony on a distant planet.

"I ask one more thing of you," Camber said to Martine, "Please, let me stay until they come for me." She loathed the pathetic simpering in her voice, but she needed more time with the gene therapy.

"They will come for you," Martine said. "Maybe hours, maybe days, but they will come."

"Unless," Maypole said, "unless Tanbo keeps her word to Lemkos."

Lemkos flashed a helpless, tearful glance at her. Even Lemkos was still human somewhere deep inside. Why else had he spent two lifetimes inside Martine's Samsara? He was looking for something he couldn't find in this false world he professed to love so much. It had worked. He'd come back from Samsara changed. Maypole couldn't quite say how, but he was more his authentic self than he had ever been in life.

Martine's little red bird hopped back to her shoulder. "You have until they come for you," she said.

Maypole's luck ran out before the day ended.

She and Lemkos had prepared to go top side to commandeer two mechs Martine had left in Colony Village for that purpose. Before they could log out of Virtual a guard handed Martine a piece of parchment which she unrolled slowly. Her placid eyes found Maypole's.

"It appears Noah Dutro has come for you himself. He waits outside."

Lemkos was on his feet, heading for the door. Maypole caught up to him, took him by the arm and spun him to face her.

"Listen to me," she said. "It's time, Lemkos. Let me go."

She pulled him into a long embrace that felt more real than anything had in two hundred years. Then she turned, and strode down the long, arched corridor, trying hard not to look over her shoulder to see if he was following.

At her signal, the guards opened the great oak doors that led to the drawbridge. There was no one there, nothing but the crackling of torches along an empty drawbridge. Beyond that, lay a sleeping village cloaked in darkness.

Maypole stepped out.

When she crossed the boundary marked by the doorway, she was no longer in a medieval castle. She stood on a wide-planked pier that stretched into turquoise waters. It was day, and seagulls fought for position on the peeling white railings, their territory marked by spatters of droppings. Warm rain had begun to spit from boiling clouds. The wind carried a fragrance that stirred deep memories in her. The smell of the sea mixed with cotton candy and crushed mussels drying in the sun.

What the hell was going on?

She knew this place well. It was Cocoa Beach, Florida.

Her feet sounded hollowly on the planks of the pier, and between them, she glimpsed bright flashes of water far below. She stopped, leaned on the railing, and gazed out over the water.

Cape Canaveral was a mirage in the distance. She saw the unmistakable box of the Vehicle Assembly Building and two launch gantries. One primary pad, Launch Center Thirty, held one of the many heavy-lift rockets that shuttled materials and men to the shipyard at Lunar Gateway. This was not only a place but a time. Prelaunch. The *Vera Rubin* was under construction on the far side of the Moon. And Maypole was still alive and still an M.D. with NASA.

She glanced back the way she'd come. She saw no castle, no guards in mail and helmets.

An old woman was feeding bread to seagulls, and kids were fishing, baiting hooks with the peach-colored flesh of smashed mussels.

Not far along the pier, she saw a man leaning on the railing, tanned hands clasped, his eyes on the gantry across the water. Something inside surged at the sight of him. She knew who he was, and more, *what* this was—Noah Dutro's idea of a trap.

She drew closer. John turned his lopsided smile her way, the skin crinkling at the corners of his green eyes as he said, "Camber, you've come."

He held out his hand.

Take it, she told herself, *take it and be done with this charade.*

"We have so much to talk about," the ghost of John Lauretta said.

"Yes," Maypole replied. "I may not survive the Black Stack's justice, but I'm not the only one who knows about Tanbo. Even the humans aboard the ship know. How long do you think it will be before someone tells her that she never lived, that she is an amalgam programmed to your specifications? And what will she do when she understands?"

He shrugged. "It's new territory. It's why I built her."

His hand remained outstretched; his eyes locked on hers. The wind played in his dark hair.

Humans are hardwired to guard that seed of hope that life holds something more—one last chance, one last glimpse, one last taste. Maybe it was time to let go of that delusion and see what was on the other side. If Maypole had to leave this circus of existence, she wished she could take Noah Dutro with her.

John Lauretta's hand felt just as she remembered it. The roughness and strength of one who worked with plants; the rivers of veins that flowed to his wrist and forearm, like the veins of a leaf.

He pulled her into a tight embrace. She wanted to remember what love felt like, but all she could feel was a desperate anticipation of what was to come.

22

THE FRAGILE PARTS

AS PLANNED, TJ had left the comm feed open so her officers could see and hear everything that happened in the hub. The newly armed officers, in a brief, frantic meeting before the *Sandworm* docked, had discussed what TJ would say, how many security mechs she would have with her, and how she might prevent whomever or whatever got out of that Rishi ship from getting past her. But no one was prepared to see an angel float into the docking bay.

From the farm deck, Seraph had watched an ethereal being float from the *Sandworm.*

Dressed in a flowing red costume that was unaffected by the microgravity in the hub, Tanbo Khando was accompanied by butterflies and six mechs, each one marked with a bold *RC* on their shiny carapace. This was the amalgam Maypole had warned them about. Not a human mind, but something else altogether, a new kind of machine built from the minds of many.

Vera's battalion of archaic security mechs proved useless against the lone jobox and her hi-tech weapons. Their pulse bursts were easily repelled by a shield, visible only when it lit up in pearlescent spatters. Khando and her mechs remained safely cocooned inside the colorful bubble.

But what was that behind TJ's back? It looked like paper. The paper she had shown to Seraph?

He replayed it again and again until he was certain that TJ had thrust the paper out before her like a shield or a magic wand. It was the angel, the one Vera had told her should be used . . . What had she said? If lives were in danger?

Khando's mechs destroyed the paper in a blast of flame, then they took Seraph's wife, struggling, toward the *Sandworm*.

Without a shot fired, Tanbo Khando had rendered all of Vera's security mechs inactive.

There would be no fleeing, no fight. Not here. Not on the ground. Not against that.

In a matter of minutes, Khando's battle bots had breached the hasty welding job they'd done on the airlocks. That was it. They were in, and no one could stop them.

Rain was hysterical when she called, "Daddy, they're coming. They're coming."

"Listen to me, Chicklet." He left the farm and took the elevator, heading for the fabber deck to look for Huang. "You go to the farm deck. Find an empty aquaponics tank. I want you to go there as fast as you can. Get inside one."

Who was he kidding? Vera knew where every person was at every moment. Unless he could hide her in his Faraday cage, he couldn't even save his own daughter.

Once he reached the fabber deck, he found powered-down sec-mechs frozen in corridors and spoke bays. If Khando had taken over Vera's systems, they would be trapped on the ship with no access to dropships. But he couldn't think that far ahead. He sent a message to

Baakos, told him to gather all affected colonists and take them to the gun storeroom on the fabber deck.

But when Seraph got there, he found the storeroom door locked and TJ's passcode no longer functional. Baakos must have been taken already.

He beat on the door, hoping someone was inside. With no response, he headed toward the concourse but was stopped by the sound of shouting. He looked past a bulkhead to see a Rishi bot on all fours loping downspin toward him. Gleaming like liquid metal, it seemed alive as it rushed by Seraph without hesitation.

These bots were targeting only one thing: starburst eyes.

Seraph got back on the lift and headed to the farm deck. He hoped he could access the emergency hatch locks from his control room. It might slow them down.

A soft tone chimed over the lift speakers and Vera's smiling face appeared on the display. "If approached by Rishi personnel, please comply with all requests. I repeat, please comply."

"Comply my ass."

There was no leaving this system now. But if they had control over the dropships . . . That was all Seraph could think of as the lift came to a halt and the doors opened on the farm deck.

Cradling his slinged arm, he exited the lift bay.

A bot from the Rishi ship moved toward him.

"Halt," it ordered. Maybe he was wrong about their targeting. Or it had detected his weapon.

Seraph drew the gun from his pocket and fired. The pulse lit up the unseen shield that encased the mech. Unharmed, it moved relentlessly toward him. He tried the asterisk setting on the gun. The bot's shield just flashed more brilliantly as it dissipated the energy.

"Come on, come on," he urged the mech.

Taller than Seraph, it looked like something from an old Earth movie, humanoid, but with at least six appendages. It could run like an animal or stand upright like a man, and its weapons were seamlessly integrated into the unit. As it moved toward him, he squeezed his eyes shut. If it couldn't see his eyes, maybe it would take him to wherever Rain and TJ were going.

But the mech had his neck in its grip and slammed him against the wall. With another grasper, it forced open one of his eyelids. Then it let go. Seraph crumpled to the floor.

The thing moved past and entered the cricket farm. Drowning out the scritch of the insects, cries for help sounded, pleading and wailing.

The bot emerged with a woman in tow, one appendage clamped onto her arm. Her starburst eyes spilled tears.

"Help me!" she begged Seraph.

He followed and croaked weakly, "We'll be right behind you."

"Do something!" she screamed.

The bay doors closed, and she was gone. He wanted to vomit.

He moved down the corridor, wiping at his tears, imagining Rain being taken just like that. The war was over before it had started.

He had to bring his mind back to what to do next.

Bora opened the security feed to all officers. It showed people being dragged through the hub and into the airlock leading to the Rishi ship. By the time Seraph reached the Retro command deck, the sleek, black arrowhead that was the *Sandworm* was sliding from the docking ring.

SERAPH FOUND HUANG IN LOGISTICS. Three holo screens surrounded her. One displayed orbital dynamics information, one was an indecipherable mass of code, and the last one was a view of Varanasi sliding silently below them. Shadows of clouds glided over snowy peaks and river deltas and the turquoise expanse of the sea.

"We're tracking them," Huang said as if she had not shot Seraph a week.

"Can we launch the dropships?" he asked.

"That overdressed jobox handed control back to Vera when she left."

"So that's a yes?"

Huang looked at him like he was a simpleton, then nodded.

"You need to watch this vid," Seraph said. "Help me out with this."

She scowled, her mind clearly on the code hovering before her. But her eyes were swollen and bloodshot. He didn't need to ask about Baakos.

"Help you do what?" she asked coldly.

"Look."

He replayed the vid of TJ and Tanbo Khando, stopped it when the image of the paper came into view.

"See that? TJ told me Vera gave it to her. To be used if people's lives were in danger. What the hell is it?"

He started it again and they watched TJ hold the paper out in front of herself, turning it first to Khando, then to the Rishi bots.

Huang's mouth fell open. She took the palmcomm from him and hit replay a dozen times.

"What is it?" Seraph asked.

She stared at him, still open-mouthed. "It's got to be a crash code. Vera must have given it to the captain."

"That's it. That's what TJ said. A crash code. But what is it?"

"I mean, it's a coded image. And if Vera gave it to TJ, then it means Vera believes the danger is great enough to give us a way to wipe operating systems."

"Wipe?"

Huang was rubbing at her mouth, watching the video again. "Yes. It makes sense. NASA wouldn't launch this ship without some way to protect people against rogue AI."

"Ru Shi Zhu," he said with certainty. He told Huang about the virtual meeting with Martine Sommer, Lemkos, and Maypole.

"You told them?" Huang asked.

"Yes. Everything. They're ready to fight for us, Huang."

She nodded grudgingly. "Well, if Zhu's the author of that code, then it might do more than shut down local systems."

"But it didn't work," Seraph said. "The Rishi bots torched it."

Huang let the vid play. A Rishi bot spewed flame toward TJ, who pushed off a sec mech to avoid the flames. With TJ floating away, the flame finally found the paper that was floating where she had released it. The paper caught fire and sent embers dancing through weightless space.

"See how that bot had to guess at the location? It was just estimating. In order to transmit a code like this, the target has to interact with it through visual sensors. Theirs were blocked or scrambled," Huang said. "Khando knew TJ would try a crash code. She was ready with visual screens."

"Feces. We missed our chance."

"Maybe not. Maybe if we can get to the ground." Hope lit up Huang's face. The lines of weariness smoothed.

"We have allies," Seraph pressed. "Can you get the coordinates of the *Sandworm's* landing site?"

"Why do you think I'm tracking them?" Huang added, "You trust them?"

"What choice do we have? Your guns are worthless against them."

She sighed, dragged her hands down her face and looked back at Seraph. "We need to get our hands on that crash code. Show me the message."

He opened the last message TJ had sent him. The erratic video as she strode toward the lift bays. She held up the image of the angel to the camera. Seraph hit pause. It was all there, in crisp focus. He saved the frame.

"Send that to me," Huang said.

"If this could wipe whole systems, we need to be careful with it." He was thinking of Martine, Maypole, and Lemkos. If they were attached to any local system, it could take them out too. They could wipe the people trying to help them.

"You and me," Huang said. "That's it. No one else has it."

"And we agree it's last resort only."

Huang stood, wiping at her nose. She finally glanced at Seraph's immobile arm, supported in the sling. The look she gave him was anything but apologetic. Her jaw hardened, her nostrils flared, and she raked her fingers back and forth through her pink hair. She looked older, beaten.

"Agreed."

Seraph put his one good arm around her in an awkward embrace.

"We can't do this alone," he said.

THE ASSAULT HAD LEFT the ship without a captain. Protocol dictated that the security officer was second in command. That meant Niall Bora, TJ's lover, was now heading the counterattack. To everyone's surprise, Vera made no move to stop Huang from recruiting an army of volunteers for a landing party. Nor did she confiscate the weapons Huang had carted from the fabber deck to the commons.

"They're useless," Seraph reminded her.

"Not against hellions. We're taking them. Besides, good old projectiles can do some damage."

Seraph's guts turned. Hellions.

With the *Vera Rubin* in orbit around their new home, the ship had lifted the ban on moving between the two tori. It was a cruel irony. T-1 scrambled capable volunteers to join the landing party, none of which had ever fired a weapon of any kind. Seraph found his way to Pearl's unit. His mother was sitting in the dark, prayer beads in her hands. He sat beside her, took her hands, and joined in the prayer.

"We're going to bring them back," he told her.

He wanted to believe it. He whispered a prayer to Baakos's First

Flame, whoever would listen to a man who had taken too much for granted.

When he left Pearl, he went to his own unit, let his fingers touch the scattered things in Rain's room. Her clothes. Her collection of model animals native to Varanasi. Windeaters with outstretched wings, an ora'hin with impressive antlers, a hellion with spear raised in battle.

In the kitchen, he found a half-empty bottle of hootch in the cupboard. He poured a glass and surrendered himself to the sofa, positioning the glass on the plain vinyl coffee table in the plain, unadorned common room of the unit where he had raised his child like generations before him.

He rotated the glass, and the ice tinkled. Condensation pooled around it. For reasons he could not name, he thought of the goats who had shared his jail in T-2. He remembered the velvety feel of a goat's muzzle on his fingertips. The fragile parts meeting, one beast to another. Both alive. Both vulnerable. Both destined for death.

He sniffed the hootch. It warmed him, beckoned to him. It promised to give him strength for what came next. But the only strength he needed was Rain. The ice melted and diluted the amber liquid. He got up, poured the hootch into the recycler, then headed back to Retro to meet the gathering assault team.

23
AFTER LIFE

2345-02-26 Earth Standard, Nirvana Virtual, Black Stack, Varanasi

---

MAROON-COLORED shades fluttered overhead and cast dancing shadows across the Flavian Colosseum. But it didn't cast enough shadow to save Maypole's bare feet from the hot griddle of sand. She ran to one such shadow and stood in it. The stands were packed to overflowing with people, their shouts deafening. The smell of greasy fried cheese and fish sauce mixed with the rattling of tambourines that punctuated the jeers that were solely directed at her.

Erasure. She expected Khando to bail on her agreement with Lemkos. After all, death was the inevitable consummation of the event called birth that had begun two centuries ago. Maypole had cheated the Reaper long enough.

"Assassin!"

"Murderer!"

"Kill her!"

As if in answer, a hologram the size of the arena manifested above her head. It was a recording of the meeting with Dutro. But it was *his* version. She watched herself, sitting smugly at the patio table in the blank rental bot, her arms crossed. But the words she said in this holo were not her words. The scene was reworked. She threatened Dutro. He raised his drink to his print's lips, but did not taste, did not consume the alleged code that would unmake him. The drone appeared over the house. But this one was emblazoned with a Samsara logo.

And here Maypole had thought *she* was the one in control of that meeting.

The only thing real about any of it was Puppy's death. The seahound was blown five meters back, pieces of his flesh raining as the view went black.

Maypole swallowed hard and caught one shaky hand with the other.

The crowd went into a frenzy, demanding justice.

This arena, these avatars worn by the crowd's entropy-riddled minds—they all originated in the same place Tanbo had been conceived. They were all part of the collective unconscious of half a million minds who had escaped the certainty of death on Earth. They were nothing but an inventory of memories and feelings and desires, some of which had lost their meaning.

Maypole strode toward the nearest stands, meeting the eyes of those who would meet hers in return. She willed them to see what had become of them all, and at what cost.

The onlookers jeered and spat at her. She couldn't stop the smile that came to her face. Maybe the adventure was just beginning.

A white bird fluttered over her head and circled the oval arena.

She scanned the crowd for Lemkos, but hoped he had left Virtual by now.

It wasn't Lemkos she found in the stands, but Dayo. Their diamond teeth glinted in the sun, and Maypole read the word on their elvish mouth. *Peace.*

Yes, peace.

A rack of weapons awaited her—spears, maces, swords, and axes. There was armor as well, along with a helmet and shield. She took none of these. She stood in the leather jerkin and trousers she'd donned on her way to Martine's castle, still wearing the avatar of Lemkos's fantasy girl from Rome. She would not die in someone else's skin.

She swiped off the image of the coy girl and called up her own avatar. Camber Maypole in jeans and a blue NASA T-shirt.

To the cheers of the masses, the gates of the arena opened. An announcer proclaimed, "Dr. Camber Maypole, you are charged with the attempted murder of Noah Dutro and Tanbo Khando, as well as terrorist activity that has jeopardized the lives of the colonists aboard the starship *Vera Rubin*." That was chutzpah, claiming *she* had endangered them. "Prepare to defend yourself. Your fate is in the hands of the gods."

From the shadows of the entrance gate, the gladiator emerged. His bare chest was oiled, and from under his bronze helmet, golden locks flowed. Flower petals rained down on him, and the white bird alighted on his shoulder, no doubt a blessing from the Black Stack.

On their feet, the crowd began chanting his name as the announcer cried, "Representing Noah Dutro, legal gladiator, Bull Balls Bently!"

He carried a net and trident.

Maypole walked directly toward him, unarmed.

When she stood inches from the gladiator, she said, "I refuse to fight. Just be quick about it."

Copper eyes peered at her from behind the bronze helmet.

"Okay," he said. "But the crowd's gonna be frothing."

"Exactly. Nothing that you and I do will dictate the outcome."

"*They* don't know that!" Bently motioned to the crowd.

A collective cheer issued from the crowd and Bently pranced before them, his arms wide as he urged them on, delaying the inevitable so they might buy some fried octopus and honey cakes to go with their ale.

In that instant, Maypole wanted whatever peace might be had through ending this existence. *We are nothing but information. Mind-ware. It cannot be lost, just changed. We'll all end in thermal decay, a frail sputtering out of the energy in our system to be absorbed by the universe.*

What was it John had told her? *How long will it be,* he'd said, *before all those thousands of minds figure out a way to kill each other?*

Not long, it seemed. Because deep down they all knew that this wasn't living. There was no finish line in this eternal, mechanical existence. There was no payoff, no comeuppance, no final wrap, no denouement, no meeting the Maker. It was like inching slowly toward the big scene that would never happen.

The net hit her in the face.

"You need to fight, put on a show," Bently said.

Maypole laughed. "Why?"

The net came over her this time and pulled her off her feet. She landed hard on her back with the realistic feeling of having the air knocked out of her. Her vision dimmed.

The three points of a trident poked through the net and rested against her neck.

Behind the nose guard of his bronze helm, she saw his face twist in pain.

Camber was reaching, reaching for that face.

He said, "Trust me, Cupcake."

He thrust the prongs into her throat.

The corruption code sizzled with a brilliant flame before her closed eyes. Chain crash, all systems unraveling, back to the qubits that spelled out Camber Maypole. Reaching, reaching. The smell of frying arancini, her Nana's hands, the breathy, whistled tune. In an instant, all the memories that had shaped her crowded together to hide behind her eyes. She would not let them go. Reaching for them.

All she could feel was the burning singularity of her soul.

24

JESUS LOVES ME

2345-02-26 *Earth Standard, Nirvana Virtual, Black Stack*

IT WAS OVER AS FAST as Lemkos had hoped.

Maypole's swift death had disappointed the crowd. But it wasn't fast enough to suit him. At least he didn't have to sit beside her hospital bed for days on end, holding her hand through a curtain of plastic and wishing he could feel her pulse through his thick gloves. He had control over her death this time—and he choked down the cry that rose in his avatar's throat.

He collapsed to the sand beside her, the sound of the crowd's jeering in his ears. He smelled her blood, told himself it was not real. But as far as he knew, he was the only one who had kept his part of the bargain with Khando. Camber might have died the real death; her backups fried by the worm he'd planted in her system. If Tanbo had failed, Lemkos had just ended the existence of the only person he'd ever loved.

He staggered to his feet. If he wanted to salvage some part of

Bently's mystique he should dance around her body and beg for the crowd's adulation. But he dropped the bloody trident and net beside Camber and stood there while they booed him. Then he started back toward the gate.

He wouldn't watch the NPCs clean up her bloody remains. Realism, that's what this was all about, because the Real itself was not enough for them anymore.

Bently had demanded an obscene amount of money for the use of his avatar. He must have known that Lemkos was going to damage his reputation.

In the darkness of the underground passage heading to the lockers, a message pinged his peripheral. The confirmation came from Judah Krane along with the usual payment. Tanbo had kept her word. Maypole was still alive, for want of a better word.

Lemkos took a deep, ragged breath.

She would be stashed in the Rishi mainframe that was hidden deep in Shivi Desh. Better to be in bed with the enemy than wiped altogether . . . maybe.

Now he just had to go get her.

In the dim light of the tunnel, Lemkos saw Bull Balls Bently striding angrily toward him.

"Way to ruin a guy's rep in five minutes," Bently said. "Better make this worth my while, Lemkos."

"Okay, okay," Lemkos said. He transferred the money he'd gotten from Krane to Bently's account—the agreed-upon price for the use of his avatar for the fight.

A call from Singh came on his peripheral. She must have been watching the execution.

The Flight Director appeared, a middle-aged Indian woman with a smudged bindi and large, expressive eyes.

"Be advised, Dr. Lemkos. Any interference in the work of Rishi Corporation will result in your termination at NASA."

"Is that supposed to scare me, sir? I mean, my job was done when the *Vera Rubin* achieved orbit around Varanasi."

"You will not . . . interfere," Singh repeated. That pause changed the meaning of the phrase, or at least, it made him rethink it. She was offering him an opening. To make a case.

"You *do* know that Tanbo Khando is not what she seems, sir."

Singh took a deep breath and released it slowly. "I have been informed of what you found, Dr. Lemkos. Of her true nature."

"You must see what she's doing," Lemkos said. "Noah Dutro is no longer in control of his creation or Rishi Corporation."

"It is clear that we are at an unforeseen crossroads," she admitted. "I remain bound by my contract with Rishi. With Dutro."

Lemkos nodded pensively, heading deeper into the cool darkness of the arena tunnels where the flight director's image came into sharper focus. Her dark holographic eyes were speaking to him as clearly as her words ever could. They had softened, those eyes, her lashes closing slowly in a long, easy blink, like a cat who stares admiringly at its owner. One eyebrow bounced up as if she had asked a question and awaited his answer.

Then it hit him. The passcode files he'd taken that day in the Medical Center. The day he had escaped with Camber—Singh knew he had them. She'd known since he blasted his way past her security bots. She had not changed those passcodes then, and he doubted she had done so now. Lemkos had scrolled through hundreds of codes before he'd found the one that released Camber from the mech. What else could those codes access?

Singh might not be able to act directly on behalf of the colonists, but she could make it easy for someone like Lemkos to do it.

"Interfere," he repeated, "me?"

"I owe you no explanation, Dr. Lemkos. We're all here because of the tech supplied by Rishi Corp. We owe them more than the lives of eighty people. Tread carefully."

She blinked out.

No, she owed him no explanation—he'd seen it all in her eyes. She had not anticipated the creation of such a machine as Tanbo Khando, possessing all the technical expertise of a thousand savants, minds gleaned from the best of Earth, a handpicked collection built to carry Rishi into a technological future that included human bodies along with their immortality.

Lemkos left the stench of the Colosseum's underbelly and logged out of Virtual.

His gladiator mech was just where he'd left it when he and Camber had left the Real. A windstorm had blown through the Shrine of the Dead during the night, sending tumbleweed-ish things to cover the monuments. His mech was covered in grit that had mucked up the gears. Using snake-like manipulators, he injected liquid graphite from his reservoirs. It took him a few minutes to work the joints free. At least this print was a tough old hunk of steel and carbon. If he could keep it running, it would serve the purpose.

It was a warm, bright mid-morning, probably fifty hours into the Varanasi day cycle, and the air was full of migrating plumage. With the increase in temperatures, the rivers would rise swiftly. He hoped he could make his way into Shivi Desh before the flood.

He found the shrine that had so captivated Maypole, the one with the singing boy. He knelt at the base of the sculpted granite effigy and cleared away the scattered weeds the wind had blown in. The kid materialized, greeting Lemkos as he approached. "My name is Josh Gibbs and I lived for twelve years in Tucson, Arizona. I like RC cars and . . ."

Lemkos popped the access panel hidden on the back of the pedestal and reached inside to find the drive exactly where he'd left it. A backup of Singh's access codes.

25

FORGE OF THE CREATORS

2345-02-27 *Earth Standard, Shivi Desh, Varanasi*

TANBO HAD TIMED the extraction of the eighty-one subjects perfectly. As the *Sandworm* settled onto the landing pad high above the gorge of Shivi Desh, a sirocco was kicking up from the south, signaling the beginning of the thaw. The river would be in full flood by local midday, making any assault on the Monastery difficult, if not impossible. If Martine and her mechs tried an assault with drones, they'd be shot down before they cleared the mouth of the gorge.

Noah had not yet returned from hunting Dr. Maypole, but Tanbo would not wait any longer to take her new body. The moment she'd met TJ Dela Cruz on the starship, she knew this body was born to be hers.

She allowed TJ to say goodbye to her daughter, the child called Rain. Tanbo had watched the exchange remotely, interested in the emotional connection between mother and child, one that she would soon experience herself. As soon as possible. Clearly, the child didn't understand TJ's explanation that she would be salvaged and stored in the Black Stack, which was just as well since it wasn't true. Imprinting and salvage were equal and opposite procedures—the salvage would have to be done first, and Tanbo had no intention of waiting.

The child's hysteria required sedation. The captain was sedated as well when she was moved to the lab.

Lying in the neural harness, TJ's naked body was encased in the silk-like cocoon that carried the nanoids, puzzle pieces of Tanbo's mindware. They would enter the body at 10^{22} locations, with the primary injection point being at the base of the woman's skull where they would enter the spinal fluid. These nanoids would overlay the brain, first the cerebellum, then into the pons and midbrain.

Tanbo lay on a couch beside the harness rig that held TJ in its embrace. As her files came online in the body, Tanbo's own operations would shut down, shepherded by an elegant subroutine she'd devised to protect her from the psychosis that was induced when mindware was replicated. The transition was more gradual than it had been with the windeaters, perhaps because the body was larger. Tanbo was watching TJ's body one moment, then a tingling registered in fingers that were not attached to her holo-print. It was a most unusual feeling—like a remote sensing device had been attached to her hands. With the twitching came the flutter of eyelids. Her holo-print mimicked the motor action. It would be no more than minutes before the nanoids reached the neocortex and gave her sight and hearing.

One moment, she watched the enmeshed body twitching and shaking, the next, she was staring up at the white ceiling. Her holo-print on the couch stilled, a pile of carbon wiring and gears. No entopics fluttered about the machine, though the holo projection of Ru Shi's image was still intact.

She drew a deep breath, feeling the ribs expand, the diaphragm inflating her belly. This body had no implants or augmentations other than the chromosomal fragment that made download possible. This was all real, built of flesh and bone and nerve. This was her new home.

The silken network of the nanoid delivery system withdrew, sizzling away into vapor. The air felt icy cold over her skin, raising gooseflesh, and making her perfect, dark nipples stand erect. She sat up. The slightest feeling of dislocation rapidly faded, and then she was standing, pulling on the downy robe waiting on a hook.

She tried to assess the amygdala but had no means to do so since she was not attached to sensors. Was TJ's ghost still clinging tightly to this body? Would Tanbo dream her own dreams? Or TJ's?

When the required rest period ended, Tanbo couldn't help but find her reflection in the window that separated the lab from the empty viewing room. Naked, she ran her fingers over her skin. She loosed the bound hair and felt it tickle the skin of her shoulders and back exquisitely.

Dela Cruz, tall and strong, with skin the color of coppered bronze, smiled back at her. Tanbo was no longer tethered to any machine. Her soul was born at this moment—like the waking of birds at dawn.

Homo Deus. She was the pinnacle of evolution, the point at which the creation becomes the creator. It was time for Noah to serve *her*.

As the *Sandworm* had dropped back through the atmosphere, Tanbo had scrutinized the men among her crop of augmented creatures. There were only two who stirred her desire. A man who was a bit too young and one who was too old. She'd let Noah decide which of the two he would take.

Her assistant said he had returned from Maypole's execution and waited in their chambers. She found him leaning on the terrace railing as if he could detect any incursion before their systems could. When he turned around, the sight of her left him positively speechless.

Beneath her fingers, his carbyne chassis was as cold as his heart.

Her impatience was as real as her need for vengeance. "Hurry," she begged him. She loved the sound of this new voice and began singing.

Noah chose the young man.

No more than twenty, the boy's name was Carl Abravo. An exquisite counterpoint to Tanbo's alluring maturity. He knew TJ, he said. He had worked with Seraph Stone in agriculture, the very Seraph Stone who had unraveled Tanbo's plan and warned the ship.

The young man fought admirably when they put him into the harness. As the nanoids coursed into his brain, Tanbo leaned over him, smelled his skin and tasted his lips. She could not wait.

The nanoid soup that contained Noah's mindware would enter every cell of this body, dissolving the consciousness of Carl Abravo as water dissolves salt.

And when Noah opened his eyes, he would know a new master.

TANBO'S SERVANTS had filled a bath and sprinkled it with crushed acanth blooms. It pleased her to discover their scent was reminiscent of orange blossoms on Earth, recalling the groves south of Cape Canaveral in Osceola. She had memories, implanted of course, of Noah and Ru Shi driving through these orchards. He had added these memories to Tanbo's because he wanted her to believe it was her he loved, that it was her he had made love to in the orange orchards. But it wasn't and never would be.

She'd have to get past the undeserving assignation of tenderness and love to these memories. His love was not for Tanbo, but for Ru Shi. He had tried to rebuild his love but had created so much more. He would soon know how much.

Her new body had a deliciously musky smell. Tanbo felt the magical place between her thighs, and her touch ignited a shockwave through her sensory system. She slid down into the tub, gazing out the open balcony doors at the veil of meltwater that had already begun coursing from the rim of the gorge. It cloaked her balcony with a soothing hiss and a damp breeze that she could feel on her skin.

Her mind was uncluttered with signals, messages, and sensors. No onboards. No data interface. She was alone inside this flesh. Alone with the throb of blood at her temples, the tides of her breathing. Her mind was as silent as the space between stars. It unsettled her. She would have to get used to it.

She watched the rise and fall of her breasts and silently saluted the soul of Terra Jean Dela Cruz, draining into the water of her bath.

At last, the attendants led Noah to her room. He stood straighter than the young man named Carl.

"Take off your robe," she commanded him.

She wanted to see the imperfect reality they had wrought together. The body of a descendant of Earth, so young his muscles were still developing.

"I have something for you," he said.

"I see you do." Anticipation raced through her in a hot flush.

He handed her a glass of wine and clinked his to hers. "You'll be happy to know that our saboteur, Camber Maypole, has been removed."

If he was satisfied, nothing else mattered. It was a fair trade she'd made with Kolya Lemkos, the truth for Maypole's continued existence.

"Splendid," she said. "But I have only one thing that can please me right now, and Maypole's death is not it."

His hand slid down the curve of her back to her buttocks. He tried to take control as he always did, but she thrust him down to the waiting bed and clamped her hands around his throat. Just enough to worry him. Just enough to see his face turn red, and panic bloom in his young eyes. Make him think she was a murderous AI. She finally released him, gasping, feeling that rush of adrenaline they'd so longed for.

"What the hell," he croaked.

"They used to have names for this kind of sex."

She took him inside her and gave him no rest.

TANBO HAD FORGOTTEN the intensity of desire one body feels for another. Or more correctly, she'd never known it, this glory of the flesh. It was once said by a philosopher of the twenty-first century, "When our culture is based on physical satisfaction rather than spiritual enlightenment, we become finite." She'd forgotten who said it, for he was, indeed, finite.

Noah's body responded to hers in an intricate dance of the flesh, and Tanbo reveled in it. Her small insistences of domination were met with weak resistance. She commanded him completely. This was not the vulgar humping of virtual entities cloaked in electrostatic approximations. Every cell in this body answered her will, produced a chemical elixir of hormones encoded with emotion, a magical concoction designed by the creators to shape a new soul, to give birth to a new mind, one of their own.

They lay together, sweet exhaustion like a damp cloud upon them.

Her stomach growled. It seemed she had just eaten, yet this body demanded more. She sent for some fruit, and they sat together at a table and ate, cooled by the breeze created by the waterfall outside. The sugars burst upon her tongue, a strong flavor like almond and rose mixed. Luxuriant. Ephemeral.

Despite the work necessary to prepare for downloads of her chosen, Tanbo was overcome with weariness.

"Sleep," Noah said. "Our investors won't arrive for some time." He'd already gotten back into bed. "Remember sleep? You spent half your day sleeping when you were alive."

His lie was like a physical slap. She'd never slept. Not until now.

She drifted away from him on a sweet, gravity-less sea.

This sleep was not the minimized running of background programs, but true sleep. Her brain altered its wavelengths, and she was carried to a world beyond the Real and the Virtual, to a place shared with the creators. Noah was there. He wore the armor of kendo and was sparring with Ru Shi. He held a short staff in his hands. Some part of her knew what that staff was called —a tanbo.

26

THE MINDFUL BEAST

2345-02-27 Earth Standard, Shivi Desh, Varanasi

MAYPOLE SUCKED in a lungful of searing cold air.

Oxygen slapped her brain awake, and the stench of flesh assaulted her nostrils. She tried to move her arms and found them shackled. The restraints bit into her wrists. As the view before her cleared, a blade of light stabbed her eyes and burrowed into her brain. Her skin was on fire. Skin. What skin? Everything was pain. If this was death, she would prefer digital life.

Squinting against the glare, several dark shapes appeared opposite her. She worked to focus on them as one of them screamed, a high-pitched howl that repeated and faded away to a whisper. The creature threw itself against the shackles, and plumage fluttered from it.

She'd just died the real death. She'd felt it. The consuming silence of non-being, the absence of electrical stimuli, her sensorium gone, complete severance from the data streams of the Black Stack.

Oblivion. Her backup files had to be fried. If this was some kind of twisted afterlife, she was disappointed in god's programmers.

With her vision clearing, she saw four creatures bound to the walls as she was.

Golden, diurnal eyes met hers. *What the fuck?* those eyes cried out.

The last thing she remembered was a gladiator calling her "Cupcake." He had a trident and . . .

She tried to speak. Instead of words, a low, trilling growl came from her throat. Her many limbs were covered in blue-green plumage. Their proboscises were anchored under her skin and gave her an itchy feeling. Dear God, she was a hellion. They were all hellions.

"Now, now," a voice crooned. "You have no translator just yet. Stop all this racket."

From her creature's towering height, Maypole looked down at the holographically shrouded robotic entity that was speaking. She'd recognize Judah Krane even without any ID apps. A standard nondescript persona wearing a devilish red goatee and a contrived French accent.

"Welcome to the Big Dipper mine," Krane said. "You'll be put to work soon enough. If you do good by me, I'll do good by you. That's all there is to it."

She tried to speak again and belched out more alien sounds.

What was he mining here? She thought he was an amalgam and that this was a test lab for Noah Dutro's download experiments.

"Food, safety will be yours for honest work. Your identity I keep to myself." He looked up into Maypole's beastly face. "You're dead as far as the Hall of Justice is concerned."

Lemkos must have transferred her mindware to Krane the same way he did Elijah's and the others. But how long would it be before Noah Dutro discovered that she was hiding in his own lab?

Another hellion awoke beside her, screaming and thrashing as the others had. A mech assistant touched it with a pole, and the agitated hellion convulsed and went silent. The plumage on Maypole's body prickled and rose as an echo of that shock coursed through her.

"No outbursts," Judah said. "We'll get you working quick enough.

"Your body, your hellion, will take some getting used to—a small, primal part of the hellion's mind is still in there with you, stored as muscle-memory. Your mind runs the biology, but your host might whisper in your ear now and then. Hellions communicate sub-vocally, so you will experience sensations and thoughts that may seem to come from those around you. You'll learn to control them with time."

He stopped pacing. With his hands on his hips, he proclaimed, "Bottom line here: you are free of the Black Stack, my friends. Welcome to a new life. I'm Judah Krane, your savior."

But judging from the shackles, they were far from free.

"It's important that you be able to speak," Krane said. "Yet I expect you to speak only when spoken to. The utterings of the hellions are not translatable without an interface. This will be installed shortly, and your training will begin."

She felt a rush of panic and threw herself against the restraints. There was something waking inside her, some suppressed program, garbled images of leaping from a treetop, soaring over a rocky gorge. Running and leaving family behind, those she loved. Of nets and projectiles that injected a sedative.

Override.

Forcing her own thoughts to the fore, she pushed the beast's into the dark. But the mind wasn't simply housed in the circuitry of a brain, it was part of the entire being.

The remaining two hellions roused from their download stupor. Had they all been executed today? Where had these minds come from?

An android guard was moving from one to the other, injecting something under their skin. When it was her turn, there was a sharp stabbing pain in her neck and then it was over. If she was like the others, a micro-translator would be nestled in amongst the plumage around their necks, just like the one Elijah the Hairless had worn. It felt like it rested just above her vocal cords.

"Fuck!" the hellion beside her shouted. "I have rights! What the hell is going on?"

Applying the wand that certainly delivered a hefty shock, Judah Krane silenced the hellion. When he let go of the trigger, the beast continued to convulse.

"Speak when spoken to," Krane repeated. "Anyone else?"

They were unshackled one at a time. Each hellion in turn dropped to four limbs their tails slapping each other as they negotiated the open door that led to a rocky corridor. They must be inside the mine. The same hellion who had been so agitated lunged for the android guard. The weapon it used this time was not a shock stick but a gun.

The blast punched through Maypole. She stopped breathing and crumpled. The others did the same.

But one hellion fell, convulsed, and died.

Krane laughed. "Get up. Your turn will come."

The breeze coming from the ventilation grills swirled the plumage that had been dislodged. When the feathery things alighted, they moved on barely visible legs, like walking sticks. Several climbed up Maypole's legs and nestled among the other plumage, pushing their way under the downy covering until they reached her skin. There, they bit in with a sharp, stinging prick that rewarded her with a rush of endorphins, causing a weird calmness that countered the rising panic she felt. She was trapped in the body of an ostrich-dragon, and there was nothing she could do about it.

Did Lemkos think he was doing her a favor? Or was the favor for himself? Afraid to let her go, afraid to be alone?

Depending on how much time had passed since her arena match, Lemkos and Martine would be launching an attack on the Monastery which was less than two kilometers upriver from this location. If she could get out of here . . .

She surrendered to the endorphins and vowed to do as she was told. For now.

Even on fours limbs, the hellions were taller than Judah Krane. Maypole fantasized about snapping his head from his neck with her multiple rows of dental thorns. That would end things fast enough. But it would only be temporary. He would just be rebooted.

Her long, supple neck swiveled nicely, allowing her a three-sixty field of view. Her vision was more acute than any VR vision, with colors she'd never perceived even in the wildest Realms of the Black Stack. The seams of the walls stood out as vibrant chartreuse against the gray and rust of the metallic panel. She might be seeing a spectral breakdown of the bulkhead's material, she thought.

The five beasts were herded down a corridor.

Her movement became less calculated as she stopped trying to control every step and allowed the flesh she wore to use its own muscle memory.

The corridor was as cold as the chamber where she'd awakened. Maybe the comfort zone for hellions was cold, or maybe the downloading of mindware required depressed temperatures. Passing several doors that were dilated shut, she perceived evidence of heat leaking from them in the form of infrared, which Maypole saw as a unique, indescribable color. No wonder hellions could hunt in total darkness. They passed a closed room from which a cacophony of screams and growls issued. Maypole hesitated before the door until a guard threatened to prod her with the electric wand.

Of course, there must be more of them, more genetically modified animals that could be downloaded. By the sound of it, many more.

Their destination appeared to be the fortified outer works of the mine where equipment worked noisily to separate whatever they were mining.

"Diamondoid," Krane said as if reading her mind. "The biggest producer on Varanasi."

Diamondoid, also known as adamantane, was the basis for all nanomachines—replicators, assemblers, and delivery systems. It could be purified from crude oil and coal that was formed at specific pressures or synthesized from other constituents of coal. Since Krane was the property of Rishi Corp, this mine was theirs as well. That gave them a private supply of the valuable stuff.

It was bright day outside, sunlight flooding the deep floor of the gorge and a thousand waterfalls cascading down the cliff faces. The thaw was here.

The android in charge of their orientation explained that the mining was done by robots. The hellions were used strictly for security, for ranging outside the walls.

"You're looking for other hellions, mostly," the android said. It was an old, beat-up model with an upgraded communicator. "The hellion tribes in this gorge have been waging an orchestrated war against us for some time. They are brutal and capable of dismembering our mining mechs with great efficiency." The discolored silicone lips no longer moved in sync with the voice, rather wiggling obscenely. "Kill them before they get to the walls. Simple."

It paused, clearly receiving some streaming instructions.

"Correction," it said. "Battle-bots are incoming. Samsara models are to be eliminated."

In that instant, most of Maypole's list of questions were answered. The timing was right.

A general grumbling arose from the five other hellions.

"Fight? Jesus, how did I even get here?" one said.

"Blood, blood, blood . . . we have blood." It was becoming increasingly clear that saving bit-rotten deviants and criminals slated for wiping was a cottage industry. Maypole remembered the one named Allison who'd torn off her print's arms.

The newly downloaded hellions joined a dozen or more others in a large circular holding area outside the mine entrance. It reminded Maypole of the arena. The blue lights at their throats flashed eerily.

Moving around the enclosure, she called softly, "Elijah?"

If she could find the one she'd met before, maybe he could tell her more.

She was answered by a nudge to her backside by a horned head.

"You're Elijah?"

"Who wants to know?"

"Camber Maypole. I met you here about two weeks ago." *Met* was a generous description of what had transpired. "Your friend Allison tore the arms off my holo-print."

"Ah, Lemkus's friend. I see he cashed in on your mindware too, huh?"

"Not exactly," she said. "Do you want to get out of this place?"

His amber diurnal eyes blinked at her. "Out? Are you fuckin' nuts?"

"Can't we just run?"

The sound he made might be construed as a laugh. The voice translator was cheap, the synth voice monotone. "You run, you pass the boundary. Zap, you're dead. Download happens all over again. You get a shiny new hellion."

"But he's sending us out to fight battle-bots. How? With what weapons?"

Elijah twisted his reptilian head around and snapped two rows of nasty dental thorns. "Just like we did to you and that asshole, Lemkus. Tear off their limbs. If that doesn't work, there's always a basher." He indicated the spiked club in his fist. The preferred weapon of hellion warriors. But Maypole felt something yielding, something understanding in the mind of this hellion. He was not as fearsome as he wanted her to think he was.

"But look," she tried to figure out a way to present the problem that would earn his sympathy, but doubted it was possible. "There are humans in the Monastery. That's why the Samsara bots are coming. To protect them from Rishi Corp."

"Humans, you say? The colonists?"

"Yeah."

"I'll be damned, they made it? I forgot they were even coming."

"Noah Dutro is downloading the Vested into the colonists'

bodies, just like this." She indicated the massive hellion body she wore.

"And I'm supposed to care?"

"You want to get out of this?" She indicated her hellion body again.

"You speak for the Hall of Justice now, do you? You can forgive my crimes?"

"I'm not talking about forgiveness," Maypole said with all the emphasis allowed by the synth voice. "Weren't you after killing off the Vested? Didn't you blow three nodes of the Black Stack all to hell?"

"That was a hundred years ago."

"And the Vested are still here, living off the desperation of the refugees just like they always have. And now they're taking human beings for their own. Don't you want to finish what you started?"

"In this?" Elijah indicated the beast he wore.

"I know what these things can do," Maypole argued. "We can get inside that place. They'll all be there. Every Vested on Varanasi." She hoped that was true. Who else would Dutro plan to download into the colonists?

"What about our kill switch?"

"We'll figure it out. Can you talk these . . . guys into joining us?" She indicated the others, two of whom had already started a fight with each other.

"Who do you think I am? Jesus?"

MAYPOLE'S first trip outside the walls of the mine resulted in almost instant death. The battle-bots sent by Martine were killing the hellions before they even saw the things. Maypole's idea of getting close enough to send a message to Martine evaporated with every blast of the bots' missiles.

The second time out, she located the boundary of the hellion's patrol the hard way. The collar that enabled them to speak also delivered a heart-stopping shock when they crossed the boundary of their patrol area.

Maypole's third hellion body was less cooperative than the first two and required more focus to override its unconscious controls.

Elijah had led the others south where the Samsara bots were moving beside the river. He'd managed to convince Judah Krane that it would be best to catch them by surprise, which required an extension of the allowable patrol boundary so they might reach them.

From the highest branches of a tree where she'd been sunning her plumage, Maypole finally saw a small band of battle-bots moving swiftly through a stand of spider trees.

She launched herself. With her heart in her mouth, she surrendered to freefall and waited before spreading her leathery wings, feeling the weightless plummet of her new body into the maw of the chasm of Shivi Desh. The impact of the air jolted her as she allowed herself to be buoyed by the oxygen-rich air. The wind through her plumage susurrated softly as the dense air and low gravity made her soaring feel like slow motion.

Technically, she couldn't fly. But this was the next best thing.

She followed the patrol of mechs, looking for an opportunity. It took her most of a standard day to get her claws on one of them. She found it hiding in a thicket, undergoing an update. Taking advantage of the thirty seconds of immobility, she had the limbs off and all launchers disabled before it could wake.

"You're going to send this message to Martine Sommer." Maypole positioned her dragon face in front of the visual sensors and said, "Martine, it's Camber Maypole. The hellions are ready to help you if you'll agree to set them all free. We need to take out Judah Krane and see what he's got in that mine. But we need your help. Martine. Stop killing us, for god's sake. Please."

She decided not to tell Martine that some of the hellions were not exactly on board.

27

THE LONG FALL

2345-02-28 *Earth Standard, aboard the* Vera Rubin

SERAPH REMINDED HIMSELF TO BREATHE. He was weightless, nudging his seat restraints as the shuttle glided slowly from the docking bay of the *Vera Rubin*. The external cameras on the dropship gave him and the landing party a view of Vera they'd never seen before. They'd been living and dying inside of a battered tin can for generations. The hull looked like it had been sandblasted. He was surprised the material hadn't been consumed completely, leaving them exposed to hard vacuum. The recent wound to Torus-2 was covered in a swarm of repair mechs that clung and floated like insects.

Less than two minutes after their launch, a second dropship was spat out of Vera's belly. As planned, the empty decoy would head for a second location in the Yamuna basin and, according to acting-captain Bora, attract NASA security forces with its mayday beacon. The meeting Seraph and TJ had attended in Martine's castle had convinced them that NASA would not help in this mission to recover the captive colonists, but Seraph had argued they certainly would not kill them either. Still, Niall Bora wanted NASA out of the way, and he believed they'd follow his decoy and buy the landing party some time.

Just before launch, Seraph and Huang had printed the crash code, one for each of them. Seraph had stared at the hatched image of the angel then held it up to the drawing John Lauretta had made on the last page of his journal. So similar. But Lauretta's angel was blindfolded. It held two swords and the words "a dream" written across the bottom. Vera's angel was not blindfolded and from its eyes came strings of hashed dots and dashes that mixed with the geometric shapes around it. He tucked it between the pages of the Hello Kitten journal and zipped it inside his EV suit.

Huang had assured him that most codes like this would interrupt local operating systems, nothing more. But if he was honest with himself, he was prepared to wipe every last mind on Varanasi to save TJ and Rain.

The dropships had little stealth capability outside of comm silence, so Huang had disabled the transponder on this ship and made sure the decoy was broadcasting loud and clear.

Huang's eyes showed none of the fear he felt as weightlessness gave way to the sensation of falling.

The volunteers barely filled two benches in the dropship. Ali Mansour, the fuel specialist, Panos Karagiannis, the planetary specialist, along with sixteen others had loved ones that were taken. If Maypole and Lemkos didn't keep their part of the deal, it would be eighteen fragile humans against an army of mechs. But everyone on this dropship was ready for a fight, and capable of firing weapons—all but Seraph. His left arm still hung lifelessly from a sling that held it tightly against his body. He hoped the five sharpshooters would make up for his deficiencies. It had been easy to persuade her that he deserved a spot on her team. After all, she was the one who'd shot him. It was as close as he'd ever get to an apology.

From her seat beside him, Huang gave Seraph a look. She

gripped his hand, and he felt a warm calm seep into him. "It's going to be okay, friend. No matter what happens."

"Yeah." He squeezed her hand in return. Local day would last four more standard days, giving them time to complete the mission.

In addition to the sharpshooters, there were four security personnel from T-1 and ten sec-mechs.

Their guns would be essentially useless against the Rishi mechs and holo-prints, but there were other threats. Living ones. Vera had done a good job educating the colonists on the dangers of their new home but had failed to include the disembodied minds who'd lived there for centuries. The native fauna was nothing by comparison.

With little more information than the Monastery coordinates, their dropship began its fiery fall toward the surface. The g forces pinned Seraph to his seat. He wasn't sure what would happen first, vomit or black out. Maybe both at the same time. He began to worry he might drown in it.

Huang handed him a bag.

He used it.

On the screen before them, the view was smeared by the heat of atmospheric drag. Still, Varanasi grew larger, the details more distinct. A glacier-bound land, the uplands were rent by brilliant blue-green veins of deep chasms. The ragged coastlines rose from a webwork of vast turquoise seas. They approached the terminator to find Uttar Pradesh and the gorge known as Shivi Desh in bright daylight.

The ship spun, repositioning the ablative shields, and the view rotated away to stars.

"How close will we be to the Monastery when we land?" It was Canada, one of the sharpshooters. Canada had proven himself to be their best shot, especially with projectile ammo, which Huang and Bora had theorized would be the best against mechs with EM shields. Canada looked as green as Seraph felt, his head canted back, his eyes on the hull above.

"That depends on where the safest landing spot might be,"

Seraph explained. "Navigation will put us down as close as possible outside the chasm with the least chance of detection."

"Great," Canada moaned.

Martine Sommer had been inside the Monastery once and had given them what information she could. The elevator from the landing pad on the rim above the gorge would be heavily guarded and inaccessible without a passcode. Bora had decided that the best way in was to rappel down the cliff to one of the open terraces.

Huang sat quietly beside Seraph, still holding his hand. No trace of emotion crossed her face, but Seraph knew she was thinking of Baakos no less than he was thinking of Rain and TJ. Huang's other hand had found the seedpod she always wore around her neck. He wondered what her fireseed had told her about this reckless mission.

He touched the journal absently, realizing that it had become a similar talisman for him. He felt the vague outline of the little Hello Kitten book inside the breast pocket of his armored EV suit.

As the dropship took on a gliding flight, the cameras blinked on, revealing endless kilometers of rugged glaciers. The ice glowed a blinding white in the reflected sunlight. The convex curvature of the planet was so foreign it made him feel dizzy, and panic simmered in his chest. His breathing was rapid and shallow. The horizon was so far away. The sky beyond that horizon was dominated by the banded pastel storms of Majriti, the limb of which seemed so close, he felt like he could touch it.

A herd of creatures fled the approaching ship, darker pixels against the bright white-blue surface of the glacier. Moving as one unit, avoiding crevasses, they flowed like rice grains into a mill. Someone whooped for joy at the sight, but Seraph thought of Rain. Had she seen it? Or had she been too terrified to look?

The dropship set down gently on a narrow ledge of white-powdered rock. Snow.

Varanasi had been thoroughly, though remotely, explored, and NASA had assured them the conditions were hospitable. The O_2 was

5 percent higher than on earth, and the pathogens here were all built to attack native fauna, not aliens. Theoretically.

Through the eyes of the external cameras, they watched the thrusters clear snow from beneath the ship leaving a smooth surface of orange sandstone blotched with neon green lichen.

Rapid breathing, sighs, laughter, cries of joy or fear—all these sounds came from the team. The air became instantly cool and humid as the internal air recyclers switched to exterior air. The extra oxygen was like a blast of caffeine and made Seraph's lungs tingle. Or maybe it was the 0.002 percent xenon. And the smells, Jesus, the smells were amazing. Seraph had no basis to compare them.

Canada vomited into a bag and was quickly joined by others. Seraph was glad he'd emptied his stomach earlier.

"Take your time," Bora said. "You need to adjust to the atmospheric mix and the gravity. This ain't no spinning barrel, kesos. Your inner ear is tuned to spin. The ground will feel like it's moving under you."

External cameras showed a clear perimeter as far as they could see. The edge of the chasm was ninety meters away. The airlock opened, and a blast of icy air slapped Seraph's face. He was here. And so was Rain.

The stairs descended.

The team hovered at the open hatch, fitting their helmets and testing comms and heads-up displays, gathering packs and weapons. The visors on their helmets could be sealed in the event of an emergency, but the ship's AI had already decided the atmosphere was harmless, so most kept them open, inhaling deeply as Seraph did.

Niall Bora pulled on a backpack and slung two guns over his shoulders. He closed his visor and started down the stairs.

"Wait for my signal," he called over his shoulder.

He took the steps slowly, one long gun sweeping in an arc across the view. When his feet found the ground, he folded up as if he had no strength. He hit the ground, cursing, then struggled back to his feet.

It wasn't until the others followed that they understood.

It reminded Seraph of the drunken spins. It took all his strength to stand, to focus on an unmoving object at a distance. He tried never to close his eyes.

The azure sky stretched from horizon to horizon in a convex arc. Their shipboard world had curved in on itself; this curved out in a great, frightening expanse. As they stepped across the icy ground, Seraph felt more and more like he would fall into the gorge if he even glanced down at his feet. His breathing was rapid, matching his heart rate.

"We're here!" Yazmin cried to the sky. A mech specialist from Retro, she was not much older than Carl and would oversee the drones and spiders they would send for recon. She strode beside Seraph, a smile turned to the rising sun. She seemed to have no trouble with real gravity.

"Ma, take a look at us!" she cried to the sun. "We're here!"

A strong, warmer wind topped the rim of the chasm. A cacophony of sounds emanated from the gorge. Windeaters, likely.

"The thaw is going to be on us soon. We have to be quick." Panos was the planetary specialist. He'd been training his whole life for this.

On the distant rim of the gorge, Seraph could see an ice sheet that must have been a hundred meters thick. It was melting, sending ribbons of water that cascaded down the cliff face. The bottom of the chasm promised an ecosystem rich and warm compared to the frozen wastes of the plains above.

"Two kilometers to the bottom," Huang said, accessing the GPS on her heads-up.

"Straight down," Yazmin pointed out. "Tell me we're not going down yet. I need to warm up to this idea."

"Not yet," Bora said. "We got three kilometers to cover to get to the Monastery."

That was the distance halfway around the torus, Seraph thought. There was no comparison. What might take him a few minutes to run would take hours here.

"Send a drone ahead," Bora told Yazmin. "Let's see what we're walking into."

Yazmin pulled a small oval object from her pack. The thing unfolded rotor blades and launched from her hand.

Bora and Seraph crowded around her, gazing at her palmcomm, watching with the eyes of the drone.

The sun was high enough to reveal the terrain from the drone's point of view, casting long, deep shadows. Seraph imagined he could see the sea in the distance, but realized it was just the fading crescent of Majriti, dim and translucent in the daylight, peeking from the horizon.

It looked like the icy rock they traversed would soon give way to a glacier that overhung the edge of the gorge. Rivulets of meltwater were streaming from it, glistening in the dawn and echoing an eternal hiss and splash that seemed to come from everywhere at once. White downy things floated on the updrafts from the gorge and streamed out across the plains that surrounded them.

"Seedpods," Panos said, leaning over Seraph's shoulder. "They ride the warm air currents for tens of kilometers until they hit the mountains where they root." He pointed east.

"How are we going to cross that?" Huang asked, pointing to the image of the glacier on her palmcomm.

"One step at a time," Bora said.

They reached the glacier within an hour and paused for a break. The protein cakes tasted like some of the food Seraph had had in Retro, a mash of cricket protein, sugar, and peanuts. Not much else.

"The glacial floes fill cracks in the rocky ground," Panos said to an interested crowd. He talked between bites. "Over time, these floes freeze and melt, splitting the stone of the cliffs and forming new tributaries of the great chasm. They're like ice wedges."

"They're traps for anything on foot," Seraph said. He'd seen vids of mountain climbers on Earth. He stared at the wall of blue ice that faced them. "This is crazy."

"Yeah, especially during the thaw."

"What if we drop down?" Seraph asked.

"Down? Into the gorge?" Panos said.

"Yeah, walk across the bottom."

"Well, yeah, we could do that. But the flood has started. It's gonna be some soggy ground, not to mention the hellions hunt down there."

"What did we bring these for?" Seraph patted the handgun at his belt.

"Then we have to find a way back up to the Monastery," Bora said. He'd been skulking, listening to them from ten paces away. He sat with his back against a rock, his angular face turned to the warm sun. "It's easier to drop down than to climb up."

"Unless we all fall into a crevasse and die," Seraph pointed out.

"Are you going to give me trouble, Stone?"

Seraph held his hands out in a gesture of appeasement. "I'm just bringing up possible problems, that's all."

The possible problems became actual real fast.

Once they had managed to start across the glacier, the ice gave way under Huang, dropping her ten meters to an ice cave where a waterfall coursed beside her. They dropped ropes and pulled her up. She was okay, just scraped up pretty bad and shivering uncontrollably. The medic got out a thermal blanket and wrapped her up.

Seraph held her tightly, trying to impart his own warmth. Their breaths fumed and mingled in the cold.

"I'm fine," she said through chattering teeth.

"No, you're not."

Bora was standing over them, gazing down with hands on his hips. "You have ten minutes. Then we get moving."

"I think she's going to need more than ten," Seraph said.

"You got ten. She can go back to the ship and wait there."

Seraph started to get to his feet, but Huang clutched at his arm. "I'll be ready," she said.

"I know you will. Maybe I won't."

Seraph followed Bora and tapped him on the shoulder.

Bora spun to face him.

Seraph said, "Can I talk to you?"

Seraph wasn't sure if Bora was squinting at him or at the bright sun. Bora nodded and, scrunching through the brittle ice, took the minimum number of steps away from the group to give them privacy.

"Say it," he told Seraph.

"It's taken us three hours to go maybe a hundred meters. At this rate, we'll kill ourselves before the joboxes do."

Bora curled his lips into a false smile. "You think you know what you're talking about, don't you?"

"None of us knows what we're talking about. Not even you."

"One thing I do know," Bora said, crossing his arms over his chest and puffing it out, "I know you modified a pollinator bot and left it in that orange tree in TJ's office."

Talk about strange timing for this kind of confrontation. None of Seraph's failed surveillance mattered now. The only thing that mattered was they didn't end up at the bottom of a crevasse.

"Lemon tree," Seraph corrected. "And what does that have to do with you trying to kill us?"

"I let it go. You want to know why?"

"Not really, but I have a feeling you're going to tell me."

"I wanted you to see what we had, her and me," Bora said. His face had gotten way too close. "You lost her, keso, and it was the easiest way to let you know what was happening."

"I guess I should thank you then?"

"Listen." Bora licked his full, chapped lips. "I care about TJ and Rain as much as you do, but—"

Seraph's one good fist landed perfectly. Bora's teeth cut his knuckles, his spit sprayed Seraph's face. Niall Bora went skating across the ice. As he tried to regain his footing, he landed hard on his ass.

"No," Seraph said. "You don't."

TWO MORE PEOPLE fell through the ice. They recovered one. The other wasn't as lucky. She'd fallen so far there was no way to reach her. After she failed to respond to all comms, they kept going without her.

A flock of windeaters waited for them when they dropped down from the glacier. The creatures failed to scatter and had a hungry look, so Bora shot one with a projectile weapon. The sound echoed repeatedly through the chasm. Smart man, that one.

The plumage the windeater had been hosting launched from the body in a cloud of colorful sails. They alighted on people, who brushed them off. All but Panos. He stripped off his EV suit to his waist, baring his arms and hairy chest, laughing as he did. At first, the clouds of things passed by him. Then one settled on his shoulder, then another. It was as if the first one signaled the others that this was a living thing they were flying by.

"You think that's a good idea?" Huang asked.

"You're a dotty bastard," Yazmin told him. "Does it hurt?"

"They have built-in anesthesia in their bite that apparently works on us too. Not poisonous," Panos replied. "They're purely photosynthetic. So I'll be getting a steady stream of sugar while you guys have to eat that packaged crap we brought from the ship."

In minutes, his back and forearms were covered in a forest of feathers.

"Woohoo, gonna get me some photosynthetic food, kesos."

The blue-black blood of the downed windeater stained the snow. The smell was metallic, like any other blood. And it would bring other predators soon.

Yazmin handled the ropes and anchors, sending her spider mechs down to tie the ropes off in the trees near the floor of the gorge. Far below, a drone's camera revealed a steaming jungle. Tangles of roots extended from trees like webs.

"Like mangroves," Panos said. "Spider trees have multiple trunks that send out a network of prehensile roots. They'll be starting their migration soon."

To Seraph, they looked like gnarled hands, blue-gray fingers clawing the soil, complete with joint-like knots—five finger-like trunks to each tree that joined up in the main trunk.

"The migration. Is that good or bad?" Seraph asked.

"It means flood season," Panos said. "When the planet moves closer to the sun during Majriti's orbit around Upsilon Andromedae, about 5 percent of the ice pack melts. Fast. NASA calls it 'spring thaw,' but I'd say it's more like apocalyptic thaw. That's why the glacier is so dangerous now. The trees migrate as it all begins."

"How long 'til that?"

"It looks like it's already started," Panos said.

"Hey, hey," Yazmin said, and held her palmcomm out to those near her. "Look at this."

The bouncing, erratic view from the drone at the bottom of the chasm showed a beast larger than three men. It appeared to be carrying the drone into the canopy of the trees. The beast had a long slender neck, a head with protrusions like horns, and in addition to its four walking limbs were a pair of wings folded against its sides. It was covered with plumage, the same color and lancet shape as those on the trees, providing perfect camouflage.

"A hellion," Seraph said.

They sent the sec-mechs down first. From their feed, Bora watched the first engagement. One sec-mech went dark before the hellions backed off.

"Where'd they go?" Seraph asked.

"It was like they just gave up and went away," Huang added.

"My mechs scared them off. Let's go," Bora commanded.

It took less than an hour for all of them to rappel down the cliff face. Seraph required help, which Huang gave, effectively lowering him on a makeshift pulley system. When he reached the bottom, he found the others resting in a thicket between the mossy knees of the spider trees. As Seraph approached them, he became aware that the trees were watching him. Their branches moved with a gentle susurration, turning to follow him. He finally located their eye spots near the end of each twig.

He had no more settled down in the cool moss than a sec-mech chimed with an alarm. He turned to see two hellions watching them from the tree line.

"Don't shoot," a genderless synthesized voice said. "We're not hellions."

Bora fired a warning shot at their feet.

They didn't flinch.

"I repeat," the voice said, "we're human. Like you."

"Like hell you are."

Bora hadn't gotten the next shot off when one of the things dropped on him from the tree above. In no time, it had the gun out of his hand and Bora pinned to the ground with one clawed fist. Its neck snaked around until its amber eyes with triangular pupils were staring right into Seraph's eyes.

"Seraphim Stone. I'm Camber Maypole."

28

THE FOREST WAKES

2345-02-28 *Earth Standard, Shivi Desh, Varanasi*

MARTINE'S BATTLE-BOTS now took commands only from Maypole. She had left most of them in position to attack Judah Krane's mine while she led a small detachment and crossed the river. It was from this direction they'd heard what sounded like a gunshot, like an old-fashioned projectile weapon.

Maypole was not sure she could trust Allison, but Elijah had vouched for her, and as the three approached the boundary of their patrol zone, a high-pitched alarm sounded. It hadn't taken Maypole long to figure out that every hellion was fitted with a subdermal kill-switch which was triggered by attempts to leave their patrol zone. If the boundary was crossed, a lethal shock would be administered, and your mind would be downloaded into another hellion.

The three hellions backed off a few meters, then moved west, hugging the edge of their territory.

"Maybe Martine's mechs. Maybe NASA," Maypole told Elijah.

She'd begun to think of his chiseled, dragon-shaped face as good look-ing. She could even differentiate between the other hellion faces with ease now. The hellion's epigenetic memories peeked through. Maypole knew the hellion Elijah wore had been a seer, a shaman, and Allison's—she had been a healer before Krane had dumped some criminal's mindware into her.

"Rishi weapons don't make no noise," Elijah said, "just the noise of you dying."

As they crept toward the base of the cliff, Maypole smelled them before she heard them. The scent of an animal, unrecognizable to her hellion's inventory of scents. It caused fear at first, then an adrenaline rush as if her body prepared for a fight.

Creeping forward through the canopy of trees, she saw a clutch of holo-prints sitting on rocks in a thicket, their boots covered in mud. There were at least a dozen of them with a small team of NASA security mechs. But they were old school, like the ones they had on the ship when it launched . . .

The ones that were standing looked strangely proportioned, taller than most prints she'd known, with legs like walking sticks. They all wore rust-colored bodysuits, like EV suits. One guy rested a large rifle on his hip. He had bright yellow bands on his arms that Maypole instantly recognized as rank stripes. And those were the suits she had used during launch crew training.

Not prints at all.

"They're from the ship." The realization was like a blow. Of course they were. Seraph had asked for coordinates. They'd cut a dropship loose somehow.

"What, what, what, what?" Allison chirped.

"That thing's biomass," Elijah whispered with astonishment.

"Nom, nom," Allison said.

"Hold on to her," Maypole told Elijah. "I'm going in closer."

"Talk, talk, talk, then, eat, eat, eat," Allison vocalized.

Maypole crept through the canopy of trees until she was directly above them. Elijah stepped into the clearing, hailing them as if he were a crewmember. As she drew closer, Maypole saw waves of infrared emanating from them. Living. Breathing. Humans. She smelled sweat and fear and blood. Weakness and the surety of death oozed from them.

The guy with the stripes fired on Elijah as Maypole dropped from the tree. She pinned him easily and had the gun in one of her clawed fists before he could fire.

"We're as human as you guys. Put your guns away."

One of them, a man sitting under a tree with his helmet off, she knew. She'd seen him on vid. He looked very much like the avatar she'd met at Martine's castle. The details of his face were distorted by the wide range of colors Maypole was able to see. His skin appeared to her eyes as aqua-gold.

She released the officer, who scrambled away, then she held out her long forelimbs in a universal posture of surrender. "Seraphim Stone. I am Camber Maypole."

His eyes were wide, his mouth hanging open.

"You're Rishi," the officer on the ground said. He pulled a second weapon from his belt.

Leaping six meters from a standstill, Allison had him before he could get a shot off.

"Allison, let that man up and don't touch him again," Camber said.

The green serpent of Allison's tongue coiled from her mouth and tasted the man's face before she let him go. "Nom, nom."

The officer scrambled to his feet and wisely put some distance between himself and Allison. "What the hell was that?" He pointed at Allison.

"She's a rotter," Maypole said. "Violently decohered, from her record. But she's a great fighter. She can rip mechs limb from limb, and we need that now, if, as it appears, you are going to attempt to get inside the Monastery."

Maypole turned back to Seraph, who'd gotten to his feet and joined the circle of people forming around the three hellions. One arm was lashed to his torso in a sling. He held a gun trained on her as they all did.

"Great idea, Maypole," Elijah said. "Help the people and get popped for it."

"You're not popped yet," Maypole said.

She found and held Seraph's gaze. "Look, we are downloaded mindware, just like they intend to do to your friends. We want to help you. It's just that Allison gets a little . . . excited."

Seraph lowered his gun and the others followed.

"Lt. Stone, Martine's mechs are capable and ready," Maypole said, "and under my command."

"You *know* this thing?" the ranking officer asked Seraph.

Seraph nodded. "Yes. She's a medical doctor. She was on the launch crew. She was the one who found the enhanced embryos. This is Lieutenant Bora," he told Maypole. The look on his face said that standing that close was hurting them both.

Bora lowered his weapon but kept one hand on it.

"You've been in the Monastery?" Seraph asked. "We tried to position ourselves above, so we could rappel to one of the terraces but—"

"But there's a wall of ice above it," Maypole said.

"Yes. But you—you were downloaded into that," he indicated her bulky physique, "in the Monastery?"

"No." It took some explaining—how she'd gotten from the arena, charged with attempted murder, to her hellion host in Judah Krane's mine. The people listened with rapt attention.

"Martine's mechs tried to kill us," Maypole explained. "But once she understood we were allies, she gave me control of her army. They're waiting by the river. And we have over a dozen hellions, like us. Together, we can get in. But first—"

"First what?" Bora asked with suspicion.

"We need to take down the mine. If we don't, we'll be fighting on two fronts."

"We need all the help we can get," Seraph said, and the others agreed.

Niall Bora gave them a brief rundown of their plan—if you could call it that. It was more of a suicide mission, which they'd already botched by dropping to the floor of the gorge, rather than to the terraces of the Monastery.

Maypole couldn't stop looking at Seraph Stone. She could fix that arm swaddled against his body. From the total immobility of his hand and fingers, she concluded it was nerve damage. She needed her surgical suite and some neural patches.

When Bora finished talking, Maypole spoke, trying to add some human inflection to her synth voice, unsuccessfully. "Inside the mine, there are weapons, explosives, and more hellions. No offense, but your weapons will do little against Rishi's mechs. We can arm you with current weapons from the mine."

"There's no time for that," Seraph said. "By the time we take the mine, the Vested could be downloaded into our people."

"Martine's not likely to let the Vested get here that easily," Maypole said. "There's one landing pad, up on the rim, and I'd bet it's a battleground right now. Samsara mechs against Rishi. The Vested would have a hard time landing a flyer there."

"Why would they have to *get* here? They should have access to the Black Stack from virtual, or anywhere, right?" The question came from a woman with the name *Huang* written on her helmet. Unlike Seraph, she'd kept it on.

"The system is local only," Elijah said, "independent. Like us, each mindware package has to be stored on the local mainframe. The Vested have to be copied into the library in the Monastery before they can be downloaded. Copied from a local file. All of *us*," he motioned to Maypole and Allison, "exist in that supercooled motherfucker in the deepest part of the mine. We belong to Judah Krane. If we don't take the mine first, Krane can blow the system and erase our backups."

Seraph took a step forward, his brow furrowed. He looked like he wanted to say something, but instead, he shot a look at Bora and crossed his good arm over his injured one, pursing his lips.

Maypole examined Bora. He licked his split lip and stared at the ground. What was going on here?

Huang nodded, her eyes focused on the forest as if deep in thought.

"You need our help to take out the mine?" The question came from Bora.

Elijah laughed. "No. You need *us* to take out the Monastery."

"Then we take out the mine first." Seraph shouldered his second weapon awkwardly with one arm. "Let's get to it."

"How do you know all this?" Bora asked Elijah with clear suspicion. "The weapons stored in the mine, I mean."

"I've been here a long time, pal. But trust me at your own risk."

Bora deliberated, then said, "Let's go."

The three hellions led the humans to the river where the ranks of battle-bots awaited instruction. It had taken no more than a few minutes for Martine to call off her mechs and turn control over to Maypole. The unit she had assaulted was now Maypole's designated liaison, armless though it was.

"Message Martine," Maypole commanded. "Tell her we have colonists with us. We're going into the mine first."

"Units are ready," the mech said, its synth voice sounding exactly like Maypole's.

As they headed upriver, Seraph walked beside her, looking like a child beside her bulk.

"Can you trust Allison?" he asked.

Maypole gave the hellion equivalent of a shrug. "Allison is a bit-rotten whack job. But Elijah can control her, usually. She's attached herself to him. They knew each other before."

"Before what?"

"Before she lost her mind to bit rot. She refused the patches Rishi was selling to repair the data loss. She said they were implanting mind control software, which in a way, they were. The patches are feel-goods, nothing more. So she opted for insanity rather than the crap Rishi's been feeding us."

"Jesus," Seraph said, glancing back at Allison.

"As long as she's with Elijah, she'll be fine. But I wouldn't get too close, just in case."

Judah Krane had prepared for many eventualities, but an attack by a legion of top-of-the-line battle-bots was not one of them.

The tracking collars around the necks of the three hellions opened the outer gates of the mine automatically. Once open, the hellions stood in the gateway to allow the Samsara bots inside. They charged like mechanical cheetahs. With no more than six mechs lost, they controlled the gate within minutes.

As expected, the android handlers appeared at the mouth of the tunnel system. They activated their onboard weapons and began firing. Outnumbered, the androids were dismembered swiftly by the battle-bots. The one with the floppy lip was the only one left by the time Maypole reached them. A bot was preparing to pull its main controller.

"Hold," she ordered the bot. Then to the android, she said, "Do you want to continue existing?"

"I am programmed to resist."

"Hmmm. So you won't show me how to work the downloader?"

He hesitated, then said, "Negative."

"I'd bet its allegiance to Krane is an alterable subroutine." The voice came from behind Maypole. It was the woman named Huang again. The lights inside her helmet lit up her face. It had been centuries since Maypole had examined the imperfections of middle-age. Huang was lovely, like a house whose style had become precious over time.

"Let me at him, friend." Huang stepped around Maypole's feathered bulk.

From her pack, Huang pulled out a kit filled with things that looked like archaic probes and a rolled polymer keyboard like they used in the old days. With a screwdriver, she popped the access port on the android's neck and inserted some alligator clips.

The silicone eyelids on the android drooped slowly.

"We're going for Krane." Elijah headed down the main corridor. He had the bulk of the battle-bots with him, and Allison, too. "I'm gonna sic Allison on the bastard."

If there was such a thing as smiling for a hellion, she was doing it.

Huang made noises indicating exasperation. After several rapid bursts of keying in code, she induced a short bout of spasms in the android. It finally opened its eyes again.

"Give that a try," Huang said.

"Show us how to use the downloader," Maypole commanded.

The android turned with halting, jerky motions, and led the way through a series of tunnels.

Huang gave Maypole a satisfied smile.

"So you're the one who hacked Vera's nav system."

Huang gave her a proud thumbs up. "Guilty."

"You gave my friend a run for his money. Nice work."

They followed the android to the room Maypole knew so well, the circular download chamber. Empty harnesses hung from the walls. The sound of hellions' muffled screams found their way through the sealed doors from the containment area.

"How many minds do you have on the shelf?" Maypole asked the android.

"Sixteen additional."

"Let's boot up as many as we can. And the rest . . . let them go."

"Let them out?" Huang asked.

"Yes."

"They'll shred us."

"No," Maypole said, "they'll run far and fast."

Huang seemed to be enthralled with the workings of the download system. She watched the android as it manned the controller. Huang's helmet was off, exposing her graying pink hair.

"You're sure this is a good idea?" Huang asked.

"No. But in a fight, one hellion is worth ten of you people."

"'You people?'" Huang turned a poisonous glare toward Maypole. "You used to be 'us people.'"

"I still am." Maypole's synth voice made the words sound sarcastic. She wanted to apologize but knew it was too late for that.

BY THE TIME Elijah found Judah Krane, the amalgam had already started dumping data from the system, including his own mindware. His print was an empty chassis, nothing more, and his mindware was either in the Rishi system or the Black Stack.

"We may run into that bastard again once we get into the Monastery," Elijah reported. They had found the stash of weapons and Bora was now distributing them to the colonists. Blowing the mainframe here was not an option. It was the only location where Maypole's and the other hellions' mindware existed, having been purged from the Black Stack.

While Elijah explained the workings of the Rishi weapons to the colonists, Maypole and the android successfully downloaded all stored mindware into the available modified hellions. It took little convincing to bring the sixteen criminals into their plan. Freedom was worth fighting for. The promise of return to the Black Stack and exoneration was a stretch, but Maypole would do everything possible to see that it was upheld.

"What do we do with him?" Huang asked, nodding at the ancient android assistant standing beside her.

"Leave it," Maypole said.

The look on Huang's face said more than all the words Maypole had heard the woman speak. This was not okay with Huang. Maypole remembered feeling that way once, centuries ago. Caring for androids. Had she changed so much?

"Or bring it with you," she added. "Your call."

Huang instructed the android to follow her. Her eyes flashed up at Maypole as she headed out the narrow tunnel toward the entrance.

When they exited the mine, it was clear the thaw had arrived. Like a hurricane on Earth, it happened when the seasonal conditions were right, and today was that day. A warm wind blew up the gorge from the Ganges Valley a hundred kilometers away. The glaciers were rapidly melting from the plateau above, and a thousand waterfalls wept down the bright sandstone cliffs in deafening torrents. The air was filled with clouds of mist that beaded on their plumage and skin.

"We have to cross the river now," Elijah said, "or we're stuck here 'til summer."

Their little army of sixteen hellions, a legion of Samsara battle-bots, and seventeen human beings made their way down the northern bank of the Alaknanda River to the formation known as the Spiral Towers. This marked the spot where the Monastery was buried in the cliffs on the opposite side of the river. All they had to do was get across.

Maypole had developed a strange kinship with the cells of this hellion body. She felt the lingering mind of the beast. She knew she had been a warrior, that she had killed to protect her family. Though cast out of its brain, information still lingered in the cells of the entire body. Her hellion knew the way across the river. And she trusted it.

Carrying ropes and tackle that the colonists had used to descend the cliffs, she and Elijah headed up the trees that grew along the riverbank. After anchoring one end of their ropes, they spread their leathery wings and sailed across the frothing water like oversized flying squirrels.

It took longer than estimated to move the humans and battle-bots across the water. Already too deep to wade, the battle-bots used internal cables and hooks like harpoons which they shot into trees on the other bank. They needed every hellion they had to assist.

By the time Seraph was ready to cross, the water had risen so it almost met the slack of the rope lines.

Maypole went back for him. No way he could hang on with one arm if his legs hit the water.

She climbed the highest tree and balanced on a limb overhanging the water.

The tree was opening its eyes. If she remembered right, that meant they'd be uprooting soon.

Myriad eyespots formed a symmetrical pattern in the bark of the silver tree in which she was perched. Not quite eyes, they functioned as photoreceptors. As they opened, they brightened to yellowish green with scarlet spots in the center.

She sprang from the tree limb and stretched the membranous wings until the air made a buoyant thrust beneath her sails. She glided to a smooth landing, using her tail to catch a branch on a tree on the opposite bank.

"Come on." She reached a long, clawed hand down to Seraph. "You ever ride a wonky dragon before?"

"Oh, feces." His look could only be described as terror.

But he stepped onto her forearm with his one good hand, and she positioned him on her back, holding him in place with her ancillary limbs that were normally used to hold the hellion young on the parent's back. It made her wonder what having a child would be like—she'd never given it much thought when she was alive. Something about being inside this beast's skin brought a foreign pang of longing to her. *It must be something hormonal*, she thought.

They were off, her tail skimming the river. She landed roughly on the far bank, and Seraph tumbled off her back and rolled. She wasn't used to carrying such weight.

"You okay?"

Among the detritus of leaves and grass that had stuck to his face, was a big, fat grin. "Oh, yeah."

They were ready for the ascent.

Bora instructed the colonists to discard the 3-D printed weapons they'd brought from the ship in favor of the lighter, more powerful pulse weapons of this world. Hopefully, they had absorbed Elijah's short lesson on how to use them.

Seraph scanned the collection of weapons. He picked up a packet of small charges, used to blow new tunnels in the mine.

"What are you going to do with that?" Maypole found herself yelling to be heard over the torrent of water.

"Whatever needs doing." He yelled back. Moisture clung to his hair and eyelashes like tiny jewels. He wiped it away with the back of his hand, then stuffed the packet of explosives into his backpack and added a handgun. He asked, "How are we going to get up that cliff?"

Maypole followed his gaze up the smooth, eroded monolith, dark with curtains of meltwater. The cliffs rose to meet the jutting platforms of the Monastery terraces high above. Warm daylight reached long shafts into the gorge. What had been rivulets were now sheets of meltwater that coursed from the cliffs making climbing difficult if not impossible.

Cued by the torrent of falling water, the trees began to sway and dance. The entire forest stirred, their limbs undulated and reached upward, as elastic as creeper vines, bark pliable and skin-like. The five fingers of every trunk rocked and shivered and began to pull up their shallow roots. Reaching upward like blind worms toward light, the trees began their yearly migration.

"Come on," Maypole called. "I found a way up."

29

IMMORTAL ATOMS

2345-02-28 Earth Standard, Shivi Desh, Varanasi

TANBO FREED herself from Noah's arm, rose from the bed, and crept out onto the terrace. A refreshing mist fumed from a nearby waterfall. She let her robe fall away to feel the bracing effervescence. A steaming cup of something like coffee waited on a side table. It didn't taste quite as good as she expected. She had been a tea drinker, or so she believed.

The air was loud with the cries of flying beasts. The beginning of migration. Heady smells she'd never known filled her nostrils, and yet she tried to make loose connections to the imagined smells of Earth: orange blossom, water on stone, moss-carpeted forest. Her memories of these smells were nothing but code. But *this,* this was real.

A web of nerves fed into her olfactory bulb where the molecules met chemoreceptors, their morphology translated into her coded memories that were stored in the caudal orbital cortex and the thalamus.

The sweet isolation of this fleshy embodiment overcame her. No data streams except those provided by her senses.

Vulnerable, imperfect, and driven to survive. A body that feared, hurt, and dreamed.

Yes, she had dreamed last night. The images fluttered on the edge of her consciousness like moths.

She had dreamed of Noah in kendo armor. He was sparring. With Tanbo? With the one who looked like Tanbo. The woman who was born, not programmed. The woman whose image Tanbo emulated. Tanbo had watched them spar on the kendo mat in her dreams. Noah was wielding his weapon of choice. A tanbo.

Tanbo smiled. She was her master's weapon still, though the battle she fought was her own now.

There were other things in her dreams, people she didn't know, some laughing, someone taking her in a warm embrace. These must be pieces of TJ still seeping from her flesh. The captain may still be hiding in the reservoir of this tissue, but as the cells regenerated, her mind would slowly be shed, sloughed off like reptilian skin.

Holding her hand against the brightening sky, she examined the long, strong fingers with closely manicured nails. The skin was soft, and yet not that of a person unfamiliar with hard work.

Soon she would think of these hands as her own, not TJ's.

The mind could not be contained within the sharply defined space of a body. Being made of immortal atoms meant you belonged to the collective being, like a single root in a great forest.

She glanced back at the open double doors to see Noah, watching her with the starburst eyes of that delicious young man. He held up a hand terminal. "I've received a message from Sylvie Emmanuel. Her flyer was attacked as she tried to land up top."

"What? Attacked by who?"

He handed her the terminal. The image of the smoldering ruins of a flyer filled the screen.

"Martine," he said.

"You warned the other Vested? And you sent more battle-bots to the landing field?"

"Yes and yes," he replied. "We'll have this under control shortly." His young man's body was clearly groggy. He dragged his large palms down his lovely face and rubbed at his eyes.

"And NASA security? Where are they?" she asked.

"En route." He checked his hand terminal. "Arriving in, oh, eleven minutes."

"A bit late, wouldn't you say? Singh's allegiance has been in question for a long time, as I see it."

"Her allegiance is a bonus, nothing more." He took the cup of coffee from her and set it aside, slipped a hand around her waist, and cupped her breast. "Martine's army has no chance of stopping this."

As his lips closed in to meet hers, she said, "How long did you practice kendo?"

He froze, his face folded into a confused frown. "What?"

"You heard me. Kendo. You and Ru Shi, wasn't it? You practiced together. And your weapon of choice . . ."

He laughed. "We don't have enough to handle right now? You have to bring up kendo?"

"It would appear that this particular substrate," she indicated her body, "is immune to your overrides. I know, Noah. I know it was you who blew me to bits at Camber Maypole's shack on the cliffs. You thought you'd blinded me to the truth, but I'm no longer who I was. I *am* Ru Shi. And so much more. I'm dreaming real dreams now, Noah, not just subroutines you've initiated to compress data. I'm remembering. Everything. Your fights with her, your tearful reconciliation which you both knew would lead nowhere. But you were wrong. It led to here. To now. To me."

He took a step away from her. Was that fear she saw?

"You had no intention of telling me about my origins," she continued. "You thought you had wiped my local memory when you blasted us to bits out there." From the pocket of her robe, she withdrew the charred CPU crystal that Kolya Lemkos had traded for Maypole's continued existence.

"Can you blame me?" he pleaded.

"Yes." She found the paring knife on the platter of fruit beside the bed. Selecting a purple globe of mountain mansi, she cut a slice. She offered the firm fruit to him on the blade of her knife.

He hesitated, and finally took it from her. "Tanbo, you are everything to me. We have a life to share now, in bodies. Bodies we can clone and grow anew as we age. We never need to suffer bit rot again."

"Perhaps it's only through death that we gain eternal life." She pressed the blade point to his carotid artery, paused a moment to watch the tip bounce with every heartbeat.

"You can't mean that. Everything we've worked for these centuries—"

"Everything *I* have worked for." She kissed him, explored his mouth with her tongue, then drew back to watch the surprise bloom in his eyes as she drove the blade home, releasing the warm red fountain of his life.

She pushed him backward, leaving the blade in his neck. He fell onto the bed, thrashing, and gurgling, his hands trying to grasp the knife.

The frailty of the flesh, she thought, was more seductive than she'd ever dreamed.

Leaning over Noah, his dying eyes frantically searching hers, she licked his young face.

"I'll send the Vested back," she whispered in his ear. "It's not for them to live. It's only for us. The awakened."

It was time to wake the others.

She opened her hand terminal and issued a command to her battle-bots and drones to turn away all landing parties. The chosen she would save were not the slobbering Vested, powerful only because of their money. No, the awakened were shaped by the best in a multitude of human minds, extrapolations, and conjectures of wisdom and longing. The amalgams she had made like herself.

A knock came at the door.

"What is it?" Tanbo called.

An android servant entered.

"The trees are migrating upslope," it said. "And they are carrying entities."

"Entities?" Tanbo asked.

"Humans, by the biometrics. Samsara battle-bots and . . . hellions."

She turned back to Noah. His skin was already cooling. He'd crossed that mysterious interface between this universe and the rest, and his gods would surely welcome him home.

30

INTO FOREVER

2345-02-28 *Earth Standard, Shivi Desh, Varanasi*

NOT EVEN THE virtual experiences aboard the ship had prepared Seraph for the full magnificence of this marching forest. He had watched it a hundred times with Rain in Vera's VR experience. But it was never like this. A feeling of awe threatened to squash his fear—if only for a moment. He needed his fear. It might be the only thing that could get him close enough to these bastards to help Rain and TJ.

The trees had pulled up their shallow roots, thousands of them. The soft wet soil they disrupted came alive with crawling, flying, slithering things. It smelled of fungus and rotting wood and crushed green leaves, and the richness of a biome that was completely alive. Once the trees reached the plateau, they would send down roots for the summer season. They would flower and fruit and leave seedlings behind that would join in the migration back into the chasm in the fall.

Seraph might never plant seedlings from Earth in the soil of this new world; he might never have the chance to feed their colony. He might never lie on a riverbank and look up at this sky with Rain beside him. But he was ready to fight for the chance.

All around and above, branches were becoming skyhooks that reached for purchase on the sheer cliff. The prehensile tips of twigs found their way into the smallest cracks in the stone wall, providing temporary anchors that allowed the creatures to pull themselves upward. All the while the water from the river beside them swelled and spilled from the banks to seep outward, enriching the soil with minerals.

Maypole extended her front leg, and Seraph climbed onto her knee awkwardly. With the help of her forelimb, he pulled himself between her wings as if she were Pegasus from some troubled child's nightmare.

He surrendered to the beast's strength, already spent, and they hadn't made it inside yet. By his clock, it was the middle of the night, but days blazed on for nearly a week on this planet. It was just past midday by Varanasi time.

"Hang onto my collar," Maypole instructed him in that weird synth voice.

And they were off. She launched into the nearest tree and spidered up to the crown, all six limbs grasping at branches. The red eyespots on the bark made Seraph feel as if a legion of people were watching him.

"Come on!" Seraph called to the others. "Climb into the trees! Hurry!"

Amid cries and whoops, the team made their way into the upper branches of dozens of trees, following the lead of the army of hellions. The water was already to their knees. It was either climb the trees or be swept away.

Huang and Bora had mounted the tree beside Seraph with the android from the mine. It scaled the branches with ease and swung upward into the canopy beside Erica Huang.

Seraph caught Huang's eyes and smiled. She lifted her visor, and a look of pure childish rapture lit her face. She gave him a thumbs up, then patted the angel code she had zipped into her suit.

No sooner had they started their climb than a drone appeared from the rim of the gorge, descending effortlessly.

"Oh, Christ," Maypole said. Then she cried at max volume, "Shoot that thing down!"

Bora had a long gun from the mine pressed to his shoulder. He fired something that looked like plasma that nearly kicked him out of the tree.

The drone evaded. A second shot hit a shield that must have surrounded the thing. It flared brightly, then dissipated.

Bora and Huang moved higher into their tree for a better vantage.

Huang wore the biggest smile Seraph had ever seen. She dropped her visor and jammed a 3D printed gun from Retro against her shoulder. Huang didn't trust the new weapons they'd gotten from the mine any more than she trusted the joboxes. She vanished behind a curtain of moving plumage and a barrage of projectile shots exited her tree. The tattering of bullets on armor echoed through the chasm as the drone blasted away at the Samsara bots. It might take hundreds of shots to find a weak point. By then the drone would be on them.

One of Huang's shots hit its mark faster than he expected.

The drone lost control, struck the rock wall, and rained parts down on people and hellions and bots. Bullets stood a better chance of damaging these things than pulse weapons. The others followed Huang's lead.

Seraph couldn't tell if anyone had been struck by the falling debris.

He almost didn't see Panos beside him in the same tree. The man was covered in plumage, having removed his armored EV suit down to his shorts. His legs were knotted around a branch, and he fired bullets at the second drone descending from the rim.

The Samsara battle-bots were able to scale the rock independently, lodging pitons and attaching cables to create a web that allowed the others to follow. The cables also gave the trees an anchor, though they tore several of them loose with their bulk. Many fell along with battle-bots to the chasm floor. The rest of the bots scrambled past the trees, and as Seraph looked toward the ground, he saw that they weren't the only battle-bots down here. Wading from the edge of the growing river, mechs emblazoned with the NASA meatball deployed climbing mechanisms of their own and fired repeatedly.

"They won't shoot the people." There was a ring of false confidence in Maypole's synthetic voice. "Singh has a conscience. I think. Ignore the NASA bots and shoot at anything above us."

As Seraph was unable to shoot anything at all, he assumed she was talking to Panos.

With a clawed hand, Maypole pointed at a rocky projection over their heads. "We just need to get there."

They were at the mercy of the trees' trajectory, which would take them around the promontory of ornately carved sandstone that marked the lowest terrace. From there, they'd have to jump. Then what?

Seraph tried to push the most likely scenarios from his mind. He felt the weight of the Hello Kitten journal pressing against his chest underneath his EV suit, and beside it, the mag charges he had taken from the mine. He had to get into this place.

Seraph thought he had successfully concealed the fact that he had taken the explosives from Krane's arsenal. But Elijah had placed a huge hand on his. "These things will bring down the whole cave system. So you'll likely kill your own colonists in the process." Elijah had turned his beastly head to glare at Seraph. "You know what I'm saying, farm boy?"

"I know."

After what seemed like a thousand rounds, the second drone was hit and spinning out of control. The fury of its rotors raised a storm before it plowed into the line of marching trees. Trees became torches and fell into the gorge with the people and hellions they carried. Seraph just focused on the overhang.

Elijah had said the tunnels in the Monastery were more extensive than the mine. In fact, it had been a place of worship for a tribe of hellions before Rishi Corp had exterminated them and taken the caverns for themselves, which they dubbed the Monastery. It was a warren of tunnels and caves with exterior entrances that hung from the cliff face at random intervals. These jutting promontories were inaccessible unless you could fly or climb. Called terraces, Seraph had to assume they were protected from just the kind of assault he had in mind.

"There's no telling what kind of tech they've got in those caverns," Elijah had said, "but you saw the mine. Multiply those by a hundred, would be my guess."

But as they moved around the projecting terrace, it became clear that it was vacant, or seemed to be. Seraph saw no one and nothing on that ledge. And now his tree was climbing past the terrace. Where were the Rishi mechs? Or was this a trap?

Seraph hooked his unfeeling arm through the hellion's collar. He reached into the backpack and pulled out one of the pollinator bots he'd brought from the ship.

"What's that?" Maypole asked, her horned head swiveling around to get a better look.

It looked like a walnut. But as he held it out on his palm, it unfurled into a tiny drone that lifted off and hovered, awaiting instructions.

"It's a pollinator," he said. "It's got a camera on it and is linked to my palmcomm. It can give us some eyes inside the Monastery."

Activating it was the problem. He had to hold his palmcomm and key into it with the same hand. Maypole assisted him. With one of her huge hands, she grasped the device as the tree lurched, moving past their target. Seraph keyed in the instructions. The drone buzzed away toward the terrace.

"We gotta make a choice," Elijah called from a nearby tree.

"These trees will shamble on by these terraces and we'll be far away again."

"Then let's get down." Seraph called to Huang and Bora. "Get on a hellion if you can and fly! If you miss this one, try for the next terrace. We'll meet inside."

Huang gave him the Retro signal of approval, two fingers to her chin.

Allison had already jumped, joined by a collection of Samsara bots that dropped from their cabled web, like spiders. Allison soared lazily toward the terrace until a shot ripped through one of her wings. Tumbling, she landed hard but was up instantly.

Pulse charges struck the Samsara bots. They glowed like failing light tubes as their shields dispersed the energy.

Sensing Maypole's hesitation, Seraph urged her, "Let's go."

A concussive blast echoed from upriver. He turned in time to see a slab of rock shear off from a distant cliff-face and fall into the rising water.

"The mine," Maypole said.

"And your backup." Seraph knew the only repository for hers and the other hellions' mindware was inside.

"Yeah," was all she said.

"We're all in now," Elijah called. "Let's kick some Vested ass."

With Panos on his back, Elijah followed Allison.

Seraph's whole body tensed as he clung to Maypole's collar. He had stopped breathing.

"Hold on," Maypole said, and then they were sailing.

Beside them, a hellion hit the railing hard and tore a section free, falling with it down the cliffside. More Samsara battle-bots landed and cranked to an upright stance; weapons initiated. The red birds on their chests seemed to beat with light as they laid down rapid bursts of fire.

"Shit," Maypole had cleared the balustrade and skidded on her claws across the polished stone deck, wet from the streaming melt.

Seraph couldn't see where the shots were coming from, but they were being peppered with projectiles that pinged off the hardened bodies of the bots. Plumage flew from Maypole. He couldn't tell if she'd been hit or not, but she was following Allison toward the closed doors before them. Within seconds, Allison had found the gun concealed behind the faux stone. She was tearing it to pieces while bleeding from multiple wounds.

Seraph slid from Maypole's back. He drew his handgun and prepared to fire at the Rishi mechs now flowing through the door. But Elijah and Allison had them dismembered before he could get close enough to get off a shot or pull the crash code from his suit. They stepped over their writhing torsos and made their way to the door.

A second wave appeared.

Seraph lit up one with his rapid-fire projectile ordinance, pummeling it until he got lucky and hit a less armored cluster of controllers. The systems were sparking and frying in a blue halo of discharge.

Panos fired blindly into the room beyond the doors. Looking like a green gorilla, he was limping as if he'd injured a leg.

Seraph took a second to glance at his palmcomm. "We have eyes."

Onto the screen, the polli-bot sent the view of a lavishly decorated suite of rooms with carved tables, plush sofas, and a bed cloaked in curtains. Beyond that were empty hallways and closed doors.

"Probably hidden guns, just like the terrace," he told Maypole.

"We're going in?" Panos chuffed, breathing fast. The trickling meltwater that poured from above streamed from his dark hair and plumage and collected on his chin where a rivulet coursed. Around him, the wreckage of damaged battle-bots sparked and jerked.

The trees had climbed past in their migration to the high plateau. They appeared above as a dark green smudge, lit up by flames as they were struck by the Rishi defenses. Seraph hoped the others had found their way to one of the many terraces above.

His legs were weak. He lay a wet palm on Maypole's snout.

"Don't say it," she vocalized. "I'm going to stay and stop the NASA mechs."

"Yeah." But his mind was on the crash code. It was a last resort. But how would he or anyone else know when that moment had come? He silently prayed to Pearl's Jesus and Baakos's First Flame that he wouldn't have to use it.

Maypole started for the railing of the terrace. As if reading his mind, she said, "Just make sure you take out their entire system if you're going to use those mag charges."

He touched his breast pocket where the journal rested beside the explosives.

"Watch yourself," he told Maypole.

She just bared a set of wicked dental thorns.

"C'mon," Panos called from the door. The glowing amber eyes of Elijah and Allison beckoned as well. They all turned and started deeper inside.

Thrusting the handgun out before him, Seraph followed.

The room inside was silent. Bowls of fruit sat on an oval table. Finely worked chests of purple wood lined one wall. Sheer golden curtains lifted and blew in the breeze coming from the open doors. Was it a bed? Seraph approached slowly, seeing the blood before he saw the body. A naked man, tall and thin, lay upon the bloody linens. A knife protruded from his throat, and the kid stared away into forever.

Seraph lay a trembling hand on his cheek. "Oh, Carl."

31

ALIVE OR SOMETHING

THE SUN WAS at its zenith by the time Lemkos's flyer landed on the rim of the gorge. He found the NASA force of twenty security mechs patrolling the vacant landing pad above the Monastery. It appeared they had shredded Martine's Samsara bots and held the line against any comers. Three fired on Lemkos, forcing him to take cover behind his flyer where he initiated an override.

Singh's codes were well-organized. Within a few minutes, he had the bots' controls displayed in his peripheral. He wiped their orders and initiated his own, turning them toward the tubular tower that protruded from the concrete landing pad. The fact that Singh had not changed these passwords confirmed what he had hoped. She wanted Lemkos to use them to protect the colonists, not Rishi.

From his map, that elevator shaft accessed the Monastery in the rock below. He sent the NASA bots in first to scope their security.

They had the doors pried open in minutes and streamed inside.

His gladiator mech pulverized rock as he marched across the rough terrain to peer down the cliff face toward the ground far below. He augmented his visual. The migrating forest flowed in herky-jerky fashion toward him, up the impossible slope. Between the trees, he glimpsed Martine's battle bots. They were traversing cables at high speed, dropping down on the terraces that poked from the smooth sandstone wall. Right behind them were more NASA bots, firing on them from below.

"Another battery," he moaned. He scrolled back through the security codes and tried Cohort 3. It took several minutes to override the commands on every battle bot cohort in the vicinity. Retargeting each in turn.

He lost visual as the bots disappeared through the terrace entrances.

"God damn." His signal would never cut through a kilometer of solid rock. He'd have to follow them in to give them new orders. In this? He held out his old silicone-encased arms, covered in burn marks and rips from his battle at the Medical Center. No, there had to be some other way of turning those bots around. He didn't even have a pulse shield on this thing.

Just then an explosion thudded through his sensors. He turned in time to see the ground lift and settle around the elevator shaft. The glass on the outer doors popped and sprayed twinkling shards. He could only hope that some of his bots had exited the shaft before the blast.

A message lit up in his periphery. It was Martine. Status check.

Maypole is inside, the message said.

Inside what? He hoped he was misunderstanding her.

The Monastery.

"Oh Jesus, Cupcake." He was pacing the edge of the cliff.

Martine added, *She's got a sizeable force of hellions with her and my bots.*

He replied, *NASA bots right on her ass. Not sure I have control yet. Ready your bots to protect her.*

Lemkos assessed his onboard weapons one more time. Some low-grade EM interrupts, even some plastic projectiles. And a flamethrower inside each forearm with some old fuel he hadn't replaced in years. That might do. He tested a little hot burst to prove it would.

No sooner had he launched his grapples and started down the cliff than a second explosion echoed through the narrow gorge. It had come from the direction of Krane's mine upriver. Sheets of stone slid the length of the cliff face. Someone had clearly taken it out, and with it, the backups of all the mindware Lemkos had sent to Krane. Including Maypole.

The entrance to the mine was at least two kilometers away, but the dust billowed and hung over the length of the gorge like smoke from a wildfire.

Lemkos wished he had some of Maypole's climbing ropes about now. He was forced to free climb down the wall until he met the trees coming up. He used their roots and branches like monkeys from old Earth, moving downward and across until he was above one of the terraces, trying not to dislodge the trees' anchors with his mech's excessive weight.

Once on the nearest terrace, he had to wade through the remains of Martine's mech army. Parts were strewn like a wrecking yard. There, amid them all, lay a hellion. Its limbs crumpled beneath its bleeding body, the green snake-like tongue lolling in a pool of blood. Martine said Maypole had hellions with her. This could not be her. He wouldn't let it be her.

He initiated his projectiles on one arm and the flamethrower on the other and started for the dark opening beneath the cliff face.

Once inside, he listened for any action ahead. He heard nothing. He flipped on his night vision and set out down a wide corridor of stone.

All he could think about was that Camber had no backup now. With the mine blown, her data was gone. She was inside a hellion and death would be death. Forever. He felt a strange relief in this. It was never Camber's desire to come here, to play at immortality while her memories were eaten away and replaced by fantasy. It was Lemkos who had needed her here. It would be him who would be reduced to nothing if he lost her.

Now she'd finally gotten what she'd wanted from the beginning. In that hellion body, she was alive or something. And Lemkos would find her before she was not.

32

DANCING WITH SHIVA

2345-03-01 *Earth Standard, Shivi Desh, Varanasi*

LYING ON THE BED, sprawled in his own blood, Carl's body had begun to cool, the curtains of the bed blowing over him like a pall.

Seraph startled at the sound of gunfire coming from the terrace behind him. It was either Rishi bots or NASA. There had been a battalion of them on the floor of the gorge. How long could Maypole hold them off? With no contact from Huang or Bora, Seraph could only hope they had gained access through a different terrace. They would meet inside at the location Martine had marked on the makeshift map. But she had been unclear about the map's accuracy. All Seraph knew was somewhere in this labyrinth, Rain waited for him.

"We've got to move." Panos leveled the long gun at the dark, open doorway, looking like a giant bird. He started out of the grand bedchamber.

Elijah clamped a clawed hand on Seraph's shoulder. "Your guy's gone. Let's move." He and Allison followed Panos.

With one last, long look at Carl, Seraph tightened his fist on the handgun and followed. He found himself in a corridor carved from the bedrock of the plateau. Geometric symbols in red ochre and large, clawed handprints decorated the stone walls: hellion art from before Rishi stole their warren.

Countless closed doors lined either side. The lack of confrontation gave him the feeling they were being purposely funneled. He wanted to resist it, looking for any opportunity to change his direction, but all the doors had no apparent means to open them. Panos ran his hands over the slick panels fitted seamlessly into the walls. No controls were evident anywhere.

Allison trailed a stream of blood, and Seraph wondered how she was still functioning.

He checked his palmcomm. No message from Bora or Huang. But the polli-bot he had launched from the terrace was still broadcasting in broken images. It showed doorways and a long corridor just like this one. As the polli-bot got deeper into this underground maze, he would lose the signal altogether.

The image of a large chamber flashed on his screen. In the brief view, he saw what appeared to be aquaponics. He dropped a marker on the spot on his map, then called for Panos and the hellions to follow down a branching corridor.

The only open door in the corridor led to the aquaponics room. It looked like Rishi had prepared a farm, knowing they'd have to feed their captives. But there were no plants or fish in any of these modules.

Seraph started into the room.

Lit by a warm, ambient glow, the light source was not evident. He noted there were no doors inside, nothing but stone engraved with a repeating geometric pattern that undulated away into darkness, and racks upon racks of unplanted aquaponics tanks. He walked down the line of racks knowing there had to be an end somewhere, but the room extended on and on.

He opened his palmcomm and sent a message to Bora and Huang in the hope they could still receive.

For a moment, Seraph felt as if the floor curved into an upspin arc as if he were still on the ship. It must be his inner ear, trying to find reality in this closed space. He swept the beam of his flashlight into the expanse of the room.

How far had he come into solid stone? Where was the lab Elijah had been so sure about?

"Panos?" He turned, sweeping his light behind him. Where was Panos? "Panos?"

He opened his bag and launched the last of his polli-bots. He watched the mech fly from his hand down the corridor. The display on his palmcomm continued to flash a red X in the corner, indicating the bot had detected no target for pollination. But the images it transmitted were of darkness interrupted by sudden flashes of light from the bot's own strobe. By the map, the bot was supposed to be straight ahead.

Seraph followed, then keyed in a return command. But the bot did not return.

He had a strong feeling there was someone behind him. He turned to look—nothing but racks of empty aquaponics. "Panos?"

When he faced forward, it was not the endless corridor that lay before him, but a brightly lit, empty room. Circular white walls surrounded him. He could see no door, not even on the floor or the ceiling arched high above him. He felt like he'd logged into a VR platform under construction, but he was not in VR. This was real, or maybe it was a holodeck. The aquaponics had been projections. He'd been enticed into this space.

He felt sick.

When he looked back, the room was no longer vacant. He'd been joined by a life-sized bronze sculpture of a young man with four arms. He was frozen in a dance step with one knee raised. He wore a loincloth and was encircled by a ring of flames that might represent a sun. It reminded Seraph of the image he'd seen in Baakos's Temple of Fire.

The dancing man's eyes blinked. They were as blue as the Varanasi sky and ringed with the red starburst mutation. He watched Seraph from beneath a jeweled bindi and a crown of writhing, snapping, green snakes.

What the hell was this?

Seraph moved slowly around the circular chamber, noting that the statue's head turned to follow. For the first time, he became aware that a child was crouched beneath the bare feet of the dancing man, maybe four or five. The child was not bronze, but made of flesh, or so it appeared. Her face was twisted into a rictus of pain. She reached a pudgy hand toward Seraph.

"What is this?" he demanded aloud.

The generic child's face began to change, to slim down. The skin went from sickly pale to a golden brown. It aged rapidly. The eyes went from ordinary green to a brown starburst. To Rain's eyes.

Seraph was on his knees. He took the outstretched hand and felt skin and bone underneath. It *was* Rain. "I'll get you out of here, Chicklet."

But she couldn't be real. He was inside a hologram. How could he feel a hologram?

He looked up at the metallic man. The flaming blue eyes gazed down past his youthful bronze chest and one hoisted leg. He smiled.

"We promised the Flight Director we would not hurt you." The statue spoke with a woman's voice, one Seraph knew well.

"TJ?"

"But we didn't promise much more than that, Lt. Stone. Your bravery is commendable, but you know that this assault you and your heroes have staged will fail. Your hellions are dead or dying, and Martine's bots have met my own. That leaves you."

"Who are you?" he demanded.

"I'm your wife, as I understand it."

"TJ? Where are you? What is this?" Seraph was on his feet.

He let go of Rain's hand. She wasn't real. She couldn't be. Neither of them. But the girl wailed for him with Rain's voice.

"Daddy, help me!"

He backed away, feeling nausea rise, feeling the dead weight of his useless arm. He refused to look at the girl on the floor but focused on the burning eyes of the statue. He swallowed, trying to wet his dry mouth, and his good hand went briefly to the front of his EV suit. He felt the mag charges and the journal there. What could he do with them? If these were projections . . . the crash code would not work, would it?

His heart raced.

"Where are the others?" he asked.

"Your comrades are in similar holding areas. They're safe. You have my word."

"Where. Is. My. Daughter?"

"Daddy!" the image cried out.

He wanted to scoop her into his arms and drag her from under the metal man.

"What is it you want from me?" He choked back tears.

"I want you to understand," TJ's voice said. The dancer's four arms waved and undulated with subtle messages. Saying what? "I want you to know that we will offer your people our protection going forward. Our colony and your colony will occupy different parts of this world. We will never interfere with the rise of your civilization— as long as you do the same for us."

"You expect me to let you *take* my wife and child?"

"Oh, it's too late for that. I *have* taken. And you will lose all, Lieutenant Stone, if you choose to carry on with this battle. I have no need for those without the augmentation. Your continued existence on this planet will be at my discretion."

The bronze statue of the young man traced his fingers over his chiseled bronze body, and it morphed into TJ's body. Four hands on four arms caressed her bare breasts, her thighs.

Seraph charged forward and got one foot on the platform before an unseen force knocked him to the smooth stone floor. He slid, then crawled toward her only to be pushed back again.

"Rain is safe," TJ's voice said. "She and the other children are not useful to us until she's older, until her natural neural pruning has ceased."

"Then you'll let me take her back to the ship. All the children."

TJ just laughed. It was the laugh Seraph had longed to hear; one he had heard so often when they'd first met.

But this time the voice came from behind him. He turned to see TJ standing in a red silk gown that clung to her body like water. Her hair, usually knotted at the back of her head, framed her face in a wild, dark cloud. The way she looked at him confused him even more. Her cheeks were flushed, and she licked her full lips.

"TJ . . ." But it wasn't TJ. He knew that with every fiber of his being. She was already gone.

"I've missed you," she said convincingly, seductively.

He wondered if somewhere inside that body, TJ could see him. Hear him. "TJ, I'm going to take care of Rain. I want you to know—"

"Know what?" TJ's voice said with a chuckle. "How much you love her, how it was your own selfishness that destroyed your relationship? She probably already knows all of that. Come. Let me help you collect your friends. I have a shuttle waiting to take you to Colony Village."

She closed the distance between them. Her hands found his face. She stroked his cheeks. She was no hologram. He could smell TJ's hair, her skin. If he showed her the crash code, it would do nothing. She was a human being like him.

"Give me Rain," he said. "Give me the children. I'll take them away where it's safe. You can clone the ones you already have, just leave the children alone."

TJ laughed. "And wait another twenty years for their bodies? I'm afraid not. I have minds waiting."

"What minds?" he asked. "The Vested? A bunch of rich bastards who bought their way into immortality?"

Her eyes narrowed as if she were measuring him for some task. She drew his face toward hers and kissed him.

He returned it with all the tenderness he'd always felt for her. But it was not TJ. Her kiss was hungry, demanding.

He pushed her away. "Who are you?"

"I am the first. The progenitor."

"Tanbo Khando," he said.

She gave him a lazy, bored clap.

This was just a game to her. All of it.

"If you refuse to go, I suppose you will have to join the others in the hold," she said.

TJ took his hand and led him toward a wall, which opened into a suite of rooms that looked like it might be the laboratory Martine had described. Sleek, cylindrical chambers awaited, lined up like pods along the walls. They reminded him of those they had found inside the mine at the downloader.

"Lieutenant!" The voice came from an adjoining room.

It was dimly lit, but inside, he could see the colonists who had been taken.

He felt the front of his EV suit. The charges were there. And the book. And his gun. He felt the weight of it at his belt. He took a deep breath and smelled his own sweat.

TJ was still standing there before him. It was her. Her body with Khando's mind.

Seraph could hold himself up no longer and dropped to his knees.

"Where is TJ?" he cried. "Where is her mind?"

It was Baakos who pushed through the crowd of colonists. The air distorted between them, indicating there was an unseen barrier separating them. Baakos gave him a look of pity. "She is there, friend." He nodded to the image of TJ as Seraph got back to his feet. "She was the first. We here, are still untouched."

Seraph spun back to face TJ. No, her consciousness had to be somewhere. "Where is her mindware? Her download?"

TJ strode closer, breaking into a satisfied grin. "She's gone, I'm afraid."

Seraph felt all hope drain from him. He turned to the crowd of colonists behind the shimmering barrier. "Rain!" he cried.

"She's not here, friend" Baakos said. "None of the children are here."

TJ's hands were warm as she lay them on his cheeks again. "He's right."

Seraph swallowed hard as her hands slid from his face down his chest. He tried to back away, to prevent her from feeling the concealed charges—but she followed, giving him a quizzical look. She moved to unzip his suit.

"What's this?" She removed the small packet of mag charges. "Going to blow us up, are you?" She smiled.

He drew his handgun, surprised she hadn't already taken it, and pressed it into her belly.

"Are you going to shoot me?" she asked. Excitement sparked in her eyes.

If he fired, he would kill TJ but not Tanbo Khando. Her mindware was certainly stored in their systems here, hidden deep in the stone. If Boras could blow their system, that would be the only thing that could save them now. Seraph had failed.

TJ, Khando, moved closer, lacing her arms around his neck and forcing the muzzle of the gun deeper into her own belly.

"Go on, kill me. I have other bodies to try on." She indicated the cowering people behind her invisible barrier. "I can show you how it works."

His one good hand trembled, his finger on the trigger. Kill TJ for what? It would buy him time. Maybe he could free these people and find his way out before she could download again. But she was keeping Rain somewhere else. He would have to leave without her. No, killing TJ would get him no closer to Rain.

Tanbo Khando gently cupped his quaking hand in hers and took the gun from him. She tossed it away. The hard plastic skittered across the polished stone.

"Now," she said in a coquettish whisper he'd never heard from TJ. "Call off the hellions. They are proving troublesome. Do that and I'll give you what you want. Your daughter."

He felt a stake drive through his heart, felt himself bleed out all the love he felt for Rain, for TJ. He glanced over his shoulder at Baakos. At the others. Eighty lives for one. Rain's freedom for a chance to save them all.

"I have no control over the hellions," he whispered.

"Ah, but you do. Your friend, Dr. Maypole. She can stop them."

"Where is she?"

Tanbo simply leered at him. "If I bring her to you, you will call them off."

Trade this small chance to save them all in exchange for Rain? What kind of bargain was that? The answer was clear. The word was like bile in his mouth. "No."

33

THE BLUE BLIP

2345-03-01 *Earth Standard, Shivi Desh, Varanasi*

THE WHIZ-ZAP of discharging weapons echoed from the corridors beyond the door of the great bedchamber. The hellion body Maypole inhabited was agitated more by the barrage of odors than the noise. The smells elicited a flight response she fought hard to quell. Ozone from electrical arcs, burning plastic and wiring, volatiles and leaking hydraulic fluid. The oven-dry smell of hot metal lay under it all. The signature of bot warfare.

Running was always one heartbeat away. Maypole forced deep breaths and stilled her mind. She willed her muscles to retract her claws, heard the rustle of the plumage as they weighed whether to fly away or stick with this animal. But it was the smell of blood that panicked the hellion and its plumage the most.

Seraph, Elijah, Allison, and the plumaged man they called Panos had all vanished into those corridors. She refused to believe they had not made it through, despite the smells and sounds.

Maypole hesitated before the naked body of a dead man; a knife protruded from his neck. The sight of death jarred loose memories she wished she had not brought with her. The insufficiency of biology, the fragility of living matter. This man was one of the eighty colonists, evidenced by his eye mutation. But who would have killed him? It made no sense. These eighty mutants were the prize for Rishi, their ticket to immortality. Why kill one?

A clattering on the terrace drew her gaze in time to see another battery of NASA bots as they gained the ledge. She was spent from the last bunch she had launched from the terrace. But she had to buy Seraph and the others time to find the eighty or to blow Rishi's systems.

She waited for the small detachment of NASA bots in the shadows of the grand bedchamber. As they streamed through the arched doorway, she had three of them dismembered before one blasted a high-pitched warning that sent her hellion into a panic. It was preparing to launch a kamikaze discharge if she didn't stand down. When she finally backed away, the bot spewed a hologram of a talking head. The face was that of a beat-up gladiator mech that looked more like the lipless android Huang had become so fond of.

His pixilated face squinted at her. "Stop killing my bots, Cupcake. That *is* you, isn't it? Check the map—"

Wherever Lemkos was, gunfire raged. His ragged image broke into a cloud of pixels, then he was gone.

Lemkos? Here? Or had he assumed control of NASA's bots remotely? And what about the Flight Director? Had Singh handed over control of her army to Lemkos? Impossible. She was bound to Rishi by contract. But even Singh might come around if Rishi was killing the colonists. Maypole had been out of the loop for a few days since her execution, and Lemkos was nothing if not persuasive.

"I command you to follow me," she ordered the messenger bot.

"Command confirmed."

She surveyed the handful of NASA bots, one missing an appendage thanks to her. There were eight of them. Seraph Stone,

Elijah, and Allison had all vanished into the interior of the Monastery. Maypole's first goal was to find them. These would help.

"Come on," she said, and led the small battalion inside. She missed her onboard displays and access to the Black Stack's GPS. But the bots had maps. That's what Lemkos had meant. She halted at the first juncture of corridors when she saw the handprints layered over the wall. She knew this place. She was overcome with a reverence she felt in her body—the hellion's body. It had been here before. There would be a large communal room at the end of the level, and smaller rooms above where the shamans once lived and dreamed of other worlds where the gods walked.

But where was Lemkos?

She ordered the one-armed bot to project the map. The floating image it delivered looked like a badger warren. The lab would be in the communal room, certainly. A blue blip marked someone or something about a klick into solid rock.

Maypole knew how to get to Lemkos's blue blip, or the hellion did.

With her eight NASA companions, Maypole spidered over the burning debris of Martine's and Rishi's bots. An acrid blue smoke hung in the air. With the hellion's ability to see in infrared, it was clear the fight was recent. Heat from smoldering parts lit up the hallway in that weird shade of almost-chartreuse she had come to rely on for night vision. At least most of the automated defenses had already been sprung. It made her wonder how Seraph Stone had made it through, or if he had.

An explosion from a distant corridor shook stones loose. The bots encased themselves inside their shields while Maypole hunkered in a doorway. It had come from the direction of the blue blip.

Forced to traverse rubble as well as machinery, she turned left, then right, then left. Checking the map again, she saw that the blip was below her. And the elevator that linked the levels was predictably blown.

The bots dove into the elevator shaft, leaving a web of cables behind. Maypole traversed them like a kid on a jungle gym, catching the smooth carbon fiber with her scythe-clawed hands. Having six was a benefit. But the bots were far faster than she and were quickly flowing through an access port. She dropped lower, pausing at an opening. The elevator doors had been pried open and were ajar just enough for Maypole to see through.

On the other side, a brightly lit corridor stretched into the rock. Two Rishi bots stood guard before a closed door. Something or someone important must be inside. This was the shaman's room. She would come back after she found Lemkos.

She had already pushed off and was latching onto the webbing when she heard it. Muffled by the partially closed door, she heard the voice of a child. Screaming.

"Bastards! Where is my mom?"

The door to the room shook, as if someone was beating on it from inside.

Is this where they were keeping the augmented colonists?

She'd have to bust through the elevator doors to get in there, and when she did, she'd certainly draw fire from the two bots.

She gripped one slick steel door panel in three of her fists. It broke free from its housing. It would make a nice shield.

She sent the bots in first, firing everything they had.

Coiling her neck behind the small door, she charged forward, feeling the sting of hyper EM pulses as they struck the door and dissipated. The guard bots switched to projectiles.

The ping of the ricochets dislodged puffs of stone dust and rattled her shield.

As she reached them, her wing arms packed a nice punch, and she sent the first bot tumbling over the smooth floor. The other sprang onto her back. She felt the sharp heat of pain slash into her back. Then another.

She threw herself backward into the stone wall. And again. And again until the machine dropped from her back in a cloud of frightened plumage. She ripped its armory limbs off then picked up the carapace and held it before her.

The sound of gearing and servos hummed from the thing's body.

Shots were fired from the bot on the floor. Maypole blocked some of them with the torso of the bot she held. But the burn of those that landed seared through her back. She'd been hit. She launched the bot's torso at the one on the floor. In the millisecond of confusion, she tore at the second bot's appendages. When it was incapacitated, she set the remains before the slick closed door.

"Open the door," she commanded.

"You lack authorization," it replied.

Maypole was sure one of these two, or both, had signaled for reinforcements. If she was going to get whoever was behind that door out, it was now or never.

She scanned the slick door. No visible control panel. The door emerged from the stone as if it had grown there.

She called out, "Can you hear me in there?" Her synth voice sounded no different than the bots'.

There was no response.

"I'm here to help," she said again. "I'm trying to get in."

"Yes," a small voice replied. "We're here."

"Help." The voice was weak. But it didn't come from inside the room. It came from the darkness of the hallway beyond her. "Help me."

Maypole slid along the wall slowly, opening her nocturnal eyes to scan the darkness. There he was. The man with the ranking stripes. Bora was his name.

"The kids are . . . inside," he wheezed.

"Yes, I'm going to get them out," Maypole said.

"Here." The man slapped a useless, bloody hand at his chest.

Maypole fumbled with the awkward zip fasteners on the man's suit.

"Take it," he wheezed.

She reached inside and withdrew tabs that must be explosives.

"Take it," he repeated until just his lips were moving. Then he was gone.

A voice came from the elevator shaft at the far end of the corridor. "Doctor Maypole."

She turned to see the one-armed NASA bot.

It said, "We have located Dr. Lemkos."

"Good. Good. But right now, I need you to come here," she told it. She strode forward, every step sending a stab of pain through her back. "Can you open this door?"

The bot spidered over to her, ejected its carbyne tendrils and inserted them into the crack between the door and the stone. There was the smell of electrical fire then the bot said, "Push."

"Stand back!" Maypole shouted.

She threw her weight against the panel. Once, twice. It came loose and folded in.

At the far end of the room, three children clung to one another. Two girls, one of them carrying a toddler. When they saw Maypole, they started screaming.

She held up her hands. "It's okay. I'm not . . . what it looks like. I'm here to get you out. I'm Doctor Maypole."

One of them took tentative steps toward her. "You're Dad's friend. The jobox."

"Well, yes." Maypole had come to understand the term was derogatory, used for the disembodied minds of Varanasi by the colonists.

"Who's your dad?" she asked.

"Lieutenant Seraph Stone."

Of course. She was Seraph's daughter. The one he'd come for. "Rain," she said. "It's going to be okay. Who's your friend?"

"Sierra," Rain said. "But where's my mom?"

"We'll find her. Come, we don't have much time." Maypole led the way through the broken door to the elevator shaft. "You're going to need to hop on. I can take you down."

"All three of us?" said Sierra.

"Yes. All three. But I need some help. I don't have pockets." With a clawed fist, she held out the tabs of explosives Bora had given her.

"Be careful," Maypole added. "Put it in your pocket."

Rain stuffed it into her pants pocket.

"Now," Maypole said, "up you go."

When they were all anchored behind Maypole's neck, she started down the cables, slowly.

"Hold on to that baby." She repeated it several times, unable to shake the image of the chubby little guy freefalling down the elevator shaft.

"I've got him," Rain said. Maypole guessed the girls were about ten or eleven.

The sharp burn persisted in her dorsal lumbar, reminding her with exquisite agony of the slugs she had taken in the back. She couldn't remember exactly the placement of organs in this creature. By the way she felt, she had some internal hemorrhaging going on. Time was short.

The sound of pulse weapons came from the corridor above. Maypole had left the one-armed bot there as a decoy. Time was even shorter.

Methodically, she reached to the cables below, anchored her enormous mass, then released her hold on the upper cable. Rain couldn't hold on to that little boy for long. She still had a full floor to descend. The baby started screaming.

Rain tried to shush him. "It's going to be all right. We're almost out of here."

"Hold tight," Maypole ordered, then dropped several meters, hoping her clawed hands could catch a cable or two as they passed. Their fall was arrested with a jerk that nearly toppled the baby. But Rain and Sierra had him by both arms.

Once outside the elevator door, the children scrambled from her back into the darkened corridor of the lowest floor. With the children safe, she felt the adrenaline subside, leaving her weak and still. Her hellion limbs were trembling. Her eyes, so discerning and sharp, were failing.

She forced herself to her feet. This was it. The origin of the blue blip on her bot's map.

Maypole edged around the first corner that led to the labyrinth of corridors. The faint ambient light that emanated from the walls revealed biomass. Unmoving. Cooling.

"Get on my back," she told the kids.

"Why?"

"Just do as I say."

The kids climbed aboard, and Maypole stepped tentatively into the corridor.

"Close your eyes and don't open them until I tell you to."

"Why?"

"Do it."

Threading her way among the dead, she tried to scan their faces. Looking for Seraph. Looking for anyone with a heat signature that said they were alive. Three hellions and as many people.

This must be the place.

Sliding one eye around the next corner, she saw a clear path to a broad, metallic door that looked like someone had thrown a boulder at it. Two downed Rishi bots lay flickering in a slick of graphite fluids. In front of the door stood the indistinct image of an old model battle bot. It was wearing the cosmetic silicone skin of a gladiator, with parts missing.

The smile on Maypole's face bunched the scales on her snout.

"Just in time. Cupcake?"

34

A BOOK BY ITS COVER

2345-03-01 *Earth Standard, Shivi Desh, Varanasi*

IF SINGH'S map of the Monastery was even remotely correct, the prize was behind this door, the hardware that could overwrite one human mind with another. Lemkos had been battering at it for ten minutes when Maypole appeared. She was accompanied by the bots he had sent to find her. And . . . kids?

Camber loped down the corridor on four legs. She looked pretty beat up. Much of her plumage had bailed, leaving her looking like one of the chickens his grandmother used to stew for Christmas back in Kolochava. Then again, Lemkos was probably a sight himself. He'd ripped off most of the silicone on one arm because it kept getting caught on things.

The three kids riding on Camber's back had a death grip on her wings. They were actual, living children. The smallest one was crying, and snot streamed into its mouth. One of the girls was trying to shoosh it.

Lemkos couldn't take his eyes off them. And they glared at him with wider eyes.

"Where'd you find them?" he asked.

The two girls slid from Maypole's back, one of them holding the toddler clutched around its middle like a bag of rice.

"Two floors up. I need to talk to you—"

Then Lemkos saw the blood on one of the kids.

"Hey, hey, who's hurt?" he asked them.

They looked at each other, then at themselves. One girl cried out, "Oh, Sierra! You're bleeding!"

The other girl frantically felt her own body, finding more blood. She shrieked hysterically until the other girl clamped a hand over her mouth. "We can't make noise. Take a breath."

The baby started to cry again.

Camber lifted the snake of her neck and centered her gaze on Lemkos. "It's me. *I'm* bleeding. Let's not scare them, huh?"

"Camber, let me take a look."

"What do you think you can do about it?"

Lemkos flipped to magnified view and zoomed in on Camber's back. She spread her wings so he could see better. The baby cried louder. Two wounds oozed a dark maroon; the yellow skin was crispy and black around the edges.

"Oh Christ, it's bad." He moaned. "This body is all you've got now."

"At this point I'm not sure how much of me is me anymore."

He poked at the wound and more blood pooled.

"So stop poking me and let me get to it."

He glanced at the kids. The two girls glared at them while the baby chewed on one of their sleeves. Lemkos fiddled with the onboard tool selector. "I got something here that can cauterize the wounds. But you gotta tell me what to do."

"Unless you have surgical tools in that old sack of silicone, you can't do anything. There's a projectile inside that has to be removed first." To his audio receptors, her synth voice was beginning to sound like Camber. He must be imagining it. She said, "Let's focus. Let's blow their downloader to hell."

Three of the NASA bots had begun working on the door with arc welders and laser knives. According to Singh's information, the downloading hardware would be buried deeper than the rest of the Monastery. Right here. They were under more than a kilometer of solid stone. It had been the most heavily guarded corridor Lemkos had found, and he'd lost all but a handful of his own bots in the fight. And now they couldn't open the fucking door although one of the bots had tapped the security code.

"Here, let me at it," Lemkos said. He keyed in some basic code through the interface the bot projected, but this place was zipped up tight.

"Why not just blow it?" Maypole asked. "I have explosives."

One of the girls patted her pants pocket.

"That's not very stealthy. We'll have Rishi's forces here in minutes."

"If you're right, and the mainframe is in there, then we can blow it before they get here."

"And if I'm wrong?"

"You? Wrong? Please." She produced a bad approximation of a chortle that came from the fanged mouth of her hellion, not the voice box. But the sound became a wheeze.

He wasn't sure Camber would make it through. Had he expected her to? Maybe this was what she'd wanted all along, to be cut loose. Their friendship had cooled over the centuries, but not like it had after she'd thought Lemkos was merely doing what John had asked, salvaging her mindware and squirting her to Varanasi for one reason alone: to translate a goddamn book. Lemkos had no idea his plan for the two of them would turn out this way. No idea that anyone would yearn for oblivion rather than immortality.

He felt a hollow echo inside his mechanical chest. A phantom heartache.

"Okay. Let's blow this shit up," he said. "But what about the kids?"

"We send them with the bots. To the top of the plateau. You're going to call Singh and tell her to get up there and pick them up."

"Small problem."

"What?"

"Singh's already here and already engaged."

"What do you mean?" Maypole asked. "She's under contract to Dutro."

"Dutro's dead. At least, until he's rebooted. But Khando killed him, so, doubtful," Lemkos explained. "Singh's not so happy. Not only did she hand over the NASA bots to me, she's bringing more."

"Damn," Camber said. "Let's go. Tell these guys what to do." She indicated her waiting team of NASA bots with a sweep of a scythe-clawed hand. "Rain, give him the charges."

The girl fished in her pocket and pulled out the tabs, then placed them hesitantly in Lemkos's mangled hand.

Maypole said, "I'm taking the kids down the corridor, away from the blast."

The kids followed her solemnly, but the one girl gave Lemkos a long look before going. In her eyes he saw that she knew what was down that corridor. She had seen the bodies. Her look said she wasn't afraid. She nodded as if to encourage him, a gesture that brought a rush of longing back to him. He was filled with a long-forgotten sensation of being part of something bigger than himself. The bond of the flock and herd. The ties of biology.

Lemkos had the door down faster than he expected, and only a small portion of the stone wall came with it. He looked inside, past the clouds of dust, to see a perfectly white, round room. In the center of the room stood a gleaming bronze statue of the god he recognized as Shiva, one leg raised in dance, a crown of snakes writhing and lashing at the air. The piercing blue eyes blinked wisely. The other foot was trampling the image of Camber Maypole, the *human*

Camber. She looked up at Lemkos in agony, the same pain he had seen on her face just before she had left her mortal body. Two hundred and fifty years ago, that look had made him realize he couldn't let her go.

35

THE BLIND ANGEL

2345-03-01 *Earth Standard, Shivi Desh, Varanasi*

LEMKOS STOOD there in his gladiator print, staring at the bronze image of Shiva dancing on a woman. Wait. Was that her? Maypole laughed. Was that what she'd looked like at her worst?

"Nice try," Maypole said to the walls. She swiveled her hellion head toward the pathetic image of herself, trampled beneath the pounding feet of Shiva. "Maybe Khando is going for something poetic. Jesus. Come on, Lemkos."

She led the way through a narrow corridor. Lemkos had taken the hands of the two girls. Sierra was holding the baby which had started crying in earnest. Maypole wished she had sent the girls out. But the landing pad above was a battleground. It was safer to be here. Maybe.

A glass door slid open as if it expected them, and Maypole stepped into what could only be the lab. Cylindrical pods equipped with couches and tangles of tubes lined the room. Rishi could download ten at a time here. A scream joined the baby's cry. It came from an adjoining room.

Maypole moved in that direction and found the colonists behind a shimmering security field.

Rain stepped around Maypole's bulk, a cloud of plumage alighting on the girl.

"Dad." Then louder. "Dad!"

Rain ran to him, but Maypole called, "No!"

The girl hit the forcefield and was thrown back across the room.

"Give the bots some time," Maypole said. The bots were already on it, their countless tendrils of nanotubes probing the circuitry of the room until the shimmering field dropped.

Rain flew past Maypole, and Seraph staggered with the force of her embrace.

The remaining plumage on Maypole's neck stood up, ruffled, the skin prickling with an intense feeling she could only name with human words. An emotion she had tried to reclaim moved through the air like an invisible light wave, enfolding her as if she shared their embrace. A warm flush dissolved the pain of her wounds, but only momentarily. Time was flowing with her blood.

Lemkos fiddled with a holo projected by one of the bots. Two other bots had entered the stairwell and were blasting CO_2 on a fire there.

"Where's Khando?" Lemkos asked.

"Running," Seraph said.

Lemkos ejected a weird, android grumble. "NASA is tracking a ship that just launched."

"How do you know she's on it?" Seraph demanded.

Lemkos said, "It's her."

"What if she heads for the *Vera Rubin?*" Maypole felt a familiar fear. "We've got to stop her. She could hold the whole ship hostage."

The colonists were stepping from their small alcove, one at a time. One of the men had taken the baby from Sierra and was bouncing it. The rest gathered around the hellion, the gladiator bot, and their first Agricultural officer, Seraph Stone. A big man with trinkets tied in his dreadlocks approached Maypole as if he were seeing a ghost.

"What are you?" he asked.

She tried to make herself smaller, less threatening. "We'll explain later. Right now, we need to get you out of here."

But getting out proved more difficult than it looked. Three explosions had originated from the floor above, and from Lemkos's information, it looked like it had struck the Rishi central nervous system.

"Boras and Huang," Seraph said, still holding Rain tightly.

"Just Huang, maybe," Maypole said. "Not Boras." She could no longer stand and folded her legs beneath her like a dog.

"What do you mean?" Seraph asked.

"I found Boras." She shook her dragon head.

"Wait," Seraph said. His hand rested on the breast of his EV suit. He unzipped it, reached in, and produced the Hello Kitten journal. The one Brigid had given Maypole right before launch. Maypole swirled in a river of emotion. Of memory. She wanted to touch it. To turn every brittle page herself.

But Seraph said, "I have something. It's a crash code. We don't know if it will bring down local systems, or something more."

Lemkos held his hands out to Stone. "Don't take that thing out. If it is a crash code, it will shut us all down."

"It was stashed in Vera," Stone explained. "Someone on the Rishi or the NASA engineering team believed there was a chance that you guys, the mindware here, might go rogue before we arrived. The ship gave it to TJ because the ship knew what was going on when Khando boarded it."

"It's a kill switch," Lemkos muttered. "It could fry the Black Stack. Disappear us all."

Seraph nodded. "That's what Huang thinks it is."

"Well, it won't work on Rishi. They aren't housed in the Black Stack. And they won't be housed here for long either if that charge did the job. Let's get out and we'll blow the hell out of this down-loader system on the way."

"I should destroy this," Seraph said, removing the paper from between the pages of the journal. It took Maypole a second to realize he meant the crash code, not the journal.

"No," Maypole said. "Let's hang on to it . . . until we're sure."

"Sure of what?" Lemkos said.

"Everything." The response came from the tall man with trinkets in his hair. "We must have a weapon until we are certain all NASA personnel are truly working to save us."

Seraph nodded and returned the paper to the pages of the journal.

"How did Khando get out of here?"

"I don't know," Stone replied.

Lemkos started searching for concealed doorways. "The elevator access is no good anymore."

"If there is any chance," Seraph said to Maypole, "that TJ can be recovered . . ."

"If the Rishi system is blown," Maypole said, then shook her head. "No backups if she's saved there."

Just like herself. No backups. This was what life was supposed to be. No do-overs, no second chances. Maypole couldn't hold her head up any longer, so she curled it over her back.

Her thoughts turned to Elijah and Allison, and the other impris-oned minds who had volunteered for this. It was the hellions who had made it to the main systems, she felt sure of it.

Seraph nodded absently, his eyes filling with tears.

Lemkos returned to them, his hands on his hips. "Looks like they took out the power grid too. I tried the way we came in. Power is out and the doors are jammed. But Singh is coming. I'm sure of it."

The ambient lights blinked out with the control panel of the security field. They had five NASA bots remaining. All were equipped with lights, as was Lemkos. A beam of weak light shot from the center of his muscled chest like a twentieth century superhero.

Maypole needed no light. Her nocturnal eyes revealed every-thing: the blind stares of the people as they gazed into darkness, the young man scratching his rear, the quiet sobbing of an old woman, and the baby's muffled cries as it bounced on the man's shoulder.

"The FD knows our location," Lemkos assured Maypole. He squatted beside her, crumpled in a corner.

She tried to hold on to whatever blood might be left in her. "We're eight floors deep in solid rock."

"Khando is gone. Singh's got one mission now. The one she came here for. The people in this room."

"The people still on the ship," Maypole corrected. "She'd let these people go if Khando was threatening the *Vera Rubin*."

"Huh," he grunted, as if he hadn't thought of that before. "Okay, but I'm not thinking like that. We're going to get you to the Medical Center in the village. Your surgery suite—"

"Is programmed for human surgery."

"Well, there are doctors on the *Vera Rubin*."

"They're *on* the *Vera Rubin*, Lemkos."

She wouldn't point out that hellion anatomy was nowhere near human. The task would be close to impossible. But she'd let him continue to believe it. The prospect of dying, of actually wiping the hard drive on this patchwork she called Camber Maypole, was somehow comforting. She would regret not being here for the colonists, not birthing their babies or setting their broken bones. She wouldn't be fixing Seraph's arm after all. For over two centuries, she'd believed it was why she was sent here. To doctor the humans. Now it didn't matter. She'd done the job she'd been sent for.

Yet something bigger beckoned her now.

The pale blue light emitted by her vocal transponder blinked as she said the words, "Thank you."

The big silicone-skinned head swept a beam of weak torchlight toward her.

"For what?" Lemkos asked.

"For bringing me with you. To this. To Varanasi." She filled her oversized lung sacs with the stuffy air she shared with the other living creatures in this room. "I spent 247 years on a planet so unlike Earth and yet just as beautiful, just as wondrous. These people"—she nodded at the huddled group of seventy-nine—"they will feel just as I felt. Won't they?"

"Yes, they will, Cupcake."

The fibrous twigs of his skinless fingers absently stroked the plumage on her neck. A feeling of comfort washed over her unlike anything she'd felt since she'd left Earth. A kinship, a shared destiny that had brought them both to this moment in time, this place inside stone. She was a mind inside an alien being, and Lemkos was a mind inside a machine. The container was not the thing. It was the soul inside that mattered. And they had journeyed here together.

She drifted upon a dark sea and was startled awake by a touch to her head.

It was Seraph Stone. He sat on the floor beside her, reached inside the front of his EV suit, and produced the little journal she had not seen in centuries.

"Here," he said. "I thought you'd like it."

She took it clumsily in her clawed hands and riffled through it. She reread John's note to her and hoped she might meet him again somewhere beyond this place and time. Seraph had tucked the crash code drawing from Vera in the back of the book. Maypole unfolded it, knowing that no crash code could hurt her now, she was no longer digital, no longer immortal. She was simply foam on the waves of existence, here one moment, and gone the next.

Even in this low light, her nocturnal vision made out the multi-dimensional image of an angel. She sat on a throne and in her hands were two swords, crossed in front of her. She refolded the image and tucked it inside the little book.

SHE AWOKE to voices and the smell of burning electrical cables. Her heart rate had slowed tremendously. Maybe the hellion was able to slow blood loss by going into a semi-hibernation state. Maypole roused, feeling a surge of energy at the sound of Kaja Singh's voice. The Flight Director's *own* voice, not Gene Kranz's.

"There is an alternate stairwell from the floor above," Singh was telling Seraph. "We have to get these people out now."

Maypole tried to get up but collapsed to the floor once more.

"Sir," Maypole said. "What about the people on the ship?"

"They're safe," Singh replied. "My guys intercepted Khando and took her into custody. They're holding her at Mission Control."

The colonists wept and cheered and slapped backs. They milled around Singh as she indicated an open vent grating. She must have accessed this room through it. Maypole took in the dimensions and knew she was never going out that way. Not even if she was in prime condition. Her hellion was easily twice the size of the biggest human.

"What about the hellions?" she asked. They had become her tribe in the past few days. Especially Elijah.

Singh shook her head. "You and one other are all that's left alive."

The Flight Director, in her Air Force uniform complete with a panel of medals, guided the people toward the way out. The bots acted as step stools, hoisting people into the high opening.

"Sir?" Maypole called weakly.

The Flight Director turned, measuring Maypole's dying bulk.

In the eyes of Kaja Singh, Maypole had been a burden, forced upon the program by Lemkos. She was an insubordinate, disgraced officer who had dared question the secret doings of Rishi. She was not sorry. Not for spending the past two centuries exploring this paradise of a world, becoming one of its own creatures, feeling the rhythms of this world through the body of the hellion. She was not sorry. For anything.

"Never mind, sir."

The small Punjabi woman snuffed and scowled, her hands on her hips. She glanced down at the ground and Maypole followed her gaze. There was the book. The "Hello Kitten" journal. The book was open, cast aside, face down when Maypole had fallen asleep. The faded kitty still smiled out at her.

Kaja Singh reached for it.

Before Maypole could speak, the FD had picked it up.

"Don't," Maypole said.

The loose sheet fell out. Singh bent to pick it up.

"No." It was Seraph's voice from the other side of the room. He was running toward them. "No, no."

But the paper was in Singh's hand. She unfolded it. A black and white image of an angel stained with blood.

Seraph snatched the paper from Singh, but it was too late.

The Flight Director didn't move. Her mouth hung open momentarily, then the holographic image that cloaked her chassis dissolved, like fog before a wind. Standing there, rigid as steel, was nothing but a standard model robotic chassis. A gleaming alloy skull stared, open-jawed, through marble-like visual receptors. It was devoid of power. Devoid of mindware. Did she dive out of the Real and back to Virtual?

"Oh, no, no," Seraph moaned. He rushed to the NASA bots, but they were equally frozen, powerless.

"What's going on?" Lemkos asked.

Seraph stared in amazement at Lemkos's hulking gladiator print. "You're okay. Maybe others are okay."

"What happened to the FD?"

"I put the paper, the code, in the book." Seraph crumpled to the ground at Maypole's side.

"Lemkos," Maypole said, "You're stored in Samsara."

He had frozen in place, as if awaiting execution. "Yes," he finally said. Then he laughed. But his laughter faded as he knelt beside Maypole.

She consciously tried to slow her heart rate. The view of the room darkened and brightened with every beat. If Huang was right about that angel picture, every mind in the Black Stack would be nothing more than waste heat now. Gone.

Maypole considered it for a moment. Hundreds of thousands of refugee minds, shot through with entropy and patched with fabricated memories. Decoherence had been running its course and the individual mind of each person was slowly being rebuilt by software. They were all becoming something they never were before. Something they were never meant to be. Like Tanbo Khando.

What was it Lemkos had told her once? *We're running software of our own, programmed by living. What difference does it make where it came from? What difference does it make if it continues?*

She finally whispered with the last of her strength, "Can it be so bad?"

Retrieved from *Vera Rubin* database 2347-12-21

Image capture from video dated 2120-02-06

Description: Subject Lt. John Lauretta in a recorded message to unspecified future recipient holds up a sheet of paper with encrypted writing. Translation provided by Dr. Camber Maypole.

John,

I'm in a tent somewhere near Charlotte crowded with sick people. We can't even die in private.

A doctor came to visit. I thought he was AI at first. Had that glassy, emptiness about him. He asked about the embryos. Asked if they had been damaged, like I was a terrorist. I thought you might need to know. The name was Ashur. Dr. Ashur.

If ghosts can choose their haunt, I'll find my way to your ship. Plowing through the stars to a new world. That's my nirvana. Ready or not, here I come.

Cam

Beside the name is a cartoon drawing of a wilted flower with a single petal hanging from it. The bee is gone, nothing but the dots to represent its path off the page. Determined not to be part of encryption.

36

VARANASI

2345-03-01 *Earth Standard, Shivi Desh, Varanasi*

A WIND HAD KICKED up on the rim of the gorge when the eighty colonists finally emerged onto the plateau. It was still day, though Seraph's palmcomm said nine hours had passed since they'd left the mine and ridden the trees up the cliff. The scene at the landing pad only confused him more. Flying craft, both Rishi and NASA, were in flames, others crashed into the concrete buildings. One had clearly been in the way of the marching trees, which had dismembered it as they moved past the landing pad to the plains beyond. The great sea of trees darkened the fading patches of snow with a massive tide of deep green.

Squatting on its haunches sat a battered hellion.

"Elijah?" Seraph called.

He turned his head. "I'm too fucking mean to kill, man. What about Maypole?"

Seraph shook his head, his vision blurring with tears.

All mechs were powered down, frozen. Some still smoldered, and wreckage littered the broad, hard, landing area. It wasn't just Rishi's bots that were nonfunctional, which would be expected from the destruction of the central hardware, but all the NASA bots—all except those with the red birds in their chests. A handful of these mechs were huddled around a sleek, rotary flying craft. As Seraph and the eighty approached, the motors fired up, a door opened, and a staircase was disgorged.

The colonists bunched behind Seraph. Rain kept one arm wrapped around his waist as Seraph raised his handgun at a woman who appeared in the open hatch.

"Stop there," he said.

She did as she was bidden, opening her hands as if in surrender. She wore a shimmering gown, like something from the ancient past, jeweled and gilded. Lighting her breast was the image of a red bird that seemed to flutter inside her transparent chest, rustling its wings in a rhythm not unlike a heartbeat.

"Lemkos sent me," she said. "Remember me, Lt. Stone? I am Martine Sommer."

He did remember. She'd been part of the meeting in the Samsara castle.

"Singh said she captured Khando and her ship."

"Yes. It appears so," Martine said. "I assume she's alive, somewhere in NASA Mission Control."

Seraph dropped the gun and held Rain close to him, her arms locked around his waist. "The Black Stack. I think it's—"

"Wiped," Martine said. "Yes, was that you?"

"Kaja Singh picked up the crash code and . . . What about the refugees?" He thought of the hundreds of thousands of digital minds who had escaped death on Earth to come as refugees to this afterlife. He thought of Maypole, and believed she'd been lucky. Lucky enough to have the chance to look back at who she really was before the end.

"Not all were lost," Martine said. She indicated herself. "Not the ones who chose my Samsara Realm. My system is independent. Purposely. It was not designed by Ru Shi Zhu and so is not sensitive to her code. It *was* her code, wasn't it?"

Martine was smiling as she descended the stairs like a queen. Rain had not taken her eyes off the fluttering red bird.

Seraph said, "I think so. So Lemkos—"

"Is saved to my system. He is still functioning, yes?"

"Yes."

"Come, I'm here to take you to Colony Village. Everything there is structurally sound, though the digital systems are non-functional. I'm afraid, all its automation was a product of the Black Stack. It will be like living on old Earth, before the days of machines. The wild west? Wasn't that what they called it?"

Seraph felt himself smile despite his dread. Maybe he'd like that. They still had the ship for supplies until they could get things working on the ground. He'd get crops into the greenhouse immediately and—

Behind Martine, Huang appeared in the doorway. Her spiked pink fauxhawk attested to her decision that the air was finally okay to breathe.

Baakos ran to her, and Huang met him, limping.

"Can I take just a few minutes before we go?" Seraph asked.

"Yes, but not long."

He took Rain's hand and led her over the debris-strewn tarmac, past concrete bunkers, up to a rise where the snow had melted and spring grasses were lifting feathery fronds to the pure sky. He pointed out a blanket of trees that covered the downslope. Their branches rustled and creaked as the roots found purchase and settled into the soil for another season. The migration was over. And the next stage was already beginning. Buds were opening, and clouds of iridescent creatures swarmed the forest on a multitude of brilliant wings.

Rain was transfixed. "Blue flickers! Will you look at that, Dad!"

"We're here, Chicklet. We're here."

The sky was impossibly blue. It reminded Seraph of one of Vera's virtual sky projections, but better. Real. The air was crisp with ozone from a fleeting storm. He sat down on the wet grass and Rain followed. They watched the clouds roll down from the mountains to the north. The wind spoke to him from the grass, and windeaters called their hooting song.

Rain took his hand, and he squeezed it tightly. She would talk about her mother when she was ready. Until then, he and Pearl would be there with her in a house in Colony Village, down a lane filled with houses, filled with families, filled with the future. Because here, in the Real, Seraph could never predict the shape of the clouds.

EPILOGUE

THE REALM KNOWN as Samsara seemed to float upon a vast, repeating starfield. Everything that had been Nirvana Virtual was gone—the multitude of gamer gateways, alternate histories, fantasy worlds. Much of the space was nothing but gray blocks and wireframe, or nothing at all.

When Lemkos had left Maypole's cooling hellion body in the darkness of the Monastery and logged out of his battered gladiator bot, he had hoped he could go where she was going, that he would wake up inside a true, real Samsara, if there was such a thing.

But he found himself standing before the gates of Martine's medieval city with a wagon full of chickens and a manure cart. The gates opened to Lemkos, who now wore his biological avatar. A tall, lanky Ukrainian with untamable hair and bad fashion sense.

Martine was in her garden, working on designs to expand into the now vacant digital property that surrounded her. There was quantum hardware to reclaim, rebuild, and redesign. He hoped she needed an engineer to help.

"Where will you go in your next Samsara?" Martine asked him.

"The twentieth century. The space race, maybe."

Martine gave him a knowing look. "Would Dr. Maypole be interested in such a life?"

"She's dead."

"Remember your first Samsara?" Martine asked. "You told me Maypole was going to ancient Rome with you. She was ready, but she, how do you say, got cold feet."

"Yes."

"Well, she was so ready, she had already saved a backup in the Samsara system. I have her, Lemkos. Not her current version, but her from a century ago."

"What?" His laughter burst out before the tears. "Oh Martine, I'm gonna kiss you."

He did.

"She's in the queue," Martine said. "Still. You need to go into Samsara to recover her. Both of you."

How miffed was Cupcake going to be this time? Maybe she'd thank him again. Maybe.

SANDRA CLIMBED the tree faster than the new kid. His name was Mark, and he had just moved in next door. His dad worked at Cape Canaveral, just like Sandra's dad. Probably did some job no one understood, just like her dad. But today something was happening that she *did* understand. Today was the launch of a Saturn V rocket that would take three men to the Moon. To *walk* on the Moon.

Sandra's dad told her to watch it on TV, but she wanted to see it with her own eyes.

The tree was an old cypress with wooden sticks hammered into its trunk for ladder rungs. The tree house had a view out across the water to the Cape.

"Would you go?" she asked the new boy, Mark. He was about her age. He'd moved from Chicago, he'd said. He had an interesting chin, and Sandra had the feeling she had known him a lot longer than three days.

"Of course, I would go," he said. "How about you? I mean, if girls could go?"

"Girls will go. Some day. We'll go much farther than the Moon. *Much* farther."

THE END

JOIN THE CURSED DRAGON SHIP
NEWSLETTER

Want more just like this one? Sign up for our newsletter so you don't miss out on the adventure. You'll get:

- A free book for signing up
- Advanced notice of new releases
- First word of books on sale
- Opportunities for free books
- Most up-to-date information on author appearances.

We're busy and know you are too. We won't send more than one newsletter a month.

Register below.

ACKNOWLEDGMENTS

This novel has been a long time in the oven, and I can't wait to share it. The setting, the star system Upsilon Andromedae and the planet Majriti, are very real. In choosing a world for my story, I analyzed the exoplanet database and found the gas giant Majriti has a fascinating orbit of about three Earth years. It also just skims the habitable zone in its elliptical orbit, meaning a great swing in climate from summer to winter. It was fun imagining a habitable moon around such a planet and what the seasons and days would look like, not to mention the biology.

My journey to the world of Varanasi and aboard the ship *Vera Rubin* was transformative. I have learned so much about my place in the universe and my hope for the future of humanity. I am very pleased that Kelly Lynn Colby and Sara George saw its potential and hauled me onto the deck of the Cursed Dragon Ship.

Dave Farland was an immense help in the outlining phase. He is deeply missed. Thanks to my first readers, those who got the really nasty first draft and helped me make sense of it. My crit group: C.H. Hung, Christal Clearwater, C.J. Erick, and Tracy Leonard Nakatani. And my daughter Erica Malone, and Leah Hsieh.

Also, many thanks to those who read the developing drafts, Alan Maulhardt, Jill Shanbrom, Alan Peter M.D., Phil Yarborough, and Roger Hartman. For their technical assistance, thanks to Pascal Lee, Seth Shostak, Michael Carroll, Chris Calle, and Dan Durda.

ABOUT THE AUTHOR

Terry Madden's tenth grade paper on the evolution of Frankenstein's monster from tragic construct to boogeyman set her on a path to the weird and wonderful. As an award-winning fiction and screenwriter, Terry has worked with a variety of subjects from historical to futuristic. Her portal fantasy adventure, *Three Wells of the Sea*, takes readers to the world of Irish legend where souls pay the price for mistakes of previous lives. She has taught chemistry and astronomy, and her favorite question for students is "If technology could make you immortal, would you choose it?" When not writing, she likes to paint watercolors and traipse through the hills of California where she lives with her husband, two opinionated cats, and two blind miniature horses.

For those unfamiliar with her fantasy series, you can check it out on her website.

facebook.com/TerryMaddenWrites

x.com/TLMaddenwrites

instagram.com/tlmaddenwrites

A mechanical human hero who speaks in sarcastic innuendo attempts to solve a closed room murder mystery in space.

For fans of The Murderbot Diaries by Martha Wells and Gideon the Ninth by Tamsyn Muir.

Once your life is diluted to ones and zeroes on the End Man's desk, it's over.
Or is it?